PRAISE FOR THE ~~NOVELS OF~~
KRISTINA FOREST

• • •

"A bighearted story about being brave enough to go for what you want, even when the rules tell you something different."
—*The New York Times*

"Pleasant, with a swoon-worthy ending straight out of the movies."
—*Kirkus Reviews*

"This book is the perfect weekend read. If you love soft books about young black romance, genuine feelings, and a few stolen kisses and moments, then this is the book for you. There are few authors that I wholeheartedly support everything they write, but Kristina Forest is now definitely one of them."
—Melanin Library

"Kristina Forest is such a ray of light . . . crafting such adorable stories that just are the book equivalent of a warm hug. The romance at the center of the book is just amazing as it has great chemistry and flirty, witty banter flying throughout."
—The Nerd Daily

"If you're looking for a heartfelt story that will leave your heart bursting at the seams by the end and is packed with adventure, then *Now That I've Found You* is the book for you."
—The Reading Chemist

The Neighbor Favor

Kristina Forest

BERKLEY ROMANCE
New York

BERKLEY ROMANCE
Published by Berkley
An imprint of Penguin Random House LLC
penguinrandomhouse.com

Library of Congress Cataloging-in-Publication Data

Names: Forest, Kristina, author.
Title: The neighbor favor / Kristina Forest.
Description: First edition. | New York: Berkley Romance, 2023.
Identifiers: LCCN 2022037544 (print) | LCCN 2022037545 (ebook) |
ISBN 9780593546437 (trade paperback) | ISBN 9780593546444 (ebook)
Subjects: LCGFT: Romance fiction. | Novels. Classification:
LCC PS3606.O74747 N45 2023 (print) | LCC PS3606.O74747 (ebook) |
DDC 813/.6—dc23/eng/20220815
LC record available at https://lccn.loc.gov/2022037544
LC ebook record available at https://lccn.loc.gov/2022037545

First Edition: February 2023

Printed in the United States of America
5th Printing

Book design by Ashley Tucker

For my literary work wife, Alison

The
Neighbor
Favor

PROLOGUE

LILY GREENE ALWAYS IMAGINED THAT IF SHE WERE TO have the tragic misfortune of dying young, it would happen in a valiant, honorable way. Similar to the heroes in her beloved fantasy novels. Maybe she'd die while rescuing a child (or cat) from a burning building. Or darting into the street to save an elderly person from being hit by a speeding truck.

She didn't imagine that at twenty-five years old her final moments would be spent drenched in sweat, dehydrated out of her mind, on a crowded New York City subway train without AC during rush hour on one of the hottest days of the year. Because this was an event that she might not survive.

Lily gripped the subway pole and tried her best to avoid touching the five other hands that were wrapped around the pole as well. With her free hand, she dug through her tote bag and pulled out her empty water canister, as if liquid would magically appear inside. Usually, she was smart about filling it before she left the office, but today, her boss, Edith, vice president and publisher of Edith Pearson Books at the esteemed Mitchell & Milton Inc., had been in a particularly terrible mood after mistakenly falling for an email phishing scam, which meant IT had taken hold of Edith's computer and she couldn't sit in her own office, which meant she'd stood over Lily's shoulder in Lily's tiny cubicle, repeatedly proclaiming that she was an "innocent victim" of a "malicious scammer." All the while, Lily wondered if when someone emailed you, claiming to be the long-lost grandson of John F. Kennedy, and said person then claimed you could read a draft of their memoir for publishing consideration by clicking an unsecure, highly suspicious link, could you really blame anyone but yourself for clicking said link and therefore unleashing a virus onto your computer?

Either way, for the rest of the afternoon, Lily suffered through Edith's complaining and micromanaging. She survived by drinking one too many cups of coffee, zero cups of water, and inhaling half a sleeve of crackers at her desk once Edith stepped away for lunch. Now Lily was hungry, dehydrated and very close to melting into a puddle right there on the downtown B train, which suddenly came to a halt. The conductor made a garbled announcement no one could understand, and a chorus of groans rang throughout the train. A man who'd already taken the liberty of removing his shirt banged on the subway doors as if the conductor could hear him. "Jesus fucking Christ, fix the AC! We're dying in here!"

A few others began to shout and complain, growing angrier as the train remained motionless. Lily grimaced. Nothing good ever happened when a bunch of people were pissed, hot and immobile. At least they'd stopped on the Manhattan Bridge, so she had cell service.

"What the fuck?" someone yelled. "Why is it so hot?"

"Global warming," a woman standing beside Lily grumbled. She was short and blonde, with flushed cheeks and a sweaty forehead. Lily could only imagine how *she* looked herself. It was only May, but this spring season was already giving unbearably hot summer vibes. Lily glanced down at her sleeveless white button-up, which now had sweat stains under her armpits. Her brown skin was dewy, but not in the cute-makeup-influencer way, and the flyaway curls that had escaped her bun were sticking to the back of her neck. Gross. She felt so horribly gross.

And nauseous? Her balance began to slip, and she clutched the pole tighter, attempting to keep the nausea and light-headedness at bay. She'd fainted a few times as a kid when heat and stress created a menacing combination, and she couldn't afford to faint today. Not when she had to rush home and feed her cat and be back in Manhattan in a matter of hours because she was meeting her older sisters, Violet and Iris, for dinner in the Meatpacking District. Violet, ever the celebrity stylist social butterfly, recently heard about a new French fusion restaurant they just *had* to try. Lily hated going to trendy spots in the city because she always felt hilariously underdressed, but Iris, a worker bee, was actually pulling herself away from the office to join them, so Lily had no excuse to miss it.

Just then, Lily's phone vibrated in her bag. It was Violet calling. Lily answered, keeping her voice low. She didn't want to be one of those people who broadcasted her entire conversation to everyone on the train.

"Lily," Violet said, her voice its usual mix of pep and confidence. "There's been a change of plans."

"What do you mean?"

"Iris can't come. She has a work thing. Big surprise. Can you—hold on." Lily listened as Violet pulled the phone away from her ear and murmured to someone in her background. Violet might have been at a photo shoot or on the set of a music video with one of her clients. Her life moved at lightning speed and Lily could never keep up. "Hey, I'm back. Sorry. No one ever *listens* to me during these things. I put her in a pair of bright pink satin Versace platform pumps and what does the photographer say? 'Put her in black.' She looks best in bright colors! Why is that so hard for everyone to understand?"

"Who are we talking about?" Lily asked, wiping the sweat from her forehead. "Just so we're on the same page."

"Karamel Kitty. I told you about her before. She's the rapper I'm working with now."

"Oh, right," Lily said, vaguely remembering. "Isn't she the one who exposed that politician who sent her dick pics?"

"What? Oh yeah, that was last year. Anyway, I want you to meet me at this bar in the Village instead of going to the restaurant. I'll send you the address."

Lily almost said okay but she hesitated. She felt a catch coming on. "Will it just be the two of us?"

"Um," Violet mumbled. "No."

Lily sighed. "Who else will be there, Vi?"

"Nobody really . . . just my new friend Damien," she said quickly. "He's the assistant photographer at the photo shoot today, and I started talking about you and I showed him your picture and he said you were beautiful, which you *are*—"

"Nope."

"But he's so cute and sweet, and he really wants to meet you! For real, you're not even going to give him a chance?"

Lily groaned. Her sisters were always trying to play matchmaker. Why couldn't they just accept that Lily was terrible at dating and leave her alone in awkward peace?

"Violet, I've had the worst day. Really. I can't deal with meeting someone new. I don't have the energy."

"I'll buy you dinner too."

Lily paused at that. On her salary, she didn't often pass up free meals.

"*Fine*," she finally said. "But don't be disappointed when Damien and I don't hit it off."

"Okay, Negative Nancy. I'll send you the address. See you in a bit. Love you!"

"Love you too," Lily said, but Violet had already hung up.

Lily let out a full-body sigh and pulled her phone away from her ear, grimacing at the sweat left behind on the screen. In all the time that she'd spent on the phone with Violet, the train still hadn't moved. How was that possible?

"Are you all right?"

Lily glanced up and the blonde girl was staring at her, sporting a concerned frown.

"You're swaying," she said. "You look like you're about to faint."

Lily noticed the people around them turn in her direction.

"I'm fine," she insisted, even though she was beginning to see spots everywhere she looked. Maybe the conversation with Violet, and agreeing to another blind date, had stressed her out more than she thought. *Why won't this freaking train move?* She forced a smile. "Thank you, though."

She'd be off this train soon. She just needed to distract herself in the meantime. Planting her feet, she dug in her bag and pulled out her copy of *The Elves of Ceradon*, her favorite fantasy novel. She'd discovered it two years ago while working at a bookstore, struggling to find a full-time job in any field that was willing to hire people with an English degree. She'd never read a book about a clan of Black elves before, a story that made it completely normal for Black people to exist in high fantasy. Lily realized then that she wanted to help bring more fantasy like this into the world, but for kids. So began her long journey to break into publishing. Currently, she was working with Edith on slightly depressing adult nonfiction, but soon she hoped she'd make the switch to children's books. And in her heart, she felt as though she had *The Elves of Ceradon* to thank for that inspiration.

The author, N.R. Strickland, was a mystery, though. The copy Lily discovered at the bookstore had been torn and tattered, published years ago by a now-defunct British press. N.R. Strickland's bio was sparse, saying that he was born and raised in London and that *The Elves of Ceradon* was his first novel. He didn't have a website or any social media. The plain, dark red book jacket didn't even have an author photo. In today's day and age, it was odd but a little admirable that he'd decided to forgo anything public-facing.

Lily carried the novel with her for moments like right now when she was stuck on a train and needed to kill time. She opened the book and tried to focus on the words in front of her instead of the heat but found it difficult. The struggle to read was giving her a headache. In a moment of blissful relief, the train started to move, only to stop after what felt like a few feet. Someone opened a window and a bit of the hot air inside the train was exchanged for the hot air outside. Lily swallowed thickly and tried to concentrate but the words began to swim on the page. Okay, so reading wasn't going to help.

Instead, she pulled out her phone and googled N.R. Strickland on a whim, as she did occasionally, hoping to read news of a sequel, but ultimately expecting to find nothing. The search engine loaded and . . . wait, N.R. Strickland had a website now.

Shocked, Lily clicked on the link and his bare-bones website appeared. It didn't provide any information that she didn't already know from the bio on the back of his book. But what the website *did* have was a contact form. *Amazing.* Lily wiped the sweat from her forehead and grinned at her phone. Giddy and increasingly delirious, she typed out a message to N.R. Strickland, telling him just how much his book meant to her, how finding his story had changed the trajectory of her life.

Her heartbeat increased, and her palms grew clammier, but she chalked it up to her excitement. Even when her breaths turned shallow and black spots aggressively clouded her vision, she continued to type. It wasn't until her phone slipped out of her hand and the train seemed to tilt off-kilter that Lily realized she was falling. Fainting, to be more accurate.

"Oh my God!" the blonde shouted as Lily hit the floor, clutching her copy of *The Elves of Ceradon*.

Minutes later, after Lily came to, and kind strangers helped her up, and someone offered her a bottle of water, and a mom forced her to eat a pack of her child's fruit snacks, Lily was busy focusing on the fact that she'd just fainted. Her mind was so far from the email she'd feverishly drafted, unaware that it had been sent prematurely and was already on its way through cyberspace for its intended recipient.

*   *   *

OVER THREE THOUSAND miles away in the city of Amsterdam, Nick Brown was trying his best not to embarrass himself and cry in a room full of people who'd been strangers to him only a month ago. But he couldn't help it. He was touched that they'd thrown him a goodbye party. And he felt slightly self-conscious to have so much attention on him.

"Remember us fondly, Nick," Jakob Davids said, raising his glass, his lips spread in a genuine smile. "We look forward to reading the article once it publishes. *Proost!*"

"*Proost!*" the rest of the Davids family shouted, clinking their glasses.

"*Proost!*" Nick said quietly, lifting his glass as well, although it was filled with only water.

Rubbing the back of his neck, feeling both grateful for

the goodbye dinner but also that he wasn't worth the trouble, Nick looked around at the Davids family and tried to commit them to memory. He'd spent the last few weeks with them. They were an Afro-Dutch family who owned a Surinamese cuisine restaurant, and he'd been writing a piece about them and their business for his column with *World Traveler*. There was Jakob and his wife, Ada, who, at thirty, were only three years older than Nick, their young children, Jolijn and Christophe, and Jakob's mother, Ruth, who'd migrated from Suriname, South America, to Amsterdam in her early twenties. They lived in a small town house a few blocks away from Sarphatipark.

Nick's job made it so that he was constantly on the go. It was what he liked most about it. His life was a revolving door of faces and places. But something about the Davidses had latched on to him. Maybe it was because they were a close-knit family who actually enjoyed spending time together, something Nick had always craved. He didn't want to leave the Davidses and wished he could soak in their togetherness for a little while longer. But he was off to Munich in the morning for his next assignment. He'd have to leave the Davidses behind.

And that was probably for the best anyway. The past few weeks had been nice. But almost *too* nice. It was making Nick anxious. He found that he was constantly waiting for the inevitable dropping of the other shoe.

"Thank you for all of this," Nick said to the Davidses. "I'm grateful that you allowed me into your home and your lives." He took a deep breath, fighting off the strong wave of surprising emotions. "I'm really going to miss you."

"We'll miss you too. You're basically family now!" Jakob barked out a laugh, unaware of the effect that his words had on Nick. He clapped his hand onto Christophe's shoulder. "Isn't he, son?"

Christophe grinned and nodded.

Nick felt a little twinge in his stomach, watching that small interaction between father and son. He shook it off and smiled at the Davidses, feeling slightly relieved when Ada began to play some music and beckoned Jakob to dance with her in the middle of the living room. Ruth, who was awake way past her normal bedtime, sat down on the couch and promptly fell asleep.

Then Christophe and Jolijn, the nine-year-old twins, suddenly appeared in front of Nick with a mischievous twinkle in their eyes.

"You won't forget us, will you?" Jolijn asked, raising an eyebrow. She was the taller of the two. She tugged on one of her thick braids. Nick noticed she did this whenever she felt especially inquisitive. "Promise you won't. Swear on your notebook."

Nick laughed. "Why my notebook?"

"Because you always carry it with you. It must be your favorite thing."

"And what will we do without your stories?" Christophe asked, hip-checking his sister out of the way to get Nick's full attention. He was young, but he already had a booming voice like his father's. "You never told us what happened to Deko the elf prince after he was bit by a life leech."

Two weeks ago, when the twins had been antsy as their parents closed the restaurant, Nick had entertained them with a story he'd written years ago about an elf prince named Deko and his journey through a magical land called Ceradon.

"You're right," Nick said, nodding. "We never finished that story, did we? What do *you* think happened to Deko?"

Christophe frowned. "I think he's gravely injured. Near death."

"Not me," Jolijn said. "I think Deko survived and then met a warrior elf queen, who is stronger and faster than him, and she becomes the ruler of the kingdom."

"That's stupid," Christophe said, rolling his eyes. "Deko is obviously going to die and then be revived by a sorceress and with her help, he'll seek vengeance on those who harmed him and his people!"

The twins began to argue, and Nick laughed. Quite honestly, they fascinated him. He'd been a lonely-ass only child, no one to bicker with.

"I'll leave the ending up to your interpretation," he said, finally intervening. "Whatever you want to happen to Deko is what happens."

"You mean you don't know the ending to your *own* story?" Jolijn asked, wide-eyed.

Nick shook his head. "Nope."

"But you must know," Christophe insisted, disappointed.

Nick wasn't lying. He'd written that story in another life and had purposely ended Deko's fate on a cliff-hanger, thinking he'd have the chance to continue Deko's journey. But now, he had no intention of doing so. As far as he was concerned, the story belonged to N.R. Strickland, the silly pen name he'd created. But he observed the twins' forlorn expressions. They didn't want to hear his sorry backstory. They wanted to know what happened to Deko. So Nick came up with a special ending, just for them.

"Okay, the truth is that Deko does die from the life leech bite," Nick said, and Jolijn gasped. "But then he's revived by a sorceress who's also a warrior queen, and she rules over the kingdom while Deko goes on a journey to kill the life leeches who murdered his clan."

"I knew it!" Christophe said, punching his fist in the air, and Jolijn grinned, satisfied.

"Okay, time for bed," Ada said, gathering the twins. "Say goodbye to Nick."

"Bye, Nick," they sang, hugging him. Nick felt himself get choked up again and wished he'd get a fucking grip on his emotions. He hugged the twins back, already missing them and their banter.

"I swear on my notebook I won't forget you," he said as they pulled away.

"Good." Jolijn nodded, very serious.

"You sure you don't want my sister's number?" Ada asked Nick, raising an eyebrow. "She's in Munich, and I'm sure she'd love to meet a handsome man like yourself."

"I heard that!" Jakob called from the kitchen, and Ada laughed.

"No, but thank you," Nick said, smiling. If Ada's sister was anything at all like Ada: kind and patient and caring, then it would be best if Nick stayed far away from her. Because he'd inevitably find a way to fuck things up.

"All right then," Ada said, giving Nick a hug. He waved goodbye to her and the twins as she ushered them upstairs.

It was almost one a.m., Amsterdam time. Nick's flight was in six hours. He at least needed to attempt to get some sleep. He stood and walked over to Jakob to say his last goodbye.

"Keep in touch," Jakob said earnestly.

Nick promised he would. But the reality was that he'd most likely never see or speak to Jakob or the rest of the Davidses again. That was just the way of things.

"Thanks for everything," Nick said, taking one final glance around the Davidses' house, already anticipating the loneliness that awaited him at his Airbnb. He flashed one last kind smile at Jakob and left.

It was drizzling when he stepped outside. He grabbed the bike he'd rented for the month and cautiously pedaled down the street. The night was still, peaceful. Just the sound of his churning tires and the rain softly hitting the ground. It was during moments like this that Nick quietly marveled over the fact that he was in a foreign country, far from North Carolina, a state he'd never thought he'd leave. Now look at him. Riding a bike through the streets of Amsterdam, leaving a goodbye party that had been thrown in his honor. *Him.* Someone who'd never even had so much as a birthday party. It had been such a good night, one of the best he'd had in a long time.

So of course right when Nick was on the brink of forming an optimistic outlook, the chain popped on his bike and he went skidding across the wet street, losing control. He crashed into a pole and tumbled off the bike, falling flat on his back. He stared up at the sky, heaving for air, wincing at the pain he felt all over his body. He took several moments to get his bearings, then he slowly stood, wincing. He wheeled his bike down the street, and right on cue, it began to pour in heavy sheets. Even in pain, all Nick could do was laugh. *Of course* this was how his last night in Amsterdam would end. Something had to bring him back down to earth and remind him that good things, be they feelings or experiences, didn't last very long in his life.

When he finally reached his Airbnb, he felt like he'd been run over by a wet truck. He stripped down to his underwear and examined his limbs. He couldn't see any bruises on his brown skin, but they'd surely appear in a few hours. Grimacing, he sat on the couch and reached for his laptop, expecting to see an email from his boss, asking why he hadn't sent in his piece about the Davidses yet, and Nick would have to say, *Sorry, Thomas, I crashed my bike into a pole because 90 percent of the time, my life just sucks that way. Can I have an extension, please?*

But when Nick opened his email, he didn't see a message from Thomas. Instead, he had a notification that someone had contacted him through his website. Or rather, the website his best friend and newly self-appointed literary agent, Marcus, had created for him. Nick stared at the screen, perplexed. Had someone really discovered his website? Was there a person in the world who'd actually read his book? *Get the fuck out of here.* If anything, it was spam. Or someone had managed to find a copy of *The Elves of Ceradon*, read it, and hated it so much they felt the need to tell him so. No good could come from checking that email.

Nick pushed his laptop aside, wishing he had a frozen bag of vegetables to put on his aching knee. And he glanced at the laptop screen again. The subject of the person's email was "You have a website!" Would a person who hated his book sound so optimistic?

Nick frowned, undecided.

Ah, fuck it. He'd let curiosity get the best of him.

He opened the message and braced himself for hate mail. Instead, to his surprise, he read the first line and felt himself smile.

PART ONE

THE EMAILS

1

FROM: Lily G. <lilyg@gmail.com>
TO: N.R. Strickland <nrs@nrstrickland.com>
DATE: May 9, 6:21pm
SUBJECT: You have a website!

Dear Mr. Strickland,

Have you ever been stuck on a subway train without air-conditioning on a 92-degree weather day? If not, count yourself lucky, because that's what I'm experiencing right now and it's absolute torture.

Okay, now that I have that off my chest, I want it to be clear that I never do stuff like this. And by stuff, I mean cold emailing a stranger. Chances are you probably won't read this message, so my nerves might be for nothing. You did *just* create a website even though *The Elves of Ceradon* was published five years ago, so my assumption is that you don't spend too much time online, which isn't really a bad thing.

My name is Lily and I read your novel almost two years ago while working at a used bookstore. I'd never heard of your book and neither had my boss, so he told me to toss it. Mostly because this particular copy looked like a dog had chewed the bottom-right corner, which basically meant we couldn't sell it. But the thought of throwing books away feels like a crime, and I was curious, so I started reading on my lunch break. Then I kept reading throughout the rest of my shift, on the bus ride home, all through dinner, and I stayed up until 3am to finish. Reading your book made me remember why I loved reading so much growing up. At the time, I'd been out of college for a year and hadn't considered working with books outside of being a bookseller, but I realized maybe I could edit books like yours, but for children. Once I had that goal, everything changed. I work in book publishing now—not in the role I want, necessarily, but it's a foot in the door. I think I have you and your book to thank, in a way. It got me through a tough and confusing time in my life.

Anyway, I won't bore you with the details of my previous existential crisis. (Again, not sure you'll even end up reading this.) I'm emailing you because I wanted to tell you that I loved your book. I thought Deko was one of the most interesting protagonists I've read in a long time. Do you plan to write a sequel? It ended on such a cliff-hanger with Deko, delirious and battle weary, finally reaching Ceradon but getting attacked by a life leech as soon as he touched the city gates! Did he survive? Did he die? I've been wondering this for two years.

I'm sure you're inundated with messages thanks to your new website and contact form, but I hope

• • •

FROM: N.R. Strickland <nrs@nrstrickland.com>
TO: Lily G. <lilyg@gmail.com>
DATE: May 14, 10:42pm
SUBJECT: Re: You have a website!

Lily—

You hope what? Did you mean to leave that sentence unfinished? Either way, thank you for your kind message. It was really nice and surprising to read. You're wrong in assuming that I'm inundated with emails. Yours is the first email I've ever received through my website, and to be honest, I thought you were someone sending me hate mail. You're probably the only person who ever visits the site, other than my agent, who made the site for me.

I'm glad that my book served as an inspiration for you and your career. That's probably the only way my book has ever inspired another person.

To answer your first question, no, I've never been stuck on a subway when it was 92 degrees outside. However, I did once find myself locked inside of a loo on a submarine in the middle of the Indian Ocean. Long story.

To answer your second question, no, I don't plan to write a sequel. I don't think of myself as an author anymore. More like a one-hit wonder, sans the hit. As far as I'm concerned, *The Elves of Ceradon* was written in another life, back when I was 22 and naive and thought I'd be the Black George R. R. Martin. Did Deko die lying there at the city gates? Did a Ceradonian elf come to his rescue? I don't know. I'll leave that up to your interpretation.

Wishing you luck in life.

~NRS

• • •

FROM: Lily G. <lilyg@gmail.com>
TO: N.R. Strickland <nrs@nrstrickland.com>
DATE: May 15, 7:13am
SUBJECT: Re: You have a website!

Dear Mr. Strickland,

Oh my God. I had no idea I actually sent that email to you. I wrote it in a delirious, dehydrated state, right before I literally fainted. I was serious about that hot subway. Reading over my email, I can tell just how out of it I was. And I didn't even finish it! I'm *mortified*.

And shocked?? I can't believe that you actually read my email and that you *replied*. I was honestly starting to think that maybe you didn't exist. I'm the only person I know who has read your book. Whenever I mention it to people, they have no idea what I'm talking about, which is really disappointing, because they don't know what they're missing, and I love my copy too much to loan it out. I have no idea where I'd find another if someone didn't give it back. It looks like the book went out of print only a few months after publication.

I'm sorry to hear that you no longer think of yourself as an author. I didn't realize how young you were when you wrote *Elves*. That's so impressive. When I was 22, I was hiding from my room-mates in our senior hall suite so that they wouldn't force me to go to parties.

Your reply came at just the right time. It's exactly the energy booster I need for my job interview later this afternoon. I'm taking it as a good omen. ☺

Sincerely,

Lily G.

...

FROM: N.R. Strickland <nrs@nrstrickland.com>
TO: Lily G. <lilyg@gmail.com>
DATE: June 12, 11:01pm
SUBJECT: Re: You have a website!

Lily—

Apologies, I'm over a month late. So you're saying you emailed me when you weren't in a clear state of mind, literal seconds before you fainted. That's mad! I hope you were okay afterward. And I have to be honest, getting an email from you in the first place makes a lot more sense now. I guess someone would have to be a little delirious to go out of their way to email me.

I'm glad you love your copy of *Elves* so much that you wouldn't let anyone else borrow it. And yes, Labyrinth Press closed its doors the same year I signed my contract. They were able to print a few copies of *Elves* beforehand. It wasn't an ideal career start, but I've come to accept my path. Again, not an author anymore.

How did that interview go?
~NRS

...

FROM: Lily G. <lilyg@gmail.com>
TO: N.R. Strickland <nrs@nrstrickland.com>
DATE: June 13, 8:21am
SUBJECT: Re: You have a website!

Dear Mr. Strickland,

I wasn't expecting you to email back the first time, and I definitely wasn't expecting to hear from you *twice*. This just made my day.

The interview didn't go so well, unfortunately. I didn't make it past the first round, which kind of sucks because it was an assistant editor position with a well-known children's publisher.

I've gone on a handful of interviews within the past year, and I never make it very far in the process. For one, even though I know so much about children's books, that knowledge leaves my brain as soon as I sit down and I just start blabbering. The other issue is that most interviewers don't think I have enough experience, which isn't wrong. For two years, I've been an editorial assistant at an adult nonfiction imprint. I spend my days reading manuscripts about plagues and genocides and dictators, among other topics. Working on a book about the Satanic Panic doesn't clearly translate to working with children's authors who could be the next Rick Riordan. At least that's what I'm told during interviews.

Anyway, that's my life career-wise. You said you were on assignment. If you're not an author anymore, what do you do?

Sincerely,

Lily G.

• • •

FROM: Lily G. <lilyg@gmail.com>
TO: N.R. Strickland <nrs@nrstrickland.com>
DATE: June 13, 8:26am
SUBJECT: Re: You have a website!

Dear Mr. Strickland,

Please let me apologize for my last email. It was so presumptuous. I'm sure you don't care to hear about my career problems. You don't even have to respond. In fact, I hope you don't, because it will save me a ton of embarrassment.

The email made me sound really ungrateful. I'm not, I swear. I have a job at one of the most well-known North American publishers. And I know how hard it is to break into publishing, especially if you're Black. I applied to hundreds of positions for a year and got nowhere, until a distant, loopy connection through my mom's church scored me an internship with my boss. Her assistant quit three weeks into my internship and she didn't want to be bothered with another interview process, so she hired me. I got this job through dumb luck and timing.

I am grateful. The work is important. It's just not the work I want to be doing, and reading that tough and depressing material every day is starting to get to me. Most days I don't leave the office until after 7pm. I go to sleep dreaming about epidemics and assassinations.

I'm only 25 and there's plenty of time for me to follow my dream to edit children's books. I know that. I just keep thinking that this would be easier to get through if my boss was at least a semidecent person.

Sincerely,

Lily G.

...

FROM: Lily G. <lilyg@gmail.com>
TO: N.R. Strickland <nrs@nrstrickland.com>
DATE: June 13, 8:27am
SUBJECT: Re: You have a website!

Dear Mr. Strickland,

SORRY. I apologized about oversharing and then overshared even more, because treating emails like taxicab confessionals is something I do now, apparently! It felt safe to share because you don't really know me, and it's not like we'll ever meet. Once I started writing, it was hard to stop.

I'm aware that I've made things incredibly awkward. I hope you've decided to stop checking your emails indefinitely, and my cringeworthy musings can be left unread in your inbox forever.

Sincerely,

Lily

...

FROM: N.R. Strickland <nrs@nrstrickland.com>

TO: Lily G. <lilyg@gmail.com>

DATE: July 15, 9:32pm

SUBJECT: Re: You have a website!

Lily—

Cringeworthy is the shitty short stories I used to submit during creative writing workshop. Your emails about your career aren't nearly as bad. You haven't made things awkward and you don't have to apologize. The subject matter you currently edit does sound bleak, though. I'd want to leave that job too.

Here's a story that will make you feel better. When I was at university, my literary agent (who wasn't my literary agent back then, just my flatmate), encouraged me to go to a novel-pitching conference. I'd been working on *Elves* for over a year in my creative writing courses, and my professors seemed to like what I was doing, so I scrounged together the conference attendance fee. I printed out copies of the first few chapters and pitched *Elves* to at least thirty editors, and no one was interested. I was told that adult fantasy wasn't selling, which I didn't think made sense because *Game of Thrones* was the biggest show on television. A few editors asked, "But the elves are *Black*?" It was an enormous waste of money. Right when I decided to leave, a man walked up to me and said he'd overheard my pitch. He was working at a small press that specifically published fantasy and science fiction. He said *Elves* sounded right up their alley. That's how I got my chance.

Eventually, this turned out to be a terrible decision because I signed a dodgy contract, and the book, along with my career, went nowhere, and then the publisher closed down by the end of the year and I never got paid my full advance. But I think you get my point. Sometimes it only takes one yes. Hopefully your yes doesn't leave you worse off like me.

About my current work, I've been writing for a travel magazine since I graduated. I often find myself having very in-depth conversations with people I don't know very well in different parts of the world, so I don't find it weird that you've shared bits of your life with me. I agree there's something cathartic about it, which I guess is why I keep responding to you now that I think about it. Other than my boss and agent, you're the only person who emails me consistently.

I'm currently on assignment in Iceland. Have you ever been? It's not as cold as I thought it would be. The name is misleading.

Attached is a picture of the waterfall Skógafoss. I read online that this is the most "stereotypical" waterfall in Iceland. Doesn't look all that stereotypical to me. I hope it cheers you up.

~NRS

P.S. You can stop calling me Mr. Strickland. It makes me sound elderly. I'm 27, only two years older than you.

...

FROM: Lily G. <lilyg@gmail.com>
TO: N.R. Strickland <nrs@nrstrickland.com>
DATE: July 15, 10:59pm
SUBJECT: Re: You have a website!

Dear [insert name],
If you don't want me to call you Mr. Strickland, what should I call you?

I'm relieved that oversharing my personal woes didn't scare you off. From my emails, you would think that I'm used to speaking so freely, but I'm really not talkative at all. In middle school, my classmates called me the Mouse. Middle school was torture for a number of reasons, and I at least wish they would have come up with a more creative nickname.

I've never been to Iceland. I've actually never traveled outside of the US. It's so cool that you write for a travel magazine. I guess you're probably never in the same place for long periods of time. Do you have any favorite cities or countries?

The waterfall definitely does *not* look stereotypical to me. Thank you for sharing the picture. It did cheer me up. That interview was almost a month ago now, and I still get sad thinking about how much I wanted that job, but there will be others. I just have to keep trying.

Getting out of the city helps (I live in Brooklyn). I've spent most of today at my parents' house in New Jersey for their annual July 15th birthday barbecue (they have the same birthday). Other than Christmas, it's the one time of year that we're all together. My sister Violet is based in New York, but at any given time, she could be anywhere in the world. And my other sister Iris lives in the same neighborhood as my parents with her daughter, but she's always working, so I hardly see her. On July 15th, everyone is home and it's nice. Violet is a stylist, so she forces us to participate in fashion shows, and my dad and uncles sit on the patio and play Spades (a card game that I have no idea how to play). It's a good time.

And yikes. I'm sorry you signed a bad contract with Labyrinth Press. I'm sad you don't think of yourself as an author and don't plan to write a sequel to *Elves*, but I'm glad you're still writing in a way with the travel magazine.

Sincerely,

Lily

P.S.—It's not a waterfall but attached is a picture of my niece's tiny feet in my sister's high heels during our "fashion show."

. . .

FROM: N.R. Strickland <nrs@nrstrickland.com>
TO: Lily G. <lilyg@gmail.com>
DATE: July 21, 12:02am
SUBJECT: You can call me Strick

Lily—

You can call me Strick.

Your niece has a cute, chubby foot. I hope she doesn't grow up to be a jaded adult with depressing worldviews. Or maybe that just happened to me. (See, I overshare too.)

So you live in Brooklyn. What's that like? What do you like about it? I've been lots of places, but never to New York, if you can believe that. My agent lives in Brooklyn too, and he's been encouraging me to move to New York for months. He has a new position at a fancy literary agency and he's decided to make me his first project. He has this idea that *Elves* can have another life with a big US publisher. He refuses to believe that I am no longer an author. I respect his dedication but hate that he's wasting his time on me.

You're right that I'm never in one place for too long. All of my valuable possessions can fit in one large backpack. It's freeing to think that I can pick up and go whenever I need to. Or rather, when there's a new assignment for me.

If I had to choose, I'd say my favorite city is Sorrento, Italy. It's right by the water and smells likes lemon trees. You should definitely visit Sorrento when you eventually leave the US. Let me know when you do so that I can give you some tips on the best restaurants and sights.

I'm currently in Thailand. Yesterday, I went to an elephant sanctuary and got pushed around by some baby elephants in the mud. Pictures of said baby elephants are attached. A reminder that the world isn't always completely terrible.

~Strick

...

FROM: Lily G. <lilyg@gmail.com>
TO: N.R. Strickland <nrs@nrstrickland.com>
DATE: July 21, 1:11am
SUBJECT: Re: You can call me Strick

Dear Strick (this is a very funny nickname, by the way),
Those baby elephants are SO CUTE. I'm jealous that you get paid to play with them. Some people truly have all the luck. And

thanks for the tip on Sorrento. If I ever do get myself together to travel there, you'll be the first person I tell.

It's amazing that your agent wants to get *Elves* republished! I, of course, agree with him that there's so much potential for your book to have a new life!

You asked for my thoughts on living in New York City: I don't think I'd actually live here if I didn't have to for my job. If I could live anywhere, it would probably be in the same neighborhood as my parents and Iris. It's peaceful and friendly and there's a ShopRite (a chain grocery store in North America; I don't think they have those in England). New York City is loud and crowded and over-whelming. I have days where I feel like I'll lose my mind if I don't get some quiet. Commuting to and from work on the subway is a pain, especially when I've had a crappy day and then a group of kids gets on the train, performing elaborate dance routines. While walking alone at night I'm always worried that a pervert is going to snatch me up off the street. Everything is expensive for no reason. The cost of living is too high and unless you're a fi-nance or tech bro, you can barely afford to live here. I have a roommate who owns two enormous St. Bernards that get slobber everywhere, so Tomcat and I mostly stick to my bedroom because I'm too anxious to remind my roommate that the apartment is my space too, and it's easier to hole up in my room than confront her about her dogs.

But New York has some of the best food, and New Yorkers band together during times of crisis in a wonderful way. I read somewhere that New Yorkers are not always nice, but they're al-ways kind, and that's the best way I can describe it.

Sometimes if I leave the office early enough, I can catch the sunset while going over the Manhattan Bridge. That's a plus.

Question: Does the traveling ever make you feel lonely?

Sincerely,

Lily

P.S. Attached is a photo of that Manhattan Bridge sunset I was talking about.

• • •

FROM: N.R. Strickland <nrs@nrstrickland.com>

TO: Lily G. <lilyg@gmail.com>

DATE: July 21, 1:41am

SUBJECT: Re: You can call me Strick

Lily—

Whenever I talk to people about living in New York City, they share a million reasons why they hate it, and then go on to describe how it's one of the best cities. It's funny that you basically had the same response. That picture of the sunset is striking. I guess after having a tough day, getting to see such beauty makes it all feel worth it.

To answer your question, I'm used to being alone, so it feels natural.

It's pretty late right now in New York, isn't it? Don't tell me you're an insomniac like me.

~Strick

P.S.—Who is Tomcat?

• • •

FROM: Lily G. <lilyg@gmail.com>
TO: N.R. Strickland <nrs@nrstrickland.com>
DATE: July 21, 2:04am
SUBJECT: Re: You can call me Strick

Dear Strick,

I can't believe I've gone this long without telling you about Tom-cat! Tomcat is my cat. He used to live at the bookstore where I worked, but when the owner remarried, his new wife had a cat allergy, so I agreed to take Tomcat home with me. He's the sweet-est, largest, fluffiest, calico cat in the world (a picture is attached for proof).

I'm not an insomniac. I *love* sleep. Probably more than the av-erage human. I'm awake right now because I had a bad date ear-lier tonight and I'm replaying it in my head because that's what I do.

If you can believe it, I'm even worse on dates than I am during job interviews. I never know what to say, because everything about my life always sounds so uninteresting. It doesn't help that I only go on dates with guys my sisters set me up with. If it's a date with one of Violet's friends, he's either a model, aspiring actor/entertainer or works in fashion. He is chic and cool and intimidat-ingly attractive to the point where looking at him for too long feels overwhelming. He is also inevitably in love with Violet and has only agreed to go out with me to get into her good graces. (This happened all the time in high school, so I'm used to it.) If it's a date with one of Iris's friends, he's someone she knows from busi-ness school. He will want to know my five-year plan and whether or not I've thought about setting up an LLC. He wears a suit, carries a smooth leather briefcase, and is at least fifteen minutes late because something important popped up at work right before he planned to leave the office. He expects me to be dynamic and driven and commanding like Iris and is disappointed when he finds out that I'm average.

Tonight's date was with one of Violet's guys, a model named Tony. He was very handsome and tall and charismatic, so I got overwhelmed looking at him and focused my attention on his collarbone while he spoke. He spent most of the night talking about himself and his recent modeling gigs. Then he mentioned Violet and kept talking about her, so I wasn't afraid to finally ask if he had feelings for her. He tried to lie at first, but then he admitted that he's in love with her and has been since they met. Violet is not the type to settle down. (I think that's why guys like her so much. They think they'll be the one to change her mind.) After telling Tony he'd have to give up on my sister, he started crying. (I should note that he'd had four Henny and Cokes at this point.) I comforted him as the entire restaurant stared. It was embarrassing, but I mostly felt bad for him.

So that's why I'm awake right now. I'm thinking about the handsome, heartbroken model who cried on my shoulder. I always know how dates set up by my sisters will end, but I go anyway.

I'd apologize for oversharing, but I think we're past that now.

Sincerely,

Lily

• • •

FROM: N.R. Strickland <nrs@nrstrickland.com>
TO: Lily G. <lilyg@gmail.com>
DATE: July 21, 2:23am
SUBJECT: Re: You can call me Strick

Lily—
Wow. That's . . . a lot. I feel sorry for him too, but I'm more concerned about you. Why do you go on these dates if you know they
won't lead to anything or that the night will end with some bloke
crying on your shoulder about your sister? Are you okay? I hope
you're asleep by now, but I'm here to talk if you need to.
~Strick

P.S.—I should have surmised that Tomcat was indeed a cat. He's
nice-looking, I guess from an objective point of view. I have to be
honest: I'm terrified of cats. When I was younger, my neighbor
had evil cats who would scratch and bite at my ankles and pounce
on me for no reason. I'm scarred for life. Can you ever really trust
a cat? Tomcat is probably plotting your demise this very minute.

• • •

FROM: Lily G. <lilyg@gmail.com>
TO: N.R. Strickland <nrs@nrstrickland.com>
DATE: July 21, 2:32am
SUBJECT: Re: You can call me Strick

Dear Strick,
I know we're friends now (or I at least assume we are?), but I will
not take any cat slander in my inbox! Cats are beautiful, majestic,

intelligent and unique creatures who get such a bad rep! Tomcat is the sweetest, cuddliest pet. He loves to plop himself down in a warm and willing lap. If you ever met him, he'd surely change your mind about cats being terrifying.

So back to my dating life. I know the obvious solution would be to stop allowing my sisters to set me up. But I guess I want to show them that I'm trying. Maybe it's a baby-of-the-family complex. I had a slower start than my sisters. Out of the womb, they were impressive, brilliant people, and that wasn't really the case for me. My family's perpetual opinion is that I don't know what I'm doing with my life and I need their help. So if going on a few bad dates is a way to get my sisters off my back, I'll do it. It's the same reason I go to career seminars every now and then, because my parents don't think I'm capable of negotiating a promotion and that I might need to find a new line of work.

But enough about me. Where are you in the world right now?

XO,

Lily

• • •

FROM: N.R. Strickland <nrs@nrstrickland.com>
TO: Lily G. <lilyg@gmail.com>
DATE: July 21, 2:41am
SUBJECT: Re: You can call me Strick

Lily—

Ah, I get it. Family dynamics are tough. I know that better than anyone. Maybe one day, you'll actually meet a decent person on one of those dates. Or maybe you'll bump into your soulmate on the street. (Does that only happen in New York City movies and not in real life?) Either way, it seems to me that you *do* know what you're doing with your life and that you have a clear goal to edit children's books. I've never met your sisters, so I can't make a comparison, but you sound impressive to me.

I promise I'll stop with the cat slander. My apologies to Tomcat. I'm sure he's nice and doesn't spend most of his time lying in wait to attack you.

I'm still in Thailand. I loved it (and the elephants) so much, I extended my stay.

I hope you're sleeping by now.

~Strick

P.S.—Yes, I think it's safe to say we are (virtual) friends by now.

• • •

FROM: N.R. Strickland <nrs@nrstrickland.com>
TO: Lily G. <lilyg@gmail.com>
DATE: July 21, 3:52am
SUBJECT: Re: You can call me Strick

Lily—

I'm guessing you're asleep since you haven't replied, and you usually reply fairly quickly. I'm leaving for Vietnam tomorrow for a few weeks and I'm not sure what the connection situation will be like where I'm staying, so if you don't hear from me for a bit, that's why.

I'm looking at the picture of Tomcat again (trying to understand what you see in cats), and I just noticed a foot beside Tomcat in the photo. Is that your foot? If so, what kind of flower is that tattoo? I'm guessing it's a lily?

~Strick

...

FROM: N.R. Strickland <nrs@nrstrickland.com>
TO: Lily G. <lilyg@gmail.com>
DATE: July 21, 3:53am
SUBJECT: Re: You can call me Strick

Shit, now it probably seems like I have a weird foot fetish and that I've been staring at your foot for hours. I have NOT been doing that. It's just that the tattoo caught my eye.

...

FROM: N.R. Strickland <nrs@nrstrickland.com>
TO: Lily G. <lilyg@gmail.com>
DATE: July 21, 3:54am
SUBJECT: Re: You can call me Strick

It's not that I don't think your foot isn't *worthy* of a foot fetish. It's a nice-looking foot.

...

FROM: N.R. Strickland <nrs@nrstrickland.com>
TO: Lily G. <lilyg@gmail.com>
DATE: July 21, 3:55am
SUBJECT: Re: You can call me Strick

I'm really buggering this up. I promise I'm not obsessed with your feet and I won't mention anything about their appearance ever again.

It's a good thing you're asleep and I'll be somewhere without service soon. Hopefully when we reconnect, you'll have forgotten about these messages.

• • •

FROM: Lily G. <lilyg@gmail.com>
TO: N.R. Strickland <nrs@nrstrickland.com>
DATE: July 22, 7:21am
SUBJECT: Re: You can call me Strick

Dear Strick,

These emails were hilarious to read, mostly because they were proof that you can be awkward sometimes too lol. You're correct: the tattoo is a drawing of a lily flower. My sisters have flower tattoos to match their names too. We got them after I turned eighteen.

I realized we've been talking about my career a lot, but not yours. What will you be writing about in Vietnam? What do you usually write about while on assignment in general?

XO,
Lily

P.S.—Thanks for saying you think I sound impressive. That really means a lot.

• • •

FROM: N.R. Strickland <nrs@nrstrickland.com>
TO: Lily G. <lilyg@gmail.com>
DATE: September 12, 10:14pm
SUBJECT: I'm alive

Lily—

It's been almost two months since I last wrote. You probably won't believe this, but my backpack fell into the water while I was on a boat in the Mekong River. Both my laptop and phone were unsalvageable. Usually, I take notes in my journal by day and transcribe them on my laptop at night, but I had to write the entire piece by hand this time (which I actually enjoyed). So that is why you haven't heard from me in so long. Sorry!

For work, I write a column called "A Day in the Life." I spend weeks with a person native to the country where I'm on assignment, and I accompany them as they go about their daily duties. I also take time to explore the area on my own. As far as jobs go, it's pretty decent. I meet a lot of people, and there is no monotony. My salary is shit, but the magazine covers travel and lodging, so I guess I can't really complain.

While in Vietnam, I stayed in the city of Cần Thơ and spent time with a family who worked at the Cai Rang Floating Market (where I stupidly dropped my bag). Other than damaging my ridiculously expensive electronics, it was a pretty great experience. I liked being completely disconnected. Maybe that's why I took a stab at writing fiction again. It was terrible and reaffirmed that part of my life is indeed over.

I landed in Budapest this morning and finally bought a new phone. My next paycheck is going toward a laptop.

How was the rest of your summer? How is Tomcat?

~Strick

. . .

FROM: Lily G. <lilyg@gmail.com>
TO: N.R. Strickland <nrs@nrstrickland.com>
DATE: September 12, 10:57pm
SUBJECT: Re: I'm alive

Strick! I'm so happy to hear from you. I thought maybe you'd felt so embarrassed after commenting on my feet that our correspondence was over. I'm sorry that you dropped your laptop in a river, but I'm glad that's the only reason you weren't talking to me.

You have the best job. You can travel and be free and do what you need to do without anyone breathing over your shoulder or micromanaging you. That must be so nice.

I don't have any interesting updates to share. I had a midyear review with my boss that didn't go so well. A couple weeks ago I forgot to add a dentist appointment to her calendar (a task that's not in my job description) and now she's written me off as useless. Would you be surprised to learn that I'm her third assistant in four years?

Tomcat is doing well! He's chunky and healthy and continues to be the best cuddler. One of my roommate's dogs ate an entire bag of Tomcat's dry food while I was at work last week, and my roommate refused to reimburse me, so that was fun. I had another bad date, this time with one of Iris's business school friends that ended with him pitching to be my life coach. I went to the beach with Iris and my niece. That was probably the highlight of August. Summer went by in the blink of an eye.

And wait. You tried to write fiction? Was it a short story? The beginning of an *Elves* sequel??? I'm sure it wasn't terrible. You can always share your writing with me if you want an opinion!

XO,

Lily

...

FROM: N.R. Strickland <nrs@nrstrickland.com>
TO: Lily G. <lilyg@gmail.com>
DATE: September 14, 9:42pm
SUBJECT: Re: I'm alive

Lily—
I haven't forgotten that you are a publishing professional. There is absolutely no chance I am sharing any of my subpar writing with you. I won't even share it with my agent.

I'm sorry to hear about your boss and the flatmate. But glad to hear Tomcat is faring well (even if I'm still skeptical about his supposed sweet nature).

I've missed reading your emails. I promise not to drop my laptop in a river and go another two months without speaking.
~Strick

...

FROM: N.R. Strickland <nrs@nrstrickland.com>
TO: Lily G. <lilyg@gmail.com>
DATE: September 29, 6:13pm
SUBJECT: Re: I'm alive

Lily—
Maybe I jinxed myself with that last email. Two weeks is nowhere near as long as two months, but I'm checking in to make sure all is well?
~Strick

. . .

FROM: Lily G. <lilyg@gmail.com>
TO: N.R. Strickland <nrs@nrstrickland.com>
DATE: October 1, 11:02am
SUBJECT: Re: I'm alive

Hi Strick,

I'm sorry about the radio silence. There's been so much going on. My boss decided to move one of her books up a season, which means I've spent every evening and some weekends for the past month fast-editing a book about the Manson Family. Then just when Iris got promoted at work (meaning she'd work even longer hours than before, including some weekends) her babysitter quit, which was bad because my two-year-old niece freaks out whenever she's around someone who isn't family. It took her months to get used to her old babysitter. Of course my parents happened to be spending the whole month in Georgia with my aunt and uncle, and Violet is always on the go, so I've been watching my niece whenever I can. Oh, and I was preparing for a job interview at another children's publisher, which I didn't get, unfortunately. Overall, though, I'm okay. Busy. But okay.

How are you? Where are you?

XO,
Lily

. . .

FROM: N.R. Strickland <nrs@nrstrickland.com>
TO: Lily G. <lilyg@gmail.com>
DATE: October 1, 6:13pm
SUBJECT: Re: I'm alive

So you've been spending the month with your toddler niece and the Manson Family. Nice. Joking. I'm sorry things have been hectic for you. I think it's admirable that you sacrifice your own time to be with your niece and that your sister is adamant on having someone babysit her. My parents would have just left me alone and not thought twice about it.

I'm in Coimbra, Portugal, on a new assignment. I've been shadowing an engineering professor at the University of Coimbra who moonlights as a baker. He brings in desserts for his students every class, so they love him, of course.

I'm attaching a picture of a pão de ló cake he made last week. It's light, like an angel cake. It was one of the best desserts I've ever had. If you were here, I would have saved you a piece.

~Strick

· · ·

FROM: Lily G. <lilyg@gmail.com>
TO: N.R. Strickland <nrs@nrstrickland.com>
DATE: October 13, 2:54am
SUBJECT: Re: I'm alive

Hi Strick,

Since I last wrote, things have gotten a bit worse. I think Iris's job is really stressing her out. She's starting to crack a little. The other day, she locked herself in the bathroom and I could hear her crying, but when she opened the door, she was fresh faced and smiling as if nothing had happened and she didn't want to talk about it. She's always been like that in a way. After my brother-in-law passed away, she became obsessed with finding the right flowers to put on every table at the repast. It was all she talked about for days.

It's almost 3am here. I'm in Iris's spare bedroom, staring at the ceiling, worrying about my family. Maybe I am turning into an insomniac like you.

What keeps you up at night?

Lily

...

FROM: N.R. Strickland <nrs@nrstrickland.com>
TO: Lily G. <lilyg@gmail.com>
DATE: October 13, 3:06am
SUBJECT: Re: I'm alive

Lily, I'm really sorry to hear that your sister and niece are struggling. They're really lucky to have you there with them and I hope things get better soon.

To answer your question about my insomnia, it started when I was young, maybe around nine or so. I was alone a lot at night, so I mostly stayed awake because I was afraid. But when I couldn't sleep, I read. I didn't have money to buy books, so I read anything I could get my hands on at the library. My favorite book was probably *A Wrinkle in Time*. I checked it out so often, the librarian at my school ended up buying a copy for me, which was kind of her but simultaneously made me feel like a charity case. Either way, the escapism saved me.

You said you read a lot when you were younger too. What did you read? Maybe you should try to read for a while. It might help you fall asleep.

~Strick

...

FROM: Lily G. <lilyg@gmail.com>
TO: N.R. Strickland <nrs@nrstrickland.com>
DATE: October 13, 3:21am
SUBJECT: Re: I'm alive

My favorite book was *Ella Enchanted*. I felt like Ella when I was younger, like I had to do everything my parents and sisters said. Violet and Iris are the opposite of evil stepsisters. They're the best sisters in the world. It's just by comparison, I came up short, and I still do. I used to think something was wrong with me because I wasn't into clubs and sports like they were, and I wasn't a great student either. Nothing about me was particularly exceptional. But whenever I was reading, I didn't think about that. The escapism saved me too. I guess we have that in common.

I do have a few e-books saved on my phone. I'll take your advice and read for a while.

Not to make it awkward, but I want to tell you how much I appreciate being your (virtual) friend. You've been a confidant for the last five months, which sounds so silly because we've never met, and I don't even know what you look like. But maybe that's the magic of it. We're two strangers who mutually decided to show each other some kindness. I feel less alone, knowing that you're only an email away.

As always, thank you for listening.

...

FROM: N.R. Strickland <nrs@nrstrickland.com>
TO: Lily G. <lilyg@gmail.com>
DATE: October 13, 3:27am
SUBJECT: Re: I'm alive

Lily, I feel the same. As I said before, you're the only person I regularly correspond with other than my boss and literary agent, and I have to admit that your emails bring me much more joy than theirs. In my line of work, I meet strangers all the time, and once we get to know each other well, I have to leave. It's funny that we've never met, but our connection has endured.

P.S.—I'm in Vilnius, Lithuania. Not sure where I'm headed next, still waiting on that assignment. Here's a picture of Vilnius's Cathedral Square. I thought the buildings were striking. I immediately felt at peace in that space. I hope that looking at this picture can do the same for you.

· · ·

FROM: Lily G. <lilyg@gmail.com>
TO: N.R. Strickland <nrs@nrstrickland.com>
DATE: November 28, 9:51pm
SUBJECT: Happy Thanksgiving

Hi Strick,
It's Thanksgiving Day here in North America. I've been cooking and baking with my mom and sisters all day.
    Where are you? How are you?
XO,
Lily

P.S.—Thank you for sending the picture of the Cathedral Square. I looked at it several times over the last month, and it did bring me peace.

. . .

FROM: N.R. Strickland <nrs@nrstrickland.com>
TO: Lily G. <lilyg@gmail.com>
DATE: November 28, 11:22pm
SUBJECT: Re: Happy Thanksgiving

Lily—

It's so good to hear from you. I'm in Plzeň, Czech Republic. I've been getting to know a couple who work at the Pilsner Urquell brewery (home of the pilsner beer; have you ever tried it?)

What did you bake? How are you doing?

~Strick

. . .

FROM: Lily G. <lilyg@gmail.com>
TO: N.R. Strickland <nrs@nrstrickland.com>
DATE: November 30, 1:34am
SUBJECT: Re: Happy Thanksgiving

Hi Strick,

Last night I fell asleep right after writing to you. I guess that's what happens when you eat seconds of Thanksgiving dinner and finish it with pie. (I baked every pie: apple cinnamon, pumpkin and sweet potato.) It was the first full night of sleep I've had in months.

I've never tried pilsner beer. I'm not much of a beer drinker, actually. Speaking of beer, earlier tonight, Violet dragged me to the bar in our hometown and we ran into two guys who were in love with her in high school (because every guy was in love with her in high school), and while Violet got drunk and ended up making out with one of the guys on the dance floor, I got stuck with his friend Devon, who was dead set on describing the ins and outs of his PhD program. I was so bored and tired that I literally fell asleep in the middle of the conversation. Devon was offended, and I felt terrible. I wish I had the heart to tell him that economics isn't as interesting as he might think.

It's kind of funny that my bad date plague continues, even when it's unplanned. It got me wondering what a *good* date would be like. My "ideal date," I guess you could say. I wouldn't mind if we did something basic, like go to the movies and get burgers. Or maybe walk around the park and stop at a bookstore (this might be asking for too much lol). Really it would be nice to spend an evening with someone who wanted to hear what I had to say, rather than talk about themselves all night, and who was patient with my nerves and lack of eloquence.

Do you date a lot while traveling? What is the best date you've ever been on? Or what does your ideal date look like?

XO,

Lily

• • •

FROM: N.R. Strickland <nrs@nrstrickland.com>
TO: Lily G. <lilyg@gmail.com>
DATE: December 5, 8:52pm
SUBJECT: Re: Happy Thanksgiving

Lily—

I'm not sure that I would call what I do "dating." It's hard to commit to someone when you know you'll be gone in a few weeks. I don't see the point in long distance.

The best date I've ever been on was during my first year at the magazine. While in Paris, I had a picnic with a girl on the grass in front of the Eiffel Tower. I don't know if I'd consider that my *ideal* date, but it was cliché and it's Paris, so there you have it.

I think the requirements of my ideal date would be equally as simple as yours: to spend time with someone I liked and who liked me.

Your bad date stories make it seem as though the men in the US are incompetent. I don't understand how they keep fumbling their chances with you.

If you were here with me in Plzeň, I'd first bring you to meet Agata and Andel (the couple I've been getting to know), we'll say we have to leave because we have dinner reservations, but Agata would encourage us to stay and eat dinner with them instead. She'll say that her rajská omáčka (beef in tomato soup) is better than anything we'll eat at a restaurant, and she'll be right. After we leave their home, we'll be so full that we'll walk around the city slowly, staring up at the clear night sky. I'll point at a constellation of stars and say they look like the shape of a dog. You'll smile, shake your head and say I'm only making things up so that you'll laugh, which would be true.

We'll walk by a bookshop, which will have just closed minutes before. But the owner recognizes that we're true book lovers, so she lets us stay late and browse the shelves. You'll choose a Czech edition of *Ella Enchanted*. I'll consider buying *A Song of Ice and Fire* but then I'll remember my failed aspirations to be like George R. R. Martin, and I'll decide against it.

Afterward, we'll come upon a park, but the benches will be occupied by other couples. You'll say, "Wouldn't it be nice if we had a blanket to sit on?" And what do you know, I'll pull a blanket out of thin air (maybe there's magic in this scenario), and we'll sit and spend the rest of the night pointing out more fake shapes in the stars.

It would make up for every bad date you'd ever had.
~Strick

P.S.—this is what Agata's rajská omáčka looks like.

• • •

FROM: Lily G. <lilyg@gmail.com>
TO: N.R. Strickland <nrs@nrstrickland.com>
DATE: December 6, 6:32pm
SUBJECT: Re: Happy Thanksgiving

Hi Strick,
Is it sad that our imaginary date is the best date I'll ever have? That sounds lovely. Seriously. And that plate of rajská omáčka looks delicious.

(Also, you might hate me for saying this, but your last email really proved that you're a natural storyteller.)

I'm here working late at the office. It's Christmastime, and our building is a ten-minute walk away from the big tree at Rockefeller Center, so the area is mobbed with tourists. I can't believe that you've traveled all over the world but haven't been to New York City. If you were here, I'd take you to every place filled with Christmastime tourists. We'd complain about the crowded sidewalks and how no one seems to know where they're going. Then your mood will brighten when I take you to the holiday market at Union Square. Because you're so cool and cultured, I'll expect you to buy something unique, like energy crystals or handwoven scarves. But you'll surprise me when you buy a Black Santa figurine and a keychain that says, "I <3 NY." Afterward, we'll sit on a Union Square park bench and drink hot chocolate, and you'll say that New York is simultaneously the most frustrating yet best city, and you can't believe you waited this long to visit.

How'd I do?

XO,

Lily

P.S.—Where do you spend the holidays?

• • •

FROM: N.R. Strickland <nrs@nrstrickland.com>
TO: Lily G. <lilyg@gmail.com>
DATE: December 17, 9:47pm
SUBJECT: Re: Happy Thanksgiving

Lily—

If I had the money, and if I weren't currently in Skopje, Macedonia, I'd fly to New York right now so that we could spend the day together just how you described. It sounds perfect, but you left out one thing. I'd like to try a famous slice of New York pizza.

I usually spend the holiday wherever I'm on assignment. My boss would let me take time off to go home if I wanted to, but I don't spend the holidays with family so there's no point in taking a break if I don't need to.

I used to spend the holidays with my best friend and his family while at university.

I know you're reading this email and thinking that I must be a truly sorry person. But, really, I prefer to be alone, so don't feel bad for me, okay?

~Strick

• • •

FROM: Lily G. <lilyg@gmail.com>
TO: N.R. Strickland <nrs@nrstrickland.com>
DATE: December 18, 10:19am
SUBJECT: Re: Happy Thanksgiving

Hi Strick,

It makes me *very sad* that you spend Christmas alone, but you asked me not to feel bad for you, so that's all I'm going to say on the subject.

I spend a lot of time baking at my parents' house over Christmas. If you were in the States, I'd save you some vanilla cookies.

XO,

Lily

• • •

FROM: N.R. Strickland <nrs@nrstrickland.com>
TO: Lily G. <lilyg@gmail.com>
DATE: December 20, 12:03am
SUBJECT: Re: Happy Thanksgiving

Thanks for the offer on the cookies. I'm sure they're amazing.

• • •

FROM: Lily G. <lilyg@gmail.com>
TO: N.R. Strickland <nrs@nrstrickland.com>
DATE: December 25, 10:19am
SUBJECT: Merry Christmas

Merry Christmas, Strick! I hope you're feeling the Christmas spirit where you are. (I know that might be cheesy, but I'm cheesy all the time and even more so over the holidays.)

• • •

FROM: N.R. Strickland <nrs@nrstrickland.com>
TO: Lily G. <lilyg@gmail.com>
DATE: December 25, 8:54pm
SUBJECT: Re: Merry Christmas

It is quite cheesy, but I'll give it a pass. Happy Christmas, Lily.

• • •

FROM: N.R. Strickland <nrs@nrstrickland.com>
TO: Lily G. <lilyg@gmail.com>
DATE: December 31, 6:01pm
SUBJECT: Happy New Year

Lily,
It's after midnight here in Macedonia, so let me be the first to wish you a happy New Year.

I was invited to a party by a friend I met at my hostel. I managed to find a half-full bottle of champagne from the kitchen, which I've decided to keep for myself.

If you were here, I'd share it with you, and we wouldn't really be able to understand the language everyone else was speaking, but that would be okay, because we'd sit in the corner, in our own world, drinking out of cheap, plastic champagne flutes. And when the clock struck midnight, we'd turn to each other and smile. I'd raise my eyebrow and you'd nod. Then we'd kiss. And we'd both think how happy we were to be there together.

· · ·

FROM: N.R. Strickland <nrs@nrstrickland.com>
TO: Lily G. <lilyg@gmail.com>
DATE: December 31, 6:11pm
SUBJECT: Re: Happy New Year

Lily, I apologize for my last email. I've had too much to drink, and I never drink. I don't know what I was thinking. I hope I haven't ruined things. This is worse than the foot comments.

Forgive me?

· · ·

FROM: Lily G. <lilyg@gmail.com>
TO: N.R. Strickland <nrs@nrstrickland.com>
DATE: January 1, 12:02am
SUBJECT: Re: Happy New Year

Hi Strick,
There's nothing to forgive. Spending New Year's with you, in the exact way you described—kiss and all—sounds pretty perfect to me.

I hope this year is good to you and that our emails continue.

Happy New Year!!!

XOXO,

Lily

• • •

FROM: N.R. Strickland <nrs@nrstrickland.com>

TO: Lily G. <lilyg@gmail.com>

DATE: January 8, 7:34pm

SUBJECT: Re: Happy New Year

Lily—

I'm glad my drunken email didn't scare you away. For the record, completely sober, it's still something I'd like to do.

This year is already off to a bizarre start. My agent might have actually done something with *Elves*, like garner legitimate interest from a US publisher. I don't want to jinx it (and let's be honest, I'm still pessimistic and doubtful), so I won't tell you details yet until it's a for-sure thing. But if it does come to fruition, you'll be the first to know.

And if this is real . . . I might move to New York. Near you. No more hypothetical scenarios. We could finally meet.

• • •

FROM: Lily G. <lilyg@gmail.com>

TO: N.R. Strickland <nrs@nrstrickland.com>

DATE: January 8, 7:38pm

SUBJECT: Re: Happy New Year

Strick, that's AMAZING! All of it! The news about *Elves* and that you might move to New York! That we might meet in person!

I've been thinking for a while that maybe we could "meet" before you move here. How do you feel about a video chat? I'd really love to see you, even if it's through a screen. Only if you're comfortable, of course.

XO,

Lily

· · ·

FROM: N.R. Strickland <nrs@nrstrickland.com>

TO: Lily G. <lilyg@gmail.com>

DATE: January 8, 9:22pm

SUBJECT: Re: Happy New Year

I'd like to see you too. I can do Sunday. How about 12pm, New York time? That's 7pm for me.

· · ·

FROM: Lily G. <lilyg@gmail.com>

TO: N.R. Strickland <nrs@nrstrickland.com>

DATE: January 8, 7:38pm

SUBJECT: Re: Happy New Year

I'm so relieved you agreed. Sunday is perfect. I'll send a link.

See you then!

XO,

Lily

. . .

FROM: Lily G. <lilyg@gmail.com>
TO: N.R. Strickland <nrs@nrstrickland.com>
DATE: January 12, 12:11pm
SUBJECT: Video chat

Hey, just checking to see if you might be having trouble logging in? I'm here!

. . .

FROM: Lily G. <lilyg@gmail.com>
TO: N.R. Strickland <nrs@nrstrickland.com>
DATE: January 12, 12:14pm
SUBJECT: Re: Video chat

Still here . . . Should we reschedule? If so, that's totally fine! I know there's a chance the connection might be spotty where you are.

. . .

FROM: Lily G. <lilyg@gmail.com>
TO: N.R. Strickland <nrs@nrstrickland.com>
DATE: January 20, 10:24pm
SUBJECT: Re: Video chat

Hey Strick,
Are you okay? It's been a little over a week since we were supposed to have our video chat, and I still haven't heard from you. Did you get a last-minute travel assignment? I'm hoping you didn't drop your laptop into a river again.

Either way, I'm still here and thinking about you. I'm also still willing to meet.

XOXO,

Lily

. . .

FROM: N.R. Strickland <nrs@nrstrickland.com>

TO: Lily G. <lilyg@gmail.com>

DATE: January 24, 9:22pm

SUBJECT: Re: Video chat

Lily, I shouldn't have let this go on for as long as I did. I would love nothing more than to meet you. But I'm not who you think I am.

We can never meet. I'm so sorry.

. . .

FROM: Lily G. <lilyg@gmail.com>

TO: N.R. Strickland <nrs@nrstrickland.com>

DATE: January 24, 9:23pm

SUBJECT: Re: Video chat

Wait . . . what? What is happening?? If you're not N.R. Strickland, then who are you? Have you just been lying to me this whole time?

. . .

FROM: Mail Delivery Subsystem <mailer-daemon@googlemail.com>

TO: Lily G. <lilyg@gmail.com>

DATE: January 24, 9:24pm

SUBJECT: Delivery Status Notification (Failure)

Delivery to the following recipient failed permanently:

nrs@nrstrickland.com

The error that the other server returned was:

The email account you tried to reach does not exist. Please try double-checking the recipient's email address for typos or any unnecessary spaces. Learn more at: https://support.google.com /mail.

PART TWO

REAL LIFE

2

Five months later

LILY WASN'T UNDER THE IMPRESSION THAT SHE WAS A woman of many talents. But she was good at hiding. *Very* good.

Phone in hand, she threw a glance over her shoulder as she snuck into the coat check room at Rosa Mexicano, the fancy restaurant in Midtown New York City. It was late June and, given the heat, there shouldn't have been many coats hanging, but Violet's fashion friends found any reason to wear elaborate, if not unnecessary, jackets. Lily crouched down and crawled behind a long, olive green leather trench coat and sat pretzel style on the floor. She opened a text from her boss, Edith.

Did you remember to print out my emails before you left

It should be illegal for bosses to text employees on a Saturday. Especially if those bosses couldn't be bothered to use punctuation. Lily sighed and quickly typed out a response.

Hi, Edith. Yes, I printed your emails and left them on
your desk. I hope you're enjoying your vacation!

Edith had this thing about emails, meaning that she
didn't like to read them on her computer. Every morning,
Lily arrived at least an hour before the rest of her colleagues, printed out Edith's emails and left them on her
desk. Edith was old-school publishing. She got her start in
the days when people were still allowed to smoke in the office and authors submitted manuscripts directly to the
company via snail mail. She'd been away at her summer
home in Vermont for the past week and had asked Lily to
print all of the "important" emails she'd missed so that
she'd be able to read them first thing Monday morning.

Edith responded: OK

No *Enjoy your weekend*. Or *Thank you for killing hundreds
of trees of my behalf every month*. Just "OK." This might have
ruffled someone else's feathers, but Lily was used to the
thanklessness of her job. It was funny that Edith struggled
with handling her own email but had no problem texting
Lily at inappropriate times. Like in the middle of her sister's engagement party.

Still shielded by the ridiculously long trench coat, Lily
dropped her phone in her lap and leaned back against the
wall. She could hear the sound of her family's voices, shouting to be heard over the music. Aunts, uncles and cousins
who all drove in from New Jersey. They weren't arguing;
they were just a loud bunch. A nosy bunch. Tonight was
Violet's night, but everyone had questions for Lily. When
was it going to be *her* turn to get married? Was she dating

anyone now? What was her job situation, still an assistant after two and a half years? Did she plan to sleep on Violet's couch forever? All of the questioning combined with the unwanted social interaction made Lily's skin crawl so badly, she honestly preferred to find a quiet corner and answer Edith's texts rather than talk to her family.

Maybe she could stay hidden here for the rest of the night and no one would notice. When the party was wrapping up, she could emerge, say her goodbyes and then hop on the subway and go home—or to Violet's apartment, which was currently her home.

Yes, that's exactly what she'd do. She opened the e-reader app on her phone and decided to take this as an opportunity to finally start *The Golem and the Jinni*, a fantasy novel she'd been wanting to read for months. She never had time to read for pleasure anymore. That's something they don't tell you when you're applying to be an editor. She grinned as she scrolled to chapter 1, eyes ready to devour text that had nothing to do with work.

Then she heard the telltale sign of click-clacking high heels.

"Lily?" a voice called, entering the room. Her sister Violet.

Lily held completely still. She used to play this game as a kid when she wanted to stay inside and read but her sisters came calling to go ride bikes or do anything remotely adventurous. If she was quiet enough, maybe she could actually become invisible.

"I know you're in here," Violet said. "Iris told me she saw you walk this way."

Lily stayed motionless and held her breath when Violet's footsteps paused. Maybe she'd give up and go back to the party being thrown in her honor. Then suddenly Violet's footsteps grew louder, and the coats shielding Lily split, exposing her. Lily looked up and smiled sheepishly at her older sister. Violet smiled back and shook her head.

"I was working," Lily said, holding up her phone by way of explanation.

"On a Saturday night?" Violet held out her hand and pulled Lily to her feet. "Come on, there's someone I want you to meet."

Lily groaned. "No thanks."

"Oh, don't start. You haven't been out in forever. And Angel is so sweet. He's one of Eddy's new clients, an R&B singer! Eddy swears he's going to be the next big thing, and he's dying to meet you."

Lily rolled her eyes. "I'm sure *dying* to meet me is an exaggeration. He won't be interested. Let's not waste anyone's time."

"What are you talking about? Of course he'll be interested in you."

"I don't know what you've told him about me, but the reality is that I'm pretty boring, and he's a singer. We won't have anything to talk about."

"Not true," Violet said, looping her arm through Lily's. "You work with books. You're both in the arts. That's something to talk about right there."

Lily looked into her sister's smiling face. Violet was the middle sister, the beautiful one. Smooth brown skin. High cheekbones and full lips. She had the kind of face that made people stop and stare. Tonight, she wore deep red lipstick, a gold halter jumpsuit and matching pointy gold pumps, all designer labels that Lily couldn't afford. Violet's thick, curly hair was smoothed back and tied into a ponytail at the nape of her neck. Lily, on the other hand, wore a simple yellow short-sleeve sundress and tan sandals, all bought on sale at H&M. Her hair was pulled into a topknot bun, her easy go-to style. A common passerby would assume the two sisters were attending completely different events and happened to run into each other in the coat check.

"Come on," Violet urged again. "You won't regret meeting him, I promise."

Lily wanted to say no. She wanted nothing to do with dating. Not after the mess she'd gotten herself into last year emailing that author, or whoever they were. But Violet was looking at her with that hopeful smile, and Lily felt the pressure not to disappoint. And she knew the rest of her family would ask why she hadn't given Angel a chance. If things didn't work out with him—which they wouldn't— Lily could at least say she'd tried and then be left alone.

"Fine," she grumbled.

"Good," Violet said, steering Lily out of the coat check.

Back in the main area, Lily spotted her parents by the bar, talking with her aunts and uncles. Her cousins were on the converted dance floor, mingling with Violet's fashion friends. It gave a country-folk-meet-city-folk vibe.

Violet's squeeze on Lily's hand tightened in excitement as they approached Eddy and Angel. Eddy, Violet's fiancé, turned toward them and smiled. Well, it was more like a smirk, really. Lily wasn't sure if she'd actually ever seen Eddy smile. This was only her second time meeting him, and he always looked rather serious. Eddy was tall and slim with dark brown skin and a bald head. Like Violet, he was dressed to the nines, a crisp white button-up and slim, black slacks. He was a talent manager for a record label in LA and traveled a lot with his clients. He and Violet got engaged back in April and he finally had the time to come to the East Coast and meet the rest of the family. Lily's parents and her oldest sister, Iris, thought Violet and Eddy were moving too fast. They'd been dating for only three months before Eddy proposed. Mostly, though, everyone was shocked that Violet, who never got serious with anyone, was suddenly a bride-to-be.

"There you are," Eddy said, reaching out and wrapping his arm around Violet's waist. She grinned and melted into him. He turned his attention to Lily. "Having a good night?"

Lily nodded and felt herself clamming up as she avoided eye contact with Angel, who was also looking at her. From a quick glance, she could tell he was tall and built. Handsome, with a friendly smile. Exactly the kind of guy that caused the words to evaporate on her tongue.

"Lily, this is our friend Angel," Violet said. "Angel, this is my sister Lily."

"It's nice to meet you," Angel said. He had short, curly hair and light brown skin. He wore a plain black T-shirt and jeans. An unassuming soon-to-be celebrity with a thousand-watt smile.

"Uh." Lily's eyes widened as she fumbled for a response. She glanced at Violet, who gave her an encouraging nod before Eddy pulled her away toward the bar, leaving Lily abandoned. "Hi."

"Violet said you're a book editor. What kind of books do you work on?"

Lily blinked. Sweat gathered at her armpits. What kind of books *did* she edit? Her thoughts began to swarm. She was too nervous to think straight.

"Um, books about dictators."

"Really?" Angel tilted his head to the side. "Like all of the dictators throughout history?"

She nodded, even though that wasn't technically true. What should she say next? Should she ask about his music? Or would that be stupid because he probably always got questions about his music? Maybe she should ask something generic, like if he was based on the East or West Coast. Or would it be creepy to ask someone you barely knew where they lived? *God*, why was this so hard for her?

An awkward silence bloomed when Lily still hadn't said anything. Her mouth was beginning to hurt from smiling. But then Angel started to tell her about the album he was working on. Something about infusing blues sounds and actual instruments, no highly produced beats.

Lily nodded like a bobblehead, trying to listen and not focus on how overwhelmed she felt, when behind Angel, she spotted Iris standing by one of the tables with her daughter, Calla, propped on her hip. She was in the middle of what was most likely a work call and Calla kept reaching for the phone.

"I'm so sorry," Lily said, interrupting Angel. "But I have to help my sister. It was, um, nice to meet you."

"Oh," Angel said, surprised. "Yeah, nice to meet you too."

Lily felt a little bad as she hurried away across the room.

But, really, she was doing Angel a favor. It was unlikely that she was his type. Plus, chances were he secretly had a thing for Violet.

She approached Iris and smoothly gathered Calla into her arms. Iris mouthed, *Thank you,* before turning away and continuing her work call.

"You're saving me from further adult interaction tonight," Lily whispered to Calla as they sat down at an empty table. Calla perched in Lily's lap and giggled, even though she probably had no idea what Lily was talking about.

"Your dress is yellow," she said, touching Lily's sleeve. "Pretty."

"Thank you." Lily beamed at her now-three-year-old niece who looked so much like her late brother-in-law, Terry, it hurt. "Your dress is pretty too."

IT WAS ALMOST ELEVEN P.M. WHEN THE PARTY FINALLY ended. Lily stood outside of the restaurant with her sisters and waved goodbye to their parents as they drove off, heading back to New Jersey.

"Don't forget what we talked about, Lily!" their mom called.

Lily nodded and forced a smile, but inwardly grimaced. After suffering through another long discussion with her mom and aunts while they tried to convince her to apply for law school or medical school or any new avenue that might result in success and decent money, Lily had reluctantly agreed to attend another EmpoWOMEN networking seminar with her mother. Her family was baffled that now at twenty-six, Lily was still someone's assistant with a meager salary, while Violet was an established celebrity stylist at only twenty-seven, and Iris was the head of partnerships at a beauty brand start-up at twenty-nine. Even her parents had opened their own plant and flower nursery in their late twenties after graduating from Brown. So what was wrong with Lily?

She personally had no idea, but she hated the narrative that in order to be a moderately successful Black person, she had to be exceptional. She didn't know if she was capable of exceptional. She simply wanted to *be*. That was already hard enough.

"Can you believe I'm getting married?" Violet said, draping Eddy's blazer over her shoulders. He'd gone to get his car, so the three sisters were alone, with Calla sleeping in Iris's arms. "I'm going to be somebody's whole-ass wife. I can't wait."

"Don't you think you *should* wait a little longer?" Iris asked. "Getting married at the end of August is pretty soon."

Violet rolled her eyes. "Not this again."

"What?" Iris switched Calla to her other hip. "You barely know him, Vi."

Violet groaned, and Iris shrugged, straight-faced.

Iris was the smart sister. Growing up, she'd juggled Model UN, debate team and year-round sports while keeping a 4.0 GPA. She graduated at the top of her class in both undergrad and business school. She was beautiful too but didn't bother with frills like Violet. Tonight, she wore a sleeveless black top and black jeans, and her curly hair was cropped close to her scalp. Even though she worked for a cosmetics company and often gave free products to Lily and Violet, she wore no makeup, just clear lip gloss. And she made only practical decisions, which was why she couldn't understand Violet's sudden choice to get married.

"I *do* know him. I love him," Violet insisted. "Why can't you just be happy for me?"

"That's the thing. I don't know if I believe that you're happy."

"I am!" Violet said. "Tell her, Lily."

Lily, ever the peacemaker, glanced back and forth between her headstrong sisters. Honestly, she wasn't quite sure what to make of Violet's engagement. It seemed that out of nowhere, she'd met Eddy and decided to get serious. But Lily had fallen for a stranger she'd met online, who hadn't even turned out to be the stranger she thought he was. Her actions had been more illogical, so how could she judge anyone?

"I don't know," she finally said. "Eddy seems nice."

"*Thank you*," Violet said.

Iris simply shook her head and frowned. "Okay, but there's still so much else to plan in a short time span. You need a wedding dress. We need bridesmaid dresses. Someone has to plan your bridal shower and bachelorette party. Do you and Eddy even have a venue? A caterer?"

"Yes, we have a venue, Iris," Violet huffed. "Eddy pulled some strings at a place in New Jersey not too far from Mom and Dad. He's taking care of the caterer too. We aren't having a traditional wedding. There will be no bridesmaids or groomsmen. Just Eddy and me, professing our love to each other in front of our loved ones. And the wedding dress search is in progress. If I know how to do anything, it's finding the right item of clothing." She paused and then sidled closer to Iris, grinning. "And as far as the bridal shower and bachelorette party, you know how wild my schedule is. Let's just do them the same weekend. And I was hoping my lovely, detail-oriented older sister would help me plan."

"Of course you were." Iris rolled her eyes but was unable to fight her smile. "Fine."

"Thank you!" Violet gave Iris a loud, smacking kiss on the cheek and Iris laughed.

Lily let out a relieved sigh. She didn't know if she had the energy to referee a sister argument tonight.

"Anyway, let's focus on more important matters," Violet said. "Like Lily's wedding date."

"True," Iris agreed.

Lily blinked. "Wait, what?"

Leave it to her sisters to find common ground with their desire to fix her life.

"What happened with Angel?" Violet asked.

Lily shrugged. "Iris needed help with Calla, so I walked away."

Iris raised an eyebrow. "Who is Angel?"

"One of Eddy's clients," Violet explained. "A singer."

"Ugh, no," Iris said. "You don't want to date someone in the entertainment industry, do you, Lily?"

"*No*," Lily said. "I do not."

"Okay, *fine*. We'll just find you someone else," Violet said. "You don't want to show up to my wedding stag, Lily. If it happens that you meet someone else at the wedding, even better, but you need to have some fun. You haven't gone out since you broke up with that guy a few months ago. You know, the one you never bothered to tell us about or introduce us to."

Lily bit her lip. She hadn't been completely honest with her sisters about what had happened with Strick. But how could she tell them the truth? That she was heartbroken after being catfished. They would pity her. And they would take that failure only as further proof that she needed their help. So she'd lied and said she'd been dating someone for a while and they'd broken up. She knew her sisters meant well, but she couldn't go on any more of their orchestrated dates. Strick might have been a hoax, but she'd finally experienced how it felt to talk to someone she actually liked, and she didn't want to settle for less now.

"I don't need to meet anyone new," Lily made herself say. She hated being combative or disagreeable, but she'd drawn a line in the sand and she wouldn't go back.

"Don't worry, we'll take care of it," Violet said. "I know this really cute sound engineer who works with one of Eddy's clients. I'll give you his number."

"I think she'd be better off with my assistant's cousin, Richard," Iris countered. "He's a law student at Cornell."

Violet groaned. "Another law student? *Boring.* This model I worked with on an *Elle* shoot has a brother who's a baseball player. She showed me pictures and he was fine. Wish I could remember the name of his team . . ."

"Lily doesn't like baseball, though." Iris frowned. In a careful attempt not to wake Calla, she reached for her purse. "Richard is sweet. I have his card here somewhere."

"I'm not bringing a date," Lily said, finally getting a word in edgewise. "You don't have to talk around me like this."

"Oh, we're only trying to help," Iris said.

"I don't need your help!" Lily burst out, shocking her sisters and herself. They stared at her, and she breathed heavily, rubbing her sweaty palms against her dress.

"I don't need your help," she repeated, more quietly. "I'll find my own date."

"Really?" Violet asked, exchanging a glance with Iris.

Lily nodded, determined. She might have been a twenty-six-year-old who was stuck at a crappy job with no idea how to move forward, been a recent victim of a catfishing that she'd walked right into, and she might have been living on her sister's couch because she'd had to escape her previous roommate's evil dogs, but *by God*, she was going to find a date on her own and finally get her sisters off her back.

"And when I do get my date, I never want either of you to try to set me up ever again," she said.

"And what if you don't get a date?" Violet asked, raising an eyebrow.

Lily paused, considering Violet's question. "Then I'll go on your dates until the day I die or I'm an old maid with a million cats. Whichever comes first. Deal?"

Lily held out her hand, and Violet looked at it, skeptical. But then she grinned, grabbed Lily's hand and shook. "Deal."

They both turned to Iris, who sighed but reluctantly shook their hands as well. "For the record, I think this is childish," she said.

But the bet wasn't childish in Lily's eyes. Because for once in her life, she was going to try her hardest not to lose.

EDDY AND VIOLET DECIDED TO GO TO A BAR, SO LILY WAS alone as she walked into Violet's fancy Union Square apartment building and got onto the elevator, pressing number 14 for their floor. It was a newer building with a housing lottery, so Violet had gotten lucky and scored a deal on the rent, and Lily was happy to temporarily live on Violet's pullout couch. She loved Union Square. It was one of her favorite parts of the city.

Lily remembered the granola bar in her tote bag, and she rummaged for it, gasping in delight once it was located. Hiding at the party meant she hadn't had much time to eat. She took a large chomp, grateful and starving. Then she jumped when someone suddenly shouted, "Hold the elevator!"

A hand shot out, keeping the elevator doors from closing. And then Lily saw him.

Her neighbor who lived down the hall.

He was slightly out of breath as he stepped into the elevator, and he flashed a quick smile at Lily, so beautiful it was nearly blinding. She tried not to openly stare at him. But that was difficult. Because he was fine as hell.

Fine as Hell Neighbor was tall. At barely five three, Lily had to tilt her head back a little to look at his face. And look she did at his smooth, medium brown complexion and his full goatee that actually connected. He was wearing a plain white T-shirt and blue jeans with black Vans.

"Thanks," he said, running a quick hand over his hair that was cut into a fade. "I appreciate you."

"Um," Lily uttered, her mouth full of granola. "You're welcome, um, yeah."

She did this every time she saw him, mumbled nonsensical replies. She was still looking at him now as he leaned back against the elevator wall, his posture indicating a slight aloofness about him. His limbs were long and muscular. Sometimes when she was lucky, she ran into him as he was leaving the gym on the ground floor of their building, and his skin would be damp and glistening with sweat. Her dignity was the only thing that kept her from drooling. She swallowed thickly at the thought now and glanced away. His presence always left her senses prickling with awareness. She felt like maybe they'd met before in passing but she couldn't remember when or where. He'd definitely popped up in her dreams a few times, dressed as an old-school, sexy elevator operator with a double-breasted jacket and matching hat.

Her confusing infatuation with him was low-key embarrassing because, in reality, they'd never exchanged more than polite greetings.

The elevator door closed, and they were alone. Lily's thoughts clambered over one another as she tried to think of something to say.

"Nutri-Grain," Fine as Hell Neighbor said, pointing at the bar in Lily's hand that she'd forgotten existed. "I love those. I hate when the crumbs get everywhere, though."

She struggled to form a response and look at him at the same time. She glanced down, and that was when she noticed he was carrying a thick paperback. Fine as Hell Neighbor always had a book or a notebook when she saw him. Once, he'd been holding a copy of *The Fifth Season* by N. K. Jemisin, and Lily had been too tongue-tied to mention that it was one of her favorite books. She angled her head slightly, trying to get a better glimpse at the book he held now, when the elevator abruptly stopped on the seventh floor. An East Asian man, who looked to be in his fifties, stepped inside, carrying a tray of cupcakes. He sighed in visible relief at the sight of Fine as Hell Neighbor.

"You're just the person I wanted to see," the man said, hurrying to her neighbor's side. "I need your advice. It's a big night for me."

"What's up, Henry?" Fine as Hell Neighbor eyed the cupcakes. "Did you make these yourself? Can I have one?" He reached for the tray and Henry slapped his hand away. Lily laughed, and her neighbor's gaze shot to her. His lips spread into an embarrassed grin, and Lily's brain short-circuited.

"No, these aren't for you," Henry said. "They're for Yolanda. Today is her half birthday. I made these for her to celebrate. And because I am going to ask her out to dinner."

"For real? That's what's up, Henry!" Fine as Hell Neighbor patted the older man on the back. "It's about time. She's been giving you hints for a while."

Henry shook his head and pulled nervously at the collar of his shirt. "What if she says no? What if she hates the cupcakes? She said cupcakes were her favorite dessert, so I found this recipe on Google. I don't like sweets, so I didn't try the cupcakes myself. Remind me what to say. I forgot everything you told me. I'm not a ladies' man like you. You talk to women so easily."

Fine as Hell Neighbor glanced at Lily and coughed, scratching the back of his neck. "I'm not—you know I'm not a ladies' man, Henry." He smiled softly and placed a reassuring hand on Henry's shoulder. "Number one, you've gotta relax. You already know Yolanda likes you and she's been waiting for you to make the first move. Just tell her the truth. You like her, and you want to take her out for a nice dinner. Be yourself. You got this. You're the man. Come on, say it."

"Say what?" Henry asked.

"That you're the man."

"I'm the man," Henry said quietly.

"Nah, say it with *feeling*."

"I'm the man," Henry repeated, slightly louder this time.

"You're the man!"

"I'm the man!"

Lily laughed, watching the two of them.

Henry glanced at her and his cheeks flushed bright red. "Sorry," he mumbled. "I hope we aren't disturbing you."

Lily shook her head. "Not at all. Um, good luck with asking her out."

Henry smiled, although he still looked nervous. "Thank you."

The elevator finally stopped on the fourteenth floor. Lily's floor. And her neighbor's.

He turned to Henry one last time. "Remember, you're the man."

Henry nodded, waving at the two of them as they stepped into the hallway. The elevator doors closed.

Lily and Fine as Hell Neighbor weren't walking together, necessarily. He was a couple feet behind her, but she felt as though he were only inches away.

That was really nice of you to help him out, she wanted to say. *To be honest, I could use one of your pep talks*. But her tongue felt leaden, covered in molasses. Why couldn't she just be normal and talk to him?

She reached Violet's apartment and pulled out her keys. Taking a deep breath, she turned to her neighbor to say something, she had no idea what. But he was already walking past her toward his apartment, exactly four doors down and across the hall.

"Have a good night," he said, smiling politely.

"Me too," Lily said. "Wait, I mean, you too." She shook her head. *God.* She was the worst.

He nodded his head before slipping inside of his apartment. Annoyed with herself and her inability to say something dazzling or memorable, Lily groaned and entered Violet's apartment, slumping against the door. *One day soon.*

One day soon, she'd get up the nerve to actually talk to him.

Lily had run into Fine as Hell Neighbor in the hallway/elevator/lobby nearly every day since she'd moved in with Violet last month. And even more lately, since the other elevator had been out of service for weeks and there was only one way up, other than the stairs. And each interaction consisted of him being friendly and attempting conversation, while she became overwhelmed by his hotness and struggled to speak.

But with Fine as Hell Neighbor, Lily actually had something to talk about. Books. She could overcome her battle with casual conversation. And . . . wait.

Wouldn't that make him the perfect date for Violet's wedding?

They could talk about books all night. And even better, she didn't have to worry about trying to make anything work long-term because apparently, he was a "ladies' man," according to Henry. Lily had never seen Fine as Hell Neighbor with a woman herself, but Henry clearly knew him better than she did. If he was a serial dater, they could have a fun night at the wedding and then go about their lives. No yearlong email chains and no messy heartbreak.

And if it happened that before they parted ways, he told Lily she was the sexiest, most fascinating woman he'd ever met, and he passionately pushed her up against the wall, grabbed her face, covered her mouth with his and then completely ravished her, who would she be to complain?

"Meow."

Lily startled and looked down at her sweet Tomcat, who was too hungry to wait for her to finish her daydream.

"Hey, bud," she said, as Tomcat affectionately bumped his head against her shin. "Let's get you fed."

Lily was the quiet sister. Or according to her family: shy. Or according to old classmates: mousy. She personally preferred the term *observant*.

She wasn't bold like Violet or strategic like Iris, but she'd have to be in order to ask out Fine as Hell Neighbor. And she'd start by learning his real name.

3

"NICK."

Nick groaned as he felt someone shaking his shoulder, trying to force him awake. He rolled over, turning away, attempting to hold on to the last remnants of his dream. In his twenty-eight years spent on this earth, Nick had rarely experienced a good night's sleep. His childhood had been filled with long, unnerving and restless nights, where he wrote *Lord of the Rings* fanfiction at three in the morning, wondering when his mother would return and if she'd managed to track down his father, who'd committed another disappearing act to (a) gamble, (b) drink, (c) steal or (d) all of the above. The insomnia had followed Nick ever since and combined with the constant jet lag from his *World Traveler* days, dreaming was rare.

But when he did manage to dream these days, he always dreamed of Lily G.

He was dreaming about her now. The same dream as always. He was running down 16th Street, trying to get to Union Square park. Lily was waiting for him and he was late. The clock ticked as he pushed his way down the crowded sidewalk. He reached the park, sweaty and out of breath, and he could see Lily waiting for him on a park bench with her back to him. Her profile was vague, but she had brown skin and dark hair. She glanced down at her watch and sighed. He was only halfway to her when she stood and began to walk away, giving up on him ever arriving. Nick called her name, but she couldn't hear him over the sound of street performers and skateboarders. He shouted louder to no avail. He sprinted forward, desperate and anxious. He finally reached Lily G. and clasped her shoulder, turning her to face him. And . . . she looked just like his neighbor from down the hall. *That* was new. Nick stared wonderingly at her pretty heart-shaped face. Her big brown eyes sparkled with joy.

"You're here," she said.

Her face broke into a smile and her obvious pleasure at his presence made Nick's heart swell. Then she leaned forward, brought his face down to hers and proceeded to lick his cheek.

Wait, what?

Nick's eyes snapped open, and a golden Pomeranian was sitting on his chest, licking his chin. It leaned away and stared at Nick with its round, black eyes. Nick's head throbbed as he stared back, too confused and groggy to even begin to understand why a tiny dog was in his room and on his bed . . . Nick looked around at the flashy gold and bright pink bedroom decor. The fluffy white comforter that covered the queen-size bed. This wasn't his bed, or his room. He lifted the comforter and discovered that he was completely naked.

Nick sat up in alarm and the dog barked at his sudden movement.

He looked at the dog again more closely, this time recognizing her glittery pink collar. "Ginger? But if you're here, then I must be . . ."

"Good, you're finally awake."

Nick looked up and his neighbor Yolanda Rivera stood in the doorway, wearing a pink silk robe and matching fuzzy slippers. Her dark hair was set in curlers. She leaned against the wall and smiled at Nick.

"You sleep like the dead. I tried to wake you more than once," she said. "We had some fun last night, huh?"

Nick blinked at her, his brain trying to compute exactly what this situation was. Did he have sex with Yolanda last night? No. Fuck. No. Yolanda was his friend. And that was important to him because she was unlike the various acquaintances he'd gathered throughout his life via his carefully practiced smoke-and-mirrors, everything-is-fine-here act. Back in March, Yolanda had spotted him moving into his apartment with nothing but a suitcase and his travel backpack. Realizing he didn't own any furniture, she'd given him one of her old armchairs and then insisted he stay for dinner. Yolanda was the same age as Nick's mother and often treated him like a son.

Nick hoped he hadn't ruined one of the few friendships he'd managed to form since meeting Marcus at UNC almost ten years ago. More than that, Yolanda had a thing for Henry, who was also his friend. So what the fuck was he doing in her bed *naked*?

He tried to recall last night's events. He remembered being on the elevator with Henry and his pretty neighbor from down the hall. He'd wanted to talk to her more and had been kicking himself about not doing so (was that why she'd shown up in his dream?), when Henry had called him and said Yolanda agreed to go out on a date. They wanted him to come up to the nineteenth floor to help celebrate her half birthday. As soon as Nick arrived, Yolanda pulled out a bottle of expensive cognac. Everything that Yolanda owned was expensive because she had real money. She and her ex-husband owned a jewelry store in Houston that was frequented by big-name rappers. Nick didn't like to drink. But Yolanda and Henry were so newly in love and happy, and Nick didn't want to disappoint Yolanda on her half birthday (which was a legit thing to her, apparently), so he'd had a sip, and that was where he planned to stop. But then one sip became two sips, then three. Somehow it turned into multiple cocktails. That was precisely why he didn't drink. Once he started, he couldn't stop.

A blurry memory finally rose to the surface of his mind. Henry had gone back down to his apartment, and Nick had stayed behind, feeling toasted. Yolanda had confided that she liked Henry a lot, but part of her had always been curious to date someone younger. She had a friend in California with a boy toy who'd just graduated from college, and she was having the time of her life.

"You don't want to date some dude fresh out of college," Nick had said. "He'll only stress you out."

"Well, maybe someone slightly older," she'd responded, winking at Nick. "Late twenties or so. Like you."

She'd leaned closer, squeezing his arm, and he'd laughed.

Now it was the morning after, and he was lying naked in her bed.

"Uh." Nick pulled the comforter up, covering his chest, although they seemed to be past propriety at this point. "Good morning."

"Good morning," Yolanda said. "I made breakfast."

She turned and walked down the hallway. Ginger hopped off the bed to follow her, and Nick flopped down and stared at the ceiling. *Fuck.* How was he going to break it to Henry that he'd slept with Yolanda? Nick had met Henry, an NYU physics professor, in their building's gym, and Henry told Nick he hadn't dated for years after a drawn-out and heartbreaking divorce, but then he'd gotten to know Yolanda and he was crazy about her. And Nick had spent weeks coaching him on how to ask her out. Nick, Henry and Yolanda had become an oddly mismatched trio in their building, and he was going to lose both of them, all because he couldn't keep his dick in his pants. It was so unlike him to slip up this way.

But then again, he wasn't surprised, really. He always found a way to fuck up a good thing.

He spotted his T-shirt and jeans folded neatly at the foot of the bed. Shit, where were his boxers? Fuck it, he'd just have to free-ball. Quietly, he crawled forward, gathered his clothes and dressed. Then he made Yolanda's bed to the best of his ability because he wasn't a complete animal.

He took a deep breath before stepping into the hall, practicing what he'd say to her. But really, was it possible to make this situation any less awkward? He walked into the living room and smelled Yolanda's huevos rancheros. His stomach grumbled painfully. Yolanda sang along to a song on the radio in the kitchen, and Nick carefully approached her.

"Yolanda . . ." he started.

She turned to him, smiling. "Are you hungry? Make a plate before Henry gets here. You know how he likes to eat."

Nick paused, weighing his words. He swallowed and tried to moisten his dry throat. "Are you going to tell him about what we did last night? Or should I?"

"What we did?" Yolanda repeated, tilting her head and raising an eyebrow. "I don't get your meaning."

"You know." He leaned closer and lowered his voice to a whisper, even though they were the only two in the room. "Us. Hooking up."

Yolanda jerked away, eyes wide. Incredulous, she gaped at Nick. Then she burst into laughter. Genuine laughter. She threw her head back and let out a true guffaw.

Nick stared at her, confused as fuck. "Was it bad sex . . . ?"

"Nick, honey," Yolanda said, gaining some composure. "You and I did *not* have sex last night."

"We *didn't*?" Nick's mind was spinning. "Then why was I naked?"

"You were too drunk to go back to your own apartment, so I let you sleep over. *I* slept downstairs at Henry's. You got into my bed fully dressed, so you must have taken off your clothes in the middle of the night. My room does get unreasonably hot. I've talked to the building manager about that."

Nick was relieved, but he felt infinitely more mortified than anything. He scratched at the back of his neck and squeezed his eyes closed, frustrated with himself.

"Yolanda, I am *so* sorry," he said. "I completely misunderstood what happened. Please forget I was ever so stupid to think you would even consider having sex with me."

Yolanda patted his cheek affectionately. "Oh, it's all right, honey. I'm a shameless flirt, but I've only got eyes for Henry Lin."

Her phone rang then, abruptly interrupting their embarrassing conversation. Yolanda grabbed her phone off the kitchen counter and began speaking in rapid-fire Spanish. She turned back to Nick and gestured for him to make a plate, but Nick knew he should take this opportunity to leave now. He'd already made things awkward enough.

"Hey, I have to go," he said quietly, so as to not interrupt her call.

Yolanda waved goodbye and Nick slipped away, grabbing his new Vans by the door on his way out. They were a recent purchase after his old sneakers had become so worn down, there were holes in the soles. Nick was still becoming used to the idea of being someone who had disposable income.

He sighed in relief once he was finally back at his apartment. The large, empty space used to overwhelm him. He'd never lived anywhere so big before, so new. His living room was sparse. There was a television mounted on the wall, and across from it sat Yolanda's mustard yellow recliner that was still covered in bits of Pomeranian dog hair. His bedroom was just as empty. Only a mattress sans bed frame and a few shirts and pants hanging up in his closet. This was the first time since college that he'd stayed in one place for longer than a month. He was still getting used to the idea.

His phone vibrated in his pocket, and he looked at an alert he'd made for Sunday mornings.

You should be writing. Don't be fucking lazy.

He wiped his hand over his face. He *should* be writing. He was trying to make a real effort to stick to a schedule and actually draft the book he'd been paid so much money to write.

He showered and threw on a T-shirt and sweats before he grabbed his laptop off the kitchen island and sat down in his only chair. He opened his document and stared at the same eight words that had been plaguing him for months.

THE ELVES OF CERADON
Book 2
By N.R. Strickland

Maybe it was the pen name that annoyed him. He'd created it when he'd been an embarrassingly naive twenty-two-year-old who'd thought he was going to be a big deal. He'd figured the pen name was necessary. Because as long as Nick had been alive, and much longer before that, Nick's dad had been terrible with money. He stole from people, he gambled, he begged and manipulated everyone around him—especially the people who loved him—until he got what he wanted. Nick had witnessed and experienced this behavior for as long as he could remember. He'd known that if he earned a decent income from his book and his dad was aware of this fact, he would chase Nick down every day, constantly asking for money that he would simply waste. And Nick figured hey, why not make his alter ego British to throw his dad further off his scent? But then the book had tanked along with his original publisher, and Nick took it as a sign from the universe that being a novelist wasn't in the cards. He'd buried that career and N.R. Strickland.

None of that had mattered to Marcus, though. Once he got his new job at a fancy literary agency, he took Nick's book and ran with it. Suddenly, in January, Marcus had resold Nick's book to a new publisher, Mitchell & Milton Inc., one of the biggest publishers in the country. And not only were they republishing *The Elves of Ceradon* in the fall, they'd signed Nick up for two sequels. They'd paid him a shit ton of money, and he'd received even more when the TV rights sold to HBO. It was why he could sit in this expensive-ass apartment. All that he'd dreamed of as a stupidly hopeful college senior was finally happening. His first draft of book two was due in November, which meant he had about five months left to complete it. But how the hell was he supposed to continue a story he'd given up on over six years ago? Not to mention that everyone at his publisher assumed he was British because of his bio.

He stared at the blinking cursor and felt like it was mocking him. He didn't even know where to begin. When he'd written the first book, he'd used his own life as inspiration. Deko might have been an elf prince, which Nick most definitely was *not*, but they were both solitary people who were trying to leave the shit in their past behind. Nick might have been trying to distance himself from his father, while Deko was escaping a vicious, deadly species of life leeches, but still. Nick had seen himself in Deko.

Maybe too much time had passed. He'd spent too many years writing for *World Traveler.* His life had become a series of starts and stops, different countries, strangers and ac- quaintances. He knew more languages now than he did at twenty-two, but his drive and desire to be an author—to be N.R. Strickland—were gone. And that was funny, because now he definitely did need the pen name and anonymity. Not even his editor knew what he looked like. Marcus han- dled in-person meetings, while Nick and his editor only spoke on the phone. His editor oddly but politely never made a comment about his lack of a British accent, but Nick was sure she wondered, and he felt like he'd look stu- pid if he told the truth now. In the deal announcement press release, his publisher had described him as an "undis- covered, obscure British talent." Being British added to the appeal. Nick was paranoid that they'd drop him if he came clean. And more than that, he wouldn't take any chances on word of his new lot in life somehow getting back to his father. Because once he found out, nothing would keep him from finding Nick and sucking all the good out of his situation because that was what he always did.

Nick had no choice but to keep the truth of his identity airtight. Even if that meant severing connections he really wished he could keep.

He drummed his fingers against his keyboard, and after a moment's hesitation, he opened a new document and be- gan to type.

Lily—

I still can't seem to write this book. I have no idea what Deko's new journey should be. I bet you'd know. I bet you'd have hundreds of ideas. I sat in Union Square park again last night and thought of you. I'm always thinking of you. I miss you. I hope you don't hate me.

He sighed and saved it to his Drafts folder, which was filled with email drafts he knew he'd never send to a woman he'd ghosted and lied to. Sometimes he wished he could go back and stop himself from replying to Lily G.'s first email. But he'd been drawn to her earnestness. He hadn't expected to want to know more about her, for them to form a real connection. He'd kept up with a shitty British accent for the first few months that they'd emailed, but somewhere along the way he'd dropped it and the real him had started to come through. He'd begun to look forward to her emails every day. But he knew that he was still lying to her about who he really was, and he'd lied to her *so easily* right from the beginning. Lying like that shouldn't come so naturally to a person. It was just like something his dad would have done, and Nick hated that about himself. He wanted to back off from Lily, but he'd grown to care for her too much, and when the moment came to video chat, he knew he couldn't show up. He wouldn't be able to take how disappointed she might be to see who he really was, that he hadn't been telling the truth entirely. And he was embarrassed for keeping up with the lie for as long as he had.

In his Drafts folder on his desktop, Nick told Lily the truth about why he used the pen name. How he'd been afraid of what she'd say when she realized he wasn't anything like the person painted in N.R. Strickland's bio.

He missed her more than he could say, and they'd never even met. That was the wild part. But it was best that he left her alone. These letters would never make it past his desktop.

His phone vibrated again, startling him. This time a text from Marcus.

See you soon for brunch. Hope you're getting some writing done!

Nick groaned. Why couldn't he just get his shit together and write the damn book?

He closed his laptop and went to stand at the window. He spotted his pretty neighbor from down the hall walking out of the bodega across the street. She was wearing a pink T-shirt and denim shorts with her hair pulled back in a bun. She always wore her hair in a bun, now that he thought about it. She carried a cup of coffee and a breakfast sandwich in either hand. She smiled politely as she moved to the side to make room for an older couple passing by. There was something so honest and open about her smile. It had intrigued Nick from the first time he saw her.

She was what Nick liked to call slim thick, petite yet curvy. He watched as she glanced over her shoulder, and the other woman from down the hall emerged from the bodega as well. She was wearing a black dress and some elaborate-looking platform boots. How did she even walk in those things? Nick figured they were sisters because they looked so much alike. He'd never spent much time talking to either of them, though, so he couldn't confirm this. The one sister with the platform boots was always on her phone whenever he saw her, not sparing him, or anyone, for that matter, a second glance. But he ran into the other sister more frequently. Nick often tried to engage her in small talk for reasons he couldn't understand, because he rarely did that with other people in their building. But he felt drawn to her. He wanted to get to know her better, and that desire increased every time they spoke, even though she always had an odd deer-in-headlights look on her face and usually just smiled and glanced away, leaving Nick to wonder if he'd said the wrong thing.

Maybe one day they'd have a real conversation. Or maybe she simply saw through his charm and wasn't interested.

He watched her laugh at something her sister said, and the way her face lit up caused Nick's chest to ache. He wanted to make her laugh like that, which made no sense because he didn't know the first thing about her, not even her name. And she seemed like a good person, so he should probably stay away from her.

He'd spent a lifetime wishing for things he couldn't have. Why dwell on that when he had so many other things to worry about? He'd rather try and forget about his problems at brunch.

HE, IN FACT, COULD NOT FORGET ABOUT HIS PROBLEMS AT brunch.

"So I talked to Zara on Friday and she asked where you

are on the draft," Marcus said, cutting his pancakes in half. "Any updates for me?"

Zara was Nick's editor. Nick suddenly became busy with gulping down his orange juice. Across the table, Marcus's fiancé, Caleb, grinned and shook his head.

"You still haven't written a word, have you?" Caleb asked.

"I'm outlining," Nick said. He ate a forkful of grits. It was true that he was eating to avoid giving a real answer, but he was also starving. He'd learned that Sunday brunch in New York City was damn near a sport. You had to arrive at an ideal time or else you'd be stuck waiting an hour and a half for a table. That was what had happened to them today. They were currently seated outside at Peaches, Marcus and Caleb's favorite soul food spot in Brooklyn.

"I can take a glance at the outline if you want," Marcus offered, scratching at his freshly twisted locs. Nick remembered when Marcus had first started growing them during their freshman year at the University of North Carolina. They'd been so short back then. Now they fell midway down his back.

Marcus and Caleb had that brown skin, happy glow about them after visiting Caleb's family in Cuba last week. Nick hated to bring the mood down and disappoint Marcus. He owed so much to him, for bettering not only his career but his life in general.

"Okay, so I don't actually have an outline," Nick admitted. "I'm trying, though. I am."

Marcus and Caleb exchanged a look.

"Do you think it might help if you bought a desk for your apartment?" Marcus asked.

"Or *any* furniture at all?" Caleb added. "I can't believe you're still sleeping on a mattress on the floor. You have money now, Nick. Why do you insist on living like a broke college student?"

"I'm gonna go to IKEA next week," Nick said. "I promise."

"IKEA? Again, you have money. Why do you insist on living like a broke college student?" Caleb shook his head. "At least let me help. You know what, this week, you and I are gonna go to IKEA and pick out a bed frame. I won't even charge you my standard interior design fee."

Nick laughed. "Wow, thanks."

Marcus and Caleb had both found their dream careers and each other shortly after college. Nick always felt like Marcus and Caleb's unruly ward, who couldn't figure out how to properly adult. It was embarrassing.

"We've been getting interview requests from some big outlets," Marcus said. "*Vanity Fair. The New Yorker.* It's not too late to claim the pen name, you know. We might even have time to get your photo taken and put on the book jacket . . ."

"No." Nick's answer was firm.

"Nick," Marcus said gently. "Your dad can't get to you or your money if you don't let him. You can't live your life trying to hide from him forever."

"Do you still not know where they are?" Caleb asked.

Nick shook his head. His parents were hard to keep track of. They moved around a lot and seldom had working phones. He rarely talked to his father, Albert, but his mom, Teresa, called him when she could. On New Year's Day, she'd called from a motel room in New Orleans. He hadn't spoken to her since. She had no idea about how much Nick's life had changed. She knew nothing of his money or the book deal, and he hated that he couldn't tell her, because then she'd tell Albert, and no good could come from that.

"Either way," Marcus said, "I think you might be missing out on a big opportunity to—"

"Is it okay if we talk about something else?" Nick asked abruptly. His headache was beginning to worsen. He didn't know whether to blame this conversation or his hangover. He looked at Marcus, feeling both tired and guilty. "Please?"

Marcus and Caleb were quiet for a few moments. Then Marcus said, "Okay. What'd you do last night?"

Nick paused, thinking of the nutty situation he'd found himself in this morning. "I woke up naked in Yolanda's bed somehow."

Marcus blinked in surprise.

Meanwhile, Caleb was cackling. "What?!" he said. "That beautiful, fashionable, classy lady who donated what is practically your only piece of furniture, slept with *you*?"

"No," Nick said, laughing, glad that he was able to both lighten the mood and change the subject. "Let me explain."

Hours later, after regaling Marcus and Caleb with what he could remember of last night and listening as they discussed plans for Marcus's twenty-ninth birthday party, Nick took the subway to the Manhattan Bridge stop and got off, choosing to walk back to Manhattan. He did a lot of walking since he'd moved here. Maybe it was the wanderlust. He could still travel if he wanted to, but he doubted he'd get any writing done that way.

As he walked over the bridge and through Lower Manhattan, he wondered about Lily and where she was, per usual. When Marcus had asked why Nick wanted to live in Union Square as opposed to Brooklyn, Nick had said he simply preferred Manhattan, but really, it was because Union Square made him think of Lily and their imaginary Christmastime date. He'd searched for Union Square apartments and came across his current building, which had been newly renovated and eagerly accepting new tenants. Nick's reasoning for moving there was silly and sentimental, something he would never share.

He reached Union Square park and sat down on a bench, looking around at the people shopping at the farmers' market. Maybe his dream would become reality one day and he'd run into Lily. Right in the middle of the park. Somehow, she'd see him and immediately know who he was, and Nick wouldn't need to explain himself. She'd forgive him and say she still wanted to know the real him anyway, that the real him was worth knowing.

But who was he kidding? They would never meet, and she would never say something like that. He'd rather think about her every day for the rest of eternity than actually insert himself into her life.

Since birth, so much about Nick's life had always been up in the air, but this one detail was indisputable: good things crumbled in his hands. Just like with his father. He'd spent a long time trying to fight against this, but now he reluctantly accepted that it was just the way of things.

Lily was better off without him, wherever she was.

4

LILY'S PHONE VIBRATED ON HER DESK, CAUSING HER MUG of pencils to shake. She'd been in the middle of a Fine as Hell Neighbor daydream, in which she'd knocked on his door and asked if she could borrow some sugar. He'd grinned at her, rugged yet charming, and immediately whipped off his shirt and pulled her into his arms. Huskily, he'd whispered in her ear, *I've got your sugar right here*, and placed his hands on either side of her face with gentle urgency and kissed her so passionately that her knees gave out.

Unfortunately, however, Lily wasn't wrapped in her hot nameless neighbor's heady embrace. She was at the office. She hurried to stop her alarm, which signaled that it was six thirty p.m., aka time for her to go home. She was making a conscious effort to be out of the building before seven p.m. every day in an attempt to achieve the elusive work-life balance people were always talking about.

Her stomach grumbled, and she leaned back and stretched her shoulders and neck, looking around at her empty floor. Almost everyone else had already gone home except for Lily and Edith. They were the only members of Editorial on the sixteenth floor because Edith had refused to give up her corner office when the rest of the editorial groups in their division had moved to the fourth and fifth floors. Lily's cubicle was smack-dab in the middle of Ad Promo and Copyediting. Her colleagues were nice enough and always greeted her in the morning, but they pretty much kept to themselves out of a sense of self-preservation. Everyone knew to avoid Edith's corner of the floor, lest they incur her wrath for simply breathing outside of her door. When she was first hired, Lily used to go to lunches once a month, organized by a couple of the other editorial assistants but then those assistants were promoted, and the lunches stopped happening. It wasn't like Lily was able to attend that many anyway. Edith always needed Lily, so she mostly ate lunch at her desk.

She could hear Edith mumbling to herself in her office now, mere feet away from Lily's cubicle. For the last three hours, Lily had been hunched over, doing line edits on a manuscript about the various infections discovered during the Renaissance. She needed to hand the line edits in to Edith at the end of the week, though, so that meant she was taking this manuscript home with her.

She gathered her things and tried to ignore the state of her messy desk. Stacks of manuscripts in various stages. Advanced reader copies piled high, and boxes of foreign editions that needed to be opened. In a beloved corner sat a small stack of children's books that she managed to snag from the free bookshelf in the hallway near the copy machine. She'd clean her desk soon. That was what she always told herself. Once they got through the summer launch presentation. Once she mailed out author copies. Once she tracked down some Lysol wipes. Once, once, once.

She grabbed her bag and switched out of her flats for her Keds, planning what she'd eat for dinner. Then: "Lily, I need you!"

Lily jerked and cringed at the sound of Edith's high-pitched voice. She quickly walked over to Edith's office and found Edith peering at her computer screen, palms pressed against her temples. Her dark blonde hair was cut into a short bob, and she wore a black button-up and a long black skirt. She always wore black, with the occasional gray sweater or slacks thrown in, which made her look even paler. She was like a distant and unpleasant cousin of the Addams Family.

"What's wrong?" Lily asked, coming around to stand by Edith.

Edith pointed at the screen. "I can't remember how to attach a document to an email."

"Oh," Lily said, fighting the urge to sigh. "I'll help you."

For what felt like the millionth time, Lily showed Edith how to properly attach a Word doc. Edith frowned and shook her head. Sometimes she pretended she was much older than someone in her early sixties, like the concept of technology simply escaped her and there was nothing to be done about it.

"This godforsaken policy to save the *environment* is really a pain in my butt," Edith said. "I miss the old days when you could mail a manuscript to an author and let that be it. Now I have to save paper and do everything electronically.

It's your generation's fault. You're always trying to crusade for something."

Lily smiled tightly and shrugged. It had actually been senior members of the finance team at Mitchell & Milton Inc. who'd realized the company could cut costs by spending less money on paper, and an added bonus was that it was good for the environment. But in Edith's eyes, millennials were to blame for everything wrong in the world.

"Have you set up a lunch with that agent from Walton Literary?" Edith asked.

Lily quickly glanced at the time on Edith's computer: 6:41 p.m. She was growing hungrier by the second. "Um, no, not yet," she said. "I haven't had a chance to, but I will."

"Lily." Edith shook her head. "You've been here for over two years and haven't even talked about acquiring anything yet. That's not how you get ahead in life, you know. You have to meet with agents and look through your submissions. Get some gumption, girl. I can't hold your hand forever. You'll never achieve what I have if you don't make the effort."

It took all of Lily's strength not to jerk her head in surprise at Edith's words. *Hold her hand forever?* There was no hand-holding taking place whatsoever. Lily had been left to fend for herself and find her own way from day one. Working with Edith was like being an abandoned toddler in a crosswalk during rush hour.

Edith always did this, though, chastised Lily about her so-called lack of effort. She never acknowledged that Lily didn't have time to set up her own agent meetings or sort through her own submissions because she was always accompanying Edith on her agent meetings and reading through Edith's submissions and editing Edith's books. Just this afternoon Lily had to catch a cab all the way downtown to SoHo to meet Edith where she was having lunch with one of her authors because she'd forgotten her favorite notepad at the office and needed Lily to bring it to her. If Lily spent her days doing things like transporting Edith's notepads across town, when was she supposed to find the time to build her own list? She was basically the only reason that the Edith Pearson Books imprint was still functioning.

Also, Edith conveniently liked to ignore the fact that her father, Edward Pearson, had been hired at M&M in the early days and she'd inherited the imprint from him.

Lily's tight smile was plastered on her face as she glanced around Edith's office, which was even messier than Lily's desk. Edith arrived at exactly eight thirty every morning and didn't leave the office until nine most nights, and Lily had no idea what Edith did during those hours, because most of the day-to-day work fell to her. Edith was surely confused if she thought Lily wanted to achieve what she had.

"I'll email the agent in the morning," Lily said, backing away. "Have a good night."

Edith grunted a goodbye, and Lily reminded herself that she needed to apply for more children's editorial positions as soon as she had the chance. She'd fallen behind lately because of her current workload, but she couldn't spend another year working with Edith. She'd quit publishing altogether if that was to be her fate.

When she stepped off the elevator into the lobby at M&M, she was accosted with an image that made her freeze. There, on the screen that rotated upcoming book covers, was the brand-new cover for *The Elves of Ceradon* by N.R. Strickland. The title was written in silver script, and behind the lettering loomed large, dark blue castles—the mythical land of Ceradon.

It wasn't like Lily hadn't seen the cover before. Back in January, the publishing world had been in a frenzy when Mitchell & Milton's sci-fi and fantasy imprint, Pathfinder, acquired *The Elves of Ceradon* for a rumored seven figures. It had been a true rags-to-riches story. Six years ago, the epic fantasy novel about a clan of Black elves had been published by a small British press, but an agent at Worldwide Artists Management had managed to resell the publishing rights to M&M, and HBO had quickly snapped it up for a television series adaption. Everyone was even more intrigued that N.R. Strickland preferred obscurity. Allegedly, even his editor didn't know what he looked like. The mystery only added to the appeal. *Elves* was crashed onto the publishing schedule with an early-September release date. M&M was making it *the* book of fall, and she'd heard a rumor that it was being highlighted at M&M's notorious, and notably exclusive, end-of-summer industry party.

Yet another reason why Lily needed to find a new job.

She averted her eyes from the screen and marched outside toward the subway.

She might never know the truth of whom she had been emailing with for the better part of a year, but whoever it was had been right about an agent trying to resell *Elves* in a big way. The same website was still up and running, so the person emailing her had to have known N.R. Strickland in some capacity. Maybe she had been emailing with his assistant, or the graphics designer who made the website. Or maybe she'd imagined the entire thing in a yearlong fever dream. Either way, she wanted it all behind her.

But she was still so angry. Angry at Strick—or whoever they were—for lying to her for months. Angry at herself for revealing so much about her life to a complete stranger. For being so lonely and vulnerable that she hadn't even thought twice about doing so. For being swept away by his imaginary date ideas and charm. God. How pathetic. How embarrassing.

She jostled her way onto the crowded subway car and managed to find a seat. As the Q train took her from Midtown to Union Square, Lily tried not to fall into old thinking patterns. Like how she used to spend so much time last year imagining her fake life with Strick. She'd pictured him to be average height and brown-skinned. Cute and approachable. For some reason, her imaginary version of Strick wore circular tortoiseshell glasses. He didn't care that Lily was awkward sometimes and he was happy to fill the silence with stories about his travels. He laughed at her jokes when she managed to make them. He was okay with spending a Friday night inside, reading beside her on the couch. And during the nights when he couldn't sleep, they'd hold hands and walk through the city. He was perfect and wonderful with a smooth British accent.

He also wasn't real.

As she got off the train and walked through Union Square park past the chess players and skateboarders, she did *not* think about that hypothetical Christmas date with Strick where they walked through this same park. She did not think about how the Christmas lights would reflect in his glasses as he leaned in to kiss her. Nope, she was not thinking about that at all.

In fact, she wasn't thinking about it so hard, she didn't even notice that Fine as Hell Neighbor was walking right toward her until he was literally feet away.

"Hey," he said, pulling open the door to their apartment building. Today, he wore a black T-shirt and black denim shorts. He looked effortlessly sexy. He stepped back to let Lily go through first and smiled.

She felt it again, that weird sensation of familiarity.

Don't just stare at him! Say something!

"Um," Lily mumbled.

No, not that!

"Thank you," she said.

Better, much better.

"No problem."

He walked a couple feet behind her through the lobby. She purposely slowed her walk so that they'd fall into step together. She took a deep breath and forced herself to look at him.

"I'm Lily, by the way," she said.

His eyebrows furrowed for a second, but his expression quickly cleared.

"Nick." He held out his hand and Lily fumbled with her bag and manuscript before clumsily offering her hand too. "Nice to meet you."

His hand was large and a little rough as it covered hers.

Her whole body felt electrified at that simple touch. When he let go, Lily discreetly rubbed her sweaty palm against her thigh with a wince. He probably thought she was a wet-handed monster.

"Nice to meet you too."

They waited for the elevator and Lily's mind went blank per usual as she stumbled for something to say next. Then she remembered their common ground.

"I like *The Fifth Season* too," she blurted.

Nick raised an eyebrow, still smiling politely, but clearly not following her train of thought.

"By, um, N. K. Jemisin, I mean," she continued. "I saw you holding it once. I assumed you'd read it . . ."

Oh God. Maybe she'd misread the situation. He could have been gifting the book to someone else. Or maybe he'd found the copy on the hallway floor and had been on his way to donate it. What if she'd somehow dropped *her* copy and he'd accidentally donated it?

"Oh yeah, I did," Nick said. "I read it in a day."

Lily's eyeballs popped. "In a day? It's over five hundred pages long!"

"I'm a fast reader." He shrugged, sporting a slightly sheepish smile, as if being a fast reader was something to be ashamed about. "I sit in the park and read for hours."

Dear Lord. Be still her heart.

The elevator doors opened, and they stepped inside.

"Do you mind?" a very tired-looking father asked, appearing seemingly out of nowhere. Behind him was a rowdy group of at least ten children wearing birthday hats. One child wore a large pin with the number 8.

The father didn't wait for Lily's and Nick's reply before he and the children were pushing onto the elevator as well. Lily and Nick crowded into one corner, swiftly surrounded by eager eight-year-olds whose birthday cake intake had them soaring on sugar highs.

Lily was standing directly in front of Nick with very little space between them. Her arm brushed against his side and she felt the warmth radiating through his shirt. She inhaled his woodsy cologne. *God*, he smelled good. She wanted to bottle his scent.

Get it together! You're behaving like an unhinged, horny freak!

"I used to read a lot when I was a bookseller," she said, attempting to continue their conversation, even though they'd been derailed by a birthday party frenzy.

Nick leaned down closer to her, angling his head to hear her over the kids. "Say that again?"

She turned slightly, and his face was right there above her shoulder. This close, she could see just how smooth his skin was, the fullness of his lips. It was sensory overload. Unconsciously, she bit her lip, and she noticed how the action caught Nick's interest. He lowered his gaze to her mouth and quickly brought his attention back to her eyes. Lily swallowed and tried to make herself focus.

"I read a lot when I worked at a bookstore," she said, slightly raising her voice. "Now I read maybe two books a year for fun and it takes me forever."

"You were a bookseller?" There he went with that quick eyebrow furrowing again. Maybe he had a tic?

"Yeah, in New Jersey," she said. "Dog-Eared Pages. You've probably never heard of it."

Nick slowly shook his head. "I'm still trying to get used to New York, to be honest. I've only been here for a few months. I moved in March."

"Oh, where'd you move from?"

He waved his hand. "All over, really. But I was born in North Carolina."

"Like Petey Pablo," she said, because of course the only North Carolina native she could think of was a rapper from the early 2000s, who was popular back when she was in middle school. She wanted to crawl under the upholstery of the elevator floor. But Nick only laughed. She felt his body shake behind her as he chuckled. He had a nice laugh, deep and full of warmth. She wondered how she could get him to laugh like that again.

"Yep," he said, grinning down at her. "Just like Petey Pablo."

She shook her head, although she was grinning too. "I should have said Nina Simone."

"Or Jermaine Dupri."

"Really? I didn't know he was from North Carolina."

Nick nodded. "And without him, we wouldn't have had Bow Wow."

"Or Mariah Carey's *The Emancipation of Mimi* album, which is one of the best albums of all time."

"Of *all time*?" Nick whistled. "That's high praise."

"Well, I mean, it's Mariah Carey." She gave him a look. "You aren't going to argue with me about Mariah Carey's talent, are you?"

Nick held up his hands in surrender, that slight grin still on his face. "No, ma'am. I don't want any problems."

Lily laughed. She was doing it! Having a full-blown conversation with Fine as Hell Neighbor—wait, no, his name was Nick. And not only were they simply conversing, the conversation was *flowing*. She barely recognized herself.

"It's my birthday, Octavius!" one little boy in the center of the birthday party group shouted. "I get to play on the PS5 first!"

"I'm still the oldest of the group, Waverly! Rules are rules!"

In a split second, a fight broke out among the kids. The birthday boy's dad only sighed, weary with exhaustion. Nick's arm shot out in front of Lily, protecting her from being hit by a scrawny, stray elbow. He gently but securely turned her away, shielding her with his body. She was enveloped by him and the scent of his heavenly cologne. It took all of her effort not to swoon. She could die right there, knowing that her last moments on earth were spent in Nick's blissful embrace. Thank the Lord for angry eight-year-olds and their temper tantrums.

The elevator finally reached the fourteenth floor and Nick shouted, "Excuse us!" creating a temporary pause in the mayhem. Wordlessly, he took Lily's hand and safely led her into the hallway. The elevator doors closed behind them, eliminating the noise of the arguing children. Lily glanced down in surprised pleasure at their intertwined fingers. Nick smiled at her, somewhat bashfully, and dropped her hand. She immediately missed his touch. It was startling how natural it felt to hold hands with him.

"Those kids were wild," he said, scratching the back of

his neck and glancing away. "Felt like we were stuck in an elevator cage match."

Lily laughed, trying to shake off how warm she'd felt at their simple skin-to-skin contact. "I almost caught an elbow to the ribs. Thanks for saving me."

He brought his eyes back to her face and smiled softly. "Anytime."

The conversation was over. Neither of them had a reason to remain in the hallway. Yet neither moved.

"You know," Nick said, "I've read *The Obelisk Gate* and *The Stone Sky* by N. K. Jemisin too. If you ever want to talk more about them, I'm always around."

He was looking at her through his lashes with a direct gaze.

Holy shit. He was asking her out.

Maybe? It seemed like that's what was happening. Lily's heartbeat accelerated, and she tried to calm herself, because this was what she wanted. This brought her one step closer to asking Nick to be her date to Violet's wedding.

Also, why would she ever turn him down, the attractive and gallant neighbor of her literal dreams, about books that he'd read?

"That would be nice," she said, making herself look Nick in the eye.

He smiled again and looked almost relieved. Had he been afraid that she'd turn him down? In what universe?

"You free tonight?" he asked. "Or maybe tomorrow if tonight is too last minute."

Lily hesitated and glanced at her bag, which held the manuscript that needed line editing.

"Tonight is perfect," she said. Her deadline be damned. "I just have to feed my cat first."

She thought she noticed him grimace at the mention of her cat, but his expression cleared so quickly she couldn't be sure.

"That's cool," he said.

They walked down the hall to her and Violet's apartment. Lily fished through her bag for her keys and was so excited she fumbled with them for a good minute before she managed to open the door.

"Do you want to come inside and wait?" she asked. Violet was in LA for the week, so they'd have privacy.

He nodded, flashing his polite smile, and her stomach somersaulted.

As soon as they stepped inside, Nick froze at the door. His eyes widened at what lay before him.

"Are you a big fan of Megan Thee Stallion and Doja Cat?" he asked.

Lily glanced at the large portraits of the female rappers that adorned Violet's walls and smirked. "No, my sister is a stylist. Those are the magazine covers she worked on this year. This is her apartment, actually. I'm just staying here for a couple months until I find a new place."

"Oh, cool."

Some of the decor in Violet's one-bedroom apartment was a little questionable. In addition to the blown-up portraits of celebrity photo shoots, there was also the dark wood coffee table in the middle of the living room that was carved into the silhouette of a naked woman. Violet had it custom made based on her own body, and that was the first thing she told people when they visited.

Lily's grand New York City plans never involved sleeping on Violet's pullout couch. She'd never had much luck with roommates, especially not her most recent roommate, Mora, whose dogs had chewed up Lily's shoes and threatened Tomcat on multiple occasions. Lily desperately wanted her own space, but she didn't make an own-space salary. So last month when Violet offered to let her move in so that she could pay less rent and save up for her own studio apartment, she'd jumped at the chance.

It wasn't a bad setup, really. Violet's apartment was spacious and there was plenty of room for Lily's clothes in the hall closet. The pullout couch in the living room was comfy, and Violet was rarely there. She spent a lot of time working in LA and staying at Eddy's. She planned to stay bicoastal until her lease was up in October, and after that, she'd move in with Eddy full-time. By October, Lily would have enough saved for her own place. Just her and Tomcat. No roommates. No more stress.

Nick stood by the kitchen island and waited as Lily put down her tote bag and looked for the stool that she used to get Tomcat's food, stored high up on top of the cabinets. But of course the stool wasn't by the fridge like it was supposed to be because Violet was always moving it to rearrange the clothes in her closet.

Lily stood on tiptoe, reaching for Tomcat's bag of dry food to no avail. She was about to go search for the stool in Violet's room, when Nick asked, "Need some help?"

"Thank you—" she began to say, and lost her train of thought as Nick reached past her, lightly brushing his chest against her back as he grabbed Tomcat's food and placed it on the counter.

Lily turned around to find Nick right behind her. He backed away, resuming a polite distance, but the air suddenly felt thick with his nearness. Lily looked up into his eyes.

"You're welcome," he said, returning her gaze. He was looking at her closely, tilting his head slightly. He let out a soft laugh and shook his head, and the sound caused Lily's stomach to seize.

"We haven't met before, have we?" he asked.

He felt a connection too? It both relieved and excited Lily at the same time.

"I don't think so," she said. *But I feel like we have*, she wanted to add. She didn't, though, because she was worried her eagerness might scare him off. So it didn't make much sense when she then said, "I had a dream about you."

Nick's eyes sparkled with curiosity. He stepped closer, almost imperceptibly. "What happened in the dream?"

"I asked you for sugar."

Was she really admitting this to him? His closeness was clouding her ability to think straight.

"It had to be a dream because I don't own sugar or hardly anything to cook with." He smiled, slow and devastating. "I had a dream about you too."

Lily blinked. "You did?" She stepped closer as well, suddenly feeling seductive and bold, and so unlike herself. "What was I doing?"

He laughed softly to himself again, like he had a secret that he wished he could share with her.

"You wouldn't believe me if I told you."

She watched the hollow of his throat pulsate with each heartbeat. Her eyes traveled up to the small scar above his top lip, where the skin was slightly raised. She wanted to touch him there, to know where the scar had come from. She wanted to know what it would feel like to kiss him, this man who felt so familiar, yet whom she hardly knew. From the way he was looking at her, hungry and mesmerized, it was clear that he felt the same way. Her whole body instantly heated. She was dizzy, staring into Nick's face. And he still wasn't looking away. If anything, he'd moved closer again. He braced his arms on either side of Lily, and she pressed her lower back into the kitchen counter and bit her lip. She wondered how things had escalated between them so quickly. Then she chose to stop wondering and just go with it.

Gently, Nick brushed a stray curl behind her ear and she closed her eyes. His lips hovered above hers and she felt his cool breath fan across her mouth.

"Is it crazy that I want to kiss you?" he asked, his voice low and husky, just like in her daydream.

"No," she whispered. And in a flash of bravado that surprised her, Lily closed the gap between them and pressed her lips to his.

The kiss was soft and tentative at first, then Nick pulled her closer, one hand cradling the side of her face and the other on her hip as he brought her flush against him.

Fireworks burst in her mind as his tongue slid into her

mouth. *What was she doing?* She didn't even know his last name.

Oh well, who cared! Because Fine as Hell Neighbor was kissing her with his fine-ass lips, and he was going to need a mop from the way she was straight up melting in his embrace.

She looped her arms around Nick's neck and angled her head to deepen the kiss. Then she heard the faint sound of Tomcat's meow, and the next thing she knew, Nick yelped and nearly jumped out of his skin. He pulled away from Lily and stared down at Tomcat, wide-eyed and wary, his chest heaving. Tomcat, who'd made his usual silent entrance, meowed and bumped his head against Lily's leg. With a curious gaze, he looked up at Nick.

"Fuck, I forgot about your cat," Nick whispered.

Lily was still in a daze. She gently brought her fingers to her tender bottom lip, which Nick had just lightly bit before Tomcat interrupted them. He finally pulled his attention away from Tomcat to look at Lily again, and his intent gaze made her feel like she might burst into flames. It took her brain a moment to string words together.

"Are—are you afraid of cats?" she asked, bending down and running a hand over Tomcat's back, attempting to regain her composure.

Nick nodded, studying Tomcat. After a beat, he said, "That looks like another cat I knew."

"I guess all calicos look similar." She stood and scooped Tomcat into her arms. "But Tomcat is special. Only one in three thousand calicos are born male. You don't have to be afraid of him. He wouldn't hurt a fly."

Nick visibly froze. "His name is Tomcat?"

"Yep," Lily said. Tomcat pushed away, wriggling to get out of her embrace. She let him go and he leaped to the floor. As Lily poured food into Tomcat's bowl, she noticed how Nick attempted to put as much space between himself and her cat as possible. Most fears people had about cats were unfounded. She wondered if he'd had a bad experience with a cat as a child.

Nick walked into the living room, and when he reached Lily's book stack against the wall, he paused, picking up her old copy of *The Elves of Ceradon* with the battered and plain, red cover. He frowned and stared at it for a long while. Finally, he turned to Lily and held up the book.

"Hey, where'd you get this?" he asked.

Of course of all the books she owned, he'd picked up that one. Lily should have thrown out her copy because looking at it was triggering. But she couldn't bear to do so. She loved the story too much.

"I got it at my old job." She walked over to him. "It's an original edition, but it's being republished now. Have you heard of it?"

He nodded, still frowning. This close again, Lily had the perfect view of his handsome face. Days before, she'd been too nervous to even speak to him and now he was inside of her (temporary) apartment and had very nearly kissed her soul out of her body.

"Do you want to sit?" She gestured to the couch, ready to pick up where they'd left off.

Nick glanced away from the book to look at Lily. "Yeah, yeah. Of course."

He followed her to the couch and sat beside her. He was still holding her copy of *The Elves of Ceradon*, then his gaze zeroed in on Tomcat, who was stretched out on the floor right in front of them. He glanced back and forth between Tomcat and the book and slowly his expression morphed into one of alarm. Was he really *that* afraid of cats? Lily didn't like shutting Tomcat up in Violet's room, especially because Violet didn't like Tomcat being on her bed, but Lily would have to temporarily remove Tomcat from her current situation if she wanted Nick to relax.

She walked to the hallway and took off her Keds. Tomcat eagerly followed behind because he had a weird obsession with smelling her shoes after she'd sweated in them all day.

She approached Nick again, but now he was staring at her bare feet with that same alarmed look. She slowed her walk, feeling self-conscious for a moment. She knew her feet were okay-looking. Plus, she'd given herself a shimmery lavender pedicure before Violet's engagement party last weekend.

He pointed at her right foot. "Is that a tattoo of a lily flower?"

"Yes," she said, lifting her foot. "My sisters have matching ones for their names. Violet and Iris."

Nick's eyes became the size of golf balls. He quickly stood and dropped her copy of *The Elves of Ceradon* in the process. He fumbled to pick it up and haphazardly put it back on top of her book stack.

"I, uh, I have to go," he said abruptly, brushing past her toward the door.

What?

Lily had the strongest feeling of whiplash. He'd just had his tongue down her throat and now he was leaving? She hadn't even brought up the wedding!

"Wait!" she called, sliding on her shoes and rushing behind him.

5

"MY SISTER VIOLET IS GETTING MARRIED AT THE END OF summer and I made a bet with her that I'd find my own date to her wedding."

It all came out like word vomit as Lily hurried behind Nick into the hallway. Where had that come from? She wasn't supposed to tell him about the bet! Whatever, it was too late. She might as well plow through while she had the chance.

"I was wondering if you wanted to go with me," she continued, right on his heels. "To the wedding, I mean. There'll be free food and an open bar. We'll have fun! What do you say?"

Nick whipped around, displaying an expression of pure panic. He stared at Lily like she'd just spoken to him in gibberish.

"I—I, no. I can't. Sorry."

His immediate rejection stabbed her right in the heart. "Oh . . . um," she stuttered.

"It's just that I remembered I'm not trying to date right now," he said quickly.

"I don't want to date anyone either!" Her painful embarrassment at being rejected was swiftly replaced with a feeling of relief. He was confused about her intentions. That was all. "It's just one night. I don't want you to be my boyfriend or anything."

Then she laughed, like the thought of Nick being her boyfriend was the most absurd idea she'd ever heard. She didn't even want to imagine how ridiculous she must seem right now.

Nick was still looking at her with that wide-eyed, confused stare. "I . . . I can't even commit to one evening. I'm kind of avoiding anything like that altogether."

Now Lily was confused. "But we just kissed."

Well, actually *she* had kissed *him* now that she thought about it.

"I'm sorry," he said. "I got caught up in the moment."

Before Lily could even process that Nick was really, truly turning her down, the stairwell door opened and a woman dressed in a dark magenta wrap dress stepped into the hallway holding a folded piece of clothing in her hands. Her diamond bracelets jangled loudly with each step as she walked toward them. Lily recognized her as the woman who owned the loud Pomeranian puppy that liked to bark at everyone.

"Nick, honey," she said, "you forgot your boxers the other morning. I washed and dried them for you."

Honey?

Nick took the navy blue boxers from the woman and cleared his throat. He glanced at Lily, looking both apologetic and embarrassed. "Thanks, Yolanda. I—uh, this is Lily."

Yolanda then turned her attention to Lily and smiled. "Hi, sweetheart. So nice to meet you. Well, I'm off to meet Henry for dinner. Have a good night." She kissed Nick on the cheek and raised an eyebrow mischievously before hurrying down the hall to get on the elevator.

Lily was slow to understand what she'd just witnessed. That woman had returned Nick's boxers . . .

"It's not what it looks like," Nick said quickly.

"Riiiight." Lily backed away from him.

"Last weekend was Yolanda's half birthday," Nick said, lowering his voice. "We had a small celebration at her apartment and I forgot my boxers."

"It's really not my business. But how could you possibly have forgotten your *boxers*, of all things?"

"It—um. It was a mistake," Nick said, shaking his head. "Just a misunderstanding."

"A misunderstanding?" Lily repeated, frowning. Maybe this was his thing. He went around trying to hook up with each of the women in their building for sport and then begged off when they expressed real interest in him. And Yolanda . . . Why did that name sound familiar? Wait a minute. Wasn't Yolanda the woman that Nick and Henry had been talking about in the elevator last weekend? The woman Henry had wanted to ask out on a date? He'd been so nervous yet excited to give Yolanda his cupcakes.

"But your friend likes her," Lily whispered, gasping. "That sweet man. You gave him that big pep talk about asking her out and everything."

"I sleep naked," Nick suddenly whispered back, looking pained. "I got drunk, fell asleep at her apartment and took off my clothes in the middle of the night. That's why she had my boxers. She wasn't even there. She was downstairs with Henry."

"Oh," Lily said. Her skin prickled with heat at the mention of him sleeping naked. Nick was looking everywhere but her face. "I'm sorry. I shouldn't have jumped to conclusions. Not that you need to care what I think."

He looked at her then, and his gaze roamed over her face in a quick, utterly absorbed manner. It was almost as if he was carefully cataloging her features. He blinked and shook his head.

"I'm really sorry," he blurted. "I have to go to IKEA."

And then, like a phantom, he rushed down the hallway, pushed open the stairwell doors and disappeared.

What in the world . . . ? Lily stood alone in the hallway, trying to figure out what had changed between her and Nick so quickly. One minute he'd been caressing her and the next he'd treated her like she had an infectious disease! What was it about her that made him realize he actually didn't want to get involved with anyone? Was he turned off by the fact that she was a cat owner? Or maybe it was something about her feet? It was true that she'd kissed him first, but he'd kissed her back. She hadn't imagined that. Either way, she'd thought Nick was a for sure wedding date candidate, but she'd been wrong. She'd followed her instincts to pursue Nick, but her instincts had led her astray. Imagine what Iris and Violet would think if they found out about this. It would just be more proof that she wasn't a good judge of men and needed them to keep intervening.

Maybe she was in a little over her head with trying to

find a date in such a short time span. She had no idea how to flirt properly. The issue was that she didn't have anyone to turn to for advice. She had very few friends in New York City, and she was closest with her sisters, but she couldn't ask them for help. She *needed* to win this bet on her own so that her sisters would stop meddling with her life. And more important, she needed to prove to them that she could do this one thing right.

The elevator doors opened again, and Lily turned, foolishly hoping to see Nick. Maybe he'd realized how weird he'd been acting and was coming to tell Lily that he'd actually love to be her date to Violet's wedding.

But it wasn't Nick that stepped out of the elevator. It was Yolanda and Henry. They were holding hands and laughing, gazing into each other's eyes as they walked down the hall. Yolanda looked up and noticed Lily standing there.

"Hi, honey," she said, then she glanced around. "Where's Nick? Henry and I were on our way to dinner and thought we should come back and invite the two of you."

"*Oh.*" Lily blinked. "He, um, he just left, actually."

"That's too bad," Yolanda said. "Next time then. Your name is Lily, right? This is my boyfriend, Henry. We're friends of Nick's."

"Nice to formally meet you," Henry said, extending his hand, smiling.

"Nice to meet you too," Lily replied, taking in his bright aura. Henry was positively beaming. He was nothing like the timid, unsure man whom she saw in the elevator only a few days ago.

Henry and Yolanda said goodbye and walked back toward the elevator. When the elevator arrived, they stepped inside, and Yolanda leaned her head against Henry's shoulder. When Henry noticed that Lily was still watching them, he gave her a secret wink before the doors closed.

That pep talk that Nick gave Henry clearly did *something* to boost his confidence. Just look at how things turned about between him and Yolanda. Lily needed someone to give her pep talks and advice, to help her the way Nick helped Henry . . .

The sensible choice would be for Lily to go back inside of Violet's apartment and lick her wounds after being rejected. But Lily wasn't thinking sensibly. She was desperate.

She ran into the stairwell and hurried to catch up with Nick.

*   *   *

NICK RACED DOWN the stairs to the lobby, quite possibly on the verge of losing his mind. The book, the cat, hell, even the fact that she used to work at a bookstore could all be coincidental. But the tattoo on her foot confirmed it.

Lily from across the hall was Lily G. from his emails.

But *how*? How was that fucking possible?

Nick was rushing down the stairs so quickly he could hardly catch his breath. If he wasn't more careful, he might slip and hurt himself. But he was too frantic to focus on his safety. He thought back and tried to remember the first time he'd seen Lily. It had been sometime last month. She'd been carrying a large stack of books as she'd stepped onto the elevator, and she'd peeked around the stack to ask if he could press 14. He'd glanced at her to say he'd already done so, but then he did a double take when he'd noticed her beautiful face behind all of those books. Her warm brown eyes and soft smile. Dumbstruck, he'd stared at her. That was the first moment he'd felt overcome with an inexplicable feeling in her presence, like a bolt of lightning had zapped him directly in the chest. Immediately, he'd thought, *Who is she? How can I get to know her?*

Well, the fucking joke was on him, because he *did* know her. She'd spent most of last year living in his inbox.

Not only did he know her, but now he knew that she smelled like the sweetest scent of vanilla. He knew how her skin tasted, and how amazing it felt to hold her soft body in his arms. He had proof that Lily was kind and smart and funny. All the things he knew she'd be. What were the odds that they lived in the same building? He had only himself to blame. He'd moved to Union Square to feel nearer to Lily. Little did he know just how near he'd get. He'd have to seclude himself in his apartment. He'd become a hermit until his lease ended so that he'd never have to run into Lily again.

He walked out onto the busy street and forgot where it was that he was supposed to be going. Oh yeah, IKEA, for unnecessary furniture. Just an excuse to get away. He hailed a taxi and as it pulled up in front of him, he heard Lily shout his name.

Nick whipped around to see her hurrying out of their building. He froze in the act of opening the backseat door of the taxi. What was he doing? He should get in the taxi and leave. But he was glued to the spot. Against his will, against his better judgment. His attention was fixated on Lily's flushed cheeks and the way her chest rose and fell with each deep breath, slightly winded from running to catch up to him. She'd looked like that right before she'd pressed her lips against his.

He was staring at her. Gawking, really. She wore tiny gold hoops in each ear, and she had a small mole underneath her right eye. He'd noticed her beauty while standing near her in the hallway or the elevator but being this close to her and taking in her features all at once was a different story. He knew he should stop trying to commit everything about her to memory, but somehow, she was right here in the flesh. It was impossible. If Nick were a normal person, he would be thrilled at a second chance to start over with Lily. But Nick wasn't normal. Every good thing he touched turned to shit. He couldn't do that to Lily. He *wouldn't*.

"I have to, uh, go," he said, climbing into the taxi. To his shock, Lily dove into the backseat right beside him, crowding his space. "What are you do—"

"I can help you look for furniture," she said quickly.

Nick shook his head, gaping at her. "I'm sorry, what?"

"Where are you going?" the cabdriver asked them impatiently.

"The IKEA in Red Hook, please," Lily said. The driver grunted in response and merged into traffic. Lily turned to face Nick. "I helped my sister Iris furnish her den when she redid it. I'm decent at that kind of thing. I just need a favor from you in return."

What he should have said was no. A simple, resolute no.

This whole situation was ridiculous. Instead, he focused on her intense and earnest expression and was compelled to ask, "What's the favor?"

"If you can't go with me to my sister's wedding, I need you to help me find a date."

Nick blinked. He remembered now that she'd asked him to be her date when he'd been in the middle of high-tailing it out of her apartment. And he'd turned her down, but he didn't have another choice. He felt like shit.

"*Me?*" he said. "I'm really sorry but I don't know anyone. My only two friends in this city are happily engaged and gay."

"I don't want you to set me up. I saw what you did for Henry. I just witnessed him and Yolanda together. They're practically lovebirds. You boosted his confidence and told him what to say to her, and it worked. Clearly you know what you're doing because . . . well, you were upstairs in my apartment and you see how that went . . ." She trailed off and glanced away. Nick felt heat creep up his neck at the memory of his hands palming Lily's thick hips. "What I'm trying to say is that I have no game. I need your help more than Henry did. I want you to show me how to talk to guys. Teach me how to flirt."

For a moment, Nick was speechless. She thought *she* needed *his* help flirting? From what had just happened up-stairs in her kitchen, she was the master and he was the nov-ice. He'd practically fallen at her feet and worshipped her.

"Lily . . ." He shook his head again, glancing down. "You don't need help, and I wouldn't be that much help to you anyway. I'm just me, a nobody. You're fine, really."

"I'm not, though," she insisted. The urgent tone in her voice made him look up at her face again. Her big brown eyes were pleading. "I'm desperate. I told you that I have a bet going with my sisters to find my own date and it's serious to me. I have to win. If I knew someone else to ask for help, I would, but I don't. I know it's awkward because I kissed you earlier, but can we just move on and forget that happened?"

"The kiss was mutual," he said, although admitting so wouldn't make things any better. He was digging himself into a hole, but he couldn't let Lily believe that he found her undesirable, that he hadn't wanted to kiss her too. "But you're right. We should move on."

This was all too ironic. If Lily knew that he was Strick, she wouldn't be asking for his help. She'd probably want to slap him, as he more than deserved.

"If you help me, I'll leave you alone afterward," she said. "I swear."

Nick's chest tightened at her words. He chose not to examine why the thought of her leaving him alone made him feel like he'd just barely survived an earthquake.

Lily sat there looking at him, anxiously awaiting his response. What he needed to do was put as much space between them as possible, for his good and hers.

"Lily, I don't—" he began.

"We'll get your furniture first, and then we'll talk strategy."

Nick felt helpless, conflicted.

There was a flashback scene in *The Elves of Ceradon*

where Prince Deko recalled being chastised by his father for sneaking away for a tryst with a maiden and therefore missing a war council meeting. Disgusted, the king called Deko a useless, besotted fool.

Nick knew better. But being the useless, besotted fool that he was, he simply stared at Lily, unsure of what to say. What could he do at this point anyway? They were already halfway to Brooklyn. She was coming with him to IKEA regardless.

6

ONCE INSIDE IKEA, NICK AND LILY WALKED THROUGH THE
maze of kitchen displays, and as they passed by a family
surrounding a long table meant for large gatherings, the
sort of thing Nick had seen only in movies, his hand hovered at the small of Lily's back, careful not to touch her but
intent on keeping others from bumping into her.

Lily's presence made him feel antsy and light-headed.
They shouldn't be here together. She glanced at him and
sent his mind scrambling again.

"So what are you looking for?" she asked.

He tried to recall the various items he needed. Enough
to furnish an entire apartment, basically.

"Just a bed frame."

"What's wrong with the one you have now?"

"I don't have one."

Lily's eyebrows quirked. "What have you been sleeping on?"

"My mattress . . . on the floor." He scratched the back of
his neck, waiting for her to make a comment similar to Caleb's. What grown man slept with his mattress on the floor
when he didn't need to?

But Lily only nodded, all businesslike. She led them to the bedroom section and plopped down on a queen-size bed with a wooden black bed frame and headboard.

"What about this one? It's nice and sleek. It'll go with anything."

Nick looked over her shoulder at the price tag and winced. "Nah, not that one."

"Okay, moving on." She stood and approached a gray upholstered bed frame, which sat low to the ground. She plunked down on this bed as well and leaned back on her elbows. Nick struggled to not gaze at the curves of her hips as she made herself comfortable. And he definitely didn't notice that from this angle, he could see her cleavage peeking out the top of her blouse. "This one has extra storage underneath and that could come in handy since our apartments don't have a ton of extra closet space."

Nick shook his thirsty-ass thoughts away and walked around to peer at the price. Even more expensive than the last.

"I don't know about this one either."

Lily glanced at the price tag herself and then looked at Nick. "What's your budget?"

Free.

"I'm not trying to spend a lot," he said, shrugging. He hated talking about money. He was desperate to change the subject, so naturally, he blurted the first thing that came to mind. "I went to an IKEA once when I was in Squid, Sweden. Weird name for a town, right? I remember I asked an employee if they ever got any of the display items for free and she gave me a look that basically said *Fuck off.*"

His rambling came to a stop, and he winced. He was being weird. Lily eyed him curiously, smiling a little. Awkwardly, he sat at the edge of the bed, putting enough space between them that they weren't touching at all, but he could still smell her intoxicating vanilla perfume.

"What do you do?" she asked. "For a living, I mean."

"I'm in between things." Technically, that was the truth. He *should* be writing, but he wasn't. It was the response he'd given Henry and Yolanda when they'd asked about his job too. "I have a good amount saved, and I'm trying to hold on to it."

What he didn't admit was that he was waiting for the other shoe to drop. At any moment his publisher could decide to scrap his contract or the television studio could cancel the adaptation and there wouldn't be any more money coming in, so he didn't need to spend what money he currently had by filling his apartment with a bunch of furniture he didn't absolutely need, when he should hold on to his money for the inevitable moment when all of his good luck came to an end.

If Marcus were here, he would tell Nick that he was overreacting. And he'd probably say that Nick was letting the memory of his old babysitter Ms. Yvette cloud his thinking. Ms. Yvette, with her bitter heart and demon cats, had often looked after Nick when his parents abandoned him, and she never missed an opportunity to remind Nick, a young impressionable child, that he came from a line of bad men who did bad things, and he'd probably grow up to be just like them because the badness was in his blood. It was easy to write her off as someone who disliked his father because he'd stolen from her before, but Nick knew that there was truth to her words. His grandfather had been a fucked-up person and so was his dad. Even when Nick tried to do something good—especially when he tried to do something good—it backfired in some way. How could he trust that the goodness from this book deal wouldn't blow up in his face?

Nick cleared his throat and glanced at Lily. She was watching him closely, and he wondered what she was thinking. He fought the urge to scratch the back of his neck again, a nervous habit he'd developed in childhood.

"I got you," she finally said. She hopped up and walked quickly between the beds. Nick watched her pause at a plain brown, wooden bed frame. No headboard, no extra storage or adornments. She waved him over and he went to her automatically, wondering again how he'd found himself here with her.

"This is the cheapest one they have," she said. "What do you think?"

He nodded, simply because the act of picking out a bed frame had become a lot more stressful than necessary.

"Perfect." Lily took out her phone and snapped a picture of the product name and number. "I work at Mitchell & Milton, by the way, since we were talking about our jobs. It's a book publishing company."

Nick felt like his whole body had just caught fire. He knew from her emails that she worked in publishing, but he had no idea that she worked at the same place that was publishing his books.

"I don't work on any of the popular stuff, though," she continued. "I edit nonfiction."

"Oh," he said, slightly relieved, remembering that detail from her emails as well. It meant that she had nothing to do with his book. But still. It reminded him that he had to stop whatever it was that they were doing here . . . even if he had enjoyed being so near to her.

"Now it's your turn to help me," she said. "Are you hungry? Let's talk over Swedish meatballs."

THE FOOD COURT AT IKEA WAS VIRTUALLY DESERTED, because it wasn't like many people wanted to eat their weeknight dinner at a furniture store. Nick sat across from Lily at an empty table, unable to understand why he couldn't say no to her. Lily poked around at her meatball for a second, then laid down her fork.

"Okay," she said, placing her hands flat on the table. He tried his hardest not to devour her face with his eyes and took a deep breath to steady himself. "So, tell me, how do you do it? What's your secret?"

"Huh?" He blinked, pulling his gaze away from her lips. "My secret?"

"How do you talk to people and flirt with them? You were so smooth with the way you encouraged Henry, and he called you a ladies' man."

"Whoa, nah. I'm not a ladies' man. Henry saw me talking to a woman outside of our building *one* time, and it was because she was asking if I was registered to vote."

"Henry probably saw the two of you together and assumed you were flirting. You have this way about you."

"What do you mean?"

"It's relaxed and unassuming. And you actually listen when people talk, like you care about what they have to say. Not to mention your body language."

Nick glanced down at his posture. "My body language?"

She leaned forward and lowered her lashes. Deepening her voice, she said, "*Is it crazy that I want to kiss you?*"

He blinked, mesmerized by the look on her face and surprised by the sudden turn in conversation. His eyes were drawn to her lips again, and damn if he didn't inch closer to her on instinct.

Then she sat up straight, backing away. "That's what you said to me in my apartment, and then I basically jumped on you . . . and then you ran away because you remembered you didn't want to get involved with anyone."

It wasn't a complete lie. Nick had casually dated—if you wanted to call it that—here and there when he worked for *World Traveler*. When both he and the person he was seeing knew he'd leave in a couple weeks, and that things could never get serious. They knew that once he was gone, there wouldn't be much further contact. In fact, the women preferred it that way. They saw Nick as an opportunity to have an exciting fling with a foreigner, and they could go back to their normal lives once he left. Of course, that all ended once he'd started emailing with Lily. He'd been so stuck on her that once he'd moved to New York, the thought of entertaining someone else hadn't even crossed his mind.

"Like I said, I don't really want to date either," Lily admitted. "I haven't had the best luck in the past. My sisters are always trying to set me up, and those dates end in varying degrees of disappointment. Violet is getting married at the end of August and I bet her and Iris that if I could find my own date to the wedding, they'd have to stay out of my love life for good."

Nick thought of the emails she'd written to him about going on dates with models and businessmen to please her sisters, and how those dates often left her feeling unhappy. He didn't like that it was still happening.

"Why don't you just say fuck it and go to the wedding by yourself?" Nick asked. "They should leave you alone regardless."

"You don't know my family," Lily said morosely. "Winning the bet is what will stop them. So can you help me?"

Nick knew she wouldn't take no for an answer, and he couldn't say no to her. A bad combination.

"I'm no expert," he said. "I'll tell you the same thing that I told Henry. Be yourself."

She gave him a look. "Being myself means being awkward."

"Someone might find that endearing." *He* found it endearing.

She shook her head. "Do you want to hear about what I'm like when I'm myself when flirting? Once, I went to a happy hour with my coworker Dani and after a few margaritas, she dared me to go talk to this guy who was sitting at the other end of the bar. He was tall and really cute and kind of looked like Jonathan Majors. Anyway, when I got to his table, my mind went completely blank. Then I glanced down at his Corona and blurted the first thing that came to my head."

"Which was?"

"I once read an article that said back in the 1980s, people thought that Corona beers had urine in them because of its odd yellowish color. But it turns out that someone at Heineken had started the rumor to hurt Corona's sales. So I asked him if he knew that if he were caught drinking that beer forty years ago, someone might tell him that he was drinking pee."

Nick snorted a laugh but stopped at the miserable look on Lily's face. "Wait, you're serious?"

"*Yes*," she groaned. "He just shook his head, and it was *very* clear that he did not want to keep talking to the girl who told him he was drinking urine." She leaned her elbows against the table and sighed. "I wasn't joking when I said I'm bad at flirting. I honestly wish I hadn't come up with the bet. Like I said, I don't *want* to date anyone."

Nick hated to see her look so dejected. Instinctively, he reached out and gently squeezed her hand in reassurance. She blinked, then he realized what he was doing and quickly snatched his hand back.

He cleared his throat. "It could have been worse."

"Oh, I've experienced worse." She laughed to herself, although her feelings of humor didn't reach her eyes. "Do you want to hear something really embarrassing?"

"Sure," Nick said. He'd listen to whatever she told him if it made her feel better.

"Last year I met someone online," she said. And Nick's

stomach fell right down to his ass. "I liked him a lot, and I thought it might go somewhere, but he ghosted me. Even though it ended badly, emailing with him made me realize how nice it was to talk to someone I actually liked. That's when I decided I couldn't be set up by my sisters anymore, so I came up with the bet." She forced a smile. "I know it probably sounds pathetic."

"It doesn't." Nick's mouth was completely dry. "I would never think that you were pathetic."

He was going to tell her the truth right now. He *had* to tell her.

"He probably feels like shit," Nick said. "I know he does . . . and I know that because—"

"Oh yeah, I *hope* he does feel like shit," she said, interrupting him. "Or, I don't know, I at least hope he regrets not getting the chance to meet me. To give us a real shot. Sometimes I think about what I'd do if I ever saw him in person."

Nick swallowed thickly. "What would you do?"

"I don't know. I'd probably be too angry to say anything. Honestly, I hope I don't meet him. I just want to move on and erase the whole thing from my memory."

Nick nodded weakly. He realized then that there would be no good in telling Lily the truth. He'd only be selfishly trying to clear his own conscience. Lily didn't want to meet Strick. What she wanted was to go forward and forget their emails ever happened. He'd separated himself because he'd felt embarrassed and shitty for lying to her, and he knew that further inserting himself into her life wouldn't result in anything good. And in the process, he'd still hurt her.

The best thing that he could do now was help her get a date to her sister's wedding so that she could find happiness with someone else.

After he helped Lily, he'd disappear from her life. He never wanted to hurt her again.

"My best friend, Marcus, is having a birthday party this weekend," Nick heard himself say. His voice felt weak as he spoke. "You should come with me. You might meet someone there."

Lily perked up somewhat. "Really? What does your friend do?"

"He's a literary agent."

"So will there be lots of book people at this party?"

"Most likely."

"Good. This is good." In much higher spirits, she speared a meatball and popped it in her mouth. "Thank you. For inviting me to the party."

She smiled at him, and Nick's stomach twisted.

"No problem."

Of course, he not only lived down the hall from Lily, but now he'd agreed to set her up with someone else, because that was the best thing for both of them.

It might just kill him in the process, though. The universe could fuck all the way off.

7

FLOWERS HAD BEEN THE SCENT OF LILY'S CHILDHOOD. And the peaceful, aesthetically pleasing environment of Greenehouse Florist and Nursery in Willow Ridge, New Jersey, had been the constant backdrop of her life. She'd spent many evenings here after school, her nose stuck in a book while her parents worked. Some of Lily's earliest memories were of sitting beside her mom as she made flower arrangements. These many years later, Greenehouse was still one of Lily's favorite places to be.

Except during wedding season. Because then everything was complete chaos.

"Where are the peonies?" Lily's mother, Dahlia, called, rushing down the aisle, rows and rows of plants and flowers on either side of her. Like the rest of the Greene women, Dahlia was petite with thick, curly hair. Although at the moment her hair was tied up in a topknot, and instead of her go-to A-line dresses and sandals, she was wearing a T-shirt and jeans, both smudged with soil.

"I have them here," Lily said at the counter, filling tall cylinder vases with white peonies and pink roses for centerpieces. She pricked her finger on a thorn, but she was moving so quickly, she didn't even wince. She'd move faster if she were dressed in something more comfortable. Her feet ached in the heels she'd put on this morning for the Empo-WOMENt career seminar she'd attended with Dahlia. Lily glanced down at her light pink button-up and groaned. She'd smeared soil on her collar somehow. This was one of the few nice blouses she owned. She'd bought it on sale at Zara.

Dahlia appeared at Lily's side and observed her work. "Looking good. But make sure you surround the peonies with the roses, not the other way around." She gave Lily's shoulder a reassuring squeeze. "Benjamin, how's that bouquet coming?" she asked, bustling over to Lily's father, who sat several feet behind Lily in the shop's office. He held up the bouquet, which looked pretty decent to Lily, but Dahlia frowned and began rearranging the flowers. Benjamin leaned his tall frame backward in the chair and used the hem of his shirt to clean his glasses' lenses, smiling ruefully as Dahlia amended his work. He caught eyes with Lily and winked. They were definitely not the perfectionists of the Greene family and were often subject to Dahlia's gentle corrections. And unfortunately, the EmpoWOMENt seminar hadn't gone as successfully for Lily as Dahlia may have hoped.

It had been pretty typical as far as career seminars went. Women who were in powerful positions at various companies spoke about how they'd climbed the corporate ladder. There'd been a networking hour afterward, and before disappearing to chat with her Alpha Kappa Alpha sorority sisters from Brown, Dahlia had encouraged Lily to introduce herself and get some business cards. Lily didn't see the point in speaking with women who worked in tech and engineering and accounting, when it had nothing to do with editing books, but for Dahlia's sake, she'd agreed to try. However, before Lily gathered the nerve to approach anyone, Edith had texted her in a frenzy because she'd discovered that their production manager, Brian, was leaving the company next month, and his replacement would be an employee who was transferring from M&M's UK office. Edith was furious that (1) Brian was leaving. She hated change and new people. And (2) not only would she have to work with a new person, but they'd be coming from an entirely different country. She wanted to know how different the production process might be at the UK office. What if this new person took too long to acclimate and the imprint's production schedule suffered? This only further supported her conspiracy theory that the president of their division was planning to shutter the imprint soon. Edith found this so stressful that she was unable to rest on her Saturday afternoon, and therefore Lily couldn't rest either.

Needless to say, Lily had stood in the corner, placating Edith and her irrational fears via text for the remainder of the seminar. She hadn't done any networking or received a single business card.

She'd felt so bad for disappointing Dahlia that she'd offered to help out at the shop. Her parents were preparing a last-minute order for a wedding a few towns away in Somerset. Apparently, the original florist backed out because they'd gotten into a physical fight with the bride. Wedding season was no joke.

Lily's phone vibrated on the counter beside her and she

grimaced, expecting to see another text from Edith. But instead it was a text from Nick.

Hey, we still good for tonight?

Lily tried to ignore how her stomach flipped at seeing his name flash across her phone's screen. They'd exchanged numbers the other day after leaving IKEA, and tonight she was joining him at his friend's birthday party with the goal of finding a potential wedding date.

Yep! Lily texted back. She'd felt a slight thrill as they'd stood outside of IKEA and she'd watched him add his number to her contacts. He'd squinted and quirked his mouth while he typed. Even his focused face was handsome, because of course it was.

Seconds later, he replied: Cool.

Then: Hope you're having a good day.

Thanks, you too!!

She cringed after hitting send. Were two exclamation points really that necessary? It sounded overeager. She didn't want Nick thinking that she liked him, especially since he'd told her that he wasn't trying to date. It was true that she still found him attractive, and his random monologue about a Swedish IKEA had only intrigued her more about the inner workings of his mind, and he was the first person she'd ever told about Strick and she appreciated that he hadn't judged or pitied her. But she wouldn't act on those feelings or let them fester and blossom. She'd decided that their kiss in Violet's kitchen had been a result of repressed horniness and overexcitement after surviving an elevator brawl. Nick was going to help her find a date to Violet's wedding, and that would be the extent of their relationship. She wasn't even sure if they were friends. She was proud of herself for jumping in and asking for Nick's help, though. Now if only she could properly apply that assertive energy to moving up in her career as well.

The bell over the front door chimed and Lily looked up to see Iris and Calla walking toward her.

"Auntie!" Calla shouted. She ran to Lily as fast as her little legs would allow, and Lily scooped her up into her arms.

"Hey, lady," she said, holding her niece close. Calla smelled like chlorine. Lily glanced at Iris, who looked sleek in her black workout tank and tights. She wore a black baseball cap, concealing her short cut. Letting out a full-body sigh, Iris sat on the empty stool behind the counter. Lily let Calla down, and she ran over to her grandparents, who showered her with hugs and kisses.

"We just left her swimming class," Iris said, rubbing her forehead. "And before that it was ballet. In an hour she has karate. I could sleep for a year straight and I'd still be tired."

"I didn't even know three-year-olds could take karate class."

"Me neither, but I looked into it because Calla was so insistent. That's what happens when you let your child watch *Cobra Kai*."

"I'm happy to help with Calla whenever you need me to," Lily said. "You know that, right?"

"Yes, and I love you for offering. But I'm okay, really. I'm tired, but it's a normal tired. Not like last fall."

Lily nodded, thinking about how exhausted and stressed Iris had been last October when she'd been promoted at work. She'd spent almost every evening and weekend entertaining clients and potential influencers for the makeup brand. Earlier this year, Iris had finally told her boss she had to cut back, even if that meant she'd need to find a new job. But her boss valued her too much to let her go. The weekend work had stopped altogether. Sometimes Iris still spent late evenings at the office, but at least she was home in time to have a late dinner with Calla and help her get ready for bed.

Without needing direction, Iris began filling the remaining vases with flowers. She moved even quicker than Lily and rarely had to readjust her arrangements. That was Iris in a nutshell. Doing everything perfectly on the first try.

Lily brushed off her hands and hugged her sister. At first, Iris stilled in Lily's arms, then she relaxed.

"What was that for?" Iris asked, smiling curiously as Lily pulled away.

"Just because." Lily shrugged. What she didn't say was that she admired Iris, who'd experienced the untimely death of her husband and college sweetheart when Calla wasn't even a year old. Lily thought Iris was a wonderful mom and that Calla was very lucky. But Iris didn't like sentimentality, so Lily added, "And you're helping me on these centerpieces."

Iris snort-laughed and shook her head. "I'm trying to decide where we should go for Violet's bachelorette party. Karamel Kitty suggested a nightclub in Miami, and she said we could stay at her South Beach mansion. She obviously didn't use the word 'mansion.' She said 'house,' but her

house is a mansion, so I'm using the correct word for ac-
curacy's sake. What do you think?"

Lily's phone chimed on the counter, startling her. Another text from Nick.

Slight change for tonight's party. It's 70s themed now.
Do you have something to wear?

The theme sounds fun, she responded. I'll pull something
together.

"Who's Nick?" Iris asked, glancing at Lily's phone.

Lily stuffed her phone in her back pocket before Iris
could see more. "He's my neighbor. What did you say about
Violet's bachelorette? Miami?"

"Yes." Iris was smiling. "So Nick the neighbor is taking
you to a party?"

"Why are you so nosy?!"

Iris smirked like that was a compliment. "Wait, do you
have a date tonight?"

"No. We're just going to a party together. It's not a date."

"Hmm. Interesting." Then Iris busied herself with fix-
ing one of Lily's arrangements. If Violet had just discovered
that Lily was texting a new guy and had plans to go out
with him that night, she would have pushed for details until Lily revealed every bit of information down to his shoe
size. But Iris was subtler. She didn't press. She waited for
you to come to her.

And as the silence stretched on, Lily realized she was
dying to finally tell someone about what had transpired between her and Nick in Violet's kitchen. So much so that she

forgot that this was a story she probably shouldn't share with one of her sisters.

"We kissed, though," she blurted.

Iris's eyes lit up. "*Really?*"

"Yes! And it was literally the best kiss of my *life*. He has the best, most wonderful lips. Oh my God."

"Lily! What?! When did this happen?"

"A couple days ago," Lily said, lowering her voice as Benjamin passed by, smiling at them over a large bouquet. "But we're just hanging out now. Friends maybe."

Iris frowned. "Why just friends?"

"Neither of us are looking for anything romantic."

She definitely wasn't going to explain that she and Nick had an agreement and he was helping her find a date to the wedding. Or how she'd originally asked *him* to be her date and he'd turned her down. She already regretted telling Iris that they'd kissed. *Ugh*, why couldn't she just have kept her mouth shut?

It didn't matter much anyway, though. Because Iris pulled out her phone and looked up the LinkedIn profile of a man named Brandon Johnson. She showed his profile picture to Lily, and he looked Professional™ with his sleek, fitted blazer and dazzling smile.

"Well, if nothing is going on between you and Nick the neighbor," Iris said, "I meant to tell you that I met this guy at an event a couple weeks ago. He works for Morgan Stanley, and he—"

"No." Lily stood and began moving the completed arrangements from the counter to the worktable in the center of the room.

"But I want to help with that wedding-date bet you have going with Violet."

"*And you*," Lily said, coming back to the counter. She frowned at Iris. "The bet is with both of you. I don't want you to try and set me up anymore either."

"Okay, okay." Iris held up her hands. "I won't bring Brandon up again."

"Or anyone else."

"Or *anyone else*," she repeated.

"Thank you."

Lily's phone buzzed in her back pocket, interrupting their conversation. Nick had finally replied to her.

Groovy.

Then another text: Because it's the 70s.

And another: I don't say groovy on a regular basis.

Finally: I'll stop texting you now.

Lily laughed and sent back the disco-dancing-man emoji.

"He's sure got you cheesing pretty hard to not be a date," Iris said, eyeing Lily.

Lily waved Iris off. So what if Nick made her smile? He was going to be the only person she knew at this party. It was an upside that she might enjoy his company. There wasn't much more to it than that.

* * *

IT WAS ONE thing for Nick to make Lily smile, but he didn't need to make her drool.

They stood on the steps of his friend's brownstone in Prospect Heights in Brooklyn, waiting for someone to answer the door, and Lily couldn't stop ogling him.

He wore a gold lamé button-up that he'd buttoned only halfway and dark denim bell-bottoms. His partially visible brown chest was strong and smooth. No matter how many times Lily tried to keep eye contact with him, her gaze inevitably drifted down to his pecs.

And they were matching. Lily borrowed the gold halter jumpsuit that Violet had worn to her engagement party. Lily hadn't realized how deep the neckline plunged, almost reaching her belly button. It wasn't something she'd usually wear, but she wanted to be on theme, and this was the only '70s-esque item she'd found in Violet's closet. She channeled '70s icon Donna Summer and left her hair out thick and curly. She finished off the look with a pair of Violet's platform pumps. Thank God for sisters who wore the same clothing and shoe size. At any moment, Lily could tip over and break her ankle, but at least she would do so looking undeniably sexy.

Beside her, Nick pulled at his collar and rang the doorbell again. He was holding a small rectangular wrapped gift. "I don't know what's taking them so long to come to the door," he said. He glanced at Lily and flashed an apologetic smile. She shrugged and smiled too, pretending as though she hadn't been staring at him on and off since they'd left their building and hopped on the subway.

"You look really nice, by the way," Nick said. He gave Lily a slow once-over, pausing at the skin visible above her belly button.

"Thank you," she said as though the way he'd looked at her hadn't threatened to send her panties ablaze. "So do you."

"Thanks." Nick cleared his throat. "Marcus's fiancé, Caleb, will be happy. He takes themes very seriously."

"Really?" she asked, and Nick nodded.

"He's an interior designer. Brooklyn moms love him. He charges the shit out of them too. I spent at least three hours searching for bell-bottoms before I found this pair at a shop in SoHo." He lifted his shirt and revealed a tag that was still attached to the waist of his jeans. "Seventy bucks for a pair of pants. Can you believe that? I'm returning these tomorrow."

Lily laughed. "You should keep them. They look good on you."

"Really?" Nick blinked, like her compliment had taken him off guard. "Well, if that's what you think, maybe I should."

He smiled, tentative but genuine. Lily couldn't help but smile in return. For several seconds, they stood on the steps grinning at each other like fools before the door finally opened and a guy with golden brown skin and wearing a tight-fitted powder blue shirt and matching high-waist bell-bottoms greeted them with a delighted shout.

"Hey now, look at you!" He pointed at Nick, and then he saw Lily and his already-wide smile grew bigger.

"Lily, this is Caleb," Nick said. "Caleb, this is Lil—"

"Lily, from the minute Nick told me you were coming over, I've been dying to meet you," Caleb said, cutting Nick off. He grabbed Lily by the hand and pulled her inside.

"You have?" she asked as they climbed the steps to the

second floor. Caleb was still holding her hand. She glanced back at Nick, who followed behind them, frowning at Caleb.

"Absolutely," Caleb assured her. He opened the door to their apartment, and Lily felt like she'd stepped through a time machine. The apartment was almost completely dark, save for the huge disco ball that hung from the living room ceiling. KC and the Sunshine Band's "Get Down Tonight" blasted from two large speakers. And the living room was already full of people dancing and talking.

Lily suddenly remembered the reason she was here. It wasn't to drool over Nick in his '70s attire. She was here to find a potential wedding date.

Lily gulped and turned to Nick. He was staring up at the disco ball in silent, amused wonder. He pointed at it. "That looks legit. Where did you find it?" he asked Caleb.

"I borrowed it from a nightclub," Caleb shouted over the music. "There's food and drinks in the kitchen . . ." he started. Then the song changed to "Boogie Oogie Oogie," and Caleb shimmied his shoulders. "Dance with me, Lily!"

Dread bloomed in the pit of Lily's stomach. She hated dancing in public. Especially surrounded by strangers. But Caleb looked so hopeful and eager, and he'd graciously invited her into his home.

"Oh," she mumbled. "Um, okay."

Caleb didn't give her a chance to second-guess her decision. Before she knew what was happening, he was pulling her across the living room floor toward the whooping crowd. Lily glanced back at Nick, who smirked and flashed her a thumbs-up. He leaned against the wall, holding his best friend's birthday present to his side, obviously harboring no plans to follow Lily and Caleb onto the dance floor.

Everyone cheered as Caleb melded into the crowd with Lily at his side. She was enveloped in a circle of sequins, bell-bottoms, and Afros. When she turned around again, Nick was no longer standing against the wall.

AT THE END OF THE DAY, NICK REALLY HAD NO IDEA WHAT he'd gotten himself into by bringing Lily to Marcus's party. As he stood against the wall, watching her dance with Caleb, he felt such a deep pang in his chest, it was honestly alarming. The way that jumpsuit hugged her breasts and hips should be illegal. She looked so fucking good. Like a golden goddess or something. If she met someone here tonight and vibed with them enough to bring them as her date to her sister's wedding, that would be great. For her. For Nick, it would be like a kick in the balls. He would put off watching that happen for as long as he could, so he went to find Marcus and discovered him inside his and Caleb's bedroom.

Marcus sat on the edge of his bed, his tortoiseshell glasses perched on the edge of his nose as he stared intently at his laptop screen. His locs hung loose down his back, and he wore a powder blue outfit that matched Caleb's. When he noticed Nick poke his head inside of the room, he smiled sheepishly, caught.

"I know, I know," Marcus said, closing his laptop. "I shouldn't be working in the middle of my own birthday party. One of my authors is stressed about missing a deadline. I was trying to figure out a new schedule for her."

"I'd tell you that you work too hard," Nick said, "but if you didn't, I wouldn't be here."

"True." Marcus pointed to the gift in Nick's hand. "That for me?"

Nick nodded. "Happy birthday, bro," he said, giving Marcus the wrapped gift. Nick never missed Marcus's birthday. In college when he was broke, he used to write Marcus funny short stories every year, and when he'd been traveling around the world, he sent small knickknacks from various countries. This year, though, he'd been able to buy him something of quality.

Marcus slowly unwrapped the gift with care, pulling the wrapping paper away to reveal a black leather-bound planner embossed with his initials: *M.W.* for Marcus Wilson. He carefully ran his fingers over the letters and glanced up at Nick with an expression of pure elation.

"Damn, this is amazing, Nick! Thank you!" Marcus was a hugger, and as was custom, he pulled Nick toward him and wrapped him in a hearty embrace. With Marcus, there were no lackluster pats on your back or quick squeezes that left you feeling cold. Through Marcus, Nick had learned that a true hug was warm and enveloping. Full of care. They separated, and Marcus continued to examine the planner. "Shit, is this from Shinola?"

Nick nodded. "I know you love that store. And if I know anything about you, it's that you love a good planner."

"Bro, I was *just* saying that I needed a new one. And it's got my initials! This is a dope gift, Nick."

"I'm glad you like it." Nick smiled. Any form of praise always made him feel self-conscious, unsure if he really deserved it. "We've been friends for ten years, so it's about time I got you an adult gift."

"*Ten years*," Marcus repeated. "Wow."

"Wild, right?"

Almost ten years ago, Nick had shown up at UNC's Chapel Hill campus alone and out of his depth. He'd been armed with a full-ride scholarship, two suitcases stuffed with all of his belongings, and no idea what to expect. The bus ride from his parents' apartment had been almost three hours long. They hadn't been around to tell him goodbye. In fact, prior to departing, he hadn't seen Teresa in three days. She was gone, running after Albert, who two weeks before had taken fifty-three dollars from her wallet while she slept and then disappeared. At eighteen, Nick no longer expected Teresa to prioritize him over Albert. But it was terrifying to show up to his first day of college with no support whatsoever.

He maneuvered his way through his dorm hall, passing fellow freshmen and their eager, helpful family members, hoping that no one questioned the whereabouts of *his* family. Once he reached his room, he discovered that Marcus had already arrived. He was sitting on his bed with his parents on either side of him. A planner lay open in his lap, and he was writing down his class schedule and the locations of each building. Marcus and both of his parents wore glasses and matching Carolina blue T-shirts. They looked like they'd stepped out of a UNC brochure.

Nick had cleared his throat and mumbled a polite hello.

Marcus quickly hopped up and introduced himself, confidently sharing that he was an English major from Pennsylvania. Less confidently, Nick replied that he was an English major as well, from North Carolina. Then Marcus's parents introduced themselves and glanced toward the hallway. When Nick realized they were expecting his family, his familiar mask of artificial ease emerged. He smiled and explained that his parents worked a lot and couldn't take time off to help him move in, but they would visit in a few weeks. Gracious and respectful, the Wilsons gave Nick space to unpack and left the room.

Hours later, Nick had sat beside Marcus during a meeting with the rest of their floor mates and their RA. Everyone seemed so relaxed, like college was another step in their lives that they'd been prepared for. Meanwhile Nick still couldn't believe that he'd been accepted in the first place. He was low-key convinced that someone in the administration office would find him and say there was a mistake with his paperwork. He hadn't won a full scholarship after all. It had all been a big misunderstanding.

After the floor meeting ended, a group had gathered to discuss which parties they wanted to hit up. Nick had lived most of his life in apprehension of getting to know people, or rather letting them get to know him. Because then they'd find out just how dysfunctional his family was. He started to walk back to his room, planning to stay in and read, but Marcus had caught up with him.

"We're gonna go out tonight," he said. "It's gonna be fun."

Again, with Marcus's effortless confidence. Nick had no choice but to believe him. It was the first hint that Marcus was the kind of person who refused to take no for an answer and that he'd refuse to give up on Nick.

"Hey, I want to ask you something," Marcus said now. His voice took on a tentative tone that warned Nick he probably wasn't going to like whatever came out of Marcus's mouth next. "Every August, M&M throws an end-of-summer party where editors present the biggest books of the fall season to tastemakers in the industry. Influencers, book reviewers and librarians, that sort of thing. I've been hearing about this party since I got my first internship years ago. It's a pretty big deal, not to mention that there's hella free food. But I bring this up because your editor will be presenting your book, and they'd like to extend an invitation to you because it helps if an author is there to speak too. Your editor knows how you value your privacy, so there's no pressure at all, and I told her I didn't know if you'd be up for it. I don't want to speak for you, though, so let me know what you want to do."

Nick made a face. "They're gonna flip when they find out I'm not some British dude."

"It might cause a tiny stir," Marcus said, shrugging. "But it isn't like you wrote a memoir and lied about your life. You used a pen name and said you were born in England. People have done worse. Your team will understand if you explain why you lied in the first place."

"I don't know . . ." Nick was doubtful that he could be so easily forgiven. The prospect of coming clean wasn't something he could wrap his mind around. He observed his best friend's hopeful expression. "You think I should go."

"Of course I do. I wouldn't be a good agent if I said no, but

I don't want you to do anything that makes you uncomfortable." Marcus removed his tortoiseshell frames and replaced them with a pair of black circular sunglasses. "Don't worry about it now, okay? You have weeks to decide. In the meantime, why don't you let me see what you've written? You can come to the office one day next week and we'll grab dinner on the company dime to talk about the draft."

Nick gulped. He had managed to write the first chapter of book two, and it was hot garbage. But it was Marcus's birthday and after all Marcus had done for him, Nick didn't want to let Marcus down, especially since he already knew he wouldn't attend M&M's party and put his face to N.R. Strickland's name.

"Yeah, cool," Nick said. "Sounds good."

Nick followed Marcus back into the living room, which was fuller than when he'd left almost fifteen minutes ago. His eyes scanned the crowd for gold. He spotted Lily bumping her hip with Caleb. She was laughing, her whole face lit up in delight. Nick's chest panged again.

"Who's that with Caleb?" Marcus asked.

Nick tore his eyes away from Lily to answer Marcus. "That's my neighbor Lily."

"Oh yeah, I forgot you said you were bringing her." Marcus paused, glancing back and forth between Lily and Nick and their matching outfits. "Is something going on there or . . ."

Nick cleared his throat. He wanted to tell Marcus the whole deal with Lily, but tonight was his birthday. He should be having fun, not listening to Nick's drama. He'd tell him soon, just . . . at another time.

"Nah," Nick said. "We're just friends."

Were they friends, though? Did Lily claim him as a friend? Should she? Probably not. This was all so fucked.

"Right, cool," Marcus said. "How much you want to bet that all the pepperoni pizza is gone?"

"Oh, um, huh?" Nick mumbled. Marcus had already moved on to a new subject, but Nick's attention was elsewhere. More accurately, his attention was approximately twenty feet away in the living room. Lily was no longer dancing with Caleb, but she was talking to some dude dressed in a skintight turtleneck with a pick stuck in an Afro that clearly looked like a wig. He was leaning down, his face several inches from Lily's, and she was nodding as he talked. The pang in Nick's chest worsened. Why, though? Wasn't this the reason he'd brought her here? To meet someone else? Mission accomplished. He should be happy! He *was* happy.

So it didn't make much sense when he found himself walking across the room, fully intending to interrupt their conversation.

* * *

LILY WAS IN the middle of talking to Caleb's friend Will about which middle-grade fantasy novels he should buy for his girlfriend's niece, when Nick suddenly materialized at her side and said, "Hey, can I show you something in the kitchen really quick?"

He had an odd look on his face, like he'd eaten a Sour Patch Kid that hadn't turned sweet as promised. He briefly nodded his head at Will before returning his gaze to her.

Lily, someone who often felt exhausted at the thought of parties, was surprised at how much she was genuinely enjoying herself tonight. Caleb took his hosting duties very seriously and he danced with Lily every few songs and was kind enough not to ask how she'd somehow gone through life without properly learning how to dance on beat. The crowd was a mix between Caleb's friends from interior design school and publishing people who knew Marcus, which basically meant that every other person knew at least one of Lily's coworkers. The men at the party were sweet and funny, but they were also either gay or had shown up with a girlfriend. Will's girlfriend had just excused herself to go smoke. That meant finding a prospective date tonight to Violet's wedding was a bust.

Lily was having fun, but she was relieved to see Nick. Talking to so many new people was exhausting. Her social battery was beginning to drain.

"Okay," she said to him, wondering what it was that he had to show her.

She said goodbye to Will and followed Nick into the kitchen. It was mostly dark, but the glow from the disco ball shed enough light on Nick's gold shirt and the table that was covered in empty pizza boxes and beer bottles. Nick paused by the fridge and glanced around before turning to face Lily. She looked at him expectantly.

"Uh," he said. Then he reached above the fridge and procured a family-size bag of Kettle Brand sour cream and onion chips. He opened the bag and held it out to Lily. "Want some?"

Bemused, she walked closer to him. "You wanted to show me a bag of chips?"

"Not just any bag of chips," he said. "Caleb's secret stash." When Lily froze, Nick laughed. "Don't worry, I'll buy him another bag. We didn't get here in time for pizza. I thought you might be hungry."

Lily was touched that he'd thought to look after her well-being. And he was right, she *was* hungry. Too hungry to think about the repercussions of eating Caleb's secret snack. She took the chips and poured a handful into her palm, trusting that Nick would make good on his promise to replace the bag.

She sat at the table and Nick took the seat beside her. Their gold clothes were illuminated. There was something calming about sitting in the dark this way, slightly removed from the party.

"Are you having fun?" he asked, looking over at Lily. His lips formed into a soft smile when he realized she was too busy chewing to respond. She wished his smile didn't have such an effect on her. "They're good, right?"

She nodded and almost wiped her hands on her thighs but remembered that Violet would murder her if she got potato chip grease on her clothes. She reached for a napkin instead.

"I am having fun. Everyone's really nice, especially Caleb." She offered him her half-full cup of rum punch. "Want some?"

"Nah, I don't drink," he said. "I mean, I try not to."

"Oh, okay." She set her cup down on the table. "I still haven't met Marcus, though."

"He's somewhere around here." Nick paused. "So . . . have you met any wedding-date contenders?"

"Sadly, you're the only single man here who is interested in women."

Nick blinked. "Really? But what about the dude with the Afro?"

"We're at a disco party. You're gonna have to be more specific."

"The one you were talking to when I walked up. He was wearing a turtleneck."

"Oh, him. He has a girlfriend."

"Huh." He leaned back in his chair and mumbled something to himself. Aloud to her, he said, "I've failed you then."

Lily grinned. "It's okay. We still have until August. Plus, as sad as it sounds, I think I've had enough socializing tonight."

"It doesn't sound sad," he said, scooping more chips out of the bag. "I've already reached my limit and I only talked to you and Marcus. Parties require too much extroverting."

Lily stared at him. He passed the chips back to her, then bit his lip self-consciously when he saw how she was looking at him.

"What?" he asked.

"I . . . Nothing. I guess I just assumed you didn't have that problem. You always talk to people so easily. At least that's what it seems like when I see you interacting with other people in our building."

"Oh, that's different," he said, chewing.

"What do you mean?"

"It's something I turn off and on."

Lily poured more chips onto her napkin "So, you turn your charm off and on like a switch? Can you explain that? I'm curious."

Nick shook his head. "I don't know if I'd call it *charm*."

"Then what would you call it?"

He shrugged. "I don't know. My secret reserve of extrovert energy? At almost any given point, I'd rather be home reading, but you can't get through life that way because there are things you have to do, like there was no way I was going to miss Marcus's birthday party tonight. And I had to participate in class as a kid or else it would affect my grades. It's just a trick I taught myself to pretend like I have energy even when I don't. It came in handy for my old job when I had to talk to people a lot."

He stopped abruptly, prompting Lily to ask, "What was your old job?"

He slid her a sidelong glance. "I was a journalist."

"Oh, what publication?"

He stared down at his hands and took such a long pause, Lily was unsure if he'd heard her question. "*World Traveler.*"

"Oh." Lily stilled. Strick had been a travel-magazine writer. Thinking of him caused her face to heat up in embarrassment. It was ridiculous to let someone who didn't exist beyond a computer screen interrupt her conversation with Nick, a flesh-and-blood person who was sitting right in front of her. She pushed the embarrassment deep down. "Basically, what you're telling me is that you're used to hiding at parties."

"I guess." Nick laughed as he scooped for more chips and held the bag open for Lily, shaking some out into her palm.

"I do it too," she said. "I've done it my whole life. After a while, I just reach this point where I can feel my body shutting down, like I need to plug into a wall and recharge or I'll malfunction. It drives my sisters nuts. There was this one time in high school when I went to a house party with Violet because she was kind of a wild child and my parents thought she might behave better if she took me out with her, but I ended up spending the entire night in the laundry room, reading *Graceling*. Then the kid's parents came home, and everyone ran out the back door, and I had no idea until his dad found me reading on a pile of fresh towels. He gave me a ride home. It was very uncool. Violet was so embarrassed."

Nick grinned, motioning for Lily to pass him the chips. "I've got a story for you. Sophomore year in English class, I finished reading *The Great Gatsby* a week before everyone else—sad-ass story, by the way—so that Friday during our period of silent reading, I brought in a book from the library to read. My teacher didn't catch on for the first half of class until she walked by my desk and noticed the book that I was reading kept mentioning a shape-shifting dragon and a lady knight named Nermana. She gave me a warning, and then because I thought I was slick, she caught me again not even twenty minutes later and gave me detention. Guess who got in trouble for reading during detention?"

Lily pictured a younger version of Nick, hunched over a book with focus, and it made her smile. "What book were you reading?"

"*The Nermana Chronicles* by Elena Masterson."

"I love Elena Masterson!" Half–Korean American and half–African American, Elena Masterson was one of the few women of color fantasy writers whose work Lily was able to read growing up. "But I haven't read that one. I haven't even heard of it."

"It's a deep cut, published before her Dragons of Blood series. I have a copy. I can lend it to you."

"Really? Thank you. I can't believe there's a book by her that I didn't know about. I'm really slacking. I rarely read for fun."

Nick tilted his head. "Why?"

"I read so much for work," she said. "I used to think I'd be a writer when I was younger. But you know what they say. If you can't do, teach. Or edit, I guess. I want to work on books like Elena Masterson's, but for children. Stories about kids of color saving the world and going on adventures."

"You'll do it," Nick said. "I believe in you."

He said this with such confident ease, as if he already knew what she was capable of. Like he saw something in her that she was struggling to see in herself. Lily was so thrown, she simply gazed at him as he scooped his hands into the bag of chips.

Girl, stop! Not with this obsessive behavior again!

Clearing her throat, she asked, "So do you think you'll go back to journalism? I remember you said you were in between things."

She noticed the way he stilled then, his hand hovering above his mouth, filled with chips. "I'm working on stuff here and there. Still trying to figure it all out, honestly."

He started fiddling with the bag of chips, rolling and unrolling the top.

It was a vague answer, but she understood him not wanting to go too in depth about his work. Edith had some authors who couldn't discuss a book until they'd completed an entire draft. She imagined it might be the same for journalists.

"Well, just putting it out there that you could share your writing with me," she said. "I do edit nonfiction. I mean, if you ever want feedback."

He quickly shook his head. "Nah. Not a chance. My stuff is trash. You'd never look at me the same."

Lily rolled her eyes, but she smirked. "I doubt it's trash."

"It is. I promise you. It's not even regular trash. Or junkyard trash. It's the kind that you can't reuse so it has no business being in the junkyard in the first place. If you read it, you'd avoid me in the hallways."

"I'd never avoid you. Who else would talk to me about early-2000s fantasy novels *and* music icons from North Carolina?"

"Good point. We share a wealth of random knowledge."

Lily laughed and was suddenly struck with a strange feeling that they'd done this before, which they most definitely hadn't. It was that deceiving sense of familiarity again, flaring up and nagging at her. She was comfortable enough to tell him things she didn't usually tell other people she'd known for only a couple weeks. Why?

When she still hadn't responded, Nick glanced over at her. He started to speak but stopped. She didn't know how she was looking at him, but something in her expression must have given him pause.

An Earth, Wind & Fire song was blasting in the living room. Lily felt the bass vibrating through the floor as she and Nick stared at each other. Nick's chest rose and fell as he breathed deeply. He began to lean closer, and she felt deliciously light-headed at the scent of his cologne. Was he going to kiss her again? This time would he pull her close, gently and carefully, before delivering soft kisses along her neck until he reached her mouth? Or would he be insistent and urgent, scooping her into his lap and grabbing either side of her face as he covered her mouth with his own? Lily squeezed her thighs together as she pictured Nick's large hands palming her butt, him biting her bottom lip.

He was giving her that look, the one that made her feel like he was cataloging her features, storing them away in his memory for safekeeping. Was it obvious that she was fantasizing about him as he sat right in front of her? He licked his lips. He had to know. How could he not?

"Lily . . ." Nick said quietly. That was it. Just her name. She leaned closer too, dying to know what he'd say next.

Then something crashed on the floor in the living room and everything went black.

"Oh shit, the disco ball!" Caleb yelled. "Party's over, you heathens!"

Someone turned off the music and turned on the lights. Lily and Nick jerked away from each other. Nick stood and ran a hand over his face, then stuffed both hands in his pockets. Lily looked everywhere but at him. What just happened? She wasn't imagining the moment they'd just had, was she?

Nick cleared his throat and she finally turned to him. He scratched the back of his neck again, a slightly panicked look in his eyes. "Are you ready to go? Should we go?"

"Yeah, sure." She stood too, feeling slightly off-kilter.

"Okay, I'll grab your coat." He started to move, then paused. "Wait, what am I talking about? It's July. You didn't wear a coat."

She forced a smile. "No coat."

"Right. Let me, uh, go see if Caleb and Marcus need help cleaning up before we leave."

Lily nodded, and Nick walked out of the kitchen. She stayed motionless for a moment to get her bearings. Her pulse had ramped into overdrive and she needed to bring herself back down to earth. No more getting physically closer to Nick. She obviously couldn't be trusted in that regard. He didn't want to date anyone, and she needed a date to the wedding. And more important, she wasn't going to chase after someone who didn't want to be involved with her. She just didn't have the room in her heart to deal with another letdown after what had happened with Strick.

She'd do better to remind herself that there was a clear boundary between herself and Nick that shouldn't be crossed.

She glanced into the living room and saw people standing by the door, hugging each other goodbye. Nick and Caleb were picking up the broken disco ball shards that littered the ground, and a very tall man with deep brown skin and long locs was walking toward her.

"Hey, you're Nick's friend Lily, right?" he asked. "I don't think we've met. I'm Marcus."

"*Oh.* Happy birthday!"

Marcus was even taller than Nick. Lily looked up, up, up at the kind smile on his face.

"Thank you." Marcus walked past her and grabbed a box of trash bags from the cabinet below the sink. He came to stand beside her again. "Nice jumpsuit."

"Thank you. I can't take full credit, though. It's my sister's."

"Well, in that case, kudos to your sister. She must have good taste in clothes."

"Oh, for sure. She's a stylist, so fashion is her whole life. She works with Karamel Kitty."

Marcus squinted. "Is that the rapper who showed up at the VMAs in a bodysuit that said, 'Eat my Kitty or Die' across her crotch?"

"Yeah. That bodysuit is one of my sister's proudest career moments."

Marcus smiled and leaned against the table. "So how long have you been friends with Nick?"

"Not that long. Only a couple weeks, really."

"Gotcha." He nodded and pulled a trash bag out of the box. "He hasn't told me much about you."

"Oh." She wasn't sure what to say to that. "I'm his neighbor from across the hall. Um, I work in publishing too."

"Really? Where?"

"At M&M, with Edith Pearson Books."

Marcus raised an eyebrow. "What's that like? I've never worked with Edith, but I've heard . . . interesting things about her."

"I'm sure every interesting thing you've heard is true.

It's not the best, but I guess it could always be worse. I want to work in children's books, actually."

"Oh yeah?" Marcus's face lit up. "I should introduce you to Francesca Ng. Francesca!"

The next thing Lily knew, Marcus was beckoning over a tall Southeast Asian woman who was wearing a bright purple minidress paired with white go-go boots. Her hair was dyed fire red and the sides of her head were shaved. Her style had an air of effortless coolness.

"Sick jumpsuit," she said, pointing at Lily. She looped her arm through Marcus's. "My Uber's almost here. What's up?"

"Francesca, this is Lily," Marcus said. "She works on adult nonfiction but wants to work in children's publishing. I thought you two should meet." To Lily, he said, "Francesca is a senior editor at Happy Go Lucky Press."

"*Oh*," Lily said. Happy Go Lucky Press was an indie children's publishing company that had been started by Anna Davidson, who used to be a vice president at M&M. Happy Go Lucky seemed to be acquiring the kind of inclusive children's fantasy and sci-fi that Lily yearned to edit.

"Only you would turn your own birthday party into a networking event," Francesca said, grinning at Marcus. She stuck her hand out to Lily. "It's nice to meet you. We should get lunch or something sometime."

Lily eagerly shook Francesca's hand. "I'd love that."

They exchanged emails and Francesca bid them goodbye. In the living room, Nick caught eyes with Lily and held up his finger, letting her know he'd be back to her in one minute. Lily nodded and ignored the inconvenient fluttering in her stomach. Marcus watched their exchange and his mouth turned up in a faint smile.

"Lily, can I share something with you?"

"Sure," she said, turning to him.

"Nick would hate me for saying this, but he's a lot softer than he likes to let on. It takes a while for him to show that side to people, if ever."

She blinked. Why was he telling her this? "Okay."

"If the two of you are getting closer, all I ask is that you be patient with him."

"Oh, it's really not like that between us," she said quickly.

"I know, I know. But in case it does turn into something more . . . just remember what I said, okay?" Marcus was looking at her so closely, waiting for her response.

"Of course," she said. "Yeah."

"Thanks, Lily. It was really nice to meet you. Thanks for coming."

Marcus walked away and joined Caleb and Nick in the living room, and Lily realized then that the main reason Marcus had introduced himself in the first place was because he'd wanted to vet Lily for Nick. Because he was trying to protect him. Because that was what friends did.

And she foolishly wondered if Nick would ever open up to her.

9

ONCE, WHEN NICK WAS A SOPHOMORE IN HIGH SCHOOL, HE sat in the back of his seventh-period geometry class, staring at the equations on his exam, wondering if he'd ever need to apply the circumference of a sphere to a real-life situation, when his name was called over the loudspeaker.

Nick stilled and looked up. With the exception of the few times he'd been caught reading in class, Nick rarely got into trouble. He kept his head down and did his schoolwork. He worked evening shifts at Jack in the Box, and then he went home. Why was he being called to the principal's office?

His teacher Mr. Kelly, a lanky white man who suffered from a constant sinus infection, stared at Nick expectantly. "Well then, get up, Mr. Brown," he said, sniffling.

Nick stood and grabbed his books, fumbling to shove them inside his backpack. He handed his unfinished exam to Mr. Kelly and headed for the main office. His stomach was in knots during the entire walk. What could he possibly have done?

He turned the corner and froze. His father, Albert, was standing in the front of the main office. The night before, he'd turned their apartment upside down looking for Teresa's car keys because he had to "handle some business." He'd totaled Teresa's last car and it had taken her two years to save up for a new one. She'd learned to hide her keys when he drank too much. After tearing through their apartment and telling both Nick and Teresa to go to hell, Albert left and didn't come back for the rest of the night. Now he was here at Nick's high school, looking well rested and pleasant. A completely different person.

Albert turned and spotted Nick standing still as a scarecrow. He smiled at Nick and beckoned him forward. Nick had no idea why his dad was there, but he looked happy. And being the sole object of Albert's attention was always something that Nick had craved. It had been a while since Albert had a good day, and although Nick was wary, hope bubbled up inside of him as he walked toward his father.

"Hey, Dad," Nick said. "What's going on?"

"I'm here to take you to your doctor's appointment."

Nick stared. He didn't have a doctor's appointment that day. "I don't . . ."

"I said I'm here to take you to your *doctor's appointment*," Albert repeated, winking. Still smiling.

Someone cleared their throat. Nick turned and noticed the office secretary, Ms. Sanford, watching him and his dad. Ms. Sanford's second most important job after giving out tardy slips was spreading gossip. Everyone in their small town of Warren already thought of Albert as the once-promising basketball star who'd turned out to be such a disappointment. Ms. Sanford was looking at Albert now with a mixture of mild disgust and intrigue. Like she was both ready to call security if necessary or give Albert her telephone number if he'd asked for it.

"Oh yeah, sorry," Nick said, turning back to Albert. Automatically, Nick's mouth stretched into a smile too, his instinct to protect his father taking over. "I forgot all about the appointment."

Wordlessly, Albert clapped Nick on the shoulder and signed him out early.

"Where are we going?" Nick asked as they walked toward the parking lot.

"I need your help with something," Albert said, his hand still on Nick's shoulder. Albert walked with a slight limp due to a poorly treated broken ankle his senior year of high school, but that didn't keep him from moving briskly. He was always in constant motion, with somewhere to be and plans to execute. "Thought we could spend some quality time."

Nick's chest warmed at Albert's words. The truth was that he cared less about where Albert was taking him and more about the fact that Albert had sought him out in the first place. Maybe after so many weeks of disappearing acts, Albert actually missed Nick and wanted to spend time with him. Should he have waited until Nick's school day had finished? Maybe, but that was Albert's spontaneous nature and Nick was used to it by now. And the two of them hadn't spent an afternoon together in ages.

Nick hurried to keep up with his dad and frowned a little when he saw his mom's Toyota in the parking lot. Albert pulled the car keys out of his pocket. Nick didn't want to ask if he'd found them or if his mom had given them to him.

"What do you need my help with?" Nick asked as Albert started the car and pulled out of the parking lot.

"Just something small," Albert said easily.

The sound of the radio drowned out any additional questions that Nick might have asked. He stayed silent in the passenger seat for the duration of the drive, taking in their surroundings until they pulled into an unfamiliar apartment complex.

"Come on," Albert said, getting out of the car. He flashed Nick another one of those warm smiles.

Nick glanced around, curious. He didn't know anyone who lived in this complex, but clearly Albert must have. Maybe he was going to see one of his friends and wanted Nick to tag along? But where did helping him come in?

Nick got out of the car and followed Albert through the apartment complex. There were kids playing in the street and people sitting on their patios. Albert waved and smiled at anyone who spared him a questioning glance. They walked around to the back of the complex and Albert approached an apartment and knocked on the door. When no one answered, he peeked through the window. He glanced over his shoulder. Back here, no one was outside to see them. He picked at the screen until the bottom gave and he partially rolled up the window.

He walked back over to Nick and gave him a direct, imploring look. "I need you to be my lookout, okay, Nicky?"

"Uh." Nick glanced around again. "But—"

"This man stole from me," Albert continued. "Last night at the pool hall. I just need to get my money back. And we'll use that to get some dinner. I'll pick up your mom from work on the way. We'll get Cook Out. Your favorite, right?"

Nick nodded, silent. Stealing was wrong. Breaking into someone else's house was illegal. But if this man had stolen from Albert first, did that change things? Nick didn't know. But Albert had asked him for help when he could have asked anyone. He trusted Nick. Nick wanted to be someone his dad felt like he could trust.

"Good." Albert squeezed Nick's shoulder. "I appreciate you, son."

Nick watched as Albert hoisted himself through the window, and Nick nervously glanced up and down the street. He heard his dad bustling around inside, cursing to himself. Whoever lived here might not have been clever enough to lock their windows, but they'd hidden Albert's money in a good-enough spot.

Soon, a black pickup truck came barreling down the street, and Nick willed the driver to keep going, but he pulled up right in front of Nick.

Nick whistled to alert Albert as a heavyset Black man climbed out of the truck. He paused at the sight of Nick.

"Hey, ain't you Albert's boy?" he asked.

"Uh." Nick looked at the man's name tag on his work shirt. FRANK was written on his left breast pocket in thick, black letters. "Um."

Then Albert opened the apartment door, grinning triumphantly, stuffing a wad of money into his back pocket. Said grin dissolved when he saw Frank.

"Albert, you son of a bitch!" Frank yelled, running toward them.

Albert took off through the complex with Nick right on his heels. Frank shouted and cursed as he chased after them.

"Come on, Nick!" Albert shouted. "Get in the car!"

Nick sprinted and then tripped over his own shoelaces and fell, busting his top lip. Albert doubled back and pulled Nick to his feet. Nick scrambled to get up and ran to the car, jumping in the passenger seat. Albert tore out of the complex, banging his fist against the ceiling. In the rearview mirror, Nick could see Frank bent over with his hands on his knees, shaking his fist at their car as they got farther away.

"That's what I'm talking about!" Albert said, gripping Nick's shoulder. "That's how you look out for your pops!"

Nick's mouth was dry, his lip swollen. He could do nothing but sit there, his heart hammering away in his chest as he watched his dad celebrate.

"Oh, damn, you got your lip there good," Albert said, looking at Nick's face. He opened the glove compartment and pulled out a wad of napkins, handing them to Nick. "Hold those over your lip for now. We'll ask your mom to bring out an ice pack. They have those at the nursing home, don't they?"

Nick shrugged. His mind was elsewhere. Something about the way that Frank had looked at Albert when he saw him walk out of his front door didn't sit right with Nick. Anyone would be pissed to see that their apartment had been broken into. But Frank had looked betrayed, hurt even.

Later, Nick found out that Frank, in fact, hadn't stolen

from Albert. He'd beaten him fair and square shooting dice, and Albert was pissed about losing the game and his money. And Nick had been so desperate to spend time with Albert and receive a little bit of his attention that he'd helped him steal and get away. How did that make him any different from his dad? He was disgusted with himself.

Nick used that experience when he drafted the final scene in *The Elves of Ceradon*. Prince Deko of the Zordoo elf clan had watched his people be murdered by life leeches, squid-like creatures with razor-sharp teeth, who sprang up from the forbidden lake to feast once every century. The last of his kind, Deko had no choice but to trek across the land of Tertia alone, in search of another clan of elves who lived in Ceradon. The Ceradonian elves were a myth, children's stories told to Deko and his sister at night. But Deko knew Ceradon was real, and finding it was his last hope after his own kingdom had been destroyed. Throughout his journey, he battled trolls and dragons, was almost drowned by a merman and lost a hand fighting with a three-horned bull snake.

All the while, he was aware that the life leeches were tracking his scent and chasing him. But in the end, he'd finally reached Ceradon's city gates. Dehydrated and weary, Deko struggled to tell the guards who he was, but before he could speak, a life leech attacked him. Deko was too weak to fight back but he used what energy he had left to throw the life leech down. He lifted his sword, thinking about his father, who had been a harsh king known for mercilessly executing those who opposed him. Deko had hated his father's ruthlessness and swore to never be the same, but if he didn't kill the life leech, it would kill him. Deko hesitated, his blade nearly piercing the life leech's throat, and in a split second, another life leech attacked him, and then everything went black.

That was how Nick ended the book. He thought a cliffhanger would have readers clamoring for more. In that, he'd been right. It was the reason so many editors had offered on his book when Marcus resold it. But now he didn't know how Deko's story should continue.

He'd struggled to write the first chapter for book two. In the opening scene, Deko has just awoken in the infirmary at the Ceradonian queen's castle. He almost died from the life leech attack and had been in a coma for three days. When he gains enough strength, he walks through the city of Ceradon, feeling lost and out of place. He mourns his people and his old life. He also worries that the life leeches will find a way to break through the gates surrounding the city.

Nick's aim with the chapter had been to establish a somber tone. Now, as he sat across from Marcus at the Redeye Grill in Midtown, a few blocks away from Marcus's office, Nick was convinced that he was in over his head, and after reading his pages, he was sure that Marcus had come to this realization too.

"So, about the first chapter," Marcus said, moving aside his empty plate.

Nick nodded. "I know."

"You know what?"

"That it's bad. I shouldn't have sent it to you without editing it first."

Marcus laughed. "It's not bad. You're really your own worst critic." He reached into his satchel and pulled out a small notebook, flipping it open to a page that was covered in his tiny, neat handwriting. "My main critique is that I think Deko should be more active. He just survived a heinous attack and he wakes up and walks around the city aimlessly. What are his goals? What does he want to happen next?"

"I don't know." Nick fidgeted with his fork. "He wants peace, I guess. He wants to start over, but he doesn't know if he can."

"Why can't he? What's stopping him?"

"He feels guilty for surviving when no one else did. He doesn't know what he has to live for."

Marcus tilted his head, looking at Nick thoughtfully. "Maybe that's your plot. Deko needs to figure out what he has to live for now. If not for himself, maybe someone else or a cause."

"Maybe." The issue was that Nick didn't even know who Deko was anymore. How could he write his story when his mind was blank? "I'm going to work on that."

"I know you will," Marcus said, waving down their server. "How about we set up another meeting next month to talk about whatever progress you've made?"

"Yeah. That sounds good." He just hoped in a month's time he'd have something more to share.

After they left the restaurant, Marcus went back to his office, and Nick opted to walk back to his apartment. He wanted to marinate on the notes Marcus had given him.

And he needed to sort out his thoughts concerning Lily.

He'd almost kissed her again last weekend at Marcus's party. Even though they'd been concealed in the darkness of the kitchen, he could see her bright gold clothes and the way she looked at him. Like she wanted him to kiss her. He'd been *this* close to doing so. He couldn't get her out of his mind. This was bad.

Lily was dangerous territory for him. And even worse, he felt shitty that he'd brought her to Marcus's party and then went all caveman and cockblocked her. Turned out that dude had a girlfriend anyway, but still. Nick had said he'd help her find someone to take to her sister's wedding, and he couldn't let her down.

He pulled out his phone and texted her.

I was thinking we should probably come up with a real game plan for finding your wedding date.

She responded right away.

Lily: Oh, I love a good game plan.
Nick: What are you doing now? We can strategize.
Lily: I'm finishing up at work.
Nick: It's almost seven. You stay at work this late all the time?
Lily: Most days.
Nick: You can't see me but I'm frowning
Lily: I know, it's bad! I'm trying to be better. What are you doing?
Nick: Walking through midtown back to our building

Lily: Wait, I work in midtown! Want to meet me and
we can walk home together?

Lily: Unless you want to be alone ofc

Nick: No, I'll meet you. What's your job's address?

Lily: I just dropped my location.

Nick: See you soon

Lily: See you soon

Despite pep-talking himself the whole walk over about
how he needed to remember that Lily was off-limits and he
should look at her as only a friend and nothing more, Nick
was a nervous wreck by the time he got to Lily's office. He
peered through Mitchell & Milton's glass doors at the large,
empty lobby. And then he saw something that made him
momentarily forget about Lily altogether.

There, on one of the large screens displaying book covers, was the new cover for *The Elves of Ceradon*. It was dark
blue and silver with the name *N.R. Strickland* written across
the bottom half in large type. In the center of the cover was
an illustration of the Ceradonian queen's castle. Nick had
no opinion on the cover one way or another when he first
saw it. But seeing it here, displayed so hugely and proudly in
his publisher's lobby, did something to him. It almost made
him want to tap a stranger on the street and point it out.
That's my book, he'd tell them. Weird. Since signing with
M&M, he'd never felt that desire.

He blinked when he saw Lily come into view. She hustled quickly through the lobby, wearing a lavender short-
sleeved dress and a gray cardigan. Her face lit up when she

smiled and waved at Nick. She looked so lovely, he felt like his heart might burst.

"Sorry," she said, meeting him on the sidewalk. "Right as I was leaving, my boss wanted to go over my notes from a meeting she missed this morning."

"It's okay." Automatically, Nick lifted his arms to hug her. But then he froze, unsure if they were at that level of friendship yet. So instead of leaning closer, he held out his arms like Frankenstein.

Lily laughed and stepped into his embrace, wrapping her arms around his torso. He held her close, inhaling her vanilla scent. When that became too overwhelming, he stepped back and stuffed his hands into his pockets.

"That flashing screen is dope," he said, nodding his head at the lobby, just to have something to say.

"Oh yeah, I guess it is." Lily glanced at the screen, and he couldn't mistake the way she frowned deeply when the image switched to *The Elves of Ceradon* cover. She turned away and readjusted her tote bag over her shoulder.

Why had he brought up the screen?! She didn't need to be reminded of how he'd caused their email correspondence to crash and burn. He needed to stay on task and help her forget all about it.

"So, your wedding date," he said as they began to walk down Seventh Avenue. "I think we've been looking in the wrong place for your man. You probably won't find him at a bar or a party."

"Oh? Where will I find him?"

"At the bookstore."

"Riiight," Lily said. "You mean the fantasy when two

people reach for the same book and end up falling in love? It's unrealistic, but I'm into it. When are we going to this bookstore?"

"Now."

"*Now?*"

Nick nodded. He wondered if she'd protest, which would be fair. She'd just finished a long workday and probably wanted to go home and see her (allegedly) sweet cat.

But instead, Lily smirked and put on her game face. "Okay. Let's go."

Relief washed over Nick. He was glad she still wanted his help.

It had *nothing* to do with the fact that she was agreeing to spend more time with him.

10

LILY AND NICK STOOD IN THE SCI-FI/FANTASY SECTION OF the Strand, waiting for . . . actually, Lily wasn't sure what they were waiting for. They'd arrived at the bookstore and got so caught up in looking at books, she forgot their plan of action.

"Remind me what this plan of yours is again," she said to Nick.

He was paging through a copy of *The Poppy War* by R. F. Kuang. He placed it under his arm and turned to Lily. "We're waiting for your Prince Charming to come into this section and lock eyes with you while you're looking at a book. He's going to think you're a like-minded person and the two of you will strike up a conversation about the book you're holding. Then that will turn into a date, and that date will turn into multiple follow-up dates, and boom. The next thing you know, he'll show up on your arm at your sister's wedding."

Lily shook her head, smiling. "Do you really think it's that easy?"

"I honestly don't know but it *should* be, and it's worth a try."

"And what if this Prince Charming sees you standing next to me and assumes we're together?"

"Good point." Nick stepped backward, putting distance between them. "Once he shows up, I'll walk away."

Lily figured the chances of someone arriving anytime soon were slim. So far, they were the only two browsing sci-fi and fantasy. It was a Wednesday evening. They probably should have enacted this plan on a Saturday afternoon for better results, but she was enjoying this, and she was genuinely interested to see if Nick's method would work.

"Are you buying that?" she asked, pointing at the book he held.

He nodded. "I've heard good things. Have you read it?"

"I inhaled it during Christmas break last year. You know what you should also read, though?" She scanned the rows of books until she found *Riot Baby*. She plucked it from the shelf and held it up for Nick to see. "*This* book. It's about two siblings, and the sister Ella has these powers—"

"Oh shit, I've read this!" Nick said excitedly, not even giving her a chance to finish her pitch. He grabbed the book from her and turned it over in his hands. "I found a copy at the American Book Center in the Netherlands. It's dope. That opening scene had me."

"When the gang member walks onto Ella's school bus, right?" Lily said, equally excited. "It sucks you right in. My boss always says that a good book will hook you instantly from the first page." She smiled ruefully and added, "That's the one useful piece of information I've learned from her."

"True." Nick walked farther away, looking closely at the

shelves. "I want to show you this other book I read a few months ago that I liked. Something about a time war."

"*This Is How You Lose the Time War?*"

"Yes! Have you read it?"

"Not yet, but I've been meaning to."

"Oh, you're not leaving here without a copy. I don't see one, though . . ." He turned the corner and she heard his voice travel to the aisle beside her. "Maybe they have it shelved in the fiction section. I'll be right back."

While Nick went in search of the customer service desk, Lily continued to browse the shelves. She spotted the third book in the Dragons of Blood series by Elena Masterson and pulled it down to show Nick once he returned. Her phone vibrated in her bag and she pulled it out to see that Iris had sent a selfie to their sister group chat. She was grinning from ear to ear and holding a charcuterie board.

Guess who's ready for the Real Housewives of Potomac reunion???

Lily: Omg I forgot that was tonight!

Iris: What?! I can't believe you almost forgot. I'm disappointed and so is the grand dame Karen Huger. I'm glad I texted you. It starts in three minutes!

Violet: I won't be home for at least another hour! No spoilers!

Lily: I'll have to watch it later too. I'm at the bookstore with Nick.

Violet: Who's Nick?

Iris: Oh, you're at the "bookstore" with Nick. Okay. ☺

Lily: Don't start.

Violet: Hello?? Who is Nick?

Iris: I didn't say anything! Quick question, is he still making you smile?

Lily: 😊 Bye!

Violet: WHO IS NICK?

Lily sighed and dropped her phone back in her bag. Why did she have to slip up and mention Nick again? It wasn't like she could tell them the real reason they were hanging out tonight. Iris still believed that Lily and Nick were more than friends because she saw Lily smile at his text *one* time . . . and Lily stupidly revealed that she and Nick had kissed weeks ago. She'd just have to let Iris think whatever she wanted. And she definitely wasn't going to give any information to Violet. She'd take it and run.

"I heard they're turning those books into a movie series."

Lily startled and glanced over. A guy with light brown skin and curly hair was standing a few feet away from her, pointing at the Elena Masterson book she held. He kind of reminded her of a shorter Michael Ealy but with brown eyes.

"I heard that too," Lily said, overcoming her nerves and finding her voice. "I've read it so many times."

The guy smiled and walked closer. "I read the first book. It was okay to me. My younger sister really likes it, though."

"She has good taste." Lily smiled too. So he didn't love Elena Masterson, which was a bit disappointing, but not completely unforgivable. Everyone was entitled to their own preferences. What was important was that the topic of

Elena Masterson had been enough to spark a conversation. Could it be that Nick's method might actually work?

"But isn't it frustrating that they always shelve her with adult fantasy?" he asked.

Lily raised an eyebrow. "No. Where else would her books go?"

"YA."

Lily blinked. "Elena Masterson doesn't write YA."

"Yes, she does."

"I—" Lily wasn't even sure what to say. He was wrong, but she didn't want to argue with a stranger. "That's actually a common misconception made about women who write fantasy. Elena Masterson writes adult fantasy and always has."

The man scoffed. "No. She writes about protagonists in their late teens and early twenties. And they're all so whiny. It's annoying when you go into a book expecting one thing and you get something else. That's all I'm saying."

Lily was speechless. He doubled down on his opinion like it was an obvious fact. *Wrong and strong*, as Iris liked to say.

"You do understand that what qualifies a book as YA is more than just a character's age, don't you?" she said. "There are specific themes addressed in YA. Esch is only fifteen in *Salvage the Bones*, but there are clear reasons why that book is adult and not YA."

He rolled his eyes. Actually rolled them! "It's okay for you to admit that Elena Masterson is just trying to cash in."

"And it's okay for you to admit that you're a literary snob."

Lily never imagined that she'd speak to a stranger this way, but she was so incensed.

"I'm not a snob," he said indignantly. "You just don't know what you're talking about. I have no idea why I'm talking to you."

"Neither do I." Lily felt a hand on her shoulder. She turned, and Nick was standing beside her. He was frowning at the guy, who'd suddenly backed farther away. "Do you work at a publishing house?"

"No," the guy mumbled.

"Then I think we should leave it to the expert who does." He nodded toward Lily.

"R-right. Whatever," he stuttered, then quickly hurried away.

"And YA characters aren't whiny!" Lily called to his retreating back.

Of course once Nick showed up, the guy suddenly scurried off and didn't have anything to say. Lily huffed out a frustrated breath. However, when she turned to Nick, she felt herself smirk.

"Just because I work in publishing doesn't mean I'm an expert," she said.

Nick's mouth was still set in a deep frown, his eyes trained on the man who was far away at the other end of the bookstore by now. When he looked at Lily, his expression softened.

"Sure it does."

"I think your plan might have backfired."

"Looks that way." He held up a copy of *This Is How You*

Lose the Time War. "It was on a display table. I bought it for you."

All of Lily's annoyance from her interaction with the pretentious guy evaporated. She almost said *You didn't have to do that.* But really, it was nice that Nick had bought her a book. And she was grateful that he loved Elena Masterson and wasn't a literary snob.

"Thank you," she said, taking the book from him.

Without needing to verbally agree, they left the Strand and walked in the direction of their building. It was dark now, and Union Square was alive and loud. Lily was thinking about how she'd been having such a good time with Nick until that guy came along, when Nick suddenly said, "I'm sorry that my plans to help you aren't working."

He looked genuinely frustrated, which was both funny and touching.

"It's okay. Honestly, it's probably me. I never have luck with dating or relationships."

"You mean with the people your sisters set you up with."

"Those guys, and even when I try to meet people on my own. In high school, I spent more time pining after boys rather than actually trying to talk to them. I didn't have my first kiss until my sophomore year of college because some boy told me that I had a nice smile, which I now realize was just a line, but at the time, I ate it *all* the way up. The next thing I knew he was my boyfriend and he ended up being my first everything. And it wasn't because I was in love with him or anything. I just felt so behind. All of my suite mates were constantly meeting people and hooking up, and I felt like this loser who couldn't hold her own. Our relationship lasted for about six months until it fizzled out over summer break."

Sex with her first college boyfriend, Darius, had been underwhelming, to say the least. Maybe Lily spent too long building up the act of losing her virginity in her head. She thought it would be beautiful and romantic, but the moment had lasted for all of two minutes, and it never improved during the months that they'd dated. After Darius, she'd hooked up with a couple more guys in college, and she'd actually had a one-night stand with one of Violet's less self-obsessed model friends over a year ago, but that had been the last time she'd had sex. She wouldn't be surprised if there were cobwebs between her legs. Her vibrator deserved a yearly salary.

"I just want to date someone who is interested in what I have to say," she said. "It would be nice if we had things in common, but that isn't a deal breaker. It's mostly important to me that he has good morals, and that he's kind to me and my sisters and the rest of my family. And I want him to accept me for who I am without wanting me to change. I don't think that's asking for a lot."

Nick had fallen quiet, and Lily realized she might have divulged a bit too much.

"Sorry if that was TMI," she said.

"It wasn't." Nick gently placed his arm on the small of her back as they maneuvered between a group of NYU students and a hot dog cart. She shivered at his touch and felt silly for doing so.

How many times do I have to tell you to get yourself together, ma'am? Stop acting like this around him!

Nick's brows were pinched together, contemplative. "I had my first kiss when I was seventeen. This girl I worked with at Jack in the Box had just broken up with her boyfriend, so she kissed me in the parking lot to make him jealous. I didn't lose my virginity until college either." He paused and glanced away. "I've never been in a serious relationship before."

"Really?" Lily slowed her walk and Nick matched her pace. "Why not? I mean, only if you want to tell me."

"I just—I don't know." He shrugged and stuffed his hands in his pockets. "My parents are all over the place. They got together in high school back when my dad was a big basketball star, and then he got injured and turned into a different kind of person. I think they turned me off from the idea of being in a relationship. Or of committing myself to someone. It's not worth the drama."

Hearing his explanation for why he wanted to stay single broke her heart a little. "Are they still together?" she asked.

"Yeah. They'll never break up. Hell would freeze over first." He took a deep breath and then forced a smile, clearly wanting to change the subject. "What about your parents? I'm hoping they're less messy."

"I think they have their own levels of mess. My mom can be pretty bossy and my dad resorts to willful ignorance when he doesn't want to be bothered with important family discussions. But they were college sweethearts. They own a florist shop and everything."

"Hence your names?"

"Hence our names. Well, actually, it started with my Grandma Rose, who named my mom Dahlia."

"Your family sounds like it's straight out of a Hallmark movie."

"It may seem that way, but we're not." Lily grinned. Then she thought about what Marcus had told her last weekend. Nick took a while to open up to people, and if she wanted to learn more about him, she'd have to be patient. He'd just revealed something about himself and his family. He trusted her enough to do that. Warming to him even more, she quietly added, "I'm sorry to hear that about your parents. Thank you for sharing with me."

"Of course." Nick laughed a little. "I didn't mean to dump all of that onto you. It just came out. You're really easy to talk to."

"Yeah," she said. "So are you."

They shared a prolonged look. Lily felt her cheeks get hot under Nick's focused gaze. It made her feel like she was the only person in the room, or, more accurately, the only person standing on the corner of University Place and 14th Street. Nick's eyes were a deep, chocolate brown. She could probably stare into them all night. But it was a foolish thought, because that wasn't what friends did.

"Don't stand in the middle of the fucking sidewalk!"

Lily and Nick both jerked to attention as the man with the hot dog cart pushed by, enveloping them in his aroma of beef and sauerkraut. "Fucking tourists," he grumbled.

Lily burst out laughing, and Nick smiled. "I've traveled all over the world and that's the first time I've ever been called a tourist."

"First time for everything," she said.

They reached their building and took the elevator up to

their floor. It wasn't lost on Lily that when she and Nick were together, she enjoyed spending time with him more than sticking to their plan to find her wedding date. If she were being honest, part of her wished Nick had just agreed to be her date in the first place. But now she knew why he'd turned her down and didn't want to date. He had a thing about commitment. A wedding date didn't equal a full-blown relationship, but maybe he was afraid of what one date could lead to. And ultimately, that was good for Lily. She didn't need to waste time again pining after someone who was unavailable. She'd only end up getting hurt and be left standing with egg on her face, and she'd already had enough of that this year. She and Nick were friend-zoning each other, and that was fine. Well, it was fine as long as she didn't have any more romanticized thoughts about staring into his eyes all night.

"I guess this is good night," Lily said reluctantly as they reached her door.

At the same time Nick said, "I can give you my copy of *The Nermana Chronicles*. It's in my apartment."

"Okay," she said quickly. Too quickly.

Jesus, could you be more of a thirst bucket?

She followed Nick down the hall, excited and intrigued that he was inviting her inside of his apartment. As he unlocked the door, he shot her a nervous glance.

"Um, so I'm still setting things up."

She started to say *Okay*, but her words caught in her throat when she witnessed the vast emptiness inside Nick's apartment. The door closed behind them in a loud *thud* and it echoed throughout the space. There was a lone yellow armchair in the middle of the room. He had a flat-screen television set up on two milk crates. A laptop was placed on the kitchen island, and stacks of books lined the living room wall. It looked like he barely lived here. Like he didn't plan to stay.

"I have to get more furniture," he said, biting his lip self-consciously. "I've never had a place to myself before. I've never been able to *afford* it before. I'm still getting used to the idea. I don't know how to fill it."

She felt bad that he sat inside like this every day. It lacked warmth. The sense of home.

"I wish you would have told me that when we were at IKEA. We could have at least picked out a nice, sturdy bookshelf."

Laughing, Nick walked over to his stack of books and grabbed *The Nermana Chronicles*, bringing it back to Lily. "You can keep it for as long as you like."

"You shouldn't say that. I read so slowly now if I'm not on vacation. You won't see this book for at least another six months."

He shrugged, smiling. "That's cool."

Lily opened his door and stepped into the hallway. "Okay, whatever you say."

Nick leaned against the doorjamb, watching her, his lips still spread in a smile. Her gaze fell to the stretch of skin visible where the hem of his shirt rose. She should definitely stop staring. She didn't, though.

"You know that offer to come over and talk about *The Fifth Season* still stands," Nick said.

Lily pulled her eyes back up to his face. "You'll have to let me know when you're free."

"I can be free whenever you want."

Lily paused. He'd be free whenever she wanted him to be? How could she possibly focus on being his friend, or trying to date someone else, when he said things like that to her?

Nick was still leaning, watching. And Lily was struggling for a response when the elevator doors opened, revealing Violet and her two enormous suitcases.

"Hi!" Violet said, beaming and pushing her sunglasses up onto her head. Only Violet was confident enough to wear sunglasses at night. She hustled toward Lily and Nick in her all-black ensemble. She glanced back and forth between the two of them, her eyebrows quirked in curiosity.

"Hey, Vi," Lily said. "Have you met our neighbor Nick?"

Lily spoke calmly. Casually. She didn't want Violet to jump to conclusions about her and Nick, or worse, try to play matchmaker.

"So *you're* the famous Nick." Violet's eyes twinkled. "I don't believe we've met. Did you just move in?"

Lily groaned, embarrassed on Violet's behalf. "He's been here for months."

"I moved back in March," Nick said. "It's nice to meet you."

"Really?" From Violet's tone, you would have thought Nick's move-in date was the most interesting piece of information she'd heard all day. "Well, it's nice to meet you too, Nick." Her eyes darted between them again. She was smirking. Lily didn't like that smirk.

"So, what were the two of you up to?" Violet asked.

"We were just talking about books," Lily said quickly, and Nick nodded in agreement.

"Books, huh? That's *so* interesting. Do you hang out in the hallway together often? Nick, I don't know if my sister has told you this but I'm bicoastal, so I miss out on a lot. I didn't find out until very recently that you and Lily were spending time together."

Now Violet's smirk had transformed into a full-on Cheshire cat grin. She was raring to go. Lily swore under breath.

"Uh, yeah, she did mention that you spend time in LA," Nick said to Violet. He glanced at Lily and flashed a smile. He had no idea that he was walking right into Violet's trap.

"Mhmm," Violet mumbled. She turned to Lily. "I just had a wonderful idea. You know what we should do?"

"What?" Lily asked, already grimacing.

"We should invite Nick to the barbecue next weekend." She turned back to Nick. "We're inviting you to our parents' July fifteenth barbecue. It's a big birthday thing that they do. It's lots of fun. Say you'll come."

Lily balked. Nick blinked, wide-eyed. He glanced back and forth between the sisters. "I don't want to intrude—"

"You won't be!" Violet said. "But you *will* disappoint me and Lily if you say no."

"*Vi*," Lily hissed. "Nick, I'm sure you have better things to do with your Saturday than join us for our parents' birthday party." She shot Violet a look, which Violet ignored.

"What's better than spending a Saturday afternoon at a

barbecue with good food and good people, am I right?" Violet said. "We'd love to have you. So, you'll come?"

"Uh. Sure, yeah," Nick sputtered. It was obvious that Violet wouldn't take no for an answer. "But only if it's all right with Lily."

They both looked at Lily. The thought of exposing Nick to her family made her want to crawl inside the deepest cavern in the Grand Canyon. But then again, possibly to her own detriment, her desire to have a reason to spend more time with him was stronger.

"It's okay with me," she said.

"Perfect!" Violet declared. "It was *lovely* meeting you, Nick."

Lily shot daggers at Violet with her eyes. Violet smiled in her dazzling way and sauntered back across the hall, letting herself into their apartment.

"So . . . she seems nice," Nick said.

Lily frowned at him. "She thinks she's being slick."

"Slick about what?"

She almost said that Violet was trying to set them up, but if that wasn't obvious to Nick, she'd leave it alone. It wasn't like Violet's efforts were going to be successful.

"Nothing," she said. "So, I guess we'll see you next Saturday."

"I'll see you next Saturday."

"Good night." She backed away, clutching his copy of *The Nermana Chronicles* to her chest.

"Good night."

He waited until she opened Violet's door and waved before he went inside his own apartment.

Later that night, as she lay on Violet's couch with Tomcat curled in her lap, she paged through Nick's book, fingering the creases of the pages he'd dog-eared. The book was old and worn, well loved. And he'd trusted her enough to let her borrow it. She placed it on Violet's coffee table and snuggled under her blanket, careful not to wake Tomcat.

Right before falling asleep, she realized she hadn't thought about Strick even once all week.

11

ON THE MORNING OF JULY 15TH, LILY SENT PRAYERS TO God, the universe and anyone who would listen that the entire day might go off without a hitch. That her family would get along. That no one would make comments in front of Nick that might embarrass her.

No such luck.

"I can't believe Eddy missed his flight," Violet groaned, smashing her thumbs into her phone as she texted. "He knew how much I wanted him to come to the barbecue today so that we could sneak away and live out my fantasy of having sex in my old bedroom. When are we going to get this chance again? We're both too busy!"

"Violet, *please*," Lily said, sighing.

Beside her, Nick laughed in surprise. They were waiting for Iris to pick them up from the train station in Willow Ridge. During the entire ride from New York, Violet had told them the whole story about Meela Baybee, Eddy's newest client. Violet had met Meela months ago when she'd been the opening act for one of Karamel Kitty's shows. Meela had a decent singing voice and a drive for success, but she'd desperately needed a better look, so Violet had swooped in and changed her image.

Meela, who used to wear tacky neon body-con dresses, now had a large and devoted following full of Gen Zers who praised her skintight snakeskin biker shorts and the playful pastel nipple pasties she wore under mesh sleeveless tops during each performance. And it had all been Violet's idea. It had also been Violet's idea to connect Meela with Eddy, since Meela's previous manager had been her cousin, who booked her only at venues that were so small, crowds inevitably broke out into fights because there wasn't enough space to dance. In the weeks since, all of Eddy's attention had been focused on launching Meela. That meant things like wedding planning, their parents' annual July 15th birthday barbecue, and joining Violet to live out her sexual fantasies, fell to the wayside when Meela needed him to attend a haircare line partnership meeting.

"He said he would try to fly in later tonight," Lily pointed out, noticing that Violet was growing increasingly upset. It was unlike her to be so agitated over a man. "He might still make it."

"I hope so. He kept disappearing in the middle of conversations at our engagement party to take calls and handle a situation with one of his clients. This is another chance for our family to get to know him. We're getting married in less than a month."

Violet let out a sigh and leaned on the extended handle of her large suitcase, which was filled with clothes for the annual barbecue fashion show. Violet was wearing a sleeveless white silk tank and white wide-legged pants. Her hair was blown out, and somehow there wasn't a strand out of place in the July heat. Lily felt like a camp counselor beside her glamourous sister. She was wearing a simple orange sundress. In this weather, she hadn't dared do more with her curls than smooth them back into a topknot.

"Maybe he's trying to surprise you," Nick offered helpfully. He wore a short-sleeve white button-up. It was the most dressed up Lily had ever seen him. He was holding a tin of cupcakes because he'd refused to show up to her parents' house empty-handed. Apparently, he'd borrowed the recipe from Henry. Lily tried not to read too deeply into this thoughtful act.

"Maybe," Violet said, still frowning. She eyed Nick's cupcakes. "Can I have one of those? I'm hangry."

Nick could barely get out, "Sure," before Violet reached over and removed the lid, grabbing a chocolate cupcake for herself. She bit into it and let out a moan. "What did you put in this? Cocaine?"

"N-no," Nick stuttered. "Just flour, sugar, milk, butter, eggs and cocoa powder."

"Please ignore her," Lily said. "She says whatever comes to her mind. It's best if you just don't respond."

Violet nodded, mouth full. "She's right. I have no filter. This cupcake is delicious, though. You should be on that baking show with those nice British people."

"Thanks." His lips turned up in a shy-yet-pleased smile. He offered the tin to Lily. "Want to try one?"

Lily nodded, reaching eagerly. Then Iris's black Mercedes pulled up in front of them, and Lily retracted her hand. "I'll try one later. Iris hates when people eat in her car."

"Sorry, I'm late," Iris said, rolling down her window and unlocking her doors. Lily took Nick's cupcakes while he grabbed Violet's suitcase and placed it in the trunk. Violet wordlessly plopped down in the passenger seat while Lily and Nick sat in the back.

Iris pivoted around and looked at Nick, giving him a quick, analyzing sweep with her eyes. "You must be Nick. I'm Iris."

"Nice to meet you," Nick said as Iris took his hand in a very businesslike handshake.

"Nice to meet you too." She flashed a brief smile at Lily and turned to Violet. "So where's Big Time Eddy?"

Lily held back a snort and Violet groaned. A couple weeks ago while the three sisters had been on FaceTime, they'd heard Eddy in Violet's background on the phone with someone saying, "Of course they want to work with me. I'm *big time*." Now it was his official nickname.

"Here you go, starting already," Violet said. "Eddy isn't coming."

"Well, that's a shame." Iris started the car and glanced at Nick in her rearview mirror. "I hope you're up for some good old Greene family fun."

Nick smiled, but he scratched the back of his neck. Lily noticed that it was something he did fairly often. Maybe he was nervous. He'd have to summon all of his extroverting powers to survive the day. *She* was nervous for him to meet her family, and she didn't know why. It wasn't like he was her boyfriend or something.

. . .

THE WOMEN IN Lily's family basically fawned over Nick. You would think she'd never brought a man home to meet them before! Well . . . actually, she hadn't.

As soon as they walked into the backyard, Lily's mom and aunts flocked to them like bees to pollen.

"Oh, who is this? Lily's boyfriend?"

"What a handsome fella you are!"

"Oh, you smell so good! What kind of cologne is that? I need to buy it for my husband."

"Ooh, he's got muscles! Feel those biceps!"

"Lily, where have you been hiding this fine man?!"

Lily wished that the ground would open up and swallow her.

"This is Nick, our *neighbor*," she explained, angling herself in front of her aunt Doreen, who was busy feeling up Nick's arm. "We're just friends."

"It's nice to meet y'all," Nick said, flashing a charming smile.

The realization that there was no romantic entanglement between Lily and Nick dulled the excitement, but Lily knew her aunts would be gossiping about them later.

The Greene clan was spread out across the patio and backyard. Lily's dad was on grill duty, and his old boom box was behind him, blasting the throwback R&B radio station. Lily's cousins in her generation were all boys, which meant she and her sisters had teamed up to do a lot of fighting as kids. Now her cousins' children ran in between the adults and some were jumping on the trampoline that Lily's parents had bought for Calla.

"You made cupcakes for us? How sweet," Dahlia said to Nick, ushering him inside the house. Lily followed behind with Violet, while Iris went to check on Calla at the trampoline.

"The cupcakes are good too, addictively so," Violet said as they entered the kitchen. "He laced them with drugs."

"*What?*" Dahlia turned to Nick, confused.

"Ma'am, I promise you that there are no drugs in the cupcakes," Nick said quickly.

Lily noticed the sudden southern twang to Nick's voice. His manners brought out his inner North Carolinian.

"Violet's kidding," Lily said, pinching her sister's arm. Violet swatted at her and went to make a plate. Lily began to prepare a plate too. Her mouth watered at the baked macaroni and cheese and potato salad. But Nick paused, standing by her mom.

"Mrs. Greene, I want to thank you for inviting me to your home today," he said. "It means a lot to me. I hope you have a wonderful birthday."

Dahlia sported a delighted smile. "Thank you, Nick. Please help yourself to some food."

As Dahlia passed Lily on her way outside, she paused and whispered, "Handsome *and* has manners? You sure you don't want him to be your boyfriend?"

"*Mom,*" Lily groaned.

Dahlia giggled and looped her arm through Violet's. "Where's Big Time Eddy?"

"*Mom.*" Violet rolled her eyes.

Outside, Lily introduced Nick to her dad. Benjamin was a simple man of few words. He stood at the grill and lowered his sunglasses to get a better look at Nick. He grasped Nick's hand in a firm shake.

"And what are you doing for work up there in New York?" he asked.

"I'm a writer, sir," Nick said.

"So you like to read?"

"Yes, sir."

"Good. Lily's a big reader." He eyed Nick for another beat and then glanced at Lily. "Y'all enjoy yourselves."

"Thanks, Dad," Lily said, kissing him on the cheek.

"It was nice to meet you, sir," Nick said.

Benjamin nodded. "Likewise."

Lily and Nick found an empty table.

"I can't tell if your dad likes me or not," Nick admitted, brows creased in worry.

"Oh, he likes you. If he didn't, he wouldn't have told you to enjoy yourself. You should see the way he used to ice out Violet's boyfriends. Well, everyone except her on-and-off-again high school sweetheart, Xavier. He and Violet got into so much trouble together, but Xavier was so charming, he always found a way back into my parents' good graces."

Nick grinned. "What about Iris? Did he like her boyfriends?"

"Iris didn't really date in high school. She was too focused on world domination. But he loved her husband, Terry. We all did." She paused. "He died a couple years ago. Car accident."

"I'm sorry to hear that," Nick said softly.

"I think he would have liked you. Terry liked everyone. I guess he was the opposite of Iris in that way."

She smiled, and Nick did too. Her pulse quickened as she stared at his upturned mouth, and she made herself look away, searching the backyard until she spotted Calla jumping on the trampoline with the other little cousins.

Iris stood close by, glancing up from her phone every now and then to check on her daughter.

Lily focused her attention on Nick again. "How's your social battery doing? Did my aunts deplete you?"

Nick laughed. "Nah, not yet. Is your aunt Doreen a masseuse? She massaged the hell out of my arm."

"No, she's a loan officer. She's just thirsty."

Nick snorted. His gaze fanned out over the bustling backyard. Lily thought back to what he'd told her about his parents and their dramatic relationship. He'd never mentioned anything else about his family. Were the Browns anything like the Greenes? Did he see them often? She wanted to know more, if he was willing to tell her.

But her plans to have a deep conversation with Nick were thwarted when her cousin Antoine strolled up to their table, holding a solo cup that was 100 percent filled with Hennessy and Coke. Antoine was twenty-nine, like Iris, and as children at family gatherings, the two of them used to argue over who was in charge. Now Antoine had his own tax firm based in Philly and argued with Iris over who'd gone to the better business school.

"This your man, Lily?" Antoine asked.

Lily sighed. "No, he's my friend. Nick, this is my cousin Antoine."

Antoine tilted his head and assessed Nick. "Can you ball?"

"I'm decent," Nick said.

"We need another person for three-on-three. Come on."

"Oh, okay. Um, sure." Nick stood, and Antoine began to walk away, not even checking to see if Nick was following.

Nick looked at Lily and shrugged. She shrugged too, smiling. If Nick was able to survive her aunts, he'd definitely survive her cousins. He jogged to keep up with Antoine and glanced back at Lily once more before they disappeared around the side of the house.

"Let me get you a napkin for that drool," Violet said, suddenly appearing over Lily's shoulder. Iris was standing beside her.

"Be quiet," Lily said.

"What? I don't blame you. He looks the fuck good, like Aunt Doreen said. You're bringing him to my wedding, aren't you? That's why I invited him today."

"He's not coming with me to the wedding."

"Okay, but why *aren't* you bringing him?" Iris asked. "He's cute, and he brought cupcakes to the barbecue. Mom practically wants you to marry him. What's up with you two?"

"*Nothing*," Lily said. "We're neighbors. Friends. Why is that so hard to believe?"

"Because you kissed him."

"What?!" Violet said.

"Iris!" Lily groaned.

"I *knew* it." Violet grinned in triumph.

"*What?*" Iris shrugged her shoulders, confused. "Sorry! I didn't know it was supposed to be a secret!"

"What's a secret, Mommy?" Calla asked, appearing at Iris's side, winded from running.

Violet leaned down and placed her hands over Calla's ears. "Iris, you should have seen the way they were eye f-u-c-k-i-n-g each other in the hallway last week."

Iris pulled Violet's hands away from Calla. "One day you're going to get my daughter in a lot of trouble at school." She looked at Lily. "But is it true? Were you eye effing?"

"No!" Lily said.

"What's effing?" Calla asked, glancing up at them curiously.

"Nothing!" Iris said quickly. "Let's go get ready for the fashion show! You love the fashion show, right? Let's see what Auntie Violet brought for us this year."

Lily and Violet followed behind Iris and Calla into the house.

"I'm not doing the fashion show," Lily declared as they climbed the steps to Violet's bedroom.

Violet turned to her sharply. "Why not?"

"Because I don't want to."

"Because you don't want Nick to see you dressed like a runway model from the early aughts. The tackiness of this year's theme is what makes it fun! He should be able to love you at your tackiest."

"He doesn't love me period. I don't love him! I wish that y'all would drop this."

"Sure." Violet smiled sweetly. "But the fashion show is tradition. Are you going to let down your favorite sister?" She looked at Lily with puppy-dog eyes.

"*I'm* her favorite sister," Iris said, opening Violet's suitcase. Calla immediately grabbed a sparkly pink tank top covered in rhinestones. Iris scrunched up her nose. "Where do you even find these clothes?"

"Thrift stores are gold mines," Violet answered. To Lily, she said, "Don't worry. I'll dress you in something sexy."

Lily very nearly rolled her eyes and walked out of the room, but she saw the gleeful look on Calla's face as she admired the pink top. It was true that Lily didn't want to do the fashion show because she'd rather not embarrass herself in front of Nick. But Violet was right. It was tradition. And a good friend *should* love you even at your tackiest. Lily hoped that she and Nick were on their way to becoming good friends.

"*Fine*," she said, relenting.

Violet and Iris cheered, and Calla joined in just because. Soon, their mom and aunts and other younger cousins joined them to get dressed in Violet's chosen pieces.

Lily hoped Nick was faring well with Antoine.

12

NICK AND LILY'S COUSINS WERE ON THEIR THIRD GAME OF three-on-three in the driveway. Nick was paired with Antoine and his younger brother, Jamil. They were playing against Lily's twin cousins, Larry and Lamont, and their nineteen-year-old nephew, Demetrius.

Nick hadn't seen Lily in over an hour. Or her sisters. Or her mom. Or any of her aunts, for that matter. They'd disappeared from the yard. He mentioned this aloud and Antoine told him that they were getting ready for the fashion show. Nick remembered Violet's heavy suitcase, and of course he thought about the picture Lily had emailed him last year of Calla's small foot in a high-heeled shoe. He wondered what Lily would wear. Since they'd parted ways earlier this afternoon, he'd thought of her constantly. Did she think he'd made a good impression with her sisters and parents? Was she happy that she'd brought him along today? It wasn't his place to care about those things, but he did.

The truth was that he shouldn't be at her parents' barbecue in the first place. He was supposed to be helping Lily fall in love with someone else because she deserved to love and be loved by a good person, a *better* person. Not someone like him. But she'd invited him to come with her, and his longing to spend an entire day with her had outweighed his logic.

"Ayo, block him, Nick!" Antoine called out, as Larry shot a three-pointer right over Nick's head.

"Shit, sorry," Nick responded, smiling sheepishly. He was guilty, lost in thoughts about Lily.

He refocused his attention on the game. They'd already lost to the twins and Demetrius twice. But who could blame them? Larry and Lamont were both six four, and Demetrius played on his college basketball team. Nick was shirtless and sweating. He'd removed his button-up because it was one of his few nice shirts and he refused to get it dirty. The afternoons he spent with Henry in their building's gym were the only reason he was able to keep up with Lily's cousins.

Demetrius dribbled the ball and Nick guarded him, watching closely as Demetrius passed the ball from hand to hand. *Never take your eyes off the ball.* Albert's voice popped into Nick's head, unwarranted. Albert was the one who'd taught Nick how to play. Basketball was one of the few things Albert loved other than money. Sometimes when Albert was around, and in a good mood, he'd pull Nick away from his books and drag him to the park. There on the basketball court, Albert showed Nick the basics. He taught him tricks. He dribbled circles around Nick and looped the ball under his thigh as he jumped and dunked. In those moments, Nick thought his dad was a superstar. And he wondered what might have happened to his dad if he hadn't

landed wrongly on his ankle during a playoff game his senior year of high school. The injury had caused him to lose
his scholarship to Duke, and he'd found himself stuck in
Warren. Basketball had been Albert's first get-rich scheme.
Injury or no, he'd never lost sight of that goal, to the detriment of himself and everyone around him.

Nick wasn't as talented a player as his dad had been. He
was adequate at best. But he took Albert's advice and watched
Demetrius's hands closely. Just when Demetrius moved to
dribble past him, Nick stole the ball and rushed down the
driveway, scoring a layup.

Antoine and Jamil whooped. "You know what," Antoine
said, giving Nick a high five, "you ain't that bad."

It was a small thing, barely a compliment. But Nick was
happy to have Antoine's approval and to feel a sense of ac-
ceptance among Lily's cousins. They'd welcomed him right
away and being around them was a new experience for
Nick. He didn't have cousins of his own or aunts and uncles
or any living grandparents, at least not on his dad's side.
His dad was an only child and his mom had been raised in
the foster care system.

"That's okay. You got lucky with that one," Larry said,
waving them off. Nick learned quickly that Larry, a middle
school teacher who also coached basketball, was a big
trash-talker. "That's, what, your first point of the game?
Congratulations! How good for you."

"Just shut up and check the ball," Antoine said.

"Hey!" a woman's voice called. They all whipped around
to find Lily at the front door, wearing a big black robe to
conceal her outfit. Her curls were loose, framing her face

like a cloud. Nick stilled, staring. This was the second time he'd seen her hair out and free like that. The last time had been at Marcus's birthday party. She always looked beautiful, but right now she looked both beautiful and relaxed. He felt the corners of his lips quirk into a smile at the sight of her. She stared back at Nick, and he didn't miss the way her gaze trailed over his bare chest. The heat in her eyes was unmistakable. Nick swallowed thickly. His pulse sped up and he silently thanked his past self who made a commitment to going to the gym because otherwise Lily would have caught him out here with a bird chest.

"You just gonna stand there or are you gonna say something?" Antoine asked.

Nick blinked, remembering that they weren't alone.

"The, uh, fashion show is going to start soon," Lily said quickly, looking away from Nick. "Can you go to the backyard?"

Lily's cousins groaned but agreed to do as she asked. She and Nick locked eyes one last time before she stepped back inside and closed the door. He grabbed his shirt and quickly began refastening his buttons, intent on following Lily to . . . do what? What did he plan to do once he found her? He had no idea, and it probably wouldn't be best to seek her out after the way she'd looked at him like he was a water fountain she'd stumbled across in the Sahara. He should take his ass to the backyard and sit down like she'd asked them to. But he still felt wrapped up in her gaze, and his desire to be closer to her beat out his more rational thoughts.

He jogged in the direction of the front door but was derailed when Jamil clapped him on the shoulder and steered him to join the rest of the group as they walked toward the backyard.

"So, what's good with you and my little cousin?" Jamil asked. He was a molecular biology PhD candidate at Princeton and was actually the same age as Lily, not older.

"We're cool," Nick said evenly.

"And you're not her man?"

Nick shook his head and used the hem of his shirt to wipe the sweat from his forehead.

"Do you wish you were?" Lamont asked, coming up on Nick's other side.

Yes, in a perfect world. Nick cleared his throat, stealing himself for their interrogation, which he should have known would happen eventually. "No, it's not like that with us."

"Uh-huh." Jamil grinned. "You know you can tell us if she friend-zoned you. This is a safe space."

"She did that with all of our friends growing up," Larry added, behind them.

"Really?" Nick twisted around to look at Larry. Lily had told him she'd spent more time pining after boys than actually talking to them. Could it be that she was oblivious to how people felt about her?

"Most definitely," Lamont said.

The chairs and tables in the backyard had been split in half to create an aisle down the middle. Lily's uncles and some of the younger kids occupied the tables in the front. Antoine went to sit with his very pregnant wife, who must not have wanted to participate in the fashion show. Nick sat down at a table near the back with the rest of Lily's cousins.

"I'm not gonna lie, though," Lamont continued, "Lily and her sisters are intimidating as hell. Iris always wants to be right, and nine times out of ten, she is. Violet doesn't give anyone the time of day, and if she does, she'll soon realize she could be doing a million other things better than chilling with you. And Lily is the sweetest for sure, but she's got high standards. Iris and Violet are always introducing her to these rich, fancy dudes and she never gives them play. You're the first dude she's brought home."

"And you're not even her man," Jamil said, laughing.

Nick smiled, unsure of what to say. He was both intrigued and flattered. Mostly flattered that Lily had brought him around her family when she'd never done so with anyone else.

"It's all good," Larry said. "If she ever takes you out of the friend zone, just make sure you're ready to lose another game the next time you come around."

Nick laughed, and then Violet opened the back patio door and walked outside, carrying a karaoke machine in one hand and a microphone in the other. She was dressed in an off-the-shoulder Baby Phat T-shirt, low-rise glittery black jeans and an Ed Hardy trucker cap turned to the side.

Jamil snorted. "What the hell are you wearing?"

"Shut it, Jamil," Violet said, although she was smirking. "It's called *fashion*."

Violet plugged the karaoke machine up to the outlet and tapped the mic.

"Good evening, Greene family!" she said. The crowd responded, but Violet was displeased with their lack of energy, so she shouted, "I said HELLO, Greene family!"

This time they answered in kind, and Violet smiled, satisfied.

"The annual Greene family fashion show is about to begin," she said. "Prepare to be dazzled by our throwback to the early 2000s."

She hooked her phone up to the speakers on the patio table, and Chingy's "Right Thurr" began to play. Lily's mom, Dahlia, was the first to walk through the patio door into the backyard. She wore a purple velour tracksuit and aviator sunglasses. Lily's dad whistled and cheered, and everyone clapped and laughed. Dahlia reached the end of the walkway and posed, blowing a kiss to Lily's dad.

"Mom is giving Juicy Couture realness, y'all!" Violet said on the mic.

Dahlia was followed by Lily's aunts, and each outfit was more ridiculous than the last. Rhinestone-covered tanks over collared shirts and sparkly pants. The song changed to Nelly's "Air Force Ones" and some of the younger boy cousins walked out wearing huge T-shirts and baggy jeans and big flat-brim fitted caps.

"I can't believe we used to dress like that," Nick said, shaking his head.

"And we were dead-ass too," Jamil added. "I still have all my fitteds stored somewhere in my mom's basement."

More of the younger cousins filed outside also wearing velour tracksuits and clothes Nick hadn't seen people wear since he was in middle school. How did Violet manage to fit all of those clothes in one large suitcase? And how did she possibly go about finding them? Nick looked around at the Greenes, who laughed and clapped along to the music, completely entertained. He hadn't realized that the fashion show was such a production. It was the highlight of the barbecue.

A family tradition.

A concept he knew nothing about. But he wished he did.

Iris and Calla were next to walk outside, wearing jersey dresses and newsboy hats. "Who remembers when Mýa wore a jersey dress in the 'Best of Me' remix video and suddenly everybody and their mom had to have one?" Violet asked. "I had a Chicago Bulls jersey dress, and everybody was jealous." Calla held Iris's hand tightly and waved shyly as everyone complimented her and Iris on how cute they looked. The matching outfits were sweet. But Nick wondered when Lily would appear.

Just then, he saw her peek her head outside and quickly withdraw. He sat up straighter, eager to get another glimpse of her.

"And our lovely Lily is the last model for tonight," Violet said. The song changed to "'03 Bonnie & Clyde." It must have been Lily's cue, but she remained unseen behind the patio doors.

Violet cleared her throat. "I said *our lovely Lily* is the last model for tonight." She placed her hands on her hips and looked pointedly at the empty doorway.

Finally, Lily emerged in a denim tube top dress and a New York Yankees fitted hat over her loose curls. The hem of her dress fell to the middle of her thighs, and Nick couldn't take his eyes off her and her smooth brown skin. He was fascinated by the simplest things, like the slope of her neck and the slight bit of cleavage peeking out at the top of her dress. How the fabric brushed against her thick thighs. The point of these outfits was obviously to poke fun at terrible fashion trends. But Lily didn't look ridiculous or tacky. She looked sexy as hell.

Nick's eyes were glued to her as she walked between the tables, smiling shyly. He willed her to look at him, and when they caught eyes, his heart climbed up his throat. Her gaze still held the heat from earlier. Like she was remembering what he looked like sweaty and shirtless. He took a deep breath, trying to steady himself.

He wondered if he could ever look at Lily and *not* feel like he'd been struck by lightning.

She'd brought him home to meet her family, and he liked all of them, even her touchy-feely aunts. Throughout the entire day he'd been asked if he were her boyfriend and he wished that were the case. He wished he'd grown up as a normal person with a normal family, without any stresses or fears. He wished he didn't have to hold Lily at bay, when all he wanted was to pull her closer. He wanted nothing more than to be worthy of her.

Lily was still looking at Nick as she turned and pivoted back toward the patio.

"Lily's look is inspired by none other than the Queen Bey herself. Are there any Jays out there in the crowd tonight?"

Lily sent a glare over her shoulder at Violet, who simply smiled innocently and shrugged.

Nick was still measuring his breathing as Violet announced that the fashion show was over. The Greenes in the audience stood and clapped, while the models bowed on the patio.

As the groups dispersed, Nick made a beeline for Lily. She stood on the patio, watching him, waiting for him to approach. She removed the Yankees cap and smiled a little.

"Hey," he said once he reached her.

"Hey. I looked silly, didn't I?"

Nick shook his head, smiling too. "Not at all. You look beautiful."

"Oh." She laughed softly and glanced away. "Thank you. It was Violet's idea. She was inspired by that time Jay-Z and Beyoncé showed up to *TRL* decked out in denim. Do you remember that? They drove through Times Square in a red convertible with the top down."

"Nah, I don't remember," he said, unable to keep from staring at her. He glanced down at her thighs again. Her skin looked so soft. He took a step forward, closing the space between them. Lily's breath hitched but she didn't retreat. She looked up into his face, her eyes on his lips. He reached forward and gently ran his hand down her arm, pausing at her elbow. What was he *doing*? He should stop. Right now. But then Lily only moved closer to him.

"Watch Calla for me for a second, please?" Iris said, suddenly appearing. "I have a stupid work call." She placed Calla in Lily's arms and hurried away, holding her phone to her ear.

Nick abruptly stepped back and blinked down at Lily's niece, who looked at him with big, quizzical brown eyes. She turned and buried her face in Lily's shoulder.

"Calla, this is my friend Nick," Lily said. "Do you want to say hi?"

Calla peeked up at Nick. He thought back to an email Lily had written once when she'd said that Calla freaked out around people who weren't family. She wasn't freaking out now, but she was being cautious. Nick couldn't blame her. He'd been a cautious kid too. He might not have lost a parent like Calla had, but he'd felt the effects of trauma at a young age.

"Hi," Nick said softly. He held out his hand. "It's nice to meet you, Calla."

Calla glanced at Nick's hand and then looked at Lily, who smiled and nodded encouragingly. Calla reached out her small hand and placed it in Nick's much larger one.

"Hi," she said, her voice barely a whisper.

Nick grinned at her and to his surprise, she smiled back.

The music abruptly stopped, and Lily's parents stood at the front of the patio, a large sheet cake placed on the table in front of them. They waited for everyone's attention.

"Dahlia and I want to thank all of you for coming out and celebrating our birthday," Benjamin said. "Today is my favorite day of the year, and not because it has anything to do with me. But because I get to see how happy Dahlia is, and how very loved we are."

"We love you!" one of Lily's aunts shouted.

"We love you too!" Dahlia yelled back.

The Greenes began to sing Stevie Wonder's version of "Happy Birthday." When the song ended, Dahlia and Benjamin held hands, smiling at their family. "Who wants cake?" Dahlia asked.

People started to line up and Lily gasped. "Wait, I should get your cupcakes too." She paused. "Do you mind keeping an eye on Calla? I'll only be gone for a minute."

"I'm okay with that if Calla is."

Lily looked at Calla. "Can you sit with Nick for a couple minutes while I go get some cupcakes for us?" Calla nodded, and Lily placed her on the ground beside Nick. "I'll be *right* back."

Nick was unsure of what to say to Calla. The last time he'd spent time around toddlers was probably when he'd been in daycare himself. He looked down at Calla and smiled tentatively. Without speaking, she reached up and linked her small fingers through his. He felt so moved by that tiny act of trust. She had that quizzical look on her face again. She said something, but her voice was so soft Nick had to bend down to hear her.

"You like cupcakes?" she asked.

"Yeah," Nick said. "Do you?"

She nodded. "I like vanilla with sprinkles. Mommy and I get them after karate on Saturdays."

Nick blinked, trying to picture the small, reserved child in front of him doing martial arts. "Do you like karate?"

She nodded again. "And swimming."

"Wow. I don't know how to swim."

Calla's eyes widened. "You don't? But you're big."

Nick laughed. "I know. No one ever taught me. I can doggy paddle, though."

"I'll teach you how to swim," she said very seriously.

"Really? Thanks, Calla."

"I have to ask my mom first, though."

"Right," Nick said, nodding. "Of course."

Lily returned, and the three of them sat down to eat Nick's cupcakes.

"Violet wasn't lying," Lily said, chewing. "These are delicious. I didn't know you could bake like this."

"My mom worked a lot when I was younger, and my dad . . . wasn't around all the time, so whenever I had school bake sales and parties, I had to bake stuff myself."

Lily looked at him, her smile slightly sad. It was the same look she'd given him when he told her about his parents' marriage.

"It's a good skill to have," she said softly. Nick only nodded and watched Lily bite into the cupcakes he'd made, simply because he wanted her and her family to think well of him.

Calla's mouth was quickly covered in frosting. Her eyes took on the glassy look of a kid who was about to ride a sugar high. And that was how Iris found her when she walked over to their table.

"Grandma wants you to come in the house for pictures," Iris said, scooping Calla into her arms and grabbing one of Nick's cupcakes before they walked away.

The backyard started to empty out as it got darker and the lightning bugs and mosquitos made an appearance.

"Thank you for bringing me with you today," Nick said.

Lily rested her chin in the palm of her hand and yawned. "You're welcome. I hope we didn't drive you nuts."

"Not at all. Your family is great."

She smiled. "I'm glad you think so."

He wanted to say more, to tell her that this was one of

the best days he'd had in a long time, but Lily's mom soon called her inside, and Lily quickly stood. "Not sure what she wants, but I'll be right back." She jogged away into the house, and Nick picked up their plates to throw them in the trash. As he began to stand, he spotted Iris walking across the backyard in his direction.

"Hi, Nick," she said, sitting beside him.

"Hi." He was trying to gauge her mood. Her eyes had an intense and inquisitive quality. It reminded him so much of Calla's expression.

"My daughter never likes new people, but she likes you," Iris said. "She just asked me if she could teach you how to swim."

Nick chuckled. "Your daughter is really sweet."

"Thank you."

Their conversation was friendly, but Nick still felt that Iris was assessing him. He rubbed the back of his neck, fighting off nerves.

"I think I like you too, Nick," she finally said. "Don't break Lily's heart."

"I won't." His words tumbled out quickly, sincerely. "The last thing I want to do is hurt her."

Iris nodded. "Good. I'm going to hold you to that."

Someone let out a loud squeal and they both startled. They turned to see Violet by the backyard gate, embracing a man in a cream-colored sweatsuit. He dropped his Louis Vuitton duffel bag and wrapped Violet in his arms.

"Looks like Big Time Eddy showed up after all," Iris said, standing. "I'd better go say hi. Apparently, I'm the mean sister. We can't all be as lovely as Lily." She smirked at Nick. "I hope to see you again soon."

"Me too," he said.

Iris's warning weighed heavy on his mind. He'd already broken Lily's heart once as Strick, and he hated himself for that. But he meant what he said. He'd never hurt her again. That was why it was time to disentangle himself from the Greene family and go home.

He found Lily talking with her parents in the kitchen.

"Hey," Lily said, turning to face him. "I'm going to stay here tonight since Eddy will be sleeping over at the apartment. Can I drive you back to the train station? I'll borrow my mom's car."

"Nick can stay too," Dahlia interjected before Nick could answer. "I'll make up the pullout couch in the living room. It's too late to catch the train back."

Nick glanced at the clock above the oven. "It's not too late, only a little after nine."

"The next train doesn't come for another hour, and then it's an hour back into the city. You won't get home until almost midnight."

"I'll be fine. Don't worry—"

Dahlia grabbed Nick's hand and led him away into the living room, not giving him a chance to turn down her offer of hospitality. She instructed Nick to sit on the couch and wait for her to return with fresh sheets and pillows. She also gave him one of Benjamin's old T-shirts and a pair of shorts to sleep in. Nick did as he was told because apparently, he simply could not refuse anything of the Greene women.

Lily came and stood by the living room mantel and smiled, amused. *Sorry,* she mouthed.

Nick shrugged. What could he do? In the grand scheme of things, being forced to spend a night on someone's comfortable pullout couch wasn't the absolute worst thing to have happened to him over the course of his life.

Then he suddenly realized he actually did have a problem on his hands.

Because staying over meant Lily would be sleeping literal feet away from him down the hall.

13

AT AROUND TWO IN THE MORNING, NICK WAS FOLDED UP like an awkward pretzel in an armchair in the corner of the living room. It turned out Lily's aunt and uncle and their three young kids from Delaware had decided to spend the night as well. Her aunt and uncle took Violet's room, and Iris's old room had been converted into an office, so Nick let the children have the pullout couch, because, after all, they were family and he wasn't. Lily's younger cousins snored quietly, wrapped up in Dahlia's soft blankets.

All things considered, the armchair wasn't too bad. He'd slept in weirder situations. Like in overcrowded hostels or spread out across chairs at airports. And it wasn't like he was sleeping tonight anyway. Between years spent struggling with insomnia and constant jet lag, stealing sleep here and there was normal for him. It was better that the pullout couch was occupied by people who would actually put it to use.

Was Lily sleeping right now? Most likely. She seemed like the kind of person who slept calmly and didn't steal covers in the middle of the night.

He stood and walked quietly into the kitchen to get a

glass of water, careful not to wake her little cousins. The Greenes' house, with their big living room and inviting kitchen, reminded Nick of the kind of homes he saw on sitcoms. Large enough to fit a family of five and a surprise fourth baby in a later season, but modest enough that viewers found their lifestyle attainable. He wondered what Teresa would think of their house. When he was younger, she'd always tried to make their apartment look nicer in small ways. Albert would probably ask Dahlia and Benjamin outright how much they paid for their mortgage. Then under the guise of forging a friendship, he might ask Lily's dad if he played cards. Or he'd ask if he liked football. Did he ever bet on games? Would he like to make some easy money? Then he'd find a way to swindle her dad out of whatever cash he had on him through a bet or a card game where he'd cheat or fudge the rules to his advantage. It sounded ridiculous, but Nick had watched Albert do just that multiple times.

Nick shook off the thoughts about his parents. He filled a glass with water and drained it in two gulps. He peered closer at the photographs covering the fridge. There was a picture of Lily and her sisters when they were little, dressed in matching pastel dresses on Easter. Another of Lily at age two, sitting on Santa's lap, crying and reaching for whoever held the camera. There was Lily and Violet standing on either side of Iris at her middle school graduation. Lily smiled brightly, while Violet stuck out her tongue. Iris's smile was slight, a determined glint in her eyes.

Nick wondered about his own childhood pictures. Some existed surely, he just didn't have much memory of seeing them. Teresa kept two photographs in her wallet. One of Nick as a baby in the hospital the day after he was born, wearing a light blue onesie and a matching newborn hat. The other was a photo of his parents in high school. Albert sported a cocky grin, his arm slung around Teresa's shoulders as she gazed up at him adoringly.

Nick spotted a more recent picture of Lily and plucked it off the fridge. It was a series of photos that she and Calla had taken in a photo booth. Calla was propped on Lily's hip and they were grinning at the camera. *Violet and Eddy's Engagement Bash* was printed at the bottom in gold lettering. He recognized the yellow dress Lily wore in the photo. She'd worn it the night they ran into each other in the elevator, when she'd witnessed him give that pep talk to Henry. And that somehow led her to believe that he could help her find a date to Violet's wedding. And *that* somehow led to him being here at her parents' house, looking at a photo she'd taken on that night weeks ago. He remembered thinking that she'd looked so pretty, that he wished he had a reason to talk to her. He'd zeroed in on her granola bar and was so nervous he made a silly comment that would probably embarrass him now if he could recall what he'd said.

"Hey."

Nick startled and turned. Lily had quietly entered the kitchen. She was barefoot, wearing an oversized TCNJ T-shirt and black shorts. He tore his eyes away from her thighs and focused on her face.

"Hey," he said. "I was just looking at your pictures."

"Oh gosh," she said, walking closer. "My parents document almost everything."

"This one's my favorite," he said, pointing to the picture of her crying on Santa's lap. "Looks like you were having a good time."

She smiled and shook her head. "If you call pure terror a good time, then sure. How's the pullout couch treating you?"

"I wouldn't know. I was willingly demoted to the armchair by your little cousins."

Lily laughed. "Oh no. Are you having trouble sleeping?"

"Yeah, but that's the norm, so it's fine."

She paused, looking at him more closely. "The norm is that you don't sleep?"

"I mean, it's not that big of a deal. I'm okay. The chair is fine. I'm not complaining."

"I didn't think you were." She walked to the pantry and pulled out a bag of Doritos. She shook a handful out into her palm and offered some to Nick. He accepted a couple, and their fingers brushed. He took a deep breath as his pulse hammered away.

"I wasn't really sleeping either," she said. "If you want to hang out."

"Yeah, hang out where?" He wondered if she might take him to one of those twenty-four-hour diners that New Jersey was known for.

"My room," she said.

Nick hesitated. His gaze shifted to the staircase that led upstairs to her parents' bedroom.

"Don't worry," she said, smirking. "We're adults. It's not like we're going to get in trouble."

He pictured Lily's dad catching him in her room and chasing him out of the house with a shotgun.

But even that image wasn't enough to deter him from spending time with her.

"Okay," he said. He followed Lily down the hall to her room, feeling like a teenager sneaking into his crush's house in the middle of the night.

Lily led him inside of her room and he immediately smiled at what he saw. Her walls were painted a soft lavender and her bed had a matching lavender comforter. There was a large white bookshelf by her window, stacked with books. A handful of teddy bears were piled in the corner. Her walls were covered in posters of Aaliyah and Destiny's Child. He walked over to the bookshelf and immediately found what he was looking for: her copy of *Ella Enchanted*.

"I love that book," she said, closing her door behind her. She came to stand beside him.

"I do too." His voice was quiet. In her emails, she'd told him it was her favorite book of all time. He placed it back on the shelf and continued to walk around, admiring her things. He reached the pile of teddy bears and picked up a pink bear holding a Valentine's Day heart in its paws.

"My dad got that for me in elementary school," she said, sitting down on her bed. "Iris keeps meaning to take them home for Calla."

"Are all of these from your dad?"

"Most. Some are from boys in high school. Just my friends."

Nick smirked. "Your cousins said you friend-zoned people all the time when you were growing up."

"That's not true," she said, snorting. "I just didn't want Violet's sloppy seconds. She wouldn't give them the time of day, so they thought I was the next best thing."

Nick turned around and walked back over to her bookshelf, leaning against it. They were directly across from each other now. She folded her legs underneath of her, pretzel style, and watched him.

"I don't know," he said. "Maybe some of them just really liked you."

She shrugged, dismissing his comment. He wished she could see what he saw. To him, she was incomparable. Not the next best thing, but *the best thing*.

"Your room is so . . ."

She waited, looking at him. "So what?"

"So you," he finished. "I can picture teenage Lily in here reading and doing her homework. Tricking herself into believing that the pile of teddy bears in her room isn't from a long list of admirers."

She laughed, and he slowly approached the foot of her bed. He sat down at the edge of the mattress, closer to her than he was before, but still far enough away that they weren't anywhere near touching.

"I'm sorry that my mom practically forced you to stay here," she said. "Sometimes she won't take no for an answer. Earlier tonight she called me into the house because she and my aunt Cherie, who's a lawyer, thought it was important to team up and convince me again that I should think about law school."

"Why law school?"

"Because lawyers make more money than I do." She sighed. "The Greenes are successful. That's what is expected. I am trying to be successful, but I guess it's hard to realize that given everything my sisters have accomplished.

I've never been as impressive as they are. I don't love my job, but I make the best of it because publishing positions are so hard to get in the first place."

"I think you're impressive." He hated to hear her talk about herself this way. "You shouldn't be so hard on yourself. Everyone is different. Not being like your sisters doesn't have to be a bad thing. You're special too, maybe even more so."

I've never met your sisters, so I can't make a comparison, but you sound impressive to me.

He'd written that to her in an email. Well, now he'd met both of her sisters. But he'd still choose Lily. He'd choose her over anyone.

"Thanks for saying that," she said. "I don't blame my mom for wanting better for me. She wants me to have a secure life. She hates that I'm living on Violet's couch. Don't get me wrong, I love my sister and I'm grateful I have a place to crash but I do want a legitimate space of my own. In a few months I'll have enough saved." She shot him a rueful smile. "That means I won't be your neighbor anymore."

Nick felt a pang at her words. No longer living in the same building as Lily was what he should want. It would make their situation much less complicated. But he'd miss her.

"You and your family remind me of another family I met a while ago," he said, thinking of the Davidses in Amsterdam. "I could tell that they genuinely loved each other. It was really wholesome."

"You should hear Iris and Violet when they argue. They're definitely the opposite of wholesome then." She paused. "Do you and your family get together often?"

He shook his head. "I haven't seen my parents in almost five years."

Lily blinked. "Really?"

"I moved around a lot with the journalism gig right after college and hardly went home. A few years into the job, my mom called me from the hospital because she'd slipped at the nursing home where she worked and fractured her shoulder. She only needed money for the hospital bill, but I flew home to see her anyway. My dad was nowhere to be found and when he finally showed up, we got into an argument about him not being there for my mom when she needed him, and the fight upset her. That was the last thing I wanted, you know? She was already in a shitty situation and she really just wanted my dad. So I gave her what I could for the bill and left. My mom and I talk on the phone briefly every now and then, but her phone's been disconnected for the past few months, so . . ." He trailed off and glanced away. "My family isn't like yours."

"Not wholesome, you mean?"

"Not good," he said. "With the exception of my mom sometimes."

She tilted her head, waiting for him to elaborate.

"I . . ." He leaned back against the wall, aware that she was watching him alertly. He didn't want to tell her the horrible truths about his family. But he'd already started to, and as always whenever he talked to Lily, he felt things pouring out of him that he didn't mean to say.

"Nobody knows where my grandfather—my biological grandfather, I mean—Maynard really came from," he said. "He was a drifter who got drafted to the Vietnam War, and while he was there, he met a man named Cassius, and they became friends. Cassius told Maynard all about his life growing up in a small town in North Carolina called Warren, and Cassius showed Maynard pictures of his fiancée, Earnestine. He told Maynard about his life working at the steel mill and how he'd been planning to save up enough to buy himself and Earnestine a house before he'd been drafted. As soon as he left Vietnam, he and Earnestine were going to be married. Maynard didn't have many stories of his own. As a kid, he'd moved around from relative to relative. He wasn't stable in the way that Cassius was. But despite their differences, they became good friends and learned to depend on each other. Or at least that's what people say."

He paused and glanced over at Lily. She was staring, listening in rapt attention.

"Cassius was a decent soldier, but Maynard wasn't," Nick continued. "I'm sure being in the Vietnam War was fucking terrifying, so I don't blame him for wanting to escape. But he shot himself in the foot and was sent home. He had nowhere to go and nowhere to be, so he went to Warren, North Carolina, the same town Cassius had told him about. And when Maynard arrived, he found Earnestine." Nick took a deep breath, then sighed. "The story goes, Maynard wormed his way into Earnestine's life, seduced her and got her pregnant. Then he left, and no one ever saw him again."

"Oh my God," Lily said quietly.

"Cassius came home from the war to a fiancée who was pregnant by someone he'd come to think of as a best friend. Warren is a small town, smaller than small. Everybody knows everybody's business. So the whole town knew about what happened. Cassius still married Earnestine because he was noble, at least he was back then. But when the baby—my dad—was born, Cassius ignored him and if he wasn't ignoring him, he was berating him for one thing or another. Cassius worked at the steel mill until he died from a stroke when my dad was a freshman in high school. As far as I know, my grandmother, Earnestine, was a cold person. She never really got over the shame of what happened to her, especially in a small town like that, and I guess my dad reminded her of that shame. She died a couple years before I was born. I feel bad that she never really had a chance to live a happy life."

Lily was still quiet, completely focused on Nick. He slumped down, his legs stretching across the edge of her bed.

"Anyway, my dad hated Warren. He hated that everyone knew the story about his parents. He spent his whole life wanting to get away, and he almost did leave on a basketball scholarship. But then he got hurt and ended up working at the same steel mill as his stepdad. He kept trying to find ways to get money and escape. That's when he started gambling, which led to the drinking, and it just got worse over time, I guess. My mom didn't really have family of her own, so when she met my dad in high school, she clung to him. They have a kind of connection that I could never really understand. He lies to her. He steals from her. He's stolen from *me*. But she stays."

Nick slumped down farther, a heavy cloud hovering above him as he thought about his parents. "My dad has this charm about him. It makes you feel like you want him to be your friend, even though you know it probably wouldn't be a good idea. I worked at Jack in the Box in high school, and my dad would show up on payday and he would get all chummy with my boss and try to convince her to give him my check since I was a minor. Luckily my boss knew he was full of shit. There were times when he'd show up the UNC campus bookstore where I worked, and he'd ask me for money. His reasons were always different. Sometimes he said it was for my mom. Sometimes they needed rent money. He'd show up sounding so earnest, I didn't know what to believe. And he'd *beg* me. I always ended up giving in, because how could I turn away my own dad? Meanwhile, he couldn't be bothered to come to campus for my graduation. That's partly why I traveled so much after college. I just wanted to get away. I needed to be in a place where my dad couldn't randomly show up and find me. Where I wouldn't be tempted to give in to him."

"I'm so sorry, Nick," Lily said softly. She was lying on her side now, looking up at him. "I had no idea."

Nick nodded and stared down at his hands. "My babysitter is the one who told me the story about my grandparents. She took care of me when no one else would, but she wasn't the kindest woman, and neither were her cats. They ruined my impression of cats for life." He smiled at Lily, and she chuckled, rolling her eyes. "One of my earliest memories is of her telling me that I came from bad people who did bad things and I'd end up just like them. It was a fucked-up thing to say to a kid, and I became obsessed with knowing right from wrong. I didn't want to be like them."

"Like your dad and grandfather?"

"Yeah," he said. "I feel like them sometimes, though. Or more so like my dad. Sometimes I fuck things up, even when I have the best intentions." *Like with you*, he wanted to say. "He's the reason I try not to drink."

"You're not like them," she said with conviction.

Nick shook his head. "You don't know that."

"I *do*," she insisted.

Nick didn't say anything. Lily's words were kind, but he didn't believe them.

"Where does your mom fit in all of this?"

"She fits wherever my dad is. That's where she wants to be." Nick sighed deeply. He felt exhausted, like a wrung-out washcloth. He slid down until he was lying on his side too, facing Lily. Her bed smelled like her hair. Vanilla.

"I've only ever told those things to Marcus," he said, his voice low.

She gently placed her hand over his. Electricity shot through his veins. "Thank you for telling me."

"Thank you for listening."

They stared at each other, their hands still touching. He noted every detail of her face. The thickness of her eyebrows and the fullness of her lips. He felt rooted to this moment, to her.

"Can I say something weird?" she asked quietly.

He smirked. "Always."

"You feel so familiar to me, like I knew you in a past life or something. I know it sounds silly. I don't even know if I believe in stuff like that."

"It doesn't sound silly." His voice grew serious.

"No?"

"No. Lily . . . I've always wanted to know you." It was as truthful as he could be. He wished he could tell her that he'd fallen for her last May when her email first hit his inbox.

Her eyes widened at his words. She inched closer and Nick did as well. His hand felt warmer under hers. He lifted it and gently kissed her knuckles. He wanted to feel his lips against her mouth, the rest of her body. The air suddenly felt thick and wired, like anything could happen. Lily stared at him, mesmerized as his hand slid down the slope of her side and rested against her hip. His hand was on fire. She moved closer again, pressing up against him. He felt the softness of her breasts against his chest and he grew hard as his fingers spread out against her hip. His mouth went dry and all he could think was that he *had* to kiss her. He leaned down, his lips hovering above hers, and he hesitated because he wanted this, but he had to know that she wanted it too. He was breathing heavily, the question hanging in between them. In the end, they met halfway, drawn to each other like magnets.

The kiss was slow and sweet, like they were both giving the other a chance to stop if they wished. When Lily didn't back away, Nick pulled her flush against his body. Her hands gripped his biceps and the kiss deepened, her tongue sliding into his mouth. Nick's hand wandered to her ass and he palmed it, bringing her even closer, leaving no space between them. Lily lifted her leg, hitching it over Nick's hip, and his hands roamed up the back of her shirt, touching her hot skin. His lips trailed from her mouth down her neck, featherlight, then deeper, sucking, loving the taste of her skin against his tongue. Lily moaned, and her hips rocked against his. He felt her brush against his hardness, and every single thought left his brain. He wanted her so badly.

He lifted her so that she was straddling him. He slowly kissed her breasts through her shirt and she moaned softly, reaching for the hem of her T-shirt. Nick held his breath, preparing to pray at the altar of her beautiful breasts when something vibrated by his head, startling him.

It was Lily's phone with a text alert from Violet.

Tomcat won't go to sleep! He keeps walking around and meowing because he misses you. Eddy and I have an early flight. Please, how do I make him stop???

"Sorry," Lily hissed, reaching past him and grabbing her phone.

Nick scrambled to stand. His breath was coming in heavy spurts. Lily's lips were swollen from kissing. Her curls were in disarray. She looked at Nick and her eyes lowered. He glanced down at his very obvious erection. *What the fuck had he just done?*

"No, I'm sorry," he said.

Lily froze. "What?"

"I—fuck, Lily. Please, you have to know that I want nothing more than this, but we can't. *I* can't—"

"You don't have to finish," she said, holding up her hand. She fixed her shirt and brushed her hair away from her face. "I know you have your thing about commitment and you don't want to get involved in anything serious with me."

"It's more than that," he said quietly. "You deserve better than me. So much better. I'm not good enough for you."

She didn't say anything, simply looked at him. He felt so fucking unworthy of her in that moment.

Finally, she said, "I don't think that's true, but if that's how you feel . . . okay then."

Nick swallowed. "I should go back in the living room."

Lily nodded. "Okay."

Silently, he left her room and shut the door behind him. He walked past her sleeping cousins, sat in the armchair and stared up at the ceiling. Was it possible for him to ever *not* fuck things up?

In the morning, he took an early train before Lily woke up. And he tried not to think about how it had felt to feel her pulse beating beneath his fingertips.

14

LILY SHOULD HAVE BEEN PAYING ATTENTION TO THE AC-quisitions meeting that was taking place before her. She sat on the outskirts of the conference table along with the rest of the assistants and junior-level staff, as Edith pitched the next book that she hoped to sign up to Christian Wexler, the president of their division, and the heads of Marketing, Publicity and Sales. The book was a memoir about one woman's experience working as the assistant to the famous primatologist Jane Goodall at the beginning of her career during the early 1960s.

With notebook and pen in hand, Lily was supposed to be ready to write down any feedback gained during this meeting, but her mind was miles from the assigned task.

She was too busy thinking about Nick.

She hadn't heard from him since last Saturday night, or rather Sunday morning. He'd left her parents' house by the time she'd woken up. She hadn't been surprised necessarily, given the look on his face after they'd kissed. He *liked* her. She knew that now. The way he'd kissed her was proof enough. She'd felt so close to him after he'd opened up to her about his family, and she'd been seconds away from ripping her top off and risking it all before Violet had texted her about Tomcat. But Nick was too afraid or unwilling to give them a fair chance. He was determined to fight his feelings for her.

You deserve better than me. So much better.

What did he even mean by that? What, in his opinion, would be better? He respected her, and he made her laugh. He was kind and cared about what she had to say. She felt like she could be herself around him. He'd navigated her family with ease, and, for goodness' sake, he'd made cupcakes for her parents' birthday party! Those were the things that were important to her.

Did he think of Lily as a princess living in an ivory tower? That he needed to be perfect in order to be worthy of her? She liked him exactly as he was. But he had such a low opinion of himself. Nothing that he'd shown her resembled the things he'd told her about his father and grandfather, but for some reason, he felt as though turning out like them was inevitable. She wished she could convince him otherwise, but she also knew that Nick was a grown man and he'd need to come to that realization himself. She thought that a relationship with Nick could work, but she knew better than to wait around for him to change his mind and see their potential. She'd promised herself that she wouldn't get caught up with Nick, and now look! She'd made a fool of herself again.

The best thing to do here was put distance between herself and Nick until she felt like she could be around him and legitimately think about only friendship.

"Lily," Edith hissed, snapping Lily back to the present. "Can you please give everyone the handouts that we made?"

From Edith's impatient tone, it was clear that she'd called Lily's name more than once. Lily jumped out of her seat and proceeded to pass out the one-sheets she'd created, which included selling points for the book Edith wanted to acquire, along with the sales numbers of books with similar content. Once Lily finished passing out the sheets, she found her seat again, annoyed with herself. She was usually hyperfocused during any meeting, regardless of how boring. It was unlike her to be distracted this way.

"The sales for these comparative books are pretty low," Christian Wexler said, sitting at the other end of the conference table. "I mean, honestly, Edith, who wants to read about Jane Goodall's first assistant? The chimps are all that people really care about."

"Can we do some sort of nonfiction photograph book of the chimps?" asked Tracy, head of Marketing.

Christian pointed at her. "Now *that* is a great idea."

"And think about the distribution we could get at zoo gift shops," added Randy, head of Sales.

Edith glowered at Christian. He was the big cheese now, but decades ago he'd been her father's assistant. And once a month, he and Edith had a cheerful breakfast across the street at Maison Kayser, where they reminisced on the good old days. At least that was what Lily assumed they did. What she knew for sure was that at their last breakfast, Christian had encouraged Edith to acquire books with more modern topics because her imprint's sales were steadily decreasing. Edith later told Lily that she thought Christian was jealous that he hadn't inherited her father's imprint himself. So began her conspiracy theory that

Christian had it out to shut down Edith Pearson Books. In Lily's opinion, Christian was smarmy and inconsiderate and often took credit for divisional achievements that he had nothing to do with. But Lily had to agree that Edith's books were becoming more niche and obscure. Their marketing budget was getting smaller, and fewer people were willing to put in the extra effort to help Edith's books succeed because she was so unpleasant to work with. Lily had tried to convince Edith to sign up books that talked about tech and global warming, and even dating apps—anything that might appeal to a wider audience. But Edith never listened. She thought Lily lacked vision.

In the weeks since Edith and Christian's last breakfast, Lily had been applying to any children's publishing position she saw, but it was like her applications were being delivered to a black hole. She'd even emailed a few children's editors at M&M in an attempt to set up informational interviews. But it was the middle of summer. Everyone was on vacation or avoiding emails that weren't urgent. She'd even emailed Francesca Ng, hoping they could finally get coffee after meeting at Marcus's birthday party. But she hadn't received a response from Francesca either.

"I am not a children's book editor," Edith said, fuming. "I don't edit books with pictures of cute animals. There are people in the world who admire Jane Goodall's work and who I'm sure would like to read a firsthand account from one of her assistants. That is who this book is for. We must be forward-thinking, like my father, Edward Pearson, always said."

Christian narrowed his eyes. "Fine, but I can't agree to

your proposed advance. How about you and Lily come up with some new figures and we'll take a look in a few days."

And with that, Christian moved on to the next editor and book on the acquisitions agenda.

Lily followed Edith out of the conference room and the minute they were alone in the hallway, Edith burst into a volcanic tirade.

"Can you believe how he tried to embarrass me in there? A book with chimpanzee photographs! How could they even suggest such nonsense?! Tracy has never been very bright, but that idea truly takes the cake. Christian is trying to push me out of the company because he doesn't understand that my imprint is about *quality* over quantity. That's what this industry needs!"

Lily sighed and remained silent, walking quickly to keep up with Edith.

"And you, Lily, with your daydreaming in the middle of the meeting. You'd better stay sharp. Because if this imprint closes, you'll be out of a job just like me."

She shot Lily a warning glare, and Lily's already-growing anxiety soared through the roof. It was just another stress to add to her life.

They took the elevator down to their floor and Edith stormed into her office, slamming her door behind her. Lily apologized on Edith's behalf to her colleagues in Ad Promo whose work had been disrupted by Edith's behavior.

Lily sat at her desk and massaged her temples. This day. When would it end?

"You left your papers in the conference room."

Lily looked up to find Dani Williams leaning against the

wall of her cubicle. Dani was a marketing manager who'd spotted Lily in the cafeteria on her first day at M&M and introduced herself immediately because she'd been glad to see another Black colleague in a sea of white faces. Dani was the type of well-connected person in publishing who had tea on everyone from assistants to vice presidents and was always attending one book party or another. She would often invite you to get lunch or drinks but consistently cancel at the last minute, and when you did manage to finally link up, you'd stay out with her until four a.m. and roll into work the next morning looking like a hot mess with a head-splitting hangover, while Dani emailed you at 9:01 a.m. saying, *Last night was SO fun!!! Let's do it again soon!!!*

The last time Lily had gone out with Dani was when she'd attempted to hit on that guy with her bad joke about Coronas and pee.

"Hey, Dani," Lily said, taking her forgotten stack of one-sheets. "Thanks for bringing this by."

"Edith is in rare form today, huh," Dani whispered. Her long silver braids hung past her waist. She tapped her matte-black stiletto nails against her notepad. "We haven't seen each other in a minute. Let's get lunch next week."

"Yeah, sure," Lily said, smiling, although she knew she probably wouldn't see Dani again for at least another month.

"Okay, cool. But, girl, now that I'm here, let me tell you about this drama I overhead. Apparently, Christian's new assistant got drunk in his office after hours and marked it down on his timesheet as overtime."

"What?"

Before Dani could continue her story, Brian in Production popped around to her cubicle, startling them both. Two visitors in one day. A record.

"Oh, good, you're here," Brian said, and Lily immediately panicked. Brian, tall and pale with bright red hair, rarely came to see her unless there was an emergency. Like that time an entire print run of one of Edith's books accidentally printed with the pages upside down. Trying to manage a crisis was already hard enough, but managing a crisis *and* Edith was nearly impossible.

"Hey, Brian, everything okay?" Lily asked, practically gulping.

"Yeah, yeah." He waved his hand and Lily sighed in relief. Then Lily realized Brian wasn't alone. Standing beside him was a Black guy with dark brown skin, about medium height. He wore a white button-up and plaid pants. And tortoiseshell glasses.

Lily blinked. Her mouth slightly fell open.

"Lily, Dani, I want to introduce you to Oliver. He'll be the production manager for Edith's books moving forward."

"Hello," Oliver said, extending his hand. He had a rich, deep voice and a British accent. "Great to meet you."

Lily stared at Oliver and his outstretched hand.

Was this a joke? Was she being messed with? Had someone at M&M hacked her personal email?

Because there was no way this new guy looked *exactly* how she'd pictured Strick.

"Hey, I'm Dani," Dani said, moving to shake Oliver's hand, discreetly nudging Lily. "I work in Marketing. And this is Lily, Edith's assistant."

"Um, hi. Um, I'm Lily. Yeah."

Oliver smiled and shook Lily's hand. If he noticed that she was being the most awkward person on the planet, he was kind enough not to let on.

"Oliver just moved here from London," Brian said, and Lily managed to tear her gaze away from Oliver's face to look at Brian. "He was a production manager with M&M UK, so he knows the ins and outs."

Lily suddenly remembered Edith's frantic texts from a few weeks ago. She'd mentioned that their new production manager would be transferring from the UK office.

"It's possible we did things completely different across the pond," Oliver said, grinning. "But it's too late to send me back now."

Brian and Dani laughed. Lily gave a delayed chuckle. Her mind was busy trying to comprehend how a cardboard cutout from her imagination was standing right in front of her. Oliver's gaze lingered on her for a beat and she felt her face get hot.

"Some of us in Production are going out for drinks after work to give Oliver a proper welcome," Brian said. "You two should join us."

"That sounds fun," Dani said.

They all looked at Lily, who was still too busy staring at Oliver. He smiled at her, relaxed and friendly. Her brain filled with a buzzing static.

Dani cleared her throat. "Lily, you want to come too?"

"Oh, um, sure. Yeah."

"Great." Brian nodded. "We're going to finish the rounds and introduce Oliver to some other folks. We'll see you at the Three Flamingos at, say, six?"

"Sounds good," Dani said, answering for both her and Lily, because apparently Lily had lost the ability to speak for herself.

"Looking forward to drinks," Oliver said, waving good-bye as he and Brian walked away.

Lily and Dani stood in silence for a second. Then they turned to each other.

At the same time that Dani said, "He's cute!" Lily said, "He looks *just* like Strick."

"Wait, what?" Dani said. "Who's Strick?"

"No one," Lily muttered. She was losing it.

"Okay, so should we meet in the lobby at five fifty?"

"Oh, I don't think I'm going to go out for drinks, actually," Lily said, shaking her head.

"Come on, it's summer! Happy hour! I'll finish telling you the story about Christian's assistant and you can tell me about how much you hate Edith and we can do it all while getting drunk and eating mozzarella sticks."

Lily bit her lip, undecided. Oliver looking so much like her imaginary version of Strick did freak her out, but what was she going to do tonight after work anyway? Go home and pine for Nick while he sat across the hall in his stubborn bubble of solitude?

"Yeah, okay," she finally said. "I'll go."

AFTER WORK, LILY AND DANI WALKED A COUPLE BLOCKS from the office to meet up with Oliver, Brian and a few others from the Production team at the Three Flamingos. As soon as they walked inside, Lily spotted Oliver standing by the bar, laughing with Brian and another colleague. She tried her hardest not to gawk at him. She really needed to shake the memory of Strick from her brain if she wanted to survive this evening.

She and Dani grabbed stools at a bar-top table by the door, then Dani's phone rang, and she quickly excused herself to take the call outside, and Lily offered to get their drinks. She approached the bar and tried to get the bartender's attention, which was difficult to do during happy hour. There were two people standing in between Lily and Oliver, and she fought the urge to shoot glances at him every few seconds.

The bartender finally came over to Lily and she ordered two glasses of rosé for herself and Dani. She idly tapped her fingers against the bar and glanced over again, this time catching Oliver's eye. The two men standing in between them walked away, and Oliver smiled at Lily, sliding down the bar closer to her.

"Hey. It's Lily, right?" he asked.

"Yes, hi."

"Thanks for coming. It's nice to know that people in the US office are so friendly."

"Oh, just give it a couple weeks. You'll see how hostile and annoying we can be."

Oliver laughed, easy and light, and Lily felt herself smile. "I was born in the US, actually. San Francisco. I still have some family there. We moved to London when I was five for my mum's work." He took a sip of his drink. "I take it we'll be doing a lot of work together."

She nodded. "Yeah. Well, with me and Edith."

"Any pieces of advice for me?"

You mean other than the fact that Edith is downright evil sometimes and you should avoid getting on her bad side at all costs?

"Advice?" she repeated. "I'm not sure."

"You can be honest. I've already been warned about Edith."

"Oh." Lily laughed. "Yeah, she can be a handful sometimes." That was putting it mildly. "Make sure you show up on time to status meetings. She *hates* when people are late. She'll hold it against you forever."

"How long have you been working for her?"

"A little over two years."

"You must know her better than anyone then."

Unfortunately. "I guess you could say that."

The bartender returned with Lily's wine, and she glanced around for Dani. She spotted her outside, holding her phone to her ear and throwing her head back in laughter.

Oliver took another swig of his drink. "I shouldn't be drinking whiskey," he said. "I'm supposed to run a 5K next month. I should probably give up alcohol altogether."

"Wow," Lily said, impressed. "A 5K, really?"

Oliver nodded. "I try to do one every few months or so. I ran a lot at university. I thought I'd become a personal trainer. Funny that I work with books now, yeah?" He leaned closer and smirked conspiratorially. "Don't tell anyone here, but I don't actually read very much. I listen to maybe two audiobooks a year, and that's because they're free through M&M's audiobook app."

Lily laughed, a mixture of delight and intense relief. She

realized part of her had still been ridiculously suspicious that Oliver not only looked like Strick, but that he *was* Strick. It made no sense because she'd already accepted that Strick was most likely someone on N.R. Strickland's team who'd thought it had been a funny joke to string Lily along. But now she could confirm that Oliver and Strick were very separate people. The Strick she knew wasn't an athlete. Well, at least he'd never mentioned anything about running. And Strick had been a lifelong reader. At least, those were the things he'd told her. They could be completely false. Either way, Strick and Oliver couldn't be more different.

"Your secret is safe with me," Lily said.

"Thanks." Oliver smiled, and Lily blushed, glancing down at her drink. He was very cute. He almost made her forget about her troubles with Nick. Almost.

Dani returned to the bar, downed her glass of rosé and handed Lily some cash. "Lily, I'm so sorry, but my roommate wants me to meet her at a gallery downtown. Free food and drinks, can't pass it up! Please don't hate me. I'll make it up to you." She hugged Lily and batted her eyes at Oliver. In a terrible British accent, she said, "And we'll have to get lunch soon, gov'na." Then she bid them a rushed goodbye and hurried out of the bar.

"You two are mates?" Oliver asked.

"Sort of." Lily grinned. "Dani is friends with everyone."

"Well, she's the opposite of me. I kind of wonder what I was thinking moving here completely alone. Most of my family are on the other side of the country. I know maybe three people in this whole city. And one of them is my ex-girlfriend's best mate, so it's not like I'll be texting her to meet up anytime soon."

His ex-girlfriend. So . . . he was single?

"My mates dared me to make the big move, actually," he continued. "There was no reason for me not to take the opportunity. I'm single, and I wanted to know how New York compared to London. I've been here for three weeks and I'm already getting tired of doing things alone. I got tickets to a comedy show this weekend because my mate's cousin who lives in Queens said he'd like to go, but he has to attend a birthday party with his wife, so now I'll be seeing Angela Lawrence by myself."

"Oh, I've seen one of her Netflix specials before. She's the one who has the joke about her Uber driver ex taking her to a date or something like that, right? She's funny."

Oliver's eyes sparkled with sudden interest. "Would you like to go to the show with me?" Lily blinked, surprised at the invitation, and Oliver quickly continued. "We just met, so if that's too weird, I completely understand. But you seem cool, and I'd hate to let the ticket go to waste." He paused. "Sorry, I'm sure you're in a relationship and your partner wouldn't want you going out with a random bloke from work." He laughed and focused his attention on his drink.

Lily slowly shook her head. "I'm not in a relationship."

"Oh . . ." Oliver's expression turned hopeful. "Would you like to go then? It doesn't have to be a date. Unless you want it to be. Sorry, that was very forward. I'm usually much smoother, I promise."

Lily looked at him. She actually appreciated his forwardness. It was a welcome change after the guessing games she'd played with Nick.

Nick . . . she'd have to let go of him. And their agreement to help her find a date to Violet's wedding. In retrospect it was kind of silly that she thought Nick would actually be able to help her. If she was being honest, she'd probably just used it as an excuse to spend more time with him.

But she had to draw a line now. She could handle getting a date to Violet's wedding on her own. And she'd start with the charming guy right in front of her.

"I'd love to go," she told Oliver.

"Brilliant." Oliver held up his tumbler, and Lily held up her glass. "Cheers."

Lily smiled, hopeful and determined. "Cheers."

15

NICK STARED AT HIS PHONE, WILLING A TEXT FROM LILY to appear. It had been almost a week since their kiss at her parents' house, and it was all he could think about. He should just call her. Or knock on her door and talk to her. But he didn't know what he'd even say. He'd revealed the rawest parts of himself to her and she hadn't turned away. If anything, she'd only brought him closer and that was terrifying. Because one day she'd wake up and see that she'd made a mistake by choosing him. He was trying to save her from that grief, which meant he most definitely should not call her.

It didn't matter anyway. After the way he'd left her room, she'd most likely already realized what a fuck-up he was and wanted nothing to do with him.

"Nick, sweetheart, do you not like my carne asada? I have to say you'd be the first. My sons love this meal."

Nick looked up from his phone at Yolanda. Fridays were usually reserved for Henry and Yolanda's date nights, but they'd invited him over. Nick, still struggling to write his book and also looking for a distraction from his constant thoughts about Lily, had been more than happy to accept.

"It's delicious," Nick said. "Best I've ever had."

"Then why are you frowning at it?" Yolanda asked.

"Oh, I—um," he stammered. "I just have a lot on my mind."

"He's having issues with his lady friend," Henry supplied.

Nick turned to him sharply. "What?"

"His lady friend?" Intrigued, Yolanda leaned forward. Her eyes twinkled. "Do tell, Nick."

"I don't know what he's talking about."

"He does," Henry said. "She's the young lady we met in the hallway a few weeks ago. I've seen them together before. They smile and stare into each other's eyes while walking down the street. They're an item. Or at least they were, and now they're not, and that's why Nick is so forlorn. He was behaving this way in the gym earlier. It's why I suggested that we invite him to dinner."

At the gym, all Henry had done was jog on the treadmill and listen to his music, while Nick lifted weights. They usually didn't talk much when they worked out, so Nick had no idea when Henry had become so perceptive.

"That's not true," Nick said. "She's my friend, not my *lady friend*. Henry, can you please stop making these blanket statements every time you see me with a woman?"

"But I'm correct in this instance," Henry said. "I haven't seen you with the young lady all week and you won't stop checking your phone." He turned to Yolanda. "They must be in a spat of some kind."

"Oh, Nick, you poor thing," Yolanda said. "What's the spat about?"

I kissed her and ruined everything between us and now I know she doesn't want anything to do with me.

"It's nothing. We just . . ." He didn't know how to finish his sentence or why he was even responding. He didn't want to get into what was going on with him and Lily. It was too complicated.

Henry and Yolanda stared at him expectantly. Nick prayed for a subject change. Then his phone vibrated in his hand, and Lily's name flashed across his screen. Nick blinked, wondering if he was seeing things. But no. Lily was calling him. His heart pounded as he quickly answered. He barely had a chance to say hello before Lily started talking.

"Hey, I'm so sorry to be calling you if you're busy," she said. "Are you home?"

"Yeah." Nick immediately stood and walked across the room for his shoes. He didn't like the slightly frantic edge to her voice. "What's going on?"

"It's Tomcat. Twenty minutes ago, I fed him and got showered and dressed and he was fine. But when I came back into the kitchen to look for my earring, he was lying on the floor moaning. I've never seen him like this before. And I don't know if I should take him to the hospital or if he'll be fine. The internet says so many different things. I don't know what I'm doing, and Violet isn't here, and I didn't know who else to call."

He slid on his sneakers. "I'm coming over now. Don't worry, okay?"

"Okay," she said weakly.

He ended his call with Lily and quickly turned to Henry

and Yolanda. "I'm so sorry, I have to go. Lily's having an emergency with her cat."

"Lily?" Yolanda said. "Oh yes, that was the young lady's name, wasn't it?" She turned to Henry and nodded, like his assessment of Nick's situation had been correct after all.

Nick didn't answer, already halfway out the door, but he heard Henry say, "Yes, that's her."

Nick sprinted down the three flights of stairs to Lily's apartment, unwilling to chance waiting for the elevator. He knocked on Lily's door and she answered right away, looking distressed.

"He ate his normal mix of wet and dry food," she explained, leading Nick inside. "And now he's lying here like he's in pain. He won't let me touch him."

Nick followed her into the kitchen. Tomcat was lying on the floor, watching Lily and Nick alertly. He didn't look like he was in pain, but when Nick crouched down closer to him, he let out a weird moan.

Nick glanced up at Lily, who was wringing her hands together. He noticed then how beautiful she looked. She was wearing dark red lipstick and a black short-sleeved minidress. She obviously had plans. He wondered what they were, but he forced himself to focus on why she'd called him over.

"Could he be allergic to anything in the food?" he asked.

She shook her head. "It's the same thing he eats every day. Should I take him to the animal hospital? I'm afraid to move him because what if it's something wrong with one of his organs? You know that's why they didn't move Princess Diana's body after her accident? They have this rule in

France that after someone is injured in a car accident you shouldn't move their body in case you make things worse."

She was blabbering. Her brown cheeks took on a slightly pinkish hue. Nick returned his attention to Tomcat, who was moaning weirdly again. Nick didn't know shit about cats—other than the fact that some liked to bite ankles—but Tomcat looked wretched, and Nick knew that if they didn't do something, Lily might regret it.

"Let's take him to the animal hospital," he said. "I'll move him."

Lily bit her lip, uncertain.

"It's okay," Nick assured her. "I'll be careful."

"All right," she finally said. "I'll get his carrier."

While she raced down the hall, Nick stared at Tomcat, who continued to groan.

"*Fuck me*," he whispered to himself. His old fear of cats was nearly causing him to break out in stress hives. "Tomcat, please don't scratch, bite or attack me, all right? I just want to help you."

Tomcat's alert gaze turned slightly wary when Nick gently slipped his hands around Tomcat's torso. The cat moaned louder, and Nick froze, but Tomcat didn't swipe at him. He lay motionless in Nick's hands as Nick picked him up and cradled him to his chest. He was terrified to hold the heavy cat so closely to him, but Tomcat was more or less docile in Nick's arms.

Lily hurried over to them. Tomcat took one look at the carrier and started squirming.

"Fuck, what's he doing?" Nick said, trying to keep a hold on the cat.

"He hates his carrier." Lily tenderly stroked Tomcat's head and he stilled. She looked up at Nick. "Do you think you could hold him instead? He seems so comfortable with you. That might be better."

Nick gulped. "I'll hold him."

They hurried to the animal hospital on 16th Street. During the harried walk, Tomcat was completely calm as Nick held him, but once they reached the hospital, he became skittish again, wriggling and groaning. Nick held on to Tomcat tighter. He had no experience with soothing a cat, but he could reassure him with his embrace.

"Shh, it's okay, buddy," Lily said, trying to placate him.

They took Tomcat inside and Lily told the front-desk receptionist that she was worried Tomcat might be having a bad reaction to his food. The receptionist, a short white woman with purple hair braided into pigtails, suggested an X-ray, and a veterinary nurse appeared and gently took Tomcat out of Nick's arms. His meow became low and guttural, but he didn't try to attack the nurse.

"It's okay, buddy, don't be upset," Lily murmured. "I'm going to be right here. They just want to make sure you're healthy."

"We'll call you back after his X-ray, okay?" the nurse said, glancing between Nick and Lily. Nick realized the nurse probably thought that Tomcat belonged to both of them. "Why don't you take a seat? It won't be long."

Nick and Lily found seats in the nearly empty waiting room. Beside him, Lily stared down at the clipboard with intake paperwork. She bounced her knees, hastily wiping tears from her eyes.

"He's gonna be okay," Nick said softly. "They're gonna take care of him."

"But what if he isn't all right?" she said, emitting a sob. "Tomcat is *my* responsibility. *I'm* supposed to take care of him. And I failed. Just like I fail at everything else. I'm a big fucking failure. If something bad happens to him I will never forgive myself."

"Hey." Nick put his arms around Lily and pulled her close. He hated seeing her like this. She cried into his shirt as he rubbed her back. "You're not a failure. How can you even say that? You're the most capable person I know, and Tomcat is lucky to have you."

She fell quiet, resting her face in the crook of Nick's neck while he continued to rub her back. Slowly, her sniffling and tears stopped. He thought she might pull away, but she remained there in his embrace. This feeling of being needed was unfamiliar to him, but it felt good. She'd called him when she could have called anyone. That meant something, right?

"Thank you," she whispered. "I'm sorry for crying all over your shirt."

He shook his head. His chin brushed against her hair. "You don't need to apologize."

"Thank you for coming with me."

"Of course."

After what felt like an eternity, but was really only about twenty minutes, the nurse returned with Tomcat. This time he sat contentedly inside his carrier and meowed as Lily and Nick approached the front desk.

"Our little friend here was so nervous that he pooped as

soon as we put him on the exam table and started the X-ray," the nurse explained. "We found a little gold hoop earring in his feces, and we think that's what was bothering him. It passed out of his system, so he should be okay now."

Before walking away, the nurse handed Lily a tiny clear bag that contained the small earring.

"No wonder I couldn't find this!" Lily said, laughing in relief. She turned her bright smile onto Nick and hugged him. He was surprised for a second, but he hugged her back on instinct. He was relieved that she was relieved. Happy that she was happy.

That is, until the receptionist gave her the bill.

"Five hundred dollars?" Lily said, gaping. "Just for the X-ray?"

"Emergency visits can be costly," the receptionist said apologetically.

Tomcat, for his part, was still meowing inside of his carrier, obviously pissed and ready to get the hell home.

"I don't have that kind of money." Lily searched through her bag for her wallet. "I just put my flights for Violet's bachelorette party on my credit card and I need to pay my part of the rent."

"I've got it," Nick said, placing down his credit card.

It was interesting, really. He'd had to force himself to buy furniture for his own apartment and new sneakers without holes in the soles. But when it came to Lily, he offered up his credit card without hesitation.

"Nick," she said, frowning. "I can't let you pay for this."

"It's okay. I told you I have a lot of money saved. I can cover it."

She gave him an apprehensive look. But then she glanced down at Tomcat, whose meowing pleas to leave hadn't stopped. "I'll pay you back."

"You don't have to." Nick picked up Tomcat's carrier as the receptionist swiped his card.

"*Thank you*," Lily said, squeezing his free hand.

"It's nothing, honestly." And that was true. He would do anything for her. She meant so much to him. It was why he was determined not to fuck up her life.

BACK AT HER APARTMENT, NICK PLACED TOMCAT'S CAR-rier on the ground. Tomcat emerged and threw an annoyed look over his shoulder. Lily refilled his water bowl and he drank loudly like he'd been abandoned in the desert. Lily cooed over him and stroked his back.

Nick stood by the door, unsure if he should leave now. Lily looked up at him and smiled tiredly.

"Come sit with me?" she asked. "If you don't have other plans, I mean."

Other plans? He'd cancel a meeting with the Dalai Lama to spend more time with her.

They sat on the couch and Nick glanced back at Tom-cat, who was busy grooming himself by his food bowl.

"He's in a better mood," he said.

"He despises the vet. It's the only time he gets out of character." She was looking at Nick intently. "Thank you for everything tonight. I don't just mean paying the bill. I mean coming to help Tomcat and holding him. Comforting me when I freaked out. All of it. I am going to pay you back, by the way."

"You really don't have to."

"I will," she said.

He let it drop. If anyone, he understood the desire to not feel indebted.

Tomcat meandered over and hopped up onto the couch. Nick stilled, then held his breath as Tomcat walked right onto his lap and started making a weird motion with his paws while he purred. It was almost like he was softly digging into the fabric of Nick's jeans.

"Uh . . . what's he doing?" Nick asked, afraid to move.

"Oh my God. He's making biscuits on you." Lily was beaming. "It means he loves you now."

"Making biscuits?"

"Yeah, look at his paws. It's like he's kneading dough. My little baker." She raised an eyebrow, smirking. "Still think all cats are evil?"

Hesitantly, Nick patted Tomcat on the head. Tomcat leaned into Nick's hand, brushing his cheek across Nick's palm. Then he curled into a ball in Nick's lap, warm and content.

"No," he finally said. "This guy's okay."

Lily smiled, satisfied. "Told you."

Nick grinned at her, and then they fell quiet. He wanted to apologize for the way he'd left things at her parents' house.

"About Saturday—" he said.

"So that kiss—" she started.

Lily laughed, and Nick did too.

"I'm sorry again," he said. "The way I handled the situation was weak. It was cowardly to leave without saying goodbye to you."

She glanced down, smoothing out her dress. "I think we should just focus on being friends. I'd like for us to be able to do that." She looked up at him. "Would you?"

"Yes," he said quickly. "I would."

"Okay. And no more wedding-date stuff either. I can take care of that on my own."

He nodded. On one hand, he was proud of her for taking control of this situation. She was still so determined for her sisters to stay out of her love life. But on the other hand, he felt shitty because he was supposed to help her find someone else, to help her find happiness, and instead he'd only screwed things up and gotten in the way.

"Of course you can do it on your own. I'm sorry I wasn't much help."

"It's okay." She shifted so that she was facing him. "I actually had a date tonight. But I had to cancel, obviously, because of Tomcat."

Nick froze. His stomach clenched. Casually, he said, "Oh yeah, with who?"

"My new coworker. It's kind of weird, actually. Physically, he looks how I pictured that guy I was emailing with last year might look. I think I told you about him? The guy who ghosted me."

Nick gulped. "I remember."

"Yeah, he's British too, and the guy I had been emailing with was British." She brushed her hair behind her ear.

"Anyway, Oliver—that's my coworker's name—had tickets to a comedy show, and I feel really bad about not being able to make it."

Fuck.

Fuck shit fuck.

Who the fuck was this Oliver dude?

But why did Nick care? This was none of his business! It was a good thing that Lily met someone else. Someone better than him. That way he couldn't hurt her, and she'd never have to find out that he was the one she'd been emailing.

He should be happy.

He was miserable.

He forced a smile anyway.

"Are you going to reschedule your date?" he asked.

"I don't see why not." She shrugged and tilted her head, looking at him. "But back to you and me. Are we cool?"

It took all of Nick's willpower to nod in agreement. "We're cool."

He was determined to do right by her.

Even if that meant breaking his own heart in the process.

16

LILY SHOULD HAVE KNOWN THAT BAD NEWS WAS COMING her way, given how Edith stormed into the office that morning after her monthly breakfast with Christian Wexler. Edith didn't spare Lily a glance or even ask her for a cup of coffee. She simply slammed her door, and for an entire hour and a half, she could be heard banging things around inside of her office. Lily didn't want to get involved. She was due to meet Dani and Oliver in the lobby at noon for lunch, which was a miracle in and of itself, because Dani rarely followed through on plans. Lily suspected it might have more to do with Dani's wanting to get to know Oliver, but she was glad to have a reason to spend an hour away from her desk, and if she called attention to herself, Edith might make the prospect of Lily leaving for lunch impossible. But she was anxious to know what Christian might have said to make Edith more upset than usual.

At eleven forty-five a.m., she knocked on Edith's door and poked her head inside her office. She was stunned to find Edith sitting at her desk with red puffy eyes, staring off into space.

Lily stepped inside and closed the door behind her. "Edith, what's wrong?"

"Hello, Lily," Edith said, sitting up straighter. "Come sit down. We have some things to discuss."

Lily's stomach tumbled in anxiety as she took the seat across from Edith. Was Edith being fired? Was *Lily* being fired? Her palms were already drenched in sweat.

"Christian is hiring a new copublisher to help me run the imprint," Edith said. "Her name is Bernice Gilman, and she's currently the editor in chief of lifestyle and nonfiction at Welford Press. Christian will make the announcement next week and Bernice will begin working with us in September."

"Oh." Lily blinked. She wasn't familiar with Bernice Gilman, but Welford Press was one of M&M's biggest competitors. It most likely meant that Christian had poached her.

"Yes. At breakfast he told me that Bernice will bring a 'fresh perspective' to the imprint, as if we needed a new perspective in the first place! How insulting. It's as if he's hired a babysitter to keep me in check." Edith took a deep breath and released it with a shudder. "We'll be doubling the number of books we publish each season, now that Bernice is joining us."

Lily stared. "Is Bernice bringing an assistant with her?"

"No." Edith gave her a look like that was the silliest question she could have asked. "You'll be assisting both of us."

"What?"

The dull pain of a tension headache began to spread across Lily's forehead.

"Now my imprint will publish books about yoga and smoothies, and whatever else your generation is obsessed with. It's ridiculous! And Christian wants me to sign up books about technology and . . . and carbon footprints or some such nonsense. *You'll* have to work on those. I won't touch them, I swear. My poor father is probably turning over in his grave!"

"Edith . . ." Lily swallowed thickly and cleared her throat. Her stomach was queasy with nerves. "If I'm going to be assisting both of you and editing my own books, I think I deserve a promotion to assistant editor."

Edith stared at Lily in pure astonishment. "How could you ask about a promotion at a time like this when the integrity of the imprint is at stake?! Christian could be bringing Bernice in like a Trojan horse to slowly change the way that we do everything and boot me out. It's so insensitive that you would even mention a promotion."

Edith proceeded to burst into tears and Lily sat there, gaping at her boss. Of course Lily deserved a promotion. The fact that Edith refused to acknowledge it only solidified what Lily already knew. Edith was a sinking ship, and if Lily didn't do something, she was going to drown right along with her.

"I have to go to lunch," Lily said, standing abruptly.

Edith blubbered an incomprehensible reply, and Lily returned to her desk. She was trying her best not to outright panic.

Once Bernice started in September, Lily would have double the work. It wasn't unheard of for an editorial assistant to assist two editors, but most editors didn't need as much hand-holding and managing as Edith. Lily was already up to her ears in stress. How could she assist someone else on top of her overflowing workload? And what would her family think once they found out that she was taking on more work without a promotion?

She opened her personal email account, hoping that she might have received a response to a job application during the last fifteen minutes, but no such luck. She even checked her spam folder and found only fake offers for credit cards. She drummed her fingers against her desk. She had to do *something*.

She couldn't sit here and let other people's decisions affect her career this way, her *life*. Her situation with Nick hadn't panned out the way she'd hoped—she still didn't have a wedding date, and any chance at a relationship with him had crashed and burned, but she'd been bold in the way that she'd taken her life into her own hands and asked for his help. That boldness was what she needed in this moment right now.

Before she could talk herself out of it, she followed up on the email she'd sent Francesca Ng a couple weeks ago.

Hi, Francesca!
I hope all is well! I'm just checking again to see if you're available for an informational interview? Coffee on me! Please let me know!

She hit send and grimaced at the amount of exclamation points she'd used, but she was desperate and didn't care if she came across as overeager.

Her phone vibrated then, startling her. It was a text from Dani, saying that she and Oliver were waiting downstairs in the lobby. Lily hurried to gather her wallet and M&M ID, but she paused when she heard the telltale *ding* of an email hitting her inbox. She blinked at her computer screen. She'd received a reply from Francesca Ng.

Hi, Lily!
I'm so sorry for the late response! You know how nuts summer can be. I'd be happy to set up an informational interview with you, but I'm hoping you might be interested in something a little better. We're expanding the editorial team here at Happy Go Lucky and hiring an assistant editor, who would work directly with me. I remember you mentioned that you wanted to switch over to children's publishing. If that's still the case and you're interested in the position, please send me your résumé and we can set up an interview. Let me know if you have any questions!
Xx,
Francesca

Lily's mouth fell open.

After the moment of shock faded, she jumped into action and responded to Francesca, saying that she would love to interview for the position and that her résumé was attached.

She felt like a million bucks. She'd put herself out there and this time it had actually worked!

Nick was the first person she wanted to share this news

with. She thought about how he'd comforted her at the animal hospital. *You're the most capable person I know.* She wanted to text him, but she wasn't sure about the boundaries of their new friendship. Maybe random messages of good news didn't need to be exchanged.

She was still pondering this as she met Dani and Oliver in the lobby. They were standing very close together, and Dani was pivoted toward Oliver, saying something with a mischievous smile on her face that caused him to laugh.

When Oliver looked up and noticed Lily approaching, he waved. Lily had felt so bad about missing the comedy show, but Oliver had been understanding about her emergency with Tomcat. She needed to figure out a way to mention a rain check date, but she wouldn't do that while Dani was standing right here . . . with her arm looped through Oliver's.

"There you are, *finally*," Dani said, leading them outside. "I heard about Edith's imprint, by the way. Is she pissed?"

Lily didn't even bother to ask how Dani already knew. "She is. But I have good news."

She pulled out her phone and showed Francesca Ng's email to Dani and Oliver.

"Lily, that's amazing!" Dani shouted, hugging her. "You might finally escape Edith!"

They squealed and jumped up and down together in the middle of the busy Midtown sidewalk. Oliver looked on, laughing, while men in business suits grumbled and stepped around them.

"I feel like celebrating," Lily said. "I feel like *dancing.*"

She was truly having an out-of-body moment of elation in order to say something like that. But she wanted to ride the wave. She hadn't felt this hopeful in . . . she didn't even remember.

"Yessss," Dani said. "Let's go out after work! There's a bar near me in Crown Heights with a DJ who's actually decent. Oliver, you have to come too, obviously."

"Oh, sure," he said, looking at Lily. "If I'm invited."

Lily nodded. "Of course."

"Perfect," Dani said. "I'll invite some of the Marketing girls. We were all just saying that we needed to blow off some steam and shake our asses. It'll be a group thing!"

As they walked to the Thai restaurant around the corner, Dani was telling them the latest publishing drama, but Lily only half listened. She was wondering if it would be weird to invite Nick tonight. Like Dani said, it was a group thing, and wasn't it normal to invite friends to group outings?

The truth was that she really wanted to share her good news with Nick, so she sent him a text.

> Hey, I have an interview with Marcus's friend
> Francesca at the children's publishing house where
> she works. I'm going out with coworkers to celebrate.
> Do you want to meet us?

Her pulse soared as the word *Delivered* appeared beneath her text. But she had no reason to be so nervous. Nick didn't like crowds or parties. He'd probably say no.

His response came right away.

Congrats! That's so dope, Lily. Yeah, I'll meet you. Just
send me the address.

ONCE THEY ARRIVED at the spot in Crown Heights that
night, Lily was running on jittery fumes. She was beginning to see the folly in inviting Nick, knowing that Oliver
would be there too.

*Nick is just your friend now. There's nothing to worry
about!*

"Let's do shots!" Dani shouted, snapping Lily out of her
nervous spiral. Dani's colleagues from Marketing, Hannah
and Emily, cheered.

Oliver leaned down and whispered to Lily, "You all right?"

"Yep!" she said quickly. A shot was exactly what she
needed to calm down. They were here to help her celebrate,
after all.

Dani waved down the bartender, who brought them a
round of tequila shots. Lily threw her shot back and felt the
tequila burn her throat and chest. She shook it off. "Another round?"

"Yes!" Dani yelled over the music.

Lily ordered more shots and they crowded closer to the
bar as the room began to fill. When their second round of
shots arrived, Lily quickly gulped hers down. She stood on
tiptoe and looked around the room, wobbling slightly. Two

shots in and she was already slightly off her rocker. It was probably because she'd eaten only a spring roll and a bowl of egg fried rice for lunch. It was all she'd been able to afford at the expensive Thai restaurant. She needed to slow down. Then she felt someone tap her shoulder. She turned to see Nick standing right behind her.

"Hi!" She threw her arms around him, surprising them both.

"Hey," he said, hugging her back.

With his arms wrapped snuggly around her, she realized how much she'd missed him, and it had been only a few days since they'd last seen each other. This was a problem.

Dani cleared her throat, and Lily stepped away from Nick, feeling herself blush. Nick smiled at her, and she brought him closer to the group.

"Nick, these are my coworkers, Dani, Hannah, Emily and Oliver," she said. "Everyone, this is my neighbor Nick."

"What's up?" Nick said.

Dani, Hannah and Emily openly gawked at Nick. Oliver was the only one who responded normally by shaking Nick's hand.

Hannah and Emily snapped out of their daze when the DJ began to play the newest Wizkid song. They ran to the dance floor, and Dani grabbed Lily's hand, bringing her along too.

"*Girl*," she whispered in Lily's ear. "When were you gonna tell me that your neighbor looks good as hell? Are y'all messing around?"

"No," Lily said, her cheeks flushing. "We're friends."

"Even if the look on your face wasn't a dead giveaway that you're lying, I wouldn't believe you after seeing the way you just hugged him."

"Stop it." Lily pushed Dani away when she saw Nick and Oliver walking toward them. They were both smiling at her. *Oh God.*

The DJ started a reggae mix and Oliver reached Lily first, smoothly sidling up beside her.

"Want to dance?" he asked, shimmying his shoulders.

"Okay," she said, careful not to look at Nick as Oliver took both of her hands and led her away from the group and closer to the DJ. Oliver continued to shimmy his shoulders and wind his hips, laughing. Lily liked that he didn't take himself too seriously. He pulled her closer, bumping his hip into hers, and Lily laughed too. Oliver was only a few inches taller than her. They fit well together.

Of course once she had this thought, she glanced back at the rest of their group and caught eyes with Nick. He was in the middle of a conversation with Dani, but he was looking right at Lily, a slightly pained expression on his face. Maybe he hated the music and wanted to leave. The look on his face couldn't have anything to do with her and Oliver. She turned away, ignoring the burning feeling in her chest.

A few songs later, she and Oliver returned to the group. Nick had disappeared, and Dani, Hannah and Emily were all yawning.

"Where's Nick?" Lily asked.

"He went to the bathroom," Dani said. "You know I love a good party, but we've got a sales conference in the morning, so we're gonna head out. This was so fun, though!

Good luck on your interview!" She hugged Lily and whispered, "And let me know who you end up choosing, because if it isn't Oliver, I want him to take me to London whenever he goes back to visit."

Lily swatted Dani's arm and she laughed. Dani hugged Oliver and then she, Hannah and Emily pushed their way to the exit.

Oliver checked the time on his Apple watch. "I should probably go too. My new running group meets at four a.m."

"Oh, of course," Lily said. But she was reluctant to leave without saying goodbye to Nick first.

Then Nick reappeared at her side.

"Where'd Dani and her friends go?" he asked.

"They left," Lily said. "Oliver is leaving too."

Nick glanced at Oliver, who was pulling up the Uber app on his phone. He turned his attention back to Lily. "What about you? Do you want to stay?"

"Yeah," she admitted. "I do. But it's cool if you're ready to go too."

"Nah, I'll stay."

Her lips spread into a grin. She couldn't have helped it if she'd tried. "Okay."

Nick looked at her, smiling too. Oliver cleared his throat.

"Um, so, Lily, I'll see you tomorrow?" he asked.

Lily blinked, tearing her gaze away from Nick. "Yeah. Thanks so much for coming."

Oliver's eyes darted between Lily and Nick. He looked like he wanted to say something else, but instead he said goodbye and told Lily he'd text her when he got home.

"So that's the new coworker you were supposed to go out with?" Nick asked, watching as Oliver made his way to the exit.

Lily nodded, intrigued by the frown on Nick's face. Was he jealous? Did it make her evil if she wanted him to be?

"He seems nice," Nick said.

"He is very nice," Lily agreed.

"Hmph," Nick mumbled flatly.

Lily turned away, hiding her grin. He *was* jealous.

The DJ was still on his reggae kick, and the song changed to "Girls Dem Sugar" by Beenie Man and Mýa. Lily hadn't heard the song in years. She started moving her hips.

Nick watched her. "Do you want to dance?"

"Yes," she said, heart quickening at his closeness.

Nick moved to stand behind her, his hands resting on her hips as she danced. She hadn't been this close to him since that night at her parents' house. Did he still think of it as much as she did? He pulled her against him and Lily continued to wind her waist. She was full-out grinding on him.

"Congrats on your interview," he whispered in her ear. Lily shivered but tried not to show the effect he had on her. "How do you feel?"

"Excited," she said. "Hopeful."

But she didn't know if she was talking about the interview or being with him.

She was enveloped by him and his embrace. There was no space between their bodies. She was beginning to sweat, and she felt Nick's grip on her hips tighten. His lips were still at her ear. She felt his breath fanning across her neck and shoulder.

She turned around to face him, and he was right there. His mouth only inches from hers. Nick was staring at her lips. He licked his own and lowered his face closer. She should back away, put space between them. But she didn't. Instead, she tipped her face up to meet his.

When Nick kissed her, she felt a jolt to her entire system. She hadn't realized just how much she'd been waiting for the chance to kiss him again until his lips were pressed to hers. She turned fully, and Nick pulled her against him, his hands sliding down to rest at the small of her back. The kiss was urgent and sloppy as their tongues knocked into each other. She gripped Nick's shoulders, wanting him closer and closer still.

Someone bumped into them, and they broke apart, gasping. They were hot and sweaty. Lily's thin button-up was sticking to her skin. Nick grabbed her hand and led her outside. The fresh air hit them, and Lily turned to Nick and burst into giddy laughter. He smiled, pulling her toward him again. He pushed her up against the brick wall and kissed her.

Who was she fooling? Nick wasn't just her friend, and she didn't want him to be.

She gently eased away from Nick, her mouth swollen and raw. She looked directly into his eyes and said what she'd been wanting to say for over a month.

"I really like you, Nick," she said plainly. "I don't want to pretend that I don't anymore."

Nick's hands were still at her waist. His gaze was glued to her face. She didn't know what she expected his reaction to be, but she didn't think he'd look so . . . nervous. Or afraid.

"Do you have feelings for me?" she asked.

"Yes," he breathed. He stepped away from her, running his hands over his face. "You have no idea how much."

"Then what's the problem? I know you think you're a bad person and you might hurt me, but I really don't think you're capable of doing that."

Nick started to pace. Lily watched him, confused. His nervousness was giving her pause. He finally stilled in front of her.

"There's something I haven't told you," he said quietly.

"What?" Her eyes searched his face. "Do you have a girlfriend or something?"

"*No*," he said. Then, "It's worse than that."

Lily blinked. What could be worse than that? Was he a murderer? Was he *married*?

"Nick." She grabbed his hand. "Just tell me."

He looked at her, almost pleadingly. An infinity passed before he spoke again.

"Lily," he said, "I'm Strick."

17

"WHAT . . . ?"

Lily's voice was low, confused. She dropped Nick's hand, and he felt the absence of her touch immediately.

"I'm Strick," he repeated. His stomach was tying itself into miserable knots. He was going to throw up. "It was me. You were emailing with me."

Lily stared at him, unblinking. She quickly shook her head, like she was trying to make sense of his words. "I was emailing with you?"

"Yes," he said weakly.

"But . . . how is that possible? How did you have access to N.R. Strickland's email?"

"*I'm* N.R. Strickland."

Lily's mouth fell open. She stood there, staring blankly. People brushed by them on the sidewalk and music blared from inside the bar, but she was focused on Nick.

"Let me explain," he said quickly. "Everything that I told you in those emails was true. I sold *The Elves of Ceradon* to a small British press when I was a senior in college. Then after the book tanked, I took a job writing for *World Trav-*

eler and I left the whole N.R. Strickland persona, along with the idea of being an author, behind. Five years later, Marcus took me on as his new client and made that website for me, and then you emailed me, and I couldn't not respond to you. There was just something about your email. I only meant to write back that one time, but the more I got to know you, the harder it became to pull away. I created the pen name so that my dad wouldn't know about my career or any money that could come from it, and I didn't want to share that with you because I'd never shared that with anyone other than Marcus. And I kept lying to you in our emails with that stupid British accent, and lying like that reminded me of something that my dad would do and I hated myself for it. I didn't want to hurt you and I kept trying to back away, but I couldn't. When I found out that Marcus sold *Elves* and I'd be moving to New York where I'd be able to see you, I knew I had to cut off contact because if I got involved with you in real life I'd find some way to fuck it up and mess with your life and I couldn't do that to you. Then I moved here and the next thing I knew you were my neighbor. I didn't realize it until the night I came to your apartment and saw Tomcat and the tattoo on your foot."

She was silent for several agonizing moments. Then she finally spoke.

"You've known for almost two months?" she asked. "Were you ever going to tell me?"

"No, not at first. I thought it would be for the best to let you move on and to help you find someone who was more deserving of you."

The music from inside of the bar grew louder, and Nick slightly raised his voice to be heard, even though the last thing he wanted was for anyone to overhear their conversation.

"It's not for you to decide who is deserving of me," she snapped. "You sat there and listened to me talk about how heartbroken I was after you stopped emailing me and you didn't say *anything*."

"I'm sorry, Lily. I'm so fucking sorry. I should have said something, you're right. My logic was fucking stupid, but I had to tell you now because . . . because . . ."

"Because *what?*"

"Because I'm so fucking into you! And I want to put all my stupid shit aside and be the partner that you deserve, and I couldn't go another second without telling you the truth."

Lily had flattened herself against the brick wall, breathing heavily as she stared at Nick, wide-eyed. He needed to know what she was thinking.

"Over half a year," she finally said. "You emailed with me for over half a year. I told you so much about my life. You *knew* me. And you pretended not to. Can you understand how betrayed I feel?"

"Yes," he breathed, tenderly taking her hand in his. "But I'm begging for your forgiveness. I was trying to protect you from me and I see now how stupid that was because you deserved the truth from the beginning. And I know this sounds ridiculous, but earlier tonight, I was thinking what are the odds that after all this time you and I would end up neighbors? That has to mean something, right? Like fate or some shit? I don't know. But I'm asking you to forgive me and if you do, I swear to God, I will never lie to you ever again in my life. I will try my best to never hurt you."

Lily stared down at their clasped hands. She was frowning, her face a storm of emotions. She pulled her hand away.

"I can't talk to you right now," she said. She began walking in the direction of the subway.

"Lily, wait." Nick went after her, and she spun on her heels and held up her hand.

"Please don't follow me."

He froze and did as she asked, letting her go.

"I'm sorry," he whispered, watching her retreating form.

He'd fucked it up, way worse than he thought was possible. Her rejection was exactly what he deserved. And he knew it.

* * *

LILY WASN'T SURE how she managed to get back to Manhattan. She moved on autopilot, staring into space as she rode the subway. She took the elevator to her floor and let herself inside her and Violet's apartment, fed Tomcat and sat on the couch. All done in a state of disbelief.

Nick was N.R. Strickland.

Nick was Strick.

She felt so stupid now that she knew the truth. It had been there right in front of her face the whole time. How had she not seen it before?

Strick wrote for a travel magazine. Nick said he was a journalist who moved from place to place. Strick had a best friend who was a literary agent. So did Nick. Neither liked to spend time with their family. They had a fear of cats. They loved books. They were the *same person*. Nick was Strick. Jesus, even their names rhymed.

No wonder he'd felt so familiar to her. No wonder she'd fallen for him so quickly, so effortlessly. She'd already fallen for him before.

She could admit that their current situation was ridiculous. What were the odds that they'd somehow ended up neighbors? She could understand how he'd be freaked out, because she was kind of freaked out too. But he'd known the truth for months and hadn't told her, and that was unfair.

He'd apologized and pleaded with her outside of the bar. He wanted to stop being afraid. He wanted to be with Lily. It was all she had wanted before. But how could she ever agree to that now? How could they start a relationship on these grounds? He'd ghosted her and concealed the truth once they met in person. She couldn't overlook that.

Her phone vibrated on her bed, jolting her to attention. It was an email from Francesca Ng, asking for Lily's interview availability. Lily responded robotically. She didn't feel like celebrating anymore.

She didn't even feel like crying over Nick. She just felt numb.

Tomcat leaped onto the couch and curled himself into a ball in her lap. She petted his smooth fur and held him closer. Before long, she heard a soft knock at the door. Somehow, she already knew who it was. She went to the door and looked through the peephole. Nick stood in the hallway, holding a stack of paper. He was staring at the ground, his shoulders slumped. Her heart pounded, and she wished he didn't have the ability to make her feel this way after everything.

She opened the door, even though she knew she shouldn't have.

"I know you don't want to talk to me and you don't have to," Nick said. His words came out quickly, tumbling over each other. He held up the stack of paper. "Since our last email exchange in January, I've kept a draft on my desktop of all the things I've wanted to tell you. The truths about me and my life. The things I kept from you. I printed them out because I want you to have them."

Lily stared at the papers. She didn't make a move to take them.

"Please," he said hoarsely.

She looked up at his face again, taking in his clear desperation. She should tell him to leave. But the honest truth was that she was curious to know what he'd written. After a prolonged silence, she took the pages.

"Thank you," he said.

She simply nodded and placed her hand on the doorknob, an obvious sign that she was done with the conversation. Nick backed away and she turned around and went inside, closing the door behind her. She peeked out the peephole again and Nick was still standing there, staring pointedly at the ground. Then he sighed and went down the hall to his apartment.

She was so angry with him. He'd lied to her. So then why did she still feel such a strong connection to him?

She sat on the couch again and flipped through the

stack of papers. The email drafts spanned from January until just last week.

With Tomcat curled beside her, Lily read Nick's first apology email, where he explained why he'd never shown up to their video chat, how he feared that she wouldn't like the real him, how nervous he'd been to tell someone else that he was N.R. Strickland. Later, he wrote to her about New York City and how overwhelming yet thrilling it felt to live there. He wondered if he might run into her, and if that happened, would she somehow know who he was right away? He mentioned his writing and how he struggled with it, and the stress of suddenly experiencing so much success and being unsure if he could deliver again.

He wrote about how much he missed talking to her. Often, he mentioned how sorry he was that he'd hurt her, and he knew he'd messed things up.

He'd written his last email draft only eight days ago.

I just left you and Tomcat. You told me you were thinking of dating one of your coworkers. I think I could hear my heart breaking when you said that. I want you to be happy. It's all I've ever wanted for you. And it's selfish that I want you to be happy with me, because I don't know if you can be. But I want to try. I would try my fucking hardest to do right by you. And that means I'll have to tell you the truth. I hope you won't hate me.

She gripped the piece of paper tighter as she reread Nick's words. She wiped her eyes. She hadn't even realized she'd been crying.

Then the door opened, startling her. To her surprise, Violet walked inside, followed by Iris.

"Hey," Lily said, clearing her throat. "I thought you were in the Bahamas for that photo shoot."

"Angel caught the flu, so they sent everyone home early," Violet said, wheeling her suitcase next to the couch.

Angel, the same R&B singer Violet had tried to hook Lily up with at her engagement party, was her newest client. Lily should have just tried her best to vibe with Angel that night. Because then maybe she wouldn't have bothered to look twice at Nick. And they wouldn't be in this messy situation.

"I picked her up from the airport," Iris said, placing her purse on the kitchen counter. "I thought I'd stop in and say hi."

"Sister night!" Violet flopped onto the couch next to Lily. Tomcat grumbled and hopped down, his serenity decidedly ruined.

"I'm hungry," Iris said, opening the fridge. "But I see that my only options are sugary Trader Joe's yogurt or wine."

"Relax. I'll order pizza." Violet pulled out her phone, then groaned, tossing it aside. "Eddy still doesn't have his tux. I know it took me a while to find my dress, but getting a tux is the one thing I asked him to do. I've done everything else for the wedding. I found the DJ even though he *works* in the music business. He booked the venue and that was it. I planned the rest by myself. Our honeymoon too."

Lily frowned. Iris immediately paused in the act of opening a yogurt carton and turned around to face them.

"He's never home," Violet said. "I spend more time at his apartment than he does."

"Vi . . ." Lily squeezed her sister's hand, her problems with Nick momentarily forgotten.

"It's okay." Violet forced a smile. "His career is taking off with his new clients, and this is what it's like when you're in love with someone who hustles as hard as you, when you're with someone who finally gets it. I've spent so many years dating men who were upset when they couldn't get more of my time, or they thought my job was stupid, like I played dress-up for a living. Eddy knows the business. He understands my life. We're both busy, but it won't always be this way."

"Violet," Iris said quietly, walking over to them. Gingerly, she sat on the arm of the couch. "Are you sure you want to get married?"

Violet didn't answer. She stared down at her hands, silent.

"Because we'd support you if you changed your mind," Lily added. "You know that, right?"

"Of course I want to get married," she said. "I love Eddy. We'll be fine." She looked up and brushed her hair over her shoulder, letting out a full-body sigh. Then she glanced at the stack of papers in Lily's lap. "What's that? Something you're editing?" Then she paused, looking at Lily more closely. "Wait. What's wrong? Have you been crying?"

Her sisters looked at her on high alert. Lily was suddenly the topic of conversation.

"I'm fine," she said, putting Nick's email drafts aside. She didn't want to tell her sisters the whole backstory with Nick. It was too complicated and embarrassing. She didn't want them feeling bad for her. But she could be vague. "Nick lied to me about something important."

"Did he cheat on you?" Violet asked.

"He'd have to be my boyfriend to cheat."

"Is he married?" Iris asked.

"No."

Violet raised an eyebrow. "Is he one of those Cash App scammers?"

"What? No. It's nothing like that. He kept something from me that I wish I'd known earlier."

Violet and Iris exchanged a glance.

"What did he keep from you?" Violet asked.

"I'd rather not get into it." Lily hoped they wouldn't push her.

"Okay," Iris said slowly. "Well, did he apologize for lying?"

Lily nodded.

"Do you think what he's done is worth forgiving?" Violet asked.

"I—" Lily paused. "I don't know."

"We don't know what happened, of course," Iris said. "But it's clear to me how much he likes you."

"Yeah, he followed you around like a puppy at Mom and Dad's," Violet added.

Iris reached over and squeezed Lily's hand. "We're not saying that you shouldn't be upset. If you never want to talk to him again because he lied, that's completely valid. We're just saying that if you *do* decide you want to give him another chance, we'd understand that too."

Lily sighed. "I don't know what I want. That's the problem."

"Then you should take all the time you need to figure it out," Violet said. "And if Nick really likes you as much as we think he does, he won't rush you to make a decision."

"Exactly," Iris said, nodding.

Lily smiled gratefully at her sisters. "Thank you for listening."

"Of course," Iris said.

"I love sister night." Violet grinned, stretching out her legs.

Then Lily realized there was something else she had to tell them. "I have a job interview next week."

"What?" Iris said. "Really?"

"Oh shit! For real?" Violet said. "Where?"

Lily told them about her upcoming interview with Francesca Ng. When Lily was finished, Iris walked around and sat on the other side of her. She threw her arm around Lily, and Violet did the same, enclosing her in a sister sandwich.

"You'll get the job," Iris said. "It would be a mistake not to hire you."

"And if they don't hire you, let me know because I will go up there and pay them a visit," Violet said.

Lily laughed, leaning on her sisters. It was exactly what she'd needed.

Iris's stomach grumbled. She sat forward and looked at Violet. "Are you gonna order the pizza, or what?"

Violet groaned. "Only you would ruin our bonding moment with your bossiness."

Iris and Violet began to bicker, and Lily welcomed the distraction. Because she still had no idea what she was going to do about Nick.

18

AFTER NICK LEFT LILY'S APARTMENT, HE PACED BACK AND forth in his bare living room. He couldn't stop thinking about the look on her face when he'd admitted that he was Strick. Just moments before she'd been telling him that she had feelings for him. He'd held her soft body close to his. Her expression had been one of raw, vulnerable hope. And then he'd told her the truth and watched in dismay as her expression morphed into confusion, then closed-off anger.

He'd betrayed her. This was why he'd wanted to avoid getting close to her. But it was too late now. She knew the truth and he was in too deep. He'd given her the email drafts because he wanted her to finally have the whole truth. He *had* to make things right with her. He had to fix this.

He wondered if he'd ever really had a choice in the matter this second time around. He'd been a goner from the moment he first spotted Lily in the elevator, before he knew who she really was. And then later when she'd invited him inside her apartment and he watched her stand on tiptoe, attempting to reach Tomcat's food, something soft and warm began to bloom inside of his chest, eroding the years of hardness. The next thing he knew, he was standing right behind her, plucking the cat food from the top of the shelf because he couldn't bear to see her struggle for even one second.

A stool. She needed a stool. How had she been getting Tomcat's food down in the weeks since their first night together? He hadn't even thought to ask. It suddenly became imperative that he find a stool for her. It was almost midnight, but that didn't matter. Wasn't he living in the city that never slept? He left his apartment in search of a stool, and he learned that the city *did* sleep at some point. Because he eventually had to go all the way to Greenpoint, Brooklyn, in order to find a twenty-four-hour hardware store. On the long subway ride back to Manhattan, he realized that Tomcat could probably use something for his digestion to avoid another trip to the ER. As soon as he got off the train he rushed to Duane Reade. It was almost three a.m. now. The only people in the store were drunk New School students congregating in the snack aisle. He went to the pet section and picked out stool softener. Then he grabbed one of those feather-stick toys because maybe Lily had been meaning to buy Tomcat a new toy, but she'd been so busy with work, she just hadn't found the time.

As Nick stood in line, one of the New School students pointed at him and grinned. Loudly, she whispered to her friends, "How sweet. He's a cat dad."

A cat dad? *Him?* Never in a million years. But as he hustled out of the store, eager to get back to his apartment building and Lily, he realized how he truly must look to them.

He didn't sleep at all that night. At seven thirty the next morning, he knocked on Lily's door with his heart in his throat. He hoped she hadn't left for work yet. He heard her feet pad to the door, then there was a slight pause as she probably looked through the peephole. She opened the door, and she was wearing a pale yellow sundress and a cream-colored cardigan. Her feet were bare, and she still hadn't put on makeup.

"Hey," he said, taking in the wary look on her face.

Lily said nothing. Her eyes drifted down to the stool and Duane Reade bag he held in his hands.

"I got these for you," he said, holding them up toward her. "A stool so that you'll be able to reach Tomcat's food since it's so high up." He opened the plastic bag and fumbled in his haste to show her the contents. "And stool softener for Tomcat in case he has more issues. And, um, this toy."

Her brows furrowed, and she blinked. "Okay...thanks."

She took the stool and bag and placed them in the hallway behind her. She turned back to him, and her face was just as closed off as it had been last night.

Nick stared at her, wishing he knew what to do, what to say, so that she could understand. "Lily ..."

"I have to finish getting ready for work," she said, her voice hard. Then she looked up at him, and he saw a bit of emotion peek through her remote veneer. "You can't just come here with gifts, thinking that's going to change everything." She stepped back and started to close the door.

"Wait." Nick's hand shot out, holding the door open. She frowned at him. "I know it won't change things. What

I did was fucked up, I know that. I hate myself for it. I hate that I hurt you. *I'm sorry.* I'm so sorry. I don't know how many times I can say that, but I will say it as many times as I need to. What can I do to make you believe me? I'll do anything."

She shook her head and looked away. "I don't know, Nick. I just don't know."

His heart thrashed in his chest at her words.

"I'm sorry," he repeated. Slowly, as if he were approaching a wounded animal, he stepped closer to her. The wary look in her eyes returned but she didn't back away. That gave him hope.

"I won't lie to you again," he said quietly. "I swear on my life."

When she still hadn't moved away from him, Nick gently pulled her into his arms and held her close. "You mean too much to me," he whispered. His lips softly grazed the top of her head. "I'm sorry, Lily."

She breathed against him, deep and slow. As the seconds ticked by, they inhaled and exhaled in tandem. Nick closed his eyes and felt the erratic energy that had been with him since last night finally begin to lift.

Suddenly, Lily jerked away. "I have to go."

She didn't look at him as she closed the door in his face.

TWO DAYS LATER, NICK WAS SLUMPED IN A CHAIR INSIDE Marcus's office. Marcus sat across from him, behind his desk, head bent as he read through Nick's revised first chapter, his red pen held at the ready. Marcus's office was small but boasted his accomplishments. His degree from UNC hung on the wall beside a framed photograph with his classmates from the Columbia Publishing Course. Copies of his clients' books were proudly displayed on his bookshelf. And to remind him of home, a framed photograph of Caleb was placed right next to his monitor.

Nick had forgotten he'd promised Marcus a revised first chapter within a month's time. To be honest, the only reason he'd managed to write anything yesterday was because he'd locked himself inside his apartment, and writing was the only way to get his mind off Lily.

His phone vibrated, and he rushed to pull it out of his pocket, hoping that it might be Lily calling. But instead *Unknown* flashed across his screen. He sighed and placed his phone facedown on Marcus's desk. He hadn't seen or heard from Lily since the other morning in the hallway outside of her apartment. He regretted giving the email drafts to her. Why would she care about what he'd written before, given the way he'd lied to her? The pages were probably lying somewhere in a dumpster outside of their building where they belonged, along with the stupid stool and cat toy.

Nick shifted in his seat and stared out the window. He could see Central Park from here. As a kid, he'd once read that Central Park had over nine thousand benches, and he'd imagined catching a bus from North Carolina, just so that he could try and sit on every bench. It had been a silly goal that he'd eventually given up on achieving.

"I think I need to leave New York," he said.

Marcus looked up sharply. "What? Why? I thought you liked it here."

"I need to start over. Somewhere else."

Marcus sighed, placing down his pen. "Don't you get tired?"

"Tired of what?"

"Running from your life. You have to stop at some point."

Nick looked away. "I'm not running from my life."

"Yes, you are," Marcus said quietly. "You have been since I met you freshman year of college. And I get it. The situation with your parents was rough. And when you were writing for *World Traveler*, you were still trying to avoid them, which I understood. But I think you've been trying to avoid any scenario that would require you to put down roots because you're afraid of what might happen if you let someone else into your life and they decide to stay."

Nick stared at Marcus silently, not wanting to admit that there was truth to his words.

"Why do you want to leave?" Marcus asked. "Does this have something to do with Lily?"

Nick froze. "What?"

"Come on, give me some credit," Marcus said. "It's very obvious that something is going on there."

Nick wanted to come clean. He took a deep breath and then he told Marcus everything. From the emails, to meeting Lily in person and not revealing his true identity, to her finding out a few nights ago.

When Nick was finished talking, Marcus looked thoughtful.

"Why don't you seem surprised?" Nick asked.

Marcus smirked. "Honestly, it tracks that you would

find yourself in this situation since you're always trying to withhold so much from everyone."

"I don't withhold from everyone," Nick said, indignant.

"It took you an entire semester to open up to me," Marcus said, laughing. "But look, I'm still here, and I've been here. Nothing about you made me want to stop being your friend. Why would you leave, when Lily might decide she wants to be there for you too?"

"That's the thing. What if she decides that I'm not worth the trouble? Or that I'm not worth it in general? That I'm not worth choosing."

He thought of his mom and the times she refused to see him if she couldn't bring his dad along too.

"Not everyone is like your parents," Marcus said, as if he'd read Nick's mind. And truthfully, after all these years, he probably could. "I guess you just have to wait and see what Lily decides. But don't make the decision for her by leaving. That's a cop-out."

Regardless of what happened with Lily, Marcus was right that he should probably stay in New York. It was where Marcus and Caleb lived, Nick's real family. He wanted to be close to them. He needed to put down roots. Long-lasting, legit roots.

"I was going to surprise you after we talked about your pages, but I guess I can give this to you now," Marcus said, reaching under his desk.

Nick sat up, intrigued. Then Marcus handed him a hardcover book with a shiny silver jacket. It was thick, like a doorstopper. Nick held the book in his palms, gazing down at the title and his pen name listed beneath the illustration of the Ceradon kingdom. This was his book. The new edition of *The Elves of Ceradon.*

"Your publisher mailed it to me this morning," Marcus said. "They'll mail the rest of your author copies soon. But I wanted you to have that copy now."

Nick ran his hands across the smooth cover and turned the book over, reading the praise from media outlets on the back. He found N.R. Strickland's brief bio on the inside of the jacket. There was no picture.

He felt it again. That sensation he'd experienced when he'd spotted his cover flash across the screen at M&M's office weeks ago. He wished his photograph were on the jacket of the book. He wanted people to know that he was N.R. Strickland, the creator of Deko's story. But then he'd be completely exposed. Albert would probably show up on his doorstep the day the book published.

"Your editor asked again if you were open to meeting," Marcus said. "And she asked if you'll be coming to M&M's party at the end of the month. What do you want me to tell her?"

Nick flipped through his book, marveling that he'd given up on this story and yet it had taken on a new life. As corny as it sounded, maybe there was some kind of analogy here about not giving up on himself either.

Even though revealing the truth to Lily had ended in disaster, he had to admit that he felt somewhat relieved it was all out in the open now. Keeping the secret had been eating him up. Coming clean to the M&M team scared the shit out of him, but he was so tired of carrying the weight of his lie.

"I still don't want to go to the party," he said. "But I want to meet my editor."

"Great," Marcus said, smiling hopefully. He didn't even sound surprised.

Nick placed the book on Marcus's desk. "Do you think you can mail this to someone in Amsterdam for me?"

"Uh, sure." Marcus raised an eyebrow and spun to face his computer screen. "Who are you sending it to?"

Nick gave him the address for Jolijn and Christophe Davids.

HOURS LATER, AFTER MARCUS TORE NICK'S CHAPTER draft apart and sent him on his way with notes, Nick walked the forty blocks back home in an attempt to jog his creativity. He had three months left until his deadline.

It was late evening by the time he reached his building. He ambled through the lobby, both physically and mentally exhausted, his mind on Deko.

So as the elevator doors began to close, and he ran forward, holding his arm out to keep the doors open, he was wholly unprepared to see Lily standing inside of the elevator with her eyes closed, leaning her head against the wall.

19

LILY HAD SPENT MOST OF HER DAY IN THE MAIL ROOM, sending books to authors. She was avoiding Edith, who'd come to work on a warpath. Unfortunately, IT was bearing the brunt of Edith's attitude. She'd locked herself out of her email account no less than three times before noon, and whenever the poor IT person came to assist her, Edith snapped at them as if it were their fault that she couldn't remember her password.

Secluded in the mail room, Lily was able to work in peace, wearing her headphones. Jazmine Sullivan blasted in her ears and she packed boxes full and taped them closed over and over again. It took all of her attention, which was a blessing. It meant she didn't have to spend the entire day thinking about Nick. She was avoiding him too.

She hadn't seen him since he'd given her the stool and items for Tomcat the other morning. She couldn't trust herself to be around him and make sensible choices. Because no matter how hard she tried not to, she kept thinking about Nick and how he'd shown up at her door the other morning with a kitchen stool and medicine and a toy for Tomcat. She'd been meaning to buy a new stool for the apartment, but she hadn't gotten around to it. Then Nick had just appeared, knowing exactly what it was that she'd needed. Tomcat usually hated toys and preferred jumping in baskets and smacking around a balled-up piece of paper as a source of entertainment but she couldn't get that feather toy away from him if she tried. And she couldn't stop thinking of Nick's face as he stood in the hallway.

I won't lie to you again. I swear on my life. You mean too much to me.

Had he really meant that? Would she ever be able to believe him again?

She wanted to. That was the problem. Because she didn't know if that made her weak or stupid or both.

She was in the middle of taping a box closed when she realized she'd printed the wrong label. Sighing, she went back to her desk to print the label again. As she rounded the corner to her desk, Oliver was walking right toward her. He smiled and waved, and Lily waved back. They met at her cubicle.

"Hey," she said. "What's up?"

"A couple of the guys in Production were talking about a restaurant they went to that's inspired by Victorian England," he said. "Lillie's Victorian Establishment. Have you heard of it?"

"I have, actually. I went once with my sister. It's near our apartment. The interior decor is great but being that you're actually English, you might find it a bit cheesy."

Oliver grinned. "See, that's why I'd like to go and give my proper assessment. And I thought maybe since you share a name with the restaurant, you might like to go too."

Then he winced. "That was worded weirdly. What I mean to say is, Would you like to have dinner with me tonight?"

"Oh." Lily blinked. She shouldn't have been surprised, but so much had happened in the last couple days, she'd forgotten that they'd agreed to reschedule their date.

Oliver was looking at her, patiently waiting for her response. He was friendly. He was direct. He *made sense*. This was a normal way to start dating someone. There were no yearlong emails or secrets or confusing feelings.

So much else in her life was currently up in the air. She didn't know where her next job would be or where she would live after she left Violet's. If she was going to date, she wanted it to be simple. Uncomplicated.

She took a deep breath and asked Oliver what time she should meet him in the lobby.

LILLIE'S VICTORIAN ESTABLISHMENT WAS CROWDED during happy hour, but after about thirty minutes, Lily and Oliver were seated at a booth near the kitchen. Oliver was delighted by the red velvet couches and Victorian era–inspired paintings on the walls. Lily was relieved that he found the decor to be good fun and not corny.

They'd both ordered burgers and fries, and Oliver spent a lot of time telling Lily about the training he was doing for his upcoming 5K race. It was fascinating, really. She'd never been an athlete herself, so hearing about how Oliver was so dedicated to getting his body into shape was inspiring.

She told him about her desire to work in children's publishing, and Oliver asked all the right questions: What were her favorite children's books growing up, and if she could work with any famous children's author, who would she choose?

It was a perfectly fine date. Lovely even.

But Lily couldn't shake the feeling that something was missing. And it wasn't Oliver's fault at all. She kept picturing the way Tomcat had smacked around his new feather toy that morning, and then she thought of the way Nick had gently carried Tomcat in his arms the entire way to the hospital a couple weeks ago.

She knew that there was no room for Oliver. Someone else had already burrowed his way into her heart first.

Oliver excused himself to use the bathroom, and when he returned, Lily knew she had to tell him the truth. She wasn't going to continue wasting his time.

"All right, I'll admit the situation in the loo is a bit weird," Oliver said as he sat down again. "I don't think I need a portrait of Prince Albert watching me the whole time."

Lily laughed, but then quickly sobered. "Oliver, I want to be honest with you."

"Okay," Oliver said, becoming serious.

"I think you are so funny and kind, and if I'd met you this time last year, I'd probably be crazy about you. But the truth is that I can't stop thinking about someone else, and you deserve to be involved with someone who is completely available in all ways. Plus, Dani likes you."

Oliver raised an eyebrow. "Does she, really?"

Lily nodded. "She wants you to bring her to London."

He laughed and, sporting a thoughtful expression, leaned

back in his chair. "Is the person you can't stop thinking about the guy from the bar the other night? The tall one?"

"Yes," Lily admitted.

"I felt like there might have been something between you two, but I wasn't sure."

"I'm really sorry."

Oliver smiled a little. "You don't have to apologize. It is what it is. And now you know way more information about the life of a runner than you probably need to."

Lily smiled too. "And now you know more about the differences between *The Princess Diaries* book and the movie adaptation."

"Can I ask you a question, though?" he said, and Lily nodded. "Why did you decide to come out tonight with me? Why aren't you with him?"

"Our situation is messy, and I don't know if it's worth trying to fix."

"If moving across an ocean has taught me anything, it's that sometimes things in life are messy, but that doesn't mean they aren't worth it."

She knew that Oliver was right, but that didn't make her feel any less afraid of trying to move forward with Nick.

"Would it be weird to ask if we could still be friends?" she said.

Oliver winced. "I'd rather not."

"Oh, of course," Lily said quickly. "I totally understand—"

He burst out laughing. "I'm joking! Of course we can still be mates. You're one of the now six people that I know in this city. I can't cut you off already."

He was grinning, and Lily sighed in relief.

"Thanks, Oliver," she said. "Really."

"So," he said. "What can you tell me about Dani?"

LATER, AFTER SHE AND OLIVER PARTED WAYS, LILY walked home. It was a beautiful New York City night. Hot, but not grossly humid. And as she passed block after block on her way toward her and Violet's apartment, she decided to accept the truth. When it came to Nick, she was a lost cause. Despite everything, she wanted to be with him.

It was possible that over the past two days he'd decided he was no longer interested. Maybe he also felt their situation was too messy. But either way, she had to tell him how she felt, no matter the outcome. It didn't make her stupid or weak to admit that she cared about him and wanted to see where things went. In fact, it made her brave. She knew the truth now and she was going into this with her eyes fully open.

She reached her building and walked through the lobby, full of nerves, the weight of her feelings pressing down on her. She got onto the elevator and pressed 14. As the doors closed, she leaned her head against the wall and sighed. Then an arm shot forward, holding the doors open.

Lily sucked in a breath as she came face-to-face with Nick.

"Hi," he said, eyes widening at the sight of her. He stepped onto the elevator and the doors slowly closed behind him. He was wearing a black T-shirt and black jeans, holding a notebook and a pen.

"Hi." Her chest constricted. She stared at him and his beautiful face.

"I've been wanting to talk to you," he said so quietly she almost couldn't hear him. "But I was trying to be respectful of your space."

She watched him. He stood at the other end of the elevator, as far away from her as he could possibly be.

"I had a date tonight," she said.

His body went still. "With who?"

"Oliver."

"Oh." He was focusing on the spot above her head. "How was it?"

"It was perfect."

He glanced down and nodded, more so to himself.

"But it wasn't right."

He looked up then. "Why not?"

She knew that there was no turning back now. "Because he wasn't you."

Nick blinked. He stared at her, motionless on his end of the small elevator. She watched his chest rise and fall.

"I know I should just try to forget you and the emails. But I can't, and the truth is that I don't want to. If I gave up on us, I'd be giving up on one of the most meaningful connections I've ever had." She paused, taking a deep breath. "I guess what I'm trying to say is that I want to be with you too."

The elevator was silent. Because Nick still hadn't responded to her. This was becoming way more awkward than she'd anticipated. Her nerves were beginning to catch up to her as the adrenaline wore off. Then Nick spoke.

"Okay," he said softly. He stepped toward her, and she

felt the air change. His voice was still a whisper. "That sounds good to me."

She leaned her head back, staring up into his face, holding her breath. He gently cradled her cheek in his hand.

"I'm going to kiss you now," he said.

She nodded wordlessly.

He bent his head and lowered his mouth to hers.

She was struck with the rightness of it immediately. The way his arms wrapped around her. The way his tongue slipped across her bottom lip. She leaned into him and fisted the sides of his T-shirt, standing up on tiptoe, trying to get closer to him in every way possible.

The elevator doors suddenly opened as they reached the fourteenth floor.

"Do you want to come over?" he asked, briefly pulling away, his voice rough and low.

"Yes."

They stopped at her place so that she could feed Tomcat. *Finally*, she thought as he took her by the hand and led her down the hall.

20

NICK'S MOUTH WAS ON LILY'S AGAIN AS SOON AS THEY were both inside of his apartment. His hands fell to the curves of her waist and he bent his head, dragging slow, heated kisses along her exposed throat and across her collarbone. Lily melted against him, loving the feel of his tongue on her skin. She sank her fingers into his back as his lips found hers again, his hands gripping her ass. He was intoxicating, mesmerizing. She never knew that kissing someone could feel this good.

He pulled away, his lips hovering above hers, his breathing short and slightly erratic. "Are you okay?" he asked in a low whisper.

"More than okay." She drew him back down to her, catching his bottom lip between her teeth. Nick groaned, squeezing her tighter, kissing her more urgently. He began backing them farther into his living room. She grazed her fingers along his lower abdomen, their mouths glued together, then coming apart.

Nick lowered himself into his yellow armchair, pulling Lily down to straddle his lap. Her skirt hitched around her waist, exposing her thighs, and Nick was already hard beneath her. She felt light-headed, drugged. He stared up at her, his chest rising and falling with each deep breath. He gently brushed his thumb across her bottom lip.

"You are so beautiful," he said.

It was reverential. Her heart was bursting.

"So are you," she whispered.

She bent down to him, capturing his mouth. Nick stroked his hands up and down her thighs. She let out a soft moan and rolled her hips against him.

"*Jesus, Lily,*" he hissed quietly.

She loved the way he sounded. Rough and a little un-controlled. She loved that she could make him sound that way. He twisted the hem of her shirt in his hands, and his fingers brushed against her stomach, making her shiver.

"I think about you all the time," he said in between kisses. "I've wanted this for so long. I've wanted *you.*"

"Me too." She was breathless, floating.

His hands were still fisted at the hem of her shirt. He tugged in question. In answer, Lily peeled her blouse over her head and let it drop to the ground beside them. She was mentally kicking herself for wearing her old, plain nude bra. She would have worn something sexier if she'd known she'd end up here with Nick. But that didn't matter. Be-cause he was looking at her like both she and her bra were made of pure gold.

He placed a soft kiss in between her breasts, causing goose bumps to spread across her skin. Then he turned his head, kissing the top of her right breast, then her left, his fingers circling her nipples through her bra.

"Your turn," she breathed.

Nick pulled off his T-shirt, and Lily stared at his bare chest and shoulders, his built arms and smooth stomach. She reached forward, faintly touching his hot skin.

"They must have made you in a lab," she murmured.

Nick laughed softly. "The same one where they made you?"

She shook her head. Because she couldn't make him understand. He was better than she'd imagined. He was real. He was everything.

He pulled her flush against him, covering her mouth with his. She pressed her chest into his and grasped his shoulders. She felt his hands pause as they smoothly roamed across her back. His fingers hovered at the hooks of her bra. "Is this okay?" he asked.

She nodded, and he unclasped her bra. She eased out of it and tossed it aside. His mouth was on her immediately, carefully caressing her nipple with his tongue. She tipped her head back, gasping. She rocked her hips against him again and Nick gripped her waist.

"Fuck," he whispered, exciting Lily. She bent down and kissed his neck, sucking on his skin. "Wait, hold on."

Lily froze, bolting upright. "Do you want to stop?"

"What? No. *No*," he said, reaching up and holding her in place. "This chair is uncomfortable. It's hurting my back."

"Oh." She laughed, relieved.

He smiled a little, then his gaze turned heated as he continued to stare at her. He looped her arms around his neck, and in one quick motion, he stood, lifting her against him. Surprised, Lily wrapped her legs around his waist as he carried her down the hall to his bedroom. Only then did she notice the small black bookshelf by the window in his living room.

Nick's bedroom was as bare as the rest of his apartment, but she recognized the bed frame she'd picked out at IKEA, which supported his neatly made mattress. And she learned how soft his mattress was when he laid her down on top of it. He began kissing her mouth and neck, lowering to kiss her breasts, down her stomach to her navel. He glanced up as he tugged at the hem of her skirt, and Lily lifted her hips, making it easier for Nick to pull the skirt off. He kissed her over top of her underwear, then he slowly slid off her panties, and he pressed his mouth between her legs.

"Nick," she moaned, waves of pleasure washing over her. His name was the only coherent thought she had. *Nick, Nick, Nick.*

He clutched her ass and she arched into him, gasping. She peered down at the top of his head, his hot mouth on her, and the sight almost sent her over the edge. Then he slowly crawled up the length of her. He eased away, and she watched as he unbuckled his pants and shrugged them off, followed by his boxers. She reached down, touching him, and he closed his eyes, moaning softly.

"Do you want to?" he managed to ask, his voice uneven and low.

"Yes," she said.

Nick kissed her, then briefly turned, reaching for the top drawer of the dresser beside his bed to grab a condom. He faced Lily again, and she inched closer, helping him slide the condom on, her fingers closed over the length of him. He groaned, biting his lip.

He moved on top of her, propping himself up on his elbows. His hands cradled either side of her face. He stared into her eyes as he slowly eased inside of her. She gasped, feeling a moment of slight discomfort, but that melted away, leaving only pleasure. They found their rhythm, and she wrapped her legs around him. He continued to thrust into her with deep strokes, unraveling her. She couldn't believe that this was finally happening after all this time. She'd been waiting for this. Waiting for Nick. Just Nick.

She whispered his name. She wanted to tell him how she felt. What this meant. But she couldn't say it. Her brain was mush. She was too stimulated. "I . . . we . . ."

"You and me," he said into her ear. Because he understood what she wasn't able to say. Of course he did. He *knew* her.

"You and me," she said back.

Then he kissed her, sliding his tongue in her mouth, moaning as he thrust harder. He said her name once, and then repeated it, his body going taut above hers as his breaths became shorter. She didn't stand a chance, and neither did he. They came undone together, their arms wrapped around each other.

Nick was careful not to collapse against her completely. He placed a gentle kiss on her shoulder, then stood. She lay there, watching as he went to the bathroom. When he came back, he lay down beside her and pulled the covers over them. He draped his arm across her, wrapping her in a cocoon.

She was exhausted suddenly. She didn't want to fall asleep, though. She wanted to be awake for every moment of this. But being wrapped up in Nick felt too good.

"You bought a bookshelf," she mumbled drowsily. She felt his body lightly shake as he laughed.

"Because you told me to."

She smiled and yawned, her eyes closing against her will.

He kissed her forehead. She moved her head to rest against his chest. She fell asleep, lulled by the sound of his heartbeat.

21

SLEEP HAD NOTORIOUSLY EVADED NICK FOR MOST OF HIS life. But that night, with Lily wrapped in his arms, he slept so hard he didn't even dream. Instead, for the first time in years, he was able to simply rest and feel at peace.

The sun peeked through the blinds when he woke a little after six the next morning. Lily was curled into a ball with her back resting against his chest. She was still asleep, her face a mask of tranquillity. Nick propped himself up on his elbow and gazed down at her. He couldn't believe that she was here with him in his bed. That she wanted to be together too. He had to prove to her that she'd made the right decision by choosing him. He'd have to hold on to her with all that he had.

An alarm sounded on her phone, which lay on the ground by his bed. Lily began to stir and let out a frustrated grumble. Nick quickly grabbed her phone and turned off the alarm. She rolled over to face him and wiped her eyes. She burrowed deeper under the covers and smiled at him. It caused Nick's breath to catch. She was so beautiful first thing in the morning, even while slightly cranky.

"Hi," she mumbled.

"Hi."

"How long have you been awake?"

"Not that long." Unable to help himself, he reached forward and began to trace soft circles on her bare shoulder. "You have to get ready for work?"

"Unfortunately." She inched closer, leaning into his touch. "I think you might be the second-best cuddler in the world."

"Who's number one?"

"Tomcat."

He laughed quietly. "A worthy competitor."

They fell silent, taking each other in. It was the first time since last night that they were able to slow down and really see each other. Nick felt that overwhelming sense of peace again that had permeated him while he slept. Everything about this moment felt right, like he and Lily had finally fallen into place.

She reached up and lightly touched the scar above his top lip. "How'd you get this?"

"I was running away from someone my dad robbed, and I fell."

Her eyes widened. Softly, she said, "The things you tell me . . ."

"What about them?" He kept her hand against his lips and placed a kiss against the inside of her palm.

"I just wish I could go back in time and protect you."

That made him smile. He lowered her hand to his chest, and she spread her fingers against his warm skin.

"So . . . you have a TV deal with HBO?" she asked.

He smirked. "I do."

"You're a big deal around the M&M office, you know. There are lots of rumors and theories about you."

"Really? Like what?"

"That N.R. Strickland isn't just one person, but multiple people writing under one pseudonym."

He snorted. "I wish that were true. Then I'd have more help writing this sequel."

"And there's a rumor that the real N.R. Strickland died shortly after *The Elves of Ceradon* originally published and they hired someone else to write the second book."

Nick shook his head, grinning. "For real?"

"Yeah," Lily said, laughing. "And people say that you've never seen or spoken to your editor before."

"That one's half-true. I've spoken to her and hadn't planned to ever meet her in person, but I'm having lunch with her and Marcus next week."

Lily tilted her head. "What made you change your mind?"

"I don't know." He paused. "I just want someone at M&M to know who I am and that the book is mine. Even if I'm still uncomfortable with sharing the information with the whole world. Telling the truth to you made me realize how I didn't want to keep lying to other people. Well, most people."

She was quiet for a moment. Her fingers drifted back and forth across his chest, giving him goose bumps. "You're nervous about your dad finding out," she said. "You mentioned that in your email drafts."

"I'm not ready for him to know yet. My life finally feels *good*. I don't want him to come along and ruin everything."

"He won't be able to if you don't give him the power."

Nick didn't want to talk about his dad, not right now

and in this moment with Lily that felt sacred. She must have picked up on his mood because she smiled and said, "I guess that means you'll skip M&M's big party in a couple weeks. They invite all the big authors. It's very elitist and I've never been able to go, but I hear that the food is good."

"Definitely skipping that." Their hands were intertwined between them now. He ran his thumb back and forth across her knuckles. "So your interview is pretty important, right?"

She nodded, smiling. "If I get this job, I can finally work on the kind of books I've been dreaming about editing. And things with my boss are reaching a real breaking point. They want me to assist her and someone else soon."

"Are they paying you more?"

"Nope."

Nick frowned. "That's some bullshit."

"*Right?* I just need this interview to go perfectly, and with the pay raise, I'll be able to move out of Violet's sooner."

His stomach sank. He didn't want her to move. Not now when they'd finally become this close.

"Don't worry," she said. "I'm not leaving New York. You won't be able to get rid of me that fast."

"I'd never get rid of you," he said quietly.

He leaned down and kissed her then. Lily pressed closer, brushing her bare breasts against his chest, and he grew hard, remembering how it felt to be inside of her. He tenderly ran his hand down to the small of her back. Just as Lily hooked her leg over his hip, her alarm went off again.

She swore under her breath, and Nick reluctantly loosened his hold on her.

"Work," he said, kissing her bottom lip, then her chin. "I know."

"No, that's my feed-Tomcat alarm," she said, easing away with a slightly guilty look on her face. "To be continued?"

"Definitely."

He watched as she climbed out of bed and got dressed. His phone vibrated beside him. *Unknown* again. He ignored it, threw on a T-shirt and pair of basketball shorts and followed her into his living room.

"I want to take you on a date," he said. "A real one."

She glanced over her shoulder as she slid on her shoes. "I'd like that."

"Even better than your ideal date," he said, walking with her to the door.

She smiled at him, picking up on the reference to their emails. "Just let me know the time and place."

"I will."

When he opened the door and Lily stepped into the hall, Violet was leaving their apartment, holding a cup of iced coffee. Her huge sunglasses were perched at the end of her nose.

"Oh, thank God," Violet said, visibly relieved at the sight of them. She walked closer, her Cheshire cat grin spreading across her face.

"Sorry," Lily said. "I should have given you a heads-up about where I was last night."

"No, I meant thank God you finally got the D." She paused. "I mean, that's what I'm assuming, given the looks on both of your faces."

"*Violet*." Lily shot Nick an apologetic glance.

"Nick, does this mean you're coming to my wedding as Lily's date?" Violet asked.

Nick looked at Lily. A question. In answer, she squeezed his hand and nodded.

Violet grinned. "You two are so freaking cute. Okay, I have to run but I'll call you later. Have a good day! Oh, and congrats on winning the bet, Lily!" She blew kisses to both of them, hustled down the hall and hopped on the elevator.

"I forgot all about the bet," Nick said.

"I did too, honestly. Thanks for helping me win." She kissed him quickly, then backed away. "I'll see you later?"

"You'll see me later."

He watched her walk away until she slipped inside of her apartment.

He went back inside of his own spot, thinking hard about where he should take Lily on their first official date. They had a lot of time to make up for. He had to take her somewhere special. Perfect.

An idea suddenly popped into his head, and he pulled out his phone and did a quick Google search. The plan unfolded before him. In a way, it was too good to be true. Like the stars had aligned just for them.

He texted Marcus.

Can I borrow your car this Saturday?

22

ON SATURDAY AFTERNOON, NICK TEXTED LILY VERY SIM-
ple, yet cryptic instructions for their date.

> Meet me outside of our building at 3:30. Bring your
> favorite Elena Masterson book.

At three thirty on the dot, Lily stepped outside, holding
the first book in the Dragons of Blood series and Nick's copy
of *The Nermana Chronicles*. And she was surprised to see
Nick parked in a red Jeep. When he spotted Lily, he hopped
out and hurried around to open the passenger door for her.

"Hi," he said, bending down to kiss her.

"Hi!" She kissed him back and pulled away slightly,
looking at the car in a mixture of delight and confusion.
"Where did you get this car?"

"It's Marcus's. He's letting me borrow it tonight."

She raised an eyebrow. "Where are we going?"

"It's a surprise." He smiled slyly. Lily was too swooned
by the idea that he'd gone through the trouble to plan a
secret date to ask additional questions.

She climbed into the passenger seat and Nick carefully

closed her door before taking his spot behind the wheel. They drove through the city and soon left it behind as they merged onto the highway.

"So which books did you bring?" Nick asked. He placed his hand on the center console, palm up. It took Lily a second to realize that he was waiting for her hand to join his. Months ago, her fear of turning into a sweaty-handed monster would have ruined this moment. But instead, she laid her hand on top of his and relaxed as their fingers interlaced. There was no reason for her to be nervous or fearful. Holding hands with Nick felt like the most natural thing in the world.

"I brought *Dragons of Blood* book one," she answered. "And your copy of *The Nermana Chronicles*."

"That's one of your favorite Elena Masterson books? I thought you hadn't finished it yet?"

"I haven't," she admitted. "But it's your favorite, so it's still special to me."

Nick glanced over at her and his mouth quirked into a smile. He gave her hand a tight squeeze.

"I'm guessing the Elena Masterson books are a hint for where we're going?"

Nick motioned zipping his lips and shrugged. "Just sit back, relax and enjoy the ride."

Lily grinned at him, more than happy to comply.

A little over an hour later, they turned off the exit for Connecticut and drove through a quaint suburban town. When they pulled into the parking lot of Old Towne Books, Lily looked at Nick and began bouncing her knees in excitement.

"Is this a bookstore date?" she asked.

He was grinning. "It's more than that."

As they walked toward the bookstore, she looped her arm through his and she started to ask what he'd meant by *more than that*, but she froze when she saw the message written on the sidewalk chalkboard in front of the store.

JOIN US FOR OUR BIMONTHLY ELENA MASTERSON READING AND SIGNING TONIGHT AT 5 PM!

Lily grabbed Nick's arm. "Oh my God, no."

He laughed, loosening her tight grip on his bicep. "Yes."

"Stop! Elena Masterson?!"

He nodded and urged her forward. In a state of awe, Lily followed Nick inside of the bookstore. At the back near the café, rows of chairs were set up and most of the seats were already taken. She and Nick managed to grab two chairs in the second-to-last row, and he explained to her that Elena Masterson hated traveling, but she still wanted to meet with her readers, so every other month she held a reading and signing at Old Towne Books, her local bookstore.

"Was this a good idea?" he asked. His brows were furrowed, like he was nervous that maybe this date didn't please her, which couldn't be further from the truth.

"Yes," she said. "A perfect idea."

She kissed him and when he pulled her closer, she lingered there in his arms, feeling like they were the only two people in the whole bookstore. Then a hush fell over the crowd as Elena Masterson was escorted to a chair in the front of the room. She was a small, slight woman with light brown skin and short curly hair and cat-eye glasses. She sat down and smiled at the crowd. Then she began to read from the second book in the Dragons of Blood series.

From the minute Elena began to speak, everyone in the room was entranced. Lily couldn't believe that she was listening to one of her favorite authors read from one of her favorite books. She'd read the Dragons of Blood series when she was a shy, friendless teenager who wanted nothing more than to escape and have a real adventure of her own. She looked over at Nick, who was watching Elena with the same wide-eyed admiration as the rest of the crowd. Bringing Lily here tonight was the nicest, most thoughtful thing anyone had ever done for her.

She was going to climb him like a tree later.

After the reading, Lily and Nick stood in line to get their books signed. While Elena signed Nick's copy of *The Nermana Chronicles*, Nick calmly told her how much he loved her work. Lily, on the other hand, stood in front of Elena and managed only to mumble that she'd been obsessed with her since high school, and she immediately regretted her inability to be relaxed and cool. But Elena thanked her and was pleased that Lily owned a first edition of *Dragons of Blood*.

Lily was still awestruck when they left the bookstore and walked to an Italian restaurant down the street.

"She was so amazing!" Lily hissed in excitement as they were seated. She flipped her book open to Elena's signature. "Just look at her penmanship. Where did she learn to write like this?"

"It must be nice to have an experience with your readers

like that." Nick leaned back in his chair and got a faraway look in his eyes. "Where you can talk to them and answer their questions."

Lily took in the contemplative expression on his face. "Is that what you want too?"

"Honestly?" he said. "Yeah. I want to stand in front of a crowd and read from my book and talk to readers and go on tour and go to the TV show premiere whenever it happens. I want all of that."

It made her heart ache that Nick craved those things but felt like he couldn't have them when they were his for the taking.

"Maybe you should just rip off the Band-Aid and call your dad first. You can tell him about this big change in your life. You can set boundaries with him."

"Boundaries aren't in my dad's vocabulary," Nick said, shaking his head. "And I couldn't call him even if I wanted to. He rarely pays his cell phone bill, and the number I had for my mom isn't working anymore. I don't even know where they're living."

"Are you worried about them?"

"My mom, yeah," he said. "But . . . sometimes I feel relieved that it isn't easy to get ahold of them, that we aren't in each other's lives. I know that sounds fucked up."

"It doesn't." Lily reached forward and placed her hand over his. "Family isn't always easy."

He stared down at their hands. Then he looked up at her. His face was open and vulnerable. "I'm glad I have you."

Her heart expanded in her chest.

"I'm glad I have you too," she said.

He flashed a warm smile and turned his attention to the menu. Lily continued to look at him. He was so dear to her, she didn't even know what to do with herself.

LATER, IN NICK'S MOONLIT BEDROOM, THEY LAY NAKED on top of his sheets. Nick trailed kisses down Lily's back. He touched her tenderly between her legs and she moaned softly, her breath hitched as he entered her from behind. He kissed her neck, and sucked on her earlobe, telling her in a jagged whisper how good she felt. He lightly bit her shoulder and gripped her hips in his hands. She was coming undone with each stroke, completely enveloped by him. The pressure mounted fast, and she came swiftly, and Nick soon followed, groaning loudly as he thrust into her one last time.

Afterward, they faced each other, exhausted, their bare legs tangled together. Nick's hand rested on her hip. He moved his thumb over her skin in soft, slow circles.

"That was the best date I've ever had," Lily said quietly. "Thank you."

Nick sported a pleased smile. "Better than your ideal date?"

"So much better. Blew my ideas out of the water."

"Good," he said. "Now I just need to figure out how to make it so that you can never leave this bed."

She inched closer to him, craving more of his warm embrace. "With the exception of Violet's bachelorette party next weekend, I'm all yours."

"Oh, right. Where is it again?"

"Miami. Karamel Kitty got us a section at a club."

"Damn," Nick said, impressed. "I hope you don't forget about me when all of her baller rapper friends show up."

"You don't need to worry about that." Lily shook her head, smiling at him. "I could never forget about you."

"Let me give you something to remember me by, just in case," he said, pulling her closer.

She laughed as he planted heated kisses across her breasts and down her stomach, showing her just how much he wanted to be remembered.

23

NICK REGRETTED NOT MEETING HIS EDITOR, ZARA SHAH, sooner. Because once they finally had lunch, and Nick told her the truth about being American and lying in his bio, she hardly blinked.

"I've heard crazier stories," she said. "You *did* write the book yourself, though, right?"

Nick confirmed that he had, and that was all Zara seemed to care about. To his further surprise, she didn't really ask about how drafting the sequel was going either. She was much more interested in discussing who she thought should be cast in *The Elves of Ceradon* television show. So far, she'd shared that she'd pictured Daniel Kaluuya as Deko.

"Can't you see it?" she said. "He's got that broody-yet-hopeful vibe. Give him some pointy ears and light green eyes, and there's Deko right there." She thought Forest Whitaker should play Deko's father. "Wise, so wise."

Nick and Marcus sat across from Zara at Eataly's restaurant section in the Flatiron district. Zara was in her early thirties with long dark hair and thick, black-framed glasses. She spun pasta around her fork in quick, jittery movements. She told them that she'd already had three cups of coffee that morning.

"Who do you think should be cast?" Zara asked, looking at Nick. "Do you have any say over that?"

"Oh, um. I'm not sure. I have an executive producer credit. So maybe?" He glanced at Marcus. "He knows this stuff better than I do."

"It's definitely something we can discuss," Marcus said. "But it's still so early. They haven't even hired someone to write the script yet."

"It sounds like Hollywood plays the hurry-up-and-wait game just like publishing," Zara said. "Nick, can I just say it's so nice to finally put a name to a face? I'm glad you finally agreed to meet me."

"Me too," Nick said, and he truly meant it. Zara was cool. He'd already thought as much during their phone calls, but it was nice to be able to confirm it in person.

Marcus leaned back in his chair, sporting a satisfied smile. After several months, Nick had finally met his editor, and they vibed. Marcus was basically the world's proudest agent. And Nick was pleased that Marcus was pleased. All around, it was a dope lunch.

Then Zara asked, albeit delicately, "How's the draft coming?"

Nick cleared his throat, eyes on his half-eaten margherita pizza. He didn't want to lie to her. "Well . . ."

"If you need more time on your deadline, just let me know," Zara said quickly. "I'd rather you give me a heads-up now so that we can pad the schedule."

Nick sighed in relief. "More time would be great."

"How much time are we talking?"

"Another few months?"

"Let's aim for next January." Zara pulled out her phone and typed a note to herself.

"I'm sorry," Nick said.

"There's no need to apologize. These things take time." She dropped her phone back into her bag. "Have you given any more thought about the company party in two weeks? The team at M&M would go nuts if you made an appearance. There's so much genuine love for your book. And curiosity."

Nick smiled to himself, thinking about the theories Lily had told him. He'd asked Lily if she knew Zara and she'd said that she didn't. They were in different divisions and on different floors. Practically worlds away in terms of M&M's inner workings.

The thought of going to M&M's party made Nick's body seize with nerves. All the required extroverting. All the people. But he remembered how he'd felt during Elena Masterson's reading. Despite his fears, he wanted to take ownership of his books in every way. He thought of how Lily had encouraged him.

"I think I'll go," he said.

Marcus froze, blinking in surprise. "Really?"

"Really?" Zara said, beaming.

"Are you sure?" Marcus asked. "You know you don't have to go."

"I'm sure," Nick said. "I want to."

"Great," Marcus said, smiling again. But this time it wasn't his pleased or proud smile. It was the encouraging, patient smile he'd reserved for Nick back in college whenever Nick had decided to join Marcus and the rest of their floor mates to chill, or any time that he was able to successfully get Nick to come out of his shell. "That's really great."

After lunch, Nick took the train with Marcus to his apartment in Brooklyn. Caleb was home, and as soon as Nick sat on the living room couch, Caleb plopped down beside him and eagerly asked about how things were going with Lily.

"Good," Nick said, unable to keep the grin off his face.

He couldn't believe that he'd tried to stay away from Lily for so long. The peace and contentment he felt at having her in his life this way was indescribable. She softened his rough edges with her carefree laughter and patience. Their moments of stillness were ones he wanted to hold on to forever. Like last night while they sat on his bed, he held her feet in his lap, massaging them, and she read aloud from a manuscript that she was editing about the evolution of shoelaces. Under any other circumstance, it would have been some of the most uninteresting shit he'd ever heard, but he listened attentively, captivated by Lily and the soothing sound of her voice. He already couldn't wait to be with her again. He was counting down the hours until he could see her after her workday ended.

"I want you to bring her over for dinner soon," Caleb said. "Marcus, what do you think?"

Marcus stood across the room at the kitchen table, sorting through their mail. "Sure. But can we have real food, and not just appetizers like that time we invited over one of your Brooklyn mom clients?"

"I'm sorry, do you mean my *hors d'oeuvres*?"

"Yeah, I was so hungry that night."

Nick laughed and sat up, pulling his phone out of his back pocket as it vibrated. Another *Unknown* caller.

"I keep getting scam calls," he said, pressing ignore.

"Well, you know what they say," Caleb said. "Scammers never sleep."

Nick gave him a dubious look. "I've never heard anyone say that before."

"Not true, because you heard me say it just now."

Nick snorted and shook his head. Then his phone vibrated again. *Unknown.*

"Fuck it," he said. "I'm just gonna answer and see what kind of scheme they've got going."

"Whatever you do, don't give them your social security number," Marcus warned.

Nick gave Marcus a look that said, *What do you take me for?* When he answered, he heard only static, followed by a rustling noise. Someone mumbling.

"Hello?" Nick repeated.

"Nick?"

Nick stilled. He almost dropped the phone as his hand went slack.

"Nick? Can you hear me?"

". . . Mom?"

Caleb and Marcus both froze, turning to look at Nick.

"Mom?" Nick repeated. His pulse quickened. He stood and walked outside. The fresh air hit him. He paused at the top of the stoop. "Mom, is that you?"

"Yeah, sweetheart. Hi."

Sweetheart.

The last time Nick saw Teresa, she'd been laid up in a hospital bed with a broken shoulder, yelling at him to leave because he'd been arguing with his father. Now she was calling him sweetheart. And with that one word, he was a boy again. Vulnerable and unsure. Seeking her acknowledgment.

"I've been calling you off this cheap prepaid phone I bought at the gas station. Barely works," she said over the static. "We've been back in Warren for a few weeks now. Are you still over there?"

Over there. That was the way she'd referred to Nick's travels. During their sporadic calls, he'd always been someplace new. He wanted to lie and keep his distance. He should tell her that he was in Asia or Australia. Far away and unreachable.

"No," he said. "I'm in the States now."

"You are? Why didn't you tell me?"

"I didn't know how to reach you." He was taken aback by the hurt in her voice. "I'm sorry."

"Where are you?"

"Is everything okay?" he asked, avoiding her question. "Do you need anything?"

"You think I'm only calling because I need something from you?"

"No, that's not what I'm saying. I just want to make sure you're all right."

Teresa sighed. "I'm calling about your father."

Nick's stomach clenched. "What happened?"

"He was in a car accident a few days ago, down there

racing with those fools at the pool hall. He broke his leg. He hit his head pretty badly too. The doctors say he'll be okay, but it's going to take some time . . ." She paused. "He's been asking for you, Nick. He wants you to come see him."

Nick said nothing. A numbness spread over him. His gaze was fixed on a crack in the stoop.

"Are you going to tell me where you are?" Teresa asked.

"New York." A voice in the back of his head reprimanded him for revealing that information, but he felt so detached from the moment. Out of body.

"Wow," she said, surprised. "How long have you been there?"

He took a deep breath and pinched the bridge of his nose. "Since March."

Teresa was silent. Most likely coming to terms with the fact that Nick had been back for five months and hadn't told her. "I hope you'll come, Nick. This is the number to reach me. Let me know what you decide."

"Okay."

She said goodbye and the line went dead. Nick let his phone drop into his lap.

Behind him, Marcus stepped outside. Caleb stood in the doorway. Both looked equally concerned.

Marcus walked closer to Nick. "Was that . . ."

"My mom," he finished. "Yeah."

Marcus was quiet for a moment. Then, "What did she say?"

"My dad got into a car accident and hurt his leg and head. They say he'll be okay, but they want me to come down to Warren."

"Are you gonna go?" Caleb asked.

Nick continued to stare at the street. A hint of panic pricked through his numbness.

"I don't know," he said.

NICK RELAYED THE PHONE CALL WITH HIS MOM TO LILY later that night. Violet was gone, so it was just the two of them and Tomcat in Lily and Violet's apartment. They sat on the couch facing each other. Tomcat was snuggled up against Nick's leg. He could see why Lily liked to cuddle with the cat for comfort.

"I think I need to go," Nick said. "I don't want to, but I wouldn't be able to forgive myself if something happened to him and I didn't see him first."

Lily nodded. "I understand. Do you want me to go with you?"

"No," he said too quickly, causing Lily to blink. He didn't want her anywhere near his parents and their drama. He couldn't let any of that shit touch her. "You have work and your interview."

"I'll figure something out."

"I'll be okay." He picked up her hand and kissed the inside of her palm. "Thank you for offering."

She eyed him quietly, then reached forward and hugged him to her. "I'm here for you, however you need me to be."

"I know." He laid his head on her shoulder and closed his eyes. "And I'm here for you."

Before Teresa called, Nick had been in the process of developing a much more positive outlook on his life. His career was stable. He had Marcus and Caleb, and his friendship with Henry and Yolanda. He had Lily.

And now by seeing his parents again, he couldn't shake his worry that his efforts to finally create a semidecent life would soon be upended.

24

THAT FOLLOWING SATURDAY NIGHT, LILY WAS SQUISHED beside Iris on the plush velvet couch of Karamel Kitty's VIP section at LIV nightclub in Miami, celebrating Violet's bachelorette.

"I see Karamel Kitty and them getting lit over there!" the DJ said on the mic. He switched to a Karamel Kitty song and the whole club shouted, "Ayyyeee!"

Violet and Karamel Kitty were standing on top of the table, surrounded by Karamel Kitty's entourage, as she poured Hennessy straight from the bottle into Violet's mouth.

It had been so interesting to spend the weekend with a celebrity. Karamel Kitty, given name Karina, was sweet and a lot calmer in real life compared to her energetic in-your-face rap persona. She'd rented out the backroom of a restaurant on South Beach for Violet's bridal shower yesterday and they'd been bombarded with a horde of fans as soon as they got out of the car. Violet was used to this and easily slipped behind Karina and her security. But Lily and Iris got lost in the chaos. Being trapped amid a crowd of Karamel Kitty stans, who were eagerly rapping the lyrics to her newest song, wasn't something Lily had expected to add to her bingo card for the year.

Tonight, Lily was wearing one of the few club-appropriate outfits she owned: a black leather bandeau top and a matching high-waist black leather miniskirt. She'd borrowed another pair of Violet's high heels and her feet were killing her, hence the sitting. She should have gone the same route as Iris, who'd paired her loose-fitting, white T-shirt dress with a pair of all-white Stan Smiths. Meanwhile, Violet and Karamel Kitty both donned spandex sleeveless catsuits. Karamel Kitty's was bubble gum pink (with a lace front, waist-length bubble gum pink wig to match), while Violet's was bride-to-be white. Lily and Iris had bought her a glittery veil that kept slipping off her head as she danced.

Violet's admission that Eddy was barely home and that she'd planned so much of the wedding alone had concerned Lily and Iris, of course. But whenever they brought it up, Violet insisted that she wanted to marry Eddy and that she was happy. She definitely *seemed* happy tonight.

Lily had gone over Violet's situation in her mind time and time again. Ultimately, there wasn't much Lily and Iris could do. It was Violet's life, and Violet was going to do exactly what she wanted, like always. They could only hope that things worked out between Violet and Eddy. And in the event that they didn't, Lily and Iris would be there for Violet no matter what.

"I'm getting motherfucking married!" Violet shouted now. She climbed off the table and stumbled over to Lily and Iris, lying across their laps.

Iris brushed Violet's hair out of her face and smiled down at her. "Are you having fun?"

"Yesshh," Violet mumbled. "Are you?"

"No, but that's okay because tonight isn't about me."

Violet flashed a lopsided grin. "I want *everyone* to have fun." She pointed at Lily. "You need to celebrate too. Your new job!"

"I don't have a new job yet," Lily reminded her, laughing.

Her interview with Francesca Ng had gone very well, though. She hadn't suffered from the things that had plagued her during interviews past: the freezing up or stumbling over her words. She spoke confidently about her love for children's books and what qualities she would bring to the assistant editor role. Now she was waiting to schedule a second interview with Francesca's boss, Anna Davidson. She was confident that she'd do well in her interview with Anna as well.

She hoped that she'd get the job, but even if she didn't, deciding to throw caution to the wind and following up with Francesca a second time had unlocked something in Lily. For the first time in a long time, she was genuinely proud of herself. She had proof that taking risks and going for what she wanted could have good results. Just look at her and Nick.

She thought of him now and wondered if he was sleeping. He'd been in North Carolina for three days. She'd talked to him earlier that morning, and he'd been at his hotel room, attempting to work on his book before he went to the hospital. He'd seemed chill, but she couldn't forget how anxious he'd looked before he left for the airport earlier that week. Nick told her that his dad was stable and mostly slept whenever he visited, and that he was helping his mom get herself better situated, because she and his dad had been living at a motel before his dad's accident. But otherwise, he didn't go into much detail about what was happening with his parents. He sweetly evaded Lily's probing questions with such skill, she ended their conversations wondering if she'd attempted to ask anything at all.

"Why am I sitting down? It's my bachelorette party!" Violet said, jumping to her feet. "I need another drink!"

She joined Karina on top of the table again, and Lily and Iris both yawned at the same time.

"Technically, I know I'm not too old for the club life," Iris said, "but I *feel* too old for the club life."

"I'm hungry," Lily said.

Iris checked the time on her phone. It was almost three a.m. "Let's get an Uber and see if they can take us to McDonald's on the way home."

"Deal."

They said goodbye to Violet, who gave them sloppy kisses on the cheek and kept dancing.

SOMEONE FROM KARINA'S SECURITY TEAM LET LILY AND Iris inside of Karina's mansion. It was so spacious, you could hear an echo when you spoke. Because Karina rarely spent extended periods of time in Miami, the entire house was pristine. The fancy marble dining table alone probably cost half of Lily's yearly salary.

After she and Iris finished eating, they migrated upstairs to their shared guest room. Iris went to shower, and Lily lay across the king-size bed and texted Nick. Are you awake? She watched three dots appear.

Nick: Hey, yeah. How's the club?

Lily: It was definitely an experience. Iris and I left,
though.

Lily: You're up late.

Nick: Oh you know, just chilling here, waiting on that
goodnight text from my lady.

She smiled. Facetime?

Her phone vibrated in her palm then with a FaceTime
call from Nick. She answered, and he was sitting on the
hotel bed, pillows stacked up behind him.

"Hi," she said, grinning.

"Hi." His smile was tired, but warm. She was hit with
how much she missed him when he said, "I miss you."

"I miss you too. How's your dad doing?"

"He still has a concussion, and he'll need physical therapy for his broken leg." He sighed and rubbed a hand over
his face. "I think I'm gonna be here for at least another
week. I need to make sure his sessions get paid for and I'm
helping my mom get approved for an apartment. She said
she's leaving my dad."

"*Really?*"

Nick nodded. He looked so exhausted.

"How are you feeling?" she asked. "Are you okay?"

"It could always be worse."

"You're a good son," Lily said.

Nick smiled faintly, but it didn't reach his eyes. She
could tell that he didn't believe her.

"Are *you* okay? You're the one who survived a whole
weekend with *XXL* magazine's rapper of the year." When

she looked at him in surprise for dropping that fact, he said, "I just googled it."

Lily smirked. Nick was trying to lighten the mood and change the subject, evading her again. She couldn't shake the feeling that after everything they'd been through, he was slowly rebuilding his defenses. He was still there with her, attentive and present for now. But she wondered if one day she'd blink and be completely shut out.

Then she had a realization.

"You're going to miss M&M's party this week," she said. "Maybe your team can put together a bookstore signing for you instead once the book publishes."

Nick fell quiet. "Nah, I don't want them to do that."

She tried to gauge what he was thinking, but his face was carefully blank.

"Why not?" she asked.

"I don't think it was ever a good idea for me to go to the party in the first place."

Lily frowned. "But what about all the things you wanted? You said you wanted to stand in front of a crowd and talk to people about your book. You wanted to take the credit."

"I changed my mind."

"Why, though?"

"I just did, Lily," he said, frustrated.

They stared at each other in silence. The explanation that he was refusing to give to her suddenly became clear.

"It's because of your parents, right? You're still afraid for them to know."

Nick didn't say anything. She watched as he moved to

scratch the back of his neck, but he checked the motion, returning his arm to his side.

"It would be different if you were someone who wanted to live in obscurity," she said. "But I saw the look on your face at Elena Masterson's reading. That was what you wanted for yourself. Keeping this secret is holding you back. I think you should tell them."

"I can't do that."

"But why not, Nick?" she asked. "This is your life. You've been blessed with an opportunity that most people only dream of, and it's what you've always wanted. How can you let it pass you by?"

"You wouldn't understand. You didn't grow up like me. You had a supportive family, not a father who acted like a parasite or a mom who couldn't function without him. You didn't have to check over your shoulder, waiting for some messed-up shit to happen because messed-up shit was *always* happening. I've had to protect myself my whole life because nobody else could. Everywhere you went you were surrounded by love, and that's how you move through life, Lily. Like someone who knows she is loved. I didn't have that."

"But you have it now," she said, growing frustrated too. "You have Marcus and Caleb, and Henry and Yolanda. You have me." She softened her voice, wanting him to know that she was on his side. "You're right, I didn't grow up like you. I hate that you had such a rough childhood, and that you've spent so much of your life alone. Every day I wish could go back in time and change things for you. But that's not an option. All we have is the present, and there is so much goodness in store for you. You just have to be willing to accept it."

Nick was staring at her, his mouth set in a frown. She didn't know if her words got through to him. He looked as miserable as she felt. Then he sighed, bone deep.

"Thank you. I know you're just trying to help," he said. "I don't want to argue."

"I don't want to argue either."

"I'm sorry," he said quietly.

"I'm sorry too." She rubbed her forehead. She felt more exhausted now than when she'd left the club.

"You should get some sleep," Nick said. "I'll call you tomorrow, okay?"

"Okay."

They hung up and Lily rolled onto her back and closed her eyes. Toward the end of their conversation, Lily had experienced a moment of clarity.

She was in love with Nick.

But she needed him to stop pushing her away. She understood that love was a risk, that it could be downright frightening. But she wanted to be with someone who knew the risks and was willing to take them anyway. She'd already spent too much of her life hiding behind her sisters and her own fears of inadequacy. She wanted Nick to be willing to open up to her instead of hiding.

The sudden sound of Violet wailing downstairs snapped Lily out of her contemplative mood. She jolted upright and saw Iris rush down the hallway, wearing one of Karina's fancy guest robes. Lily hurried behind her.

Violet, Karina and one of Karina's security guards were walking toward the living room. Violet was sobbing onto Karina's arm as they wobbled to the couch.

"What happened?" Iris asked.

Lily sat on the other side of Violet and hugged her. She didn't know what the issue was, but she knew that her sister needed comfort. Violet began blubbering, too emotional to speak. Karina held up her phone, and Lily bent forward, peering at the screen. She gasped when she realized what she was looking at. TMZ had posted a picture of Meela Baybee and Eddy, kissing on a beach. The headline read, *Meela Baybee Gets Hot and Heavy with Her Manager.*

"Oh no," Lily whispered.

"That motherfucker," Violet cried. "He said they were in Jamaica for a video shoot, but he was there because he was having a fucking affair."

Iris scrolled through the article, her face grim. "It says here they've been secretly together since July."

"Jesus," Lily said.

"He didn't even try to deny it!" Violet was sobbing again, burying her face in the couch cushion.

"Fuck him, girl!" Karina said. "He's no-account! I been telling you that!"

Violet sat up and fiercely wiped her eyes, smearing her makeup. "The wedding is *off*. Fuck him. Fuck Meela Baybee. I should have never introduced them. I hope she does something stupid and gets canceled so that she can drag Eddy's career down with her."

"What do you need us to do?" Iris asked, crouching in front of Violet. "I'll start canceling things in the morning. I'll call the caterer and the DJ. Lily can call Mom and Dad." Iris looked at Lily for assistance. "Right?"

"Yes, anything," Lily said, jumping in. "Anything you need."

"No," Violet said, standing. She had a bright-eyed, feral look in her eyes. "Don't cancel a thing. Because we're still going to have a party. An *anti-wedding* party."

"Um," Lily said. She and Iris exchanged worried glances.

"Shit, that sounds good to me," Karina said.

Violet abruptly left the living room. The squishy movements of her spandex catsuit echoed throughout the house.

"Let's just give her a minute," Iris said. "Do you have lavender tea, Karina? That always makes her feel better."

"We might. Let me check."

Iris followed Karina into the kitchen, and Lily glanced at Karina's stoic, beefy bodyguard, who was seemingly unmoved by the hysteria.

When she could no longer hear the sound of Violet's footsteps, Lily went upstairs to Violet's guest bedroom. The lights were out, and Violet was curled in a ball in the center of the bed. Her shoulders were shaking. Quietly, Lily walked to the bed and crawled beside Violet, drawing the comforter up to cover both of them.

"I feel sick to my stomach," Violet mumbled quietly.

Lily snuggled closer. "I'm so sorry, Vi."

They lay there not speaking, breathing in tandem. After a while Iris appeared, holding a mug of tea. She encouraged Violet to sit up and drink a little. Then wordlessly, Iris climbed into bed too, and Lily thought about how they used to sleep in the same room on Christmas Eve when they were kids. Times were so much simpler then. Their years of heartbreak were miles away.

Their flight back to New York tomorrow morning couldn't come soon enough.

25

NICK SLOWLY PUSHED A SHOPPING CART DOWN THE JUICE aisle at Piggly Wiggly, waiting patiently as Teresa picked the items she needed.

In some ways, being back in Warren made Nick feel like he'd stepped through a time machine. Piggly Wiggly was still the place where everyone shopped. He'd already bumped into three high school classmates. The Jack in the Box where he'd worked was still across the street. It was strange to return to a place where much hadn't changed, when he felt like a different person.

Teresa stood beside Nick, glancing back and forth between two different bottles of apple juice. Welch's and store brand. She looked almost exactly the same as the last time he'd seen her. Slight and petite with light brown skin and large round eyes. The only difference was that her hair was shorter and styled into a pixie cut.

When Nick first arrived at the hospital days ago, Teresa had hugged him more tightly than he'd expected. He remembered how fragile she'd always seemed to him as a kid.

His parents had spent the better part of the last five years bouncing around the Bible Belt. And to Nick's surprise, the reason they'd come back to Warren was because Teresa was divorcing Albert. After almost three decades, she'd finally had enough of running after him. She'd left Albert behind in Memphis and returned to Warren. Soon after, Albert had arrived too, but Teresa remained adamant on the divorce, even though she let him stay with her at the extended-stay motel. Theirs was a relationship that Nick still didn't understand and probably never would.

While Teresa had been rehired at the nursing home, Albert dragged his feet about finding work. He spent too much time down at the pool hall, drinking and betting like before, and a few nights ago he'd gotten into the car with an associate who'd been too drunk to drive, and now Albert was in the hospital, concussed and injured.

That morning Nick had given Teresa the money to apply for an apartment. In another move that surprised him, Teresa chose to list only her name on the lease. He didn't know where his father would live. He didn't know if he believed Teresa would actually go through with the divorce. But he couldn't have imagined Teresa making that kind of act of independence when he was younger.

So now, while they waited for Teresa to be approved for the apartment, Nick took her grocery shopping. Their relationship was awkward and stilted. But she was his mother and Nick had the money. The very least he could do was buy her food.

"This one's cheaper," Teresa said, finally placing the store brand apple juice into the cart.

"Get whichever one you want," Nick said. "Don't worry about the price."

"You sure?" Teresa frowned, glancing at the cart, which was already full. After couponing her whole life, she was unused to the concept of not needing to tally up costs while she shopped.

"I'm sure."

"All right," she said after a prolonged moment. She switched out the apple juices and indicated for Nick to move the cart farther down the aisle.

Nick still hadn't told her about how much money he had or how he'd gained it. He could tell that Teresa was curious to know how he'd been able to give her money for the apartment security deposit, and how he'd offered to pay for his dad's physical therapy without question. But Teresa wasn't Albert. She would observe Nick's actions instead of asking for an outright explanation.

Keeping this secret is holding you back. I think you should tell them.

Lily's voice popped into his head then. He hated how they'd left things after their phone call the other night. They'd spoken to each other a few times since, but something was off, and it made *him* feel off. He didn't like feeling disconnected from her. Neither of them brought it up, but M&M's party tomorrow night, and Nick's refusal to go, was an elephant in the room.

Nick knew that everything Lily said had been right. He *was* afraid. He was fucking terrified to finally grasp on to the things that he wanted. He'd always thought it would be safer if he managed his expectations. But how could he live a full life that way? He'd thought he'd stopped running from his life by choosing to stay in New York, but really, he'd just been running in place.

The other night, Lily couldn't understand where Nick had been coming from because when she looked at him, she didn't think in terms of limitations. She was always thinking the best of him. His own self-perception wasn't so positive yet, but he could work to improve it. He wanted to be better for Lily. He wanted to be better for himself. He couldn't let this shit hold him back anymore.

"Mom," he said, swallowing thickly. He waited until she turned away from the shelf of condiments and gave him her full attention. "I wrote a book. I—the book was sold to a publisher, and that's how I make a living. I'm an author."

She looked at him for a moment. "Does that explain all of this?" she asked, gesturing at the nearly overflowing cart.

He nodded. "I didn't want to tell you or Dad, because I was nervous about what Dad would do once he found out about my new life. I thought he'd find a way to ruin everything." He breathed deeply and added, "And I was unwilling to accept that something good had happened to me."

Teresa eyed him closely, taking in what he'd just told her.

"You were always writing in those notebooks of yours every chance you got," she said. "I remember you loved those Ring Lord books."

Nick smiled. "*Lord of the Rings.*"

"Yeah, those." She took over pushing the cart, and Nick walked beside her. "So, are you going to tell me what your book's about?"

"Oh yeah, sure," Nick said, surprised that she wanted to

know. He told her the name of his book and his pen name. Her eyes glazed over when he attempted to explain the plot, but he didn't hold it against her. High fantasy wasn't everyone's forte. But she looked at him with renewed interest when he mentioned the television show adaptation.

"When can I watch it?" she asked.

"Not for a while. Years probably."

"Well, when can I buy a copy of the book?"

"In a couple weeks," he said. "I'll send you one."

"Good."

She didn't say anything else as she steered the cart toward the checkout. Nick's heart rate slowly returned to a normal pace. It was over. He'd told her. He'd built this moment up for so long in his head, and in the end, it had been so much easier than he'd thought it would be. There was still the matter of Albert and how he'd react to the news, but half the battle had been fought.

At the register, the cashier, a young girl with two nose rings and box braids, placed a thick paperback book aside in order to ring them up.

"You like to read?" Teresa asked the cashier, who nodded. "My son's an author." Teresa nudged Nick. "Go on. Tell her about your book."

Nick paused in the act of swiping his credit card and glanced at his mom. Then he looked at the cashier, who stared back at him expectantly.

"Oh, uh, okay." Nick proceeded to struggle through an elevator pitch that he'd definitely need to improve at a later date. But when he was finished, the cashier simply nodded again.

"Cool," she said. "I'll buy it."

Teresa was smiling softly as they loaded the groceries into Nick's rental car. He didn't know if his mom would ever flat-out say that she was proud of him. That wasn't exactly her way. But her smile let Nick know how she felt.

They dropped off her groceries, then Nick drove Teresa to the nursing home for her evening shift. She thanked Nick for the ride and opened her door. Then she seemed to rethink her decision and closed the door just as quickly.

"I met your dad when I had no one," she said, turning to him. "He was the first person who really cared about me. When I found out I was pregnant with you, my priority was keeping my family together. I didn't want you to feel the way I'd felt as a child. I wanted you to grow up with both of your parents. That's why I always did everything I could to bring your father back home whenever he left. I wanted you to have stability. It took me a long time to realize that my behavior was the opposite of stable."

Nick leaned back in his seat, his hands at ten and two on the steering wheel. He was shocked that his mother, who'd always been so stoic, was sharing these things with him.

"Given the way that your father and I were, it makes sense that you'd want to stay away," she continued. "I wasn't there for you when I should have been, and I'm sorry. But people can change. I'm trying to, at least."

There was a part of Nick that was hesitant to trust Teresa's earnestness. She could be saying this now only because Nick had helped her so much or because Albert wasn't there to keep her attention. Trusting Teresa didn't come naturally to him.

But he thought about what Lily would do. He knew that she'd give Teresa the chance to prove herself.

"Okay," he said.

"You're not up there in New York alone, are you?" she asked. "Do you have someone?"

His knee-jerk reaction to keep Lily separate from his parents flared up. But he didn't want to hide his past from his present anymore.

"I do," he said. "Her name's Lily."

Teresa smiled a little, tilting her head. "Tell me about her."

And so he did.

LATER, AT THE HOSPITAL, NICK WAS WAITING TO SPEAK with Albert's doctor about next steps for his recovery and at-home care. Albert had been in the hospital for almost a week and a half, and the surgery a few days ago for his broken leg had been successful. He was recuperating now and would be discharged soon.

While Albert slept, Nick sat in a chair by the window with his notebook propped open in his lap. He was trying to write, but his mind was on Lily.

"I don't think I've ever seen you without a notebook in your hand."

Nick glanced up, and Albert was awake, looking at him. His voice was groggy, and his movements were sluggish as he slowly sat upright.

"You the one paying for this hospital bill?" he asked. He attempted a lopsided grin.

Nick cleared his throat and closed his notebook. "I can."

Over the past couple days when Nick had visited Albert, he'd been asleep or so high on painkillers, he'd barely registered that Nick was even there. Now they stared at each other, assessing. It had been years since they'd spoken directly, receiving updates on each other's lives only through Teresa. The last time they spoke they'd been in this same hospital after Teresa had fractured her shoulder. They'd been arguing, shouting.

Nick had spent so many years in constant anxiety, anticipating Albert's behavior, wondering if he was going to pop up at his school or his job to ask for money or to make him do something that he didn't want to. As a kid, Nick had both feared the possibility of Albert's presence and craved it, because on his rare good days, Albert had been larger than life. Now he looked so small and fragile in his hospital bed, and Nick wondered why he'd ever thought to feel so afraid.

"Why you looking at me like that?" Albert asked. His gaze suddenly turned hard.

Nick shook his head. "I'm not looking at you any kind of way."

"Yes, you are. You think you better than me or something?"

"No," Nick said. Then he paused. "I just think you need help, Dad."

Albert sighed, his anger deflating. "Don't we all?"

The simplicity of that question struck Nick.

He'd fought his whole life to be nothing like Albert, despite the qualities they had in common. Their ambition, their sense of survival. Their desire to be loved. But what they most had in common was something that Nick had no control over: they were imperfect human beings.

Despite everything, Nick loved his dad, but doubted he'd be able to build a new relationship with him, and honestly, he wasn't sure if he wanted to. But what Albert had said was true. Nick also needed help in his own way. He decided right then that he'd find a therapist as soon as he got back to New York.

By the time Nick thought to reply, Albert was already snoring.

He didn't know when he'd talk to Albert about his book, but he was no longer afraid about him finding out. That was what mattered most.

Albert's doctor appeared in the hallway then, gesturing to Nick. He left Albert's room quietly, careful to close the door behind him without a sound.

THAT NIGHT IN HIS HOTEL ROOM, NICK SAT IN FRONT OF his glowing laptop screen and pulled up his current draft of *The Elves of Ceradon* book two. He stared at the blinking cursor and realized something.

The story he'd started for Deko no longer fit. It didn't make sense for Deko to stay in Ceradon. It was true that he'd found a new home there, a safer home. But Deko would need to return to his old kingdom eventually. He'd need to build an army to rid the land of life leeches for good.

Deko might not be successful in his venture, but he had to try. He'd come too far not to.

Nick highlighted and deleted the handful of chapters he'd managed to write over the last few weeks. With a clear vision in mind, he began again.

Hours later, when most people in his part of the world were sleeping, Nick was bleary-eyed and exhausted. He wanted to text Lily, but he'd wait until first thing tomorrow morning when she was awake.

26

THE ONE UPSIDE ABOUT NOT BEING INVITED TO M&M'S party as a junior-level employee was that Lily was able to leave the office an hour early shortly after Edith left to meet other executives for pre-party drinks.

On the subway ride home, Lily sighed impatiently, looking at her dead cell phone. She'd stayed up late with Violet last night, helping her curate the perfect post-breakup playlist, including songs from SZA, Summer Walker and Jhené Aiko, aka the men-ain't-shit holy trinity. She'd forgotten to charge her phone and it had died on her morning commute seconds after Nick had texted at 7:34 a.m.

Hey, can I call you later during your lunch?

Of course she'd forgotten her charger at home and didn't have a spare one at her desk, and she surely couldn't ask Edith if she could borrow *her* charger because Edith refused to upgrade her flip phone. And then during lunch, Edith pulled Lily into her office and spent forty-five minutes complaining about how their imprint wouldn't have any titles featured at the party.

Lily had no idea what Nick wanted to say to her. Even with the weirdness since their FaceTime call the other night, she missed him something bad. She wanted to hear the sound of his voice. She needed her freaking charger.

When she got home, Violet was sitting at the kitchen island in her black silk pajamas, typing away on her laptop.

"What do you think of this invite?" she asked, spinning her laptop around so that Lily could see the e-vite on her screen.

Violet's Anti-Wedding Party
When: Same day the wedding was supposed to be
Where: Same place the wedding was supposed to be
Wear black!
Fuck cheaters!

"Oh, so you're really going through with this?" Lily asked.

"I'll be damned if I let that man, who has an obsession with Supreme sweatsuits and being *big time*, ruin what could otherwise be an amazing day with my family and friends. This party will be a celebration. A *liberation*."

Lily looked at the bags under Violet's eyes. She hadn't seen a good night's sleep since Miami. Would Lily throw a party after finding out that her fiancé cheated two weeks before her wedding? Unlikely, because she'd probably be somewhere crying her eyes out. Everyone dealt with heartbreak differently. Lily could only admire that Violet was choosing to handle her heartbreak in style.

"I'll be there," she said. "In all black."

"Good." Violet beamed, spinning her laptop back around, and hit send on the e-vite. "You didn't weigh in on a dinner spot for tonight, by the way. Did you get Mom's texts? She feels bad for me and wants to have family time."

"No, my phone died." Lily walked to the couch and searched for her charger, checking between the cushions. She checked by her book stack and crouched down, looking under the coffee table. "Have you seen my charger?"

"Oh shit," Violet said with a weighty pause. "Is that it right there?"

Lily sat up, alert. "Where?"

She followed Violet's line of sight and watched as Tomcat sauntered toward her, holding her mangled charger in his mouth. He dropped the charger at Lily's feet like an offering and blinked at her sweetly. A look that said, *Hello, Mother, look what I destroyed just for you.*

"Nooo," Lily groaned, holding the chewed-up charger in her hand. "I thought you grew out of this."

"Use my charger," Violet said. "It's somewhere in my room."

Lily dashed down the hall and groaned again, because every inch of Violet's room was covered in clothes, strewn across her bed and floor. Racks were lined up in front of her closet. It was like being stuck in a department store maze. Lily maneuvered to the outlet by Violet's bed, but saw only the charger for Violet's laptop.

"I can't find it!" she shouted. But the apartment phone rang with a call from the front desk, drowning out her voice.

Lily hurried back into the living room, growing more anxious by the second to find a charger, any charger, so that she could finally call Nick. Then there was a knock at the door, and Violet opened it, letting in Dahlia, Benjamin, Iris and Calla.

"Violet, what is this anti-wedding party email you've sent to the whole family?" Dahlia asked. "Do you know that your great-aunt Portia received that email? It's filled with profanity!"

"I only used the F-word once," Violet clarified. "And I'm sure it's not the first time Great-Aunt Portia has heard it. Didn't she sing at a speakeasy back in the day?"

Dahlia frowned at her. Iris and Calla went to sit on the couch and were immediately joined by Tomcat, who could always count on Calla to show him extra attention. Benjamin hugged Violet and Lily hello and sat on the couch as well, but Dahlia stayed where she was by the kitchen island.

"Violet, are you sure your charger is in your room?" Lily asked, growing desperate.

Violet looked puzzled. "Yeah. Isn't it plugged up by my bed?"

"No," Lily said.

"I don't understand how you girls can stand living in such a small space," Dahlia said, casting a skeptical glance around the apartment. Her gaze snagged on Lily's shoes, lined up by the heater and her basket of fresh laundry by the coffee table. "Lily, honey, don't you want your own room again? Why don't you move back home for a little while? You can reassess your career and find a job where you can afford your own apartment. We haven't discussed business school yet. That's an option."

"Mom, *no*." Lily couldn't take another second of this. Not from her mom, not from anyone. If she'd learned anything over the past couple months, it was that she was done with being pushed, pulled and managed by those around her. She had a voice and a life vision, and she believed in herself. It was time that everyone else learned that too. Starting with her family.

"I'm not moving back home," she said, "and I'm not going to business school or law school or any other school. I know that you do this because you care, and I know that it's confusing to you because I haven't really accomplished anything great yet like Iris or Violet. I have a second interview next week with a dream publisher, and I hope I get the job, but even if I don't, I'm going to keep trying. I might progress at a slower pace and I might not get everything right on the first try, but you have to give me the space to figure things out on my own."

Dahlia blinked, momentarily speechless. "I'm sorry, honey. I thought I was helping. I wasn't trying to make things worse."

"I know that's right," Violet said. "Stand up for yourself, Lily."

"It's not just Mom," Lily said, whipping around to face Violet, then looking at Iris. "It's both of you too. I lied to you about having a boyfriend earlier this year because it was the only way I could get you to stop trying to fix my love life. I never had a boyfriend. I was emailing with someone I'd never even met in person! And . . . well, it turns out he was actually Nick—"

"*What?*" Iris and Violet said.

"—but that's neither here nor there. He and I already moved past that. He believes in me and accepts me for who I am, and that's why I love him, but—"

"*Love?*" they said.

"—my *point* is that I didn't want to tell you the truth because I didn't want you to pity me or think that I was helpless." Lily looked around at each of them. "I love all of you. I'm so grateful to be part of this family. But if I need your help, I will ask for it, okay?"

The Greenes nodded in silence, stunned by soft-spoken Lily and her not-so-soft-spoken behavior. Calla's laughter at Tomcat lightly bumping his head against her chin broke the silence.

"For the record, we love all three of you equally," Benjamin said, speaking for the first time since he'd entered the apartment. "Regardless of what you have or haven't accomplished."

"Thanks, Dad." Lily smiled at her father and took a deep breath. "Now that that's settled, does anybody have an iPhone charger?"

Everyone shook their heads. Violet, who was still intrigued by Lily's revelation about her emails with Nick, smiled slyly. "What kind of emails were y'all sending, though?" she asked, wiggling her eyebrows. "Kinky stuff?"

"*Violet.*" This from Dahlia, Benjamin and Iris.

"No, the emails were . . ." Lily started. Wait. *Email.*

She could email Nick! Why hadn't she thought of that before?

She ran to open her laptop, pulling up her personal email account. And the first thing she saw was a message from Edith.

I've been trying to reach you every way possible, and I'm hoping that you regularly check your personal email, unlike the way you've been ignoring your work account. I need my new business cards! Please bring them to the party!

Was she *serious*? She wanted Lily to go back to the office and bring her business cards across town, just so that she could hand them out at a party that happened every year?

Forget that. Lily wasn't going out of her way for Edith like this anymore.

But then she thought about how Edith had bullied their poor book cover designer Jeremy into designing those business cards. Jeremy was kind and patient and never gave Lily grief over the many comments Edith made about his cover sketches. Lily didn't want his hard, unpaid work to go to waste.

"Where are we going for dinner?" she asked, grabbing her tote bag and useless, dead phone. "I'll meet you there. I have to do something for work first."

Iris gave Lily the address for Osteria 57 in the Village, and Lily rushed out the door.

• • •

THE PARTY WAS being held on the rooftop at the Moxy hotel in Times Square. Lily spent a good five minutes in the lobby trying to explain that no, she didn't have an invitation, she simply needed to bring business cards to someone in attendance. After she was finally allowed entry, she took the elevator up to the rooftop. When she exited the elevator, her steps faltered. This party was packed. Clusters of people were spread out across the rooftop. Hotel staff milled among the crowd, holding trays of appetizers. To the far left, there was a large projector screen, displaying a book cover that Lily didn't recognize. A short white man, who was sweating in his blazer, stood behind a makeshift podium, gesturing to the screen as everyone listened. He must have been an author.

Lily maneuvered through the crowd, searching for Edith. She heard someone call her name, and she turned, spotting Dani and Oliver by the bar. They waved at her, and Lily laughed, waving back. Of course Dani had found a way to score *two* invites for junior-level staff. Lily kept moving through the crowd. Along the way, she spotted Marcus standing by the rooftop railing, speaking to a tall, brown-skinned woman with long, dark hair. Lily would have to find him and say hi before she left.

She finally located Edith near the back of the party by the bathrooms. Edith was talking with another white woman, who was short like Edith, but her strawberry blonde hair hung loose to her shoulders. She wore a bright orange, sleeveless A-line dress in contrast to Edith's all-black outfit. They looked like night and day.

When Edith noticed Lily, she waved her forward impatiently. Lily fought the urge to roll her eyes and slipped through the crowd.

"Here you go," Lily said, handing over the business cards.

Edith didn't even say thank you. She took the cards and dropped them into her purse. "Lily, this is Bernice Gilman."

"Oh," Lily said, looking at the woman who would be her second boss if Lily was unfortunate enough to be stuck at this job by the time Bernice started. "Nice to meet you."

"It's nice to meet you too." With a warm smile, Bernice shook Lily's hand. "Did you really come all this way to drop off Edith's business cards? That's dedication."

"She's decent most days," Edith said, waving her hand in dismissal. "Lily is a career assistant type. She'll be with us for a long time."

Lily smarted at Edith's words. Not just her words, but the way she'd said them. Lily had literally just asked for a promotion. She obviously didn't want to be a career assistant!

She thought again about what Nick had said to her. *You're the most capable person I know.* He was right. Lily *was* capable. Months ago, she'd been a mumbling, hesitant girl in the elevator who couldn't even look Nick in the eye. And now she was in love with him. If she hadn't taken the leap all those days ago, who knew where they would be. Life was about the leap.

Fuck it. No more of this bullshit. Lily owed Edith nothing. If she could finally stand up to her family, she could surely stand up to Edith.

She took a deep breath. "Actually, I quit."

Edith gawked at her. Bernice looked on in confusion.

"You what?" Edith sputtered.

"I *quit.*"

Maybe the job with Francesca Ng would pan out or maybe it wouldn't. Lily had other options while she continued to apply to other publishing jobs. She could go back to being a bookseller. She could freelance edit. She'd take temp jobs. She'd be without healthcare for some time and that would suck, but *anything* would be better than working for Edith. She deserved respect and to work with someone who believed in her. She deserved peace.

What the hell was she still doing at this self-indulgent, elitist party? She couldn't spend another second wasting her time, doing things that made her unhappy.

"I'll hand in my official notice tomorrow morning," Lily said. "Good luck with her, Bernice."

Bernice's jaw was on the floor. Edith's pale cheeks flushed red as she struggled to come up with a reply. Lily wasn't going to stay long enough to hear it. Feeling weightless and free, she turned on her heels and began to make her way back to the elevator.

Her first order of business was going to Duane Reade to buy a new phone charger, and *then* she'd call Nick and hop her ass on the first flight to North Carolina because she loved him, and she wanted to be there for him, and she wasn't going to let him push her away.

She was halfway to the elevator when the doors opened, and Nick stepped out, wearing a black T-shirt and Adidas joggers. Definitely not party attire. He looked like he'd just gotten off a flight. His gaze immediately fanned out across the crowd, searching.

Lily froze in place, blinking at him, wondering if he was really there or if he was a figment of her willful imagination.

She called his name, not caring if she interrupted whoever was speaking at the front of the rooftop. Nick's attention snapped in the direction of her voice. But before he could see Lily, the woman who'd been speaking with Marcus appeared and pulled Nick away toward the podium.

27

"NICK!" ZARA HISSED EXCITEDLY INTO HIS EAR. HER hands were clasped around his arm as she ushered him across the rooftop and through the crowd. "You're here! Marcus told me you weren't coming!"

Oh fuck.

Given the way things looked, it might seem like Nick had made a last-minute decision to come to the party after all, but the truth was that he'd been trying to get in touch with Lily since seven thirty that morning, and as the hours ticked by and he continued to not hear from her, he became more and more certain that talking to her over the phone simply wasn't enough. He needed to see her in person. That way he could tell Lily to her face that he loved her, and he was working his shit out.

The next thing he knew, he was waiting on standby at the airport for a flight back to New York. And then he was on a plane, rehearsing exactly what he'd say to her. When he landed, he called Lily and got her voice mail again, and once he reached their building, he went straight to her apartment only to be greeted by her entire family, who then told him that Lily had gone to some work event. Immediately, he knew that work event had to be M&M's party.

He ran into his apartment and grabbed his invitation. It wasn't until he was on the elevator that he looked down at his joggers and swore. He was embarrassingly underdressed for any professional gathering, but his plan was simple: he'd go to the party, find Lily, talk to her and go completely unnoticed by his editor or Marcus. He'd have to pick another day to introduce himself to the world as N.R. Strickland. Speaking to Lily was high-key more important right now.

The elevator stopped on the tenth floor, and Nick huffed out a frustrated breath. When the doors opened, Henry and Yolanda stepped into the elevator, holding hands and grinning at each other like lovesick teenagers.

"Hi, sweetheart," Yolanda said, hugging Nick. "Where are you off to?"

"Hi. A party," he said, distracted. "I'm sorry, excuse me." He reached past Yolanda and pressed a button to make the doors close faster. Yolanda and Henry exchanged a glance.

"Are you all right, honey?" Yolanda asked. "You look quite anxious."

"I have something really important to say to Lily, and I've never done something like this before, and I low-key wanna puke, but I've got this. I think."

"Ah, the lady friend," Yolanda said with a knowing smile. "If you are genuine and earnest, whatever you say will be well received."

"Don't worry," Henry said. "You're the man, remember?"

Nick let out a surprised laugh. He was definitely in need

of a pep talk. He just hoped it had the same effect on him that his pep talk had on Henry months ago.

"Thank you," Nick said, looking at both of them. He was thanking Henry for more than the pep talk, and he was thanking Yolanda for more than her advice. He planned to be around for a lot longer to show them how grateful he was that they'd welcomed him into their lives.

They wished him luck as he rushed out of the elevator through the lobby and hopped in a cab.

Now he was here at the party, and he thought he'd heard Lily call his name a second ago, but Zara thought Nick had arrived for a completely different reason.

"I, um, that's not why—" Nick stumbled over his words, attempting to disentangle himself from Zara's tight grasp.

"Mary!" Zara whispered loudly to a redhead in front of them. "N.R. Strickland is here. Nick, this is Mary. She's your publicist!"

Mary turned around and gasped, causing the others in their vicinity to look at Nick too. "We have to get him to the podium!"

"Ah no, no. Wait," Nick said, backing up.

"This is amazing. Everyone will be so excited," Zara said, talking over him. "The head of our division basically made it seem like I ruined the party when I told her you weren't coming. I was honestly afraid she might fire me."

Shit. Nick could easily pull away from Zara and Mary, but how could he do that after what Zara just shared? He couldn't leave her hanging.

He spared one more glance around the party, looking for Lily, but instead he spotted Marcus, cutting across the party toward him, sporting a puzzled expression at Nick's presence.

They reached the podium, and Zara hurried to whisper something to a blonde-haired woman, who then rushed to the podium and whispered something into the ear of a tall, balding white guy who had been in the middle of telling everyone how this fall was going to be M&M's best season yet.

The man paused and listened to the blonde woman. Then he flashed a surprised smile.

"Folks," he said, turning back to the microphone. "We've got a real treat for you tonight. N.R. Strickland, the author of one of our major fall books, *The Elves of Ceradon*, is here after all."

There was a collective gasp from the crowd, which was followed by a flurry of whispers.

Zara ushered Nick up to the podium, and the white guy eagerly shook Nick's hand.

"So nice to meet you, Mr. Strickland," he said. "I'm Vincent Meyer, the CEO of M&M. Thank you for joining us."

Holy shit. The CEO?

"Nice to meet you too," Nick managed to say. Then Vincent stepped aside and left the floor to Nick.

Nick stared out at the crowd. A sea of blurring faces waiting for him to speak. *The Elves of Ceradon* cover flashed on the screen behind him. He cleared his throat. Where was his special reserve of extrovert energy when he needed it?

He started to break out into a sweat. If only he'd had time to plan what he'd say. He noticed a few people holding up their phones, recording him. This would end up on the internet for everyone to see. Down in front, Zara gave him an encouraging thumbs-up, but looking at her made him feel only more pressure. He'd have to deliver, because that meant she would deliver too.

He took a deep breath, trying to steady his erratic heartbeat.

And then he saw her.

Lily was on the outskirts of the crowd, staring back at him. And then it was like everyone else on the rooftop faded away. She smiled at him, soft and warm and so *her*. She nodded her head. It was all he'd needed. He could do this.

He leaned down toward the mic. "Hi," he said, then immediately winced at the loud burst of feedback. "Uh, I'm N.R. Strickland. I wrote *The Elves of Ceradon* ... which all of you know because Vincent just said that. I'm obviously not British, as you might have been told. I grew up in North Carolina eating barbecue and hot dogs and apple pie, and all the other stereotypical American foods." There were a few chuckles, and that loosened him up. "Um, just to clear up some rumors, I'm not dead. I'm only one person, not multiple people. And I have spoken to Zara before, who is amazing, by the way."

He cleared his throat and glanced at Lily, steadying himself again.

"I wrote this book when I was twenty-two years old," he continued. "I was a college senior with grand plans that didn't come to fruition. I lied about my backstory for several personal reasons. I'm sorry that I made you all believe

I was someone that I'm not. What's true is that I am the author of *The Elves of Ceradon*. This story and its characters came from deep inside of me. I needed Deko to survive despite the many life challenges he experienced, because I needed to survive the challenges in my life too. I gave up on this book and the idea of being an author, but I've learned that sometimes we're lucky enough to get a second chance. I'm so thankful for everyone here who had a hand giving *Elves* a new life." He paused. "But I didn't come here tonight to talk about my book."

There were a few confused murmurs, but Nick focused his gaze on Lily again. She was beautiful and still. He didn't take his eyes off her as he continued to speak.

"I came to the party because I was looking for someone who means a lot to me," he said. "More than my career. More than anything, really. She is the best part of my life, and I want her to know that if she'll let me, I'll spend forever returning the favor." He stepped away from the podium, eyes still on Lily. Then he awkwardly leaned toward the mic again and said, "Thank you. Have a good night."

There was a spattering of enthusiastic if not bemused applause. Zara was patting Nick on his shoulder, but he didn't register any of it. He was moving toward Lily, and those in the crowd watched him curiously, stepping out of his way.

◾ ◾ ◾

LILY STOOD THERE, waiting for Nick. She grinned at him, shaking her head in delighted wonder. She couldn't believe that he was here. Her heart was bursting.

Nick reached her and stepped close, leaving but a breath of space between them. She stared up into his face. His gaze was soft and intent as he took her hands in his.

"I love you," he said. "I've loved you since you sent me that first email last year. You found me when I didn't want to be found. You saved me."

Lily blinked at him, speechless.

"I'm sorry about what I said on the phone the other day," he continued. "All of the things you said were right." He lifted his hand to cradle her cheek. "I told my parents about everything, including you. I just want you to know that I'm trying."

"I know you are," she said, her chest filling with lightness. "And so am I." She brought his face down closer to hers. "I love you too."

Then she kissed him, and Nick held his hands on either side of her face, deepening the kiss. The crowd whistled and cheered, and it was only then that she remembered they weren't alone. Lily laughed and blushed.

"You two are absolutely *adorable*," Zara gushed, materializing next to them. "Just imagine what that heartfelt speech is going to do for your career, Nick! You had everyone eating out of the palm of your hand! Our first-week sales will be through the roof!"

"I can't believe you showed up!" Marcus said, popping up on Nick's other side. "I'm so proud of you, bro. And hey, Lily, is it true that you just quit? Somebody said they heard Edith throwing a tantrum about it in the bathroom."

Nick turned to Lily, eyes wide. "You quit?"

"Yes." She beamed.

"Proud of you," he said, smiling too. Then, "Wanna get out of here?"

She nodded. "Definitely."

Once they were outside in front of the hotel, neither knew what to say. They were both overwhelmed in the best way.

"I wanted to tell you that I was flying back today," Nick said. "I tried calling you, but—"

"My phone died!" Lily pulled her phone out of her bag and showed him her blank screen. "*I* was going to fly to *you*, actually. Right after I bought a new charger."

He smiled. "I didn't want you to have to seek me out this time. I wanted to show up for you. And for myself."

His smile was so breathtakingly beautiful and tender, it made Lily's heart ache. "I'm glad you did."

"I needed to see you," he said. "But I have to go back to North Carolina for a few more days. They still need my help."

"I know." Lily gently laced her fingers through his. "I'll be here when you get back."

Nick brought her hand to his mouth and kissed it.

"So, you really quit," he said. She grinned, nodding, and he laughed. "You wanna tell me that story?"

"I can tell you all about it on the way to dinner with my family," she said. "If you want to join us."

She gazed up at him, patient and encouraging.

With a grin on his face and love in his eyes, he said, "Of course."

28

IN THE END, VIOLET'S ENGAGEMENT PARTY AND HER ANTI-wedding party were proof that sometimes celebrating a breakup could be a lot more fun than celebrating an impending marriage. For one thing, the anti-wedding party had live entertainment.

"If you a bad bitch, lemme hear you say ayyyyeee!" Karamel Kitty shouted into the mic.

"*Ayyyeee!*" Lily, Iris and Violet hollered, along with Violet's fashion friends and the members of the Greene family on the dance floor who chose to identify as bad bitches.

"That's what I'm talking about!" Karamel Kitty yelled. Then she proceeded to perform her newest number one single, "Bad Bitch Antics."

In a last-minute change, Violet was able to keep the same catering and event teams from her wedding. This time, there were black tablecloths, and she convinced Dahlia to dip every flower for the floral arrangements in black. The guests were dressed in black, just how Violet had envisioned. Violet wore a custom black V-neck halter ball gown, and Lily had even bought a new black sleeveless minidress from Aritzia for the occasion.

The new purchase was one of the splurges she'd treated herself to after landing the job at Happy Go Lucky Press. Working with Francesca and Anna would be a dream. A busy dream because they were a small but mighty team. But Lily had the feeling that she would finally learn what it was like to work with people who were invested in her growth and saw value in her work.

Months ago, if you would have told Lily that this would be her life, she wouldn't have believed it. It would sound too good to be true. But she was allowing herself to bask in the happiness. Because she deserved to.

"I'm going to get some water," she shouted to her sisters, who were busy dancing and laughing. The sight made Lily's heart swell. "Do either of you want anything from the bar?"

"A rum and Coke," Iris said, but Violet shook her head and kept dancing.

Lily made her way to the bar, passing her family and Violet's friends who'd come together to help turn what had started as a terrible situation into something joyful. She waited for the bartender to mix Iris's rum and Coke and jumped when she heard someone say her name.

"Hi, Lily."

She looked over in surprise at Angel, who'd appeared beside her. He looked just as handsome as the first time she'd met him earlier this summer at Violet's engagement party. But his presence no longer scrambled her brain or made her heart flutter. There was only one person who had that effect on her. And he was standing outside the venue somewhere quiet, giving his first-ever press interview over the phone for his book.

"Hey, Angel," Lily said. "How are you? I didn't expect you to be here."

"I took Violet's side in the breakup. Eddy wasn't a good dude." He shrugged. "Are you still working on books about dictators?"

Lily laughed. "Thankfully, no. How's the album coming along?"

"*Great*. I've been collaborating with this new producer who—"

Angel abruptly stopped talking. Lily raised an eyebrow, waiting for him to continue. He was staring at something beyond Lily's shoulder. She turned around and spotted Iris approaching them. Iris looked quite beautiful tonight with her dark plum lipstick and her skintight black lamé turtleneck dress. She'd let Calla stick a black rose behind her ear.

"I think Karamel Kitty's lyrics are going to give Great-Aunt Portia a heart attack," Iris said, once she reached the bar. She took her drink from the counter and glanced past Lily at Angel. "Hello."

"Hey, what's up, what's good?" Angel blurted.

"Iris, this is Violet's friend Angel," Lily said, trying not to laugh at Angel's besotted expression. "Angel, this is our other sister, Iris."

Iris squinted at him. "You're the musician."

"Yes." Angel's eyes lit up as he eagerly leaned forward. "You've heard my music before?"

"No." Iris sipped her drink and turned to Lily. "Calla's sitting with Mom. I'm going outside to get some air if anyone's looking for me."

Iris walked away, and Lily hid her smile as Angel stared after her sister.

"It was nice seeing you again, Lily," he said, hurrying to finish his drink. "I have to . . . go check on something."

Lily grinned. "Nice seeing you too."

Then he was gone, walking off in the same direction as Iris. He'd have his work cut out for him, but Lily hoped Angel might be successful in bagging Iris. She could use some fun in her life.

Her phone vibrated with a text from Nick.

Interview just wrapped up. Save me a dance?

Lily stood up straighter, her eyes searching. And there was Nick, striding right toward her. He cut a devastatingly handsome figure in his all-black tux. Lily could have melted on the spot.

They met each other halfway. It was unclear who reached for whom first, but they were immediately glued together, magnetic, like they hadn't just been in each other's presence thirty minutes ago. Lily kissed him, and he wrapped his arms around her waist, holding her close.

"How'd the interview go?" Lily asked once she pulled away.

"It was cool." Nick pushed a stray curl behind her ear and settled his hand at the nape of her neck. "I need more practice, but I think I'll be better once they send me on tour."

"Don't worry. I'll give you some media training before then."

Nick laughed, and the sound washed over her like a warm balm.

He backed away toward the dance floor and held out his hand. "Wanna dance?"

Violet instructed the DJ to play only fast songs that went with her fuck-cheaters anthem, but that didn't matter to Lily. She nodded and placed her hand in Nick's as he led her out onto the dance floor. She looped her arms around his neck, and they swayed slowly from side to side, gazing at each other. His embrace was her forever favorite place to be.

"Looks like I was your date after all," he said softly.

"Looks like it." Lily couldn't help smiling.

She wouldn't have had it any other way.

EPILOGUE

Four months later

SOMEWHERE ALONG THE WAY, LILY HAD LOST NICK AT THE Union Square holiday market. She figured he was trying to find a moment of quiet amid the chaotic New York City holiday rush. It was mid-December, and they'd had a true day of holiday tourism, including a trip to the tree at Rockefeller Center, attempting to ice-skate at Bryant Park, and viewing the window displays at Saks Fifth Avenue. They'd been surrounded by tourists at every turn. Funny enough, it had all been Nick's idea. He'd finished his sequel draft and wanted to celebrate by exploring what New York City had to offer at Christmastime.

Lily had been all too eager to agree. She was editing a middle-grade fantasy novel about a Black girl from New York who finds out that her great-grandfather was the real Jack Frost. She figured she could use the day as editing research. But really, she just wanted to watch Nick experience the mayhem and magic of Christmas in the city.

Armed with newly purchased holiday place mats, Lily moved on to browse a stand with various Christmas tree ornaments. She had a teeny-tiny tree in her teeny-tiny studio apartment in Crown Heights, only a fifteen-minute walk away from Marcus and Caleb. The following weekend, she was hosting Nick and his mom for dinner, and she wanted to make sure it looked as festive as possible. Teresa was visiting Nick for the first time ever. He and his dad still weren't there. But it was something Nick was working out in therapy.

Lily was in the middle of choosing between a set of silver snowmen and red Santa hat ornaments when she felt a cold, wet kiss on her cheek.

"I went on the hunt for hot chocolate," Nick said, holding out a steaming cup to her. Like Lily, he was bundled up in a wool peacoat, a thick scarf wrapped around his neck.

Lily smiled at him, accepting the cup gratefully. "Thanks. I was wondering where you'd gone."

"After I got the chocolate, I was on the phone with Violet for almost ten minutes. She had hella questions about what Marcus and Caleb considered ugly for their Christmas sweater party. I think she's overthinking it."

Lily laughed and held up the ornament sets for him. "Which one do you like better?"

Nick grinned and shrugged. He pointed at the snowmen. "Those."

"Great, that's what I was thinking too." Lily moved to pay for the ornaments, but Nick gently turned her to face him again.

"I got you something," he said, reaching into his pocket.

"Don't give it to me yet!"

They were going to exchange gifts on Christmas Eve before they went to her parents' house for dinner. It was going to be Nick's first stateside Christmas in years, and she wanted it to be special. She'd bought him a vintage typewriter. It was already wrapped and hidden away in the hall closet at her apartment. And because Nick wasn't so good at hiding gifts, she knew that he'd already bought her a signed, illustrated edition of the Dragons of Blood series.

"Don't worry, it's not your real gift," he said. "Just something small."

He placed a small black bag in her hand. Lily glanced up at him curiously and he nodded, urging her to open it. Lily reached inside the bag. She grabbed two small items. A Black Santa figurine and an I <3 NY keychain.

She laughed out loud then, remembering the imaginary date from their emails.

"This is perfect," she said, grinning up at him. She kissed him softly. His mouth tasted sweetly of hot chocolate. "Thank you."

"You're welcome." He smiled back and wrapped his arms around her, moving his hands up and down her arms to generate warmth. "It's freezing. How about we go back to my place now?"

"Okay," Lily said, snuggling closer.

Nick wasn't a figment of her imagination or a faceless stranger behind her computer screen. He was right there in front of her. The realest thing in the world.

She kissed him again to prove just how real he was.

Acknowledgments

Writing adult romance has always been a huge dream of mine, and for a long time I was afraid to pursue this dream because writing in a new genre/age group can be very intimidating! I love this book so much, and I'm so grateful for everyone who helped bring this story to fruition.

Thank you to my agent, Sara Crowe, for always believing in me and my stories and my ability to tell these stories, regardless of how afraid I might be to write them.

Thank you to my editors, Cindy Hwang and Angela Kim, who guided me (and Lily and Nick!) on this journey in the most supportive way. I'm thankful for the rest of the team at Berkley as well: Adam Auerbach, Stacy Edwards, Christine Legon, Daniela Riedlova, Dache' Rogers, Lila Selle and Randie Lipkin.

Thank you to my friend and critique partner, Alison Doherty, who listened to my pitch about Lily and Nick years ago and encouraged me to take the leap and write their story. And thank you to my work wife, Dana Carey, who made my days of working in publishing so much more worthwhile.

Finally, thank you to my family for being so supportive. Especially my grandma Peggy, who always made a point to ask if I was still planning to write a story about sisters named after flowers.

The
Neighbor
Favor

Kristina Forest

Questions for Discussion

1. Lily and Nick initially grow close without even having seen each other. Have you ever had a pen pal who became a close friend or romantic partner?

2. Lily struggles to move forward in her career, due to both internal and external circumstances. In what ways do you think she could've stood up for herself earlier? What did you find admirable throughout her journey?

3. Lily and Nick's relationship begins with an underlying deceit on Nick's part. Do you think you could forgive, like Lily did? Or would that have been a dealbreaker?

4. What is your ideal date?

5. Would you want to be a travel writer, like Nick? What are some of the pros and cons of this job?

6. Nick and Lily's families are extremely different and helped shape the people they became.

What are some character strengths and flaws they both have due to the way they grew up?

7. Nick ultimately returns to North Carolina to see his parents and has some sort of closure, or possibly a new beginning, with them. Do you think you would do the same? Or are Nick's dad's actions unforgivable to you?

8. Lily lies to her sisters about what really happened between her and Nick when they were corresponding online because she doesn't want them to feel bad for her or think she further needs their help in her love life. Do you think she should have told them the truth from the beginning or do you think her lie gives her a sense of independence from her sisters?

9. Lily's favorite genre to read is high fantasy because she loves the escapism and the bravery of the main characters. What is your favorite genre to read and why?

10. At the end of the book, Nick agrees to have dinner with Lily and her family. What is the significance of this commitment?

KEEP READING FOR AN EXCERPT
FROM KRISTINA FOREST'S NEXT NOVEL,
ABOUT LILY'S SISTER, VIOLET!

VALENTINE'S DAY WAS NOTHING BUT A CAPITALIST SCAM, and the world would be a much better place if everyone accepted this simple truth about this senseless holiday.

At least, that was Violet Greene's new philosophy.

She'd never thought of herself as a love cynic or someone who crapped on things that most of the population enjoyed for the sake of being difficult or edgy, but Valentine's Day could kick rocks this year. It might be a pessimistic outlook to hate the day of love, but Violet figured she deserved to revel in her animosity. Being that five months ago, just two weeks shy of her wedding day, she'd discovered that her charming, successful and seemingly dedicated husband-to-be had been sleeping with someone else. Now, it was the middle of January and she was standing in line at a Walgreens in Las Vegas, surrounded by Valentine's Day balloons and teddy bears and silly cards with weird romantic puns, like *Thanks for bacon my Valentine's Day eggstraordinary!* She imagined each of the fluffy, red and pink teddy bears laughing at her and the silly life she'd imagined for herself that had so easily gone up in flames. It was all a huge joke. *Love* was a joke. At least the romantic variety.

But she wasn't at Walgreens to shoot the stink eye at innocent teddy bears. She needed Advil to dull her killer headache, because her day was far from over. In fact, in many ways, she was just getting started.

"Did you have any trouble finding what you needed?" the cashier asked, when it was finally Violet's turn to be rung up.

She kept her Dior aviator sunglasses perched carefully on the bridge of her nose as she shook her head. The cashier, a youngish guy with shaggy blond hair and forehead acne, looked her up and down in a slightly suggestive manner. Violet sighed and rolled her eyes behind her glasses. Men had been objectifying her since she'd sprouted boobs in the seventh grade, so while his behavior was exhausting, it wasn't new. This guy was really reaching, though, because you could hardly see anything about her figure underneath her oversized, black Off-White T-shirt and matching joggers.

"Nope," she said, rubbing her temples.

Then, as he was bagging up her painkillers, Violet spotted something behind his head.

"Wait." She pointed at the latest edition of *Cosmopolitan*. "I want that too."

He scanned the magazine and started to slip it into the bag, but Violet quickly grabbed it from his hands. "I'm going to read it now. Thank you."

She barely heard him tell her to have a good day as she hustled out of the store toward the black Mercedes SUV waiting for her in the parking lot. Her eyes were glued to the photo of *Cosmo*'s January cover star, Meela Baybee, the up-and-coming R&B singer everyone seemed to be obsessed with lately. Meela's silver hair was cut into an asymmetrical bob, and she was wearing her signature biker shorts and nipple pasties combo—a look that Violet had created specifically for her. Violet flipped to the interview, quickly skimming over the uninteresting sections about Meela's new haircare venture, and when she reached the inevitable question about Meela's love life, Violet narrowed her eyes.

> *Cosmo: There's been a lot of talk about your relationship with your manager, Eddy Coltrane. Can you speak to that?*
> *Meela coyly takes a sip from her drink and laughs.*
> *Meela: We're together. I'm happy. That's all I'm going to say.*

Eddy Coltrane, Meela's manager turned boyfriend, was otherwise known as Violet's ex-fiancé.

Otherwise known as the world's biggest asshole.

"Damn, girl, I thought somebody went and kidnapped you inside that store."

Violet snapped her head up, and her best friend, Karina, aka Karamel Kitty, the number one rap artist in the country *and* Violet's number one client, was leaning out the SUV window, beckoning Violet forward. The glittery polish on her long stiletto nails shimmered in the sunlight.

"We've got things to do, mama!" Karina said. "Hurry that cute ass up."

"I'm coming. I'm coming." Violet grinned and tossed the magazine in the trash before sliding in the backseat beside Karina, who was busy lathering her light brown arms and legs with sunblock. Violet raised an eyebrow at her.

"What?" Karina said, placing the SPF back in her orange, snakeskin Birkin. "This Vegas sun is wild."

"True." Violet downed two Advil and took a swig of water, waiting for the pills do their job.

Karina's driver peeled out of the parking lot, and Karina reached past her bodyguard in the passenger seat to turn up the radio. Of course, they were playing Karina's hit single "Bad Bitch Antics." Vegas was showing Karina all the love because she had an appearance tonight at the opening of the brand-new Luxe Grande casino.

But they'd only be in Vegas for less than twenty-four hours. Tomorrow, they'd be on the first flight to New York to begin the press tour for Karina's new visual album, *The Kat House*. Just three weeks ago, they'd finally wrapped the shoot, and the whole team had worked tirelessly on the visual album for over a month, filming in places like Egypt, Brazil and Paris. Violet had acted as head stylist. At only twenty-eight years old, she was one of the youngest stylists to ever achieve such an accomplishment with an in-demand star. Now, Violet was in-demand too. Her client roster was growing, and every other day her agent was emailing her about potential new clients.

Violet's younger sister, Lily, always said that Violet's life moved at lightning speed. She wasn't wrong. Violet was rarely in the same place for longer than a week. Her job required her to be on the go constantly. More often than not, she was running on empty. But she wouldn't complain. She was living her dream.

She couldn't believe there had been a point where she'd

considered slowing down in order to spend more time with Eddy.

Back at the hotel, controlled chaos ensued—the norm for Violet's line of work. Thankfully, her headache was finally beginning to subside. Music blasted as Karina talked to fans on her Instagram Live, while simultaneously getting her hair and makeup done. Violet and her assistant, Alex, were on the other side of the suite surveying Karina's many dress options for the night. Karina was voluptuous, with big boobs and big hips and she loved showing off her figure. Violet was personally invited to the showrooms of top high fashion designers who specifically wanted Karina to be seen donning their clothes.

Violet pulled two dresses off the rack: a floor-length Versace leopard-print gown with zebra-print lining and a thigh-high slit, and a rose gold LaQuan Smith corset minidress. Alex snapped a few photographs for Violet's archives and frowned when she didn't capture the right kind of lighting that she wanted. Alex was short, soft-spoken, and a hard worker. With her pixie cut and serious personality, she reminded Violet of her older sister, Iris. She'd met Alex at a FIDM career fair and had hired her as soon as she graduated last spring.

After Alex took more photos then uploaded them to her laptop, Violet brought the dresses over to Karina after she ended her Instagram Live.

"Okay, so what are we feeling tonight?" Violet shouted over the music. She held up the dresses side by side. The plan was for Karina to walk the red carpet with the other celebrities who were invited to the Luxe Grande's opening, and later she'd have a section at the club inside of the casino. "I was thinking the Versace for the red carpet and the LaQuan Smith for the club."

Karina turned toward Violet to view the dresses.

"Feel free to weigh in," Violet said to Brian, Karina's hairstylist, and Melody, her makeup artist.

"It's giving jungle queen," Brian said, pointing at the animal print.

"*What?*" Violet scowled at him. "Do not come for my taste, Brian! This dress is bomb."

"It can be cute and a jungle queen at the same time."

Violet huffed and looked at Melody. "Mel, do you have a smart comment too or will you be helpful?"

Melody kept her eyes on her makeup brushes and pulled her silky black hair into a ponytail at the nape of her neck. "Don't drag me into this. I like both. Karina will look good regardless."

"I know that's right," Karina said. "I'm always on the best-dressed lists at the end of the night, okay? Vi, Versace for the red carpet and LaQuan Smith for the club is perfect. Brian's just salty because somebody on my Live said he looked like a bootleg John Boyega."

Violet snorted and looked at Brian. "Oh my God, you do kind of look like him! Why have I never noticed this?"

"But he doesn't have a sexy British accent, sadly," Melody said.

"And none of the *Star Wars* fame," Alex added, coming over to take the dresses from Violet to hang them up again.

"Or money," Violet noted.

"Okay, keep it up," Brian said, "and after I'm done with Karina's hair, I won't be doing freebie touch-ups for any of you." He shot a pointed look at Violet specifically.

She blew him a kiss. "Then I won't help with your outfit. Have fun at the club sweating in your velour tracksuit."

"We do not need you sweating in VIP, Brian," Karina said, swiveling back toward Melody, who began painting Karina's lips in a deep fuchsia shade.

Brian gave Karina the finger and stuck his tongue out at Violet, and she laughed. Their crew was like a little family. Given how often they traveled together, Violet spent more time with them than she did with her own sisters. In fact, after the breakup, Violet let the lease run out on her New York City apartment, took whatever items she'd had at Eddy's downtown LA condo, and moved her things into the spare bedroom in Brian's Echo Park loft. She'd gotten used to her sister, Lily, staying with her for the better half of last year, and after leaving Eddy, she didn't want to live alone. This meant that sometimes she heard Brian and his boyfriend hooking up across the hall, but she'd put up with that if it meant she didn't have to be stuck with the sound of her own thoughts at night.

After deciding on Karina's shoes and jewelry, Violet went to her own room to get dressed. She often joined Karina on the red carpet and followed behind discreetly to make sure Karina's dresses weren't dragging or twisted, because she needed to look good for photographs. At the end of the night, Violet posted those photos to her social media and added them to her portfolio. Last summer, she'd scored a feature in the *Hollywood Reporter*'s Most Powerful Stylists issue. Her seventeen-year-old self, who'd been desperate to escape New Jersey, would be so geeked to see her now.

As she slid on her own dress, a black Valentino halter with intricate cutouts on her hips, her phone buzzed nonstop. There were emails from her agent about interviews surrounding *The Kat House* premiere in March, and a series of texts from one of her other clients, Angel, a neo-soul singer, who treated Violet like a big sister and was more interested in asking her for dating advice than about what he should wear on the red carpet. Violet slipped her phone into her clutch, promising herself that she'd reply to everyone during the flight to New York the following morning. She just had to get through tonight first.

Brian came to her room and quickly swooped her curls into a chic topknot. Then she helped him put together his outfit (a chambray button-down with dark blue jeans), and they met the rest of the team at the elevator bank.

"Okay, whole team looking good," Karina said, angling her phone to record a video as they crowded together in the elevator. Karina's bodyguard, Raymond, pressed the button for the lobby and down they went.

Alex, who hated being on camera, ducked behind Violet to avoid being seen on Karina's vlog. She pointed at the visible skin on Violet's left hip.

"I don't think I've ever seen that tattoo," she said. "What's the X for?"

Violet glanced down, seeing that her small tattoo was in plain view thanks to the design of her dress. Sometimes she forgot the tattoo was there. And other times, when she was in the shower or putting on lotion before bed, she stared at the X for a while and wondered whether or not the boy she'd gotten this tattoo for still had the image of a violet flower on his inner bicep. And if so, she wondered if he'd considered getting it removed. She thought about removing the X sometimes, but she could never bring herself to actually go through with it.

Everyone thought that Violet's breakup with Eddy had been devastating. And it had been, to a certain degree. Mostly because Hollywood was a small town and Eddy had played Violet for a woman who used to be her client, and that was embarrassing. So much so, Violet had even thrown herself an anti-wedding party in order to save face.

But the truth was that what had happened with Eddy didn't scratch the surface of how she knew heartbreak could *really* feel. Like your chest was caving in and half of you was missing. She knew what it was like to be in love where nothing else mattered, and your life seemed utterly pointless without that other person. She'd felt that way for someone once, and he hadn't been Eddy. That person was from a past life.

"It's just this thing I did in high school," she finally answered, adjusting her dress to cover the tattoo as much as she could.

Then the elevator doors opened and the paparazzi in the hotel lobby descended, shouting for Karamel Kitty. The bulbs of their cameras flashed, snapping Violet out of her melancholy trip down high school memory lane.

She didn't have time to think about lost love or old ghosts.

She reached down to grab the train of Karina's dress.

The show must go on.

Steven Forest

Kristina Forest is the author of romance books for both teens and adults. She earned her MFA in creative writing at the New School and she can often be found rearranging her bookshelf. Visit her online at kristinaforest.com.

Ready to find
your next great read?

Let us help.

Visit prh.com/nextread

Penguin
Random
House